A Novel

by

Jackie Ullerich

Published by
Brighton Publishing LLC
501 W. Ray Rd.
Suite 4
Chandler, Arizona 85225

Invitation to Death

A Novel

by

Jackie Ullerich

Published by
Brighton Publishing LLC
501 W. Ray Road
Suite 4
Chandler, Arizona 85225
www.BrightonPublishing.com

Printed in the United States of America

ISBN 13: 978-1-62183-024-5
ISBN 10: 1-621-83024-1

First Edition

Cover Design: Tom Rodriguez

Books by Jackie Ullerich

The Bride Stands Alone - At Risk

Reviews and Comments

A Page Turner!

"The Bride Stands Alone is a page turner filled with love, mystery, and deception. The story begins with a beautiful romance that leads to an exotic wedding in Acapulco. Then the unthinkable happens. The bride's new husband disappears. Her heartbreak only deepens when it appears he was living a double life. Confusion and intrigue follow. I highly recommend this book!"

Interesting Twists!

"First of all, the cover says a lot about this book. One of the most interesting and well-done covers I have seen. If you can't figure it out, it's not necessarily an everybody lives happily ever after, the author takes us yet again to exotic places, and turns the story with some interesting twists. I don't want to spoil the story, so read it yourself!"

Talented Author!

"In the early chapters of The Bride Stands Alone, author Jackie Ullerich introduces an array of characters, each of whom has his or her own complex story realistically and are as expansively described as the story scenes, near and far. The characters are then neatly woven into the mystery that is unfolding, leading ultimately to a surprising ending. In reviewing this second Jackie Ullerich novel it is clear to me that this talented author will be heard from again."

This Is A Fantastic Read!

"Imagine finding your true love. Next comes a fairy-tale wedding. Everything seems perfect, but then your whole world turns upside down. Your new husband disappears and you begin to find out he might be very different from the person you thought you knew. The Bride Stands Alone takes the reader through the excitement of new love, the heartache that follows, and unexpected twists that continue to unfold. The author's beautiful, exotic, and dramatic descriptions make the story come to life. This is a fantastic read."

Great Book...I Hope She Writes More!

"I've never taken a cruise, but now I'm pretty sure I'll just stay home and read more books from Jackie Ullerich! Imagine being trapped on a cruise ship with people who suddenly decide they hate you...and there isn't anything you can do about it? No way out! This was a pretty great read, and always fun to read novelist I haven't read before. Good suspense, good dialogue, great intensity!"

Great Suspense—Fun Reading

"At Risk is a page turner filled with suspense. The cruise ship provides the perfect backdrop for an exotic adventure that, for some passengers, leads to romance—and for others... takes an unexpected murderous turn."

Compelling New Author

"I found author Jackie Ullerich's book At Risk to be a compelling read. Her in-depth development of a diverse group of characters made their intriguing experiences come alive. The sharp dialogue held my interest from start to finish. The research and knowledge of the variety of locales brought reality to this suspenseful story. I recommend this book and will seek out additional works from this new author."

An Intriguing Plot

"Jackie introduces several couples that will be taking the same cruise, each with a challenging situation in their marriages. The complexity of the plot challenges the reader to visualize the reasons behind their motives. The development of the characters and their interactions keeps the reader involved. A great read."

Talented Author!

"I enjoyed this book very much! New author and talented. Am looking forward to her next book."

Romance, Intrigue, Suspense!

"This sounds like a lovely, exotic cruise but has some nice twists and turns. Romance, or is there more to this than meets the eye? Will read her next book, The Bride Stands Alone, for sure."

Her Own Voice!

"She has created a voice all her own in mystery fiction, unmistakably her own, down to every plot twist, every barb, every bit of wit and wry humor which keep the pages turning and readers guessing what might possibly happen next."

Impossible To Stop Reading!

"Jackie delights in stringing together a series of twists and turns that make it impossible to stop reading until yet another page has been feverishly read."

As Good As Anything Published In The Last Decade!

"Jackie Ullerich weaves a tale of high seas suspense as good as anything published in the last decade, with a plot that will keep readers turning the pages wondering what she'll come up with next."

It's Party Time!

Join Us For: Barry's Birthday Bash (# 43)

Date: Friday, June 20
Time: 8:00 p.m. Cocktail/Buffet
Place:* 87 Park Meadows Drive
Regrets Only Kim and Barry Williams
(213) 784-5152

No Gifts Please

*Take entrance to Griffith Park - not L.A. Zoo!

Chapter One

The sound of shattering glass followed by muttered expletives rose above diminished party chatter and a woman's fluty laugh.

Kimberly Williams stood at the front door, ankle deep in confetti, ribbons and the remnants of popped balloons. She raised her eyebrows but remained attentive to Jenna Price, her partner at their art gallery.

"Uh, oh," Jenna said. "Something just bit the dust." She peered beyond Kim's shoulder. "I'd better let you survey the damage."

"Right. Broken glass is no joke."

"But honey, the party was a blast. And I'm just a *leetle* bit wobbly to prove it."

Kim laughed and blew Jenna a kiss. "See you on Monday," she said as she shut the door.

Raised voices drew Kim toward the center of the room, only to be blocked by more departing guests. Oh, well, she'd let Barry deal with the broken glass, but a quick visual sweep of the room revealed that her husband was nowhere in sight.

More goodbyes, more hugs, until just a few guests remained–George Anderson at the bar and a couple seated on the couch with two women hovering over them. One of the women–Myra, Barry's secretary–spotted Kim and broke away from the foursome. "He might need stitches," she said, pointing to the man on the couch.

As Kim moved closer, she struggled to contain herself. "Oh no, not my ballerina. Shit," she muttered.

"Jeez, I'm sorry." The man pointed to the glass sculpture that lay broken on the floor. His other hand was wrapped in a handkerchief, soaked with blood.

Kim tried to stay calm and addressed the woman sitting next to him. "You'd better get him to the emergency room."

"Naw. I'm okay. Patty'll get me home. Sorry about the mess."

He attempted to get up, but failed; and then with Patty's help, lurched to his feet.

"Here we go again," Patty muttered. "Sorry about that," she said to Kim. "We're only up the hill from you. I'll drive us home, and we'll take it from there. Oh, and be sure to send us the bill for the broken knick knack."

Myra had hung back as the couple and the other woman made their exits. Approaching Kim she said, "Knick knack, huh? Apparently, the woman has a limited vocabulary. Well, it was a great party, sweetie. Too bad that drunken S.O.B. had to ruin it for you and Barry. Say, where is our host?"

Kim shrugged. "Darned if I know. Maybe he went for a swim. That's his nightly routine."

"Well, you deserve to kick off your shoes and join that handsome husband of yours. Oops." She gestured toward the living room, "Looks like I'm not the last to leave after all."

She rolled her eyes. "I'll let you deal with George. Bye, now."

George Anderson sauntered over to Kim, baring his gleaming white teeth, his one bow to cosmetic enhancement on an otherwise lumpy face that revealed years of hard drinking and recreational drug use.

"Kim, what a beautiful soiree," he gestured grandly. "You look ravishing. Always do."

"Oh, come on, George. You can save that line for the glamour goddesses you pamper and sweet-talk."

"OK, maybe wholesome suits you better than ravishing, but I like your style. You're easy to be with; you go with the tide, kiddo."

"Hah. Don't I wish. Appearances can be deceiving."

A gesture of dismissal, and he was out the door, only to come right back. "Where's the host? Where's our birthday boy?"

"Good question."

"Oh?" A slyness crept into his expression, or was it a knowingness? "Well. Tell Barry to call me. It's important. We need his input on some damage control. One of our clients–big name in TV–has been a bad boy," he grinned. "Thanks, doll. Great party."

Oh, to work at a public relations firm. Never a dull moment. Kim kicked off her shoes and rubbed her toes against one of the soft flokati throw rugs they had purchased in Greece. Sure, it was nice. But a rug was a rug. The ruined dancer was, for her, a gigantic loss.

Despite birthday paraphernalia, napkins, and glasses strewn about, the room maintained a certain formality. Kim liked the effect of soft blues accentuated by touches of navy and silver in the cushioned furniture and draperies that contrasted with their white rugs. But she would have preferred that the end tables and large cocktail table that fronted the three-piece sectional were crafted in glass, rather than mahogany—a more casual, California look. Barry's taste, however, had prevailed.

Barry. Where could he be? Surely, he hadn't gone to bed. Maybe he *was* at the pool. She slipped on her shoes and started for the rear of the house, only to pause at the corridor leading to the den and bedrooms. Was that music coming from the den?

Kim followed the sound down the hall. The closed door to the den loomed like an intractable barrier, allowing only a ribbon of light to escape from beneath.

With the careful, deliberate moves of an intruder, she nudged open the door. Barry and a woman were dancing–if you could call it that. Kim flipped the switch for the overhead light. "The party's over," she said, hearing the stridency in her tone.

As they broke apart, the harsh light underscored the woman's disheveled appearance–lipstick smeared, mascara smudged under her eyes, chin reddened by whisker burn, blouse partially unbuttoned. Barry regarded his wife. "Oh, hi Kim. This is Felicia. Felicia, meet my wife."

Felicia trailed her fingers over Barry's cheek in a caress, and then turned to Kim. "Guess you're right; the party's over. Boo hoo." She brushed past Kim but not before giving her the once-over. "Cute," she murmured as she left the room.

Barry used his handkerchief to wipe his lips, and then smoothed his hair. "Kim, wow, what a knockout you are tonight. We all know you're the poster girl for preppy, but this low cut dress–silk is it?–proves you can retire Kimberly the co-ed collegian. Yep. Turquoise is your color."

"You have the nerve to stand there and make a fashion statement? Who is Felicia, and what in the hell was going on in here?"

"Felicia is a member of our legal staff. We were dancing."

"Welded together. You call that dancing?" She strode to the entertainment center to shut off the CD. Ironically, it was playing "*Breaking Up is Hard to Do*."

"Oh, grow up, Kim."

She turned to face him. "You're the one who needs to grow up, Barry. Why weren't you out there to see our guests out? Everyone was asking for the host. But the host was engaged in his own dirty little sideshow with Ms. Sleaze. Oh. And one of your drunken colleagues was so smashed he practically fell out the front door. That is, after he bumped into the ballerina sculpture, which is now broken into pieces."

He chuckled. "I'll bet it was Ben Stewart. Nice guy, but the man can't hold his liquor."

"You miserable bastard." She broke into sobs.

"Kim, that isn't very becoming language for a lady, is it? Well," he shrugged, "happy birthday to me."

His exit was jaunty, if a little unsteady.

She wanted to pummel him with her fists, but as her rage subsided, so did her tears. She couldn't let it go like this.

She figured he was headed for the pool, and if she could catch him before he changed for his swim, they might talk it out.

Wrong. Light and movement in the kitchen confirmed what she should have surmised—that Barry, true to custom, was making a drink to take out to the pool.

She stood in the doorway and watched as he reached for the bottle of Drambuie. Surely he sensed her presence. She took a few halting steps forward. "George Anderson told me tonight that he likes my style, that I go with the tide, that I'm easy to be with." Inwardly, she cringed. Was she that desperate?

Barry turned to face her. "You do give that impression." He nodded. "You can be—well, soothing to be around."

Soothing, she thought? "I wouldn't say I'm feeling very soothing right now. Barry, for God's sake, what should I think when I see you close to vertical intercourse with some tramp?"

Barry opened, and then closed his mouth. If she read his expression correctly, her choice of words had surprised him. He raised his hands, palms upward. "Felicia means nothing to me. Okay, we got a little carried away. Maybe it was the booze, the excitement of the party." He paused, "On second thought, am I old enough to be entering into a mid-life crisis?"

Kim smiled in spite of herself and as if on cue, her husband came to her and placed his hands on her shoulders. He spoke softly. "Consider it simply a birthday bonus."

He smiled, and the warmth in his expressive dark eyes melted dregs of conflicting emotions. She tilted her face toward him, but he turned from her to return to the sink, leaving her there like an uninvited guest.

Kim waited until he'd poured his Drambuie, and then said, "Maybe I'll have a nightcap, too."

"You know you can't drink scotch."

"I'll fix myself a Cointreau."

"Sure. Help yourself. I'm going for my swim."

Just like that. Well, maybe she'd take her drink out to the patio. Better yet, why not join God's gift to women in the pool sans suit. Call it another birthday bonus.

Sliding glass doors in the family room led outside to the patio and pool. But Kim didn't make it that far, wrinkling her nose at the sight of lipstick stained glasses and crumpled cocktail napkins scattered across tables that needed to be wiped clean. The lingering stench of cigar smoke made her gag. Forget about the swim. Suit or no suit.

She set her drink on the cocktail table and then gathered some of the debris as well as a few glasses. Gracie, their housekeeper, had agreed to come by in the morning to clean up.

When Kim returned from the kitchen, she stepped gingerly around splinters of glass and ballerina body parts that were still intact. The head retained its classic features and serene expression; the arms that had stretched in a graceful pose were now severed and lay at grotesque angles from the fractured body.

The ballerina had been more than a piece of art, a mere trinket. It had marked a very special occasion.

Seated now, Kim bowed her head as memories surfaced, then lifted her glass to sip the sweet orange flavor. She was doing it again, retreating into the past, searching for clues that would restore the passion and depth of feeling that seemed to be fading from her marriage.

Her sister, not always an ardent supporter of Kim, had introduced her to Barry. Dana, at that time, was head buyer for the better dresses department at I. Magnin on Wilshire Boulevard. She was married to Kyle Sterling, whose membership at the Riviera Country Club brought him into contact with Barry Williams, a VIP at a public relations firm on Sunset Boulevard.

When Dana learned that Barry was an art collector, she suggested he visit the gallery in Beverly Hills where Kim worked acquiring and selling paintings. "This could mean a really good commission for you," Dana had said to Kim. "You tell the rest of the staff you have dibs on this man because your brother-in-law is sending him over."

"Wow," Kim had responded. "You'd do this for me?"

"Well, I haven't always been the best big sister. But I'm not all bad," she paused. "Incidentally, this man is single."

And so it began. When Barry Williams walked into the gallery at the appointed time, Kim took one look and felt a physical attraction so overpowering that she had to clutch a chair to steady herself.

Conventionally handsome, with dark hair and eyes, his attire and demeanor suggested East Coast establishment, rather than California-casual.

And while Kim might have been drawn to any man of polish and sophistication, when Barry made eye contact, he projected a singular awareness of her that took her breath away.

Of course, she had rallied to snuff out her thirteen-year-old alter ego and assumed the poised stance of a thirty-year-old business woman. She had even made a sale and managed to entice this man into attending an art exhibit and wine tasting event the following week. They were married three months later.

Now, reflecting on their time together, Kim wondered how others perceived them as a couple. Certainly they were a study in contrasts—she, with her flaxen hair and green eyes, and a light dusting of freckles over her cheekbones.

Barry's appearance had stayed much the same in the five years they'd been married. His hair was still dark and lustrous, his sculptured features softening just a bit. Without making a big deal of it, he maintained a good body weight for his height which was just under six feet.

As for their personalities—that was another story. All this thinking, this rambling mental discourse, had been prompted by the loss of what had been to her, an exquisite piece of art.

The ballerina sculpture had been her husband's gift to her on their first wedding anniversary.

Routine, the day-to-day repetition of acts can be comforting, Kim thought as she slipped under the covers, waiting for Barry to come to bed. And indeed, Barry was all about routine. Take, for example, his evening nightcap and swim, the order in which he arranged clothes and shoes in his closet, the precise timing and duration of his daily shower.

Though at times she found his behavior irritating, it was comfortable. It was familiar and set the tone for a stable marriage.

She broke off her thoughts as Barry entered his side of the bed, positioning himself with his back to her. She snuggled close to him, only to receive a pat from his outstretched hand, and a muffled, "Good night."

So be it. She inched to the other side of the bed and stared into the darkness. It wasn't only tonight. Something was seriously wrong. She gnawed at her lower lip, fighting tears.

She had to talk to Dana. Now. This minute. Okay, first thing tomorrow morning. Though she and Dana had clashed over attitudes, values, and ethics, her sister could be kind and generous. But more importantly, Dana could—and would—assess her situation and without mincing words, advise her, calmly and objectively. Even in spite of the open hostility between Dana and Barry.

Glamorous, clever, abrasive: that was Dana. Kim's sister lived in a penthouse on Wilshire Boulevard with her second husband, Jasper James, an Australian who ran a successful import-export business in downtown Los Angeles.

It saddened Kim that she and Dana seldom got together, even though they lived a short distance apart. But now she had an excuse for a visit and she knew she could count on Dana for some straight answers.

Ah, good. The light of consciousness was winding down to a mere glimmer, dimming, dimming...

And then she remembered: she had failed to give Barry the message from George Anderson.

Still, she turned away from her husband. Let TV's bad boy take his lumps. And if her negligence resulted in a misunderstanding between the two men—tough. Barry could suffer the consequences of his behavior.

She stirred restlessly, and then glanced over at her sleeping husband, wanting him to hold her close. Jesus. She struck the bed with the flat of her hand. How could she love, yet feel such fury at the same time? It wasn't like her to be mean spirited. That was more Dana's domain.

On the other hand, she'd rather see Barry dead, than in the arms of another woman.

Chapter Two

Dana James took pleasure in strolling through the lobby of the Wilshire Marquis building, with its massive crystal chandelier presiding over thick gold carpeting and oyster white leather sofas that straddled antique gold legs.

The revolving door, with accompanying doorman, evoked images of tree shaded mansions she had observed along New York's 5th Avenue. Not that the Wilshire Marquis was on par with Manhattan's priciest accommodations, but most of these apartments, including her own, were in the million dollar range.

As she entered the small room that served as a mail distribution center for residents, she saw she had company. A man stood at the box adjoining hers.

He turned as she approached and smiled.

Nice. His smile was easy, attractive. He wasn't her type, but still…

She smiled back, and then inserted her key to retrieve her mail. A quick perusal revealed the postman had made an error.

"Excuse me," she said. "Would you happen to be Mark Hampton?" She held out an envelope.

"I am," he smiled again, "but if it's a bill, it's all yours."

"I only accept checks, not bills. Here you go."

"Thank you." His hand grazed hers as he accepted the envelope. "Actually, I owe you for arriving when you did. I'm only here a day or two during the week and sometimes on Saturdays."

"Oh. So you're not a tenant?"

"I work in one of the offices off the lobby. And you are?"

"Dana James. I live here."

"Lucky you." He looked at his watch. "I'd better get going. I have a patient in ten minutes." He didn't move. Apparently not in any hurry. "I hope to see you again." He held her gaze for a second or two longer than necessary, obviously flirting.

After he left the room, she waited a beat or two, and then followed him through the lobby at a careful distance. He was tall with a robust build, though softness around the edges suggested he wasn't a frequent visitor at the gym. She couldn't remember the color of his eyes but had taken a quick inventory of his features: high forehead, thick brown hair with an exaggerated widow's peak, a generous but masculine mouth, a sexy yet refined deep baritone voice. She waited until he was in his office, and then moved in to inspect the lettering on the door. The small print read:

MARK HAMPTON, Ph.D

Psychological Services

She prided herself on her accuracy in judging people on first impressions. This man, she sensed, was strong on compassion and undoubtedly doled out a ton of tissues to weepy, befuddled souls.

Backtracking across the lobby, Dana glanced idly in the direction of the revolving doors, and then did a double take. The woman entering the lobby was Susan Connelly, Dana's nemesis from her short-lived college days. Dana's rage intensified at the thought of Susan writing out her annual smug, infuriating, rub-it-in-your-face Christmas newsletter. The only thing holding Dana back from returning the letters in shreds was Ted, Susan's husband, and Dana's financial advisor.

Dana stood still as the woman, now only a few yards away, walked past her. Susan held her arms tightly to her sides, her gaze focused on the carpet, like someone bent on disappearing.

Dana followed her at a discreet distance to the office of Dr. Mark Hampton. Susan, it appeared was the patient he'd been expecting.

Why in the world was Ms. Perfect seeing a psychologist? What could be the problem? Marital doldrums? Depression? Drugs? Alcohol? Sex addiction? All of the above would make Dana's day, though she seriously doubted sex addiction was the issue.

Dana flexed her fingers from their clenched position and headed for the elevator. Though it seemed highly unlikely, for some reason, she had a hunch Dr. Hampton and that bitch were destined to play a future role in the life of Dana James.

Once inside her apartment, Dana made a bee-line for the kitchen. She grabbed a Coke from the refrigerator, poured it into a glass, and then settled in at her desk at the far end of the great room.

The blinking light on her phone indicated a voice message. She sipped her second Coke of the morning, enjoying the jolt of caffeine, and then pushed the message button. "Dana, it's Kim. I need to talk to you. It's really urgent. Please call as soon as possible."

Good God. She wondered if her sister's call had something to do with that bastard, Barry.

A couple more swigs of Coke, and she reached for the phone. Kim answered on the first ring.

"Oh, hi, Dana."

Oh, hi? That's it? "Kim, what's going on? You sounded upset on your message."

"Upset and then some. I'll get to that in a minute. What's happening with you? How's Jasper?"

"Jasper is in Australia, Sydney to be exact."

"Business?"

"That too, but he's also looking for a place for us to live."

"Tell me you mean part time."

"I expect it would be full time."

Dana waited. The silence that greeted her announcement puzzled her. She'd expected an outpouring of protest, for Christ's sake. "Kim?"

"I'm in shock. I can't think. You're telling me you'd give up your country, your friends, *me,* to live half way around the world?"

"Oh, come on, Kim. I'm married to an Aussie."

"You'd be miserable. It's different over there–quirky, bizarre; it's even harsh." She gulped. "When would I see you?"

"When people want to get together, they find a way. As for living conditions, we wouldn't be settling in the Outback or on a sheep farm, for God's sake."

"I suppose." A big sigh. "And here I've been complaining about Barry's wanting us to move to Malibu."

"What's wrong with Malibu? You'd have a house on the ocean and share grocery aisles with the flavor-of-the-month celebrity."

"I'm perfectly satisfied with the home I'm in, plus it's close to

Melrose Avenue."

"Art galleries are everywhere. Think Beverly Hills, Westwood, Pacific Palisades, Santa Monica."

"You don't understand. Jenna and I are finally building up our clientele. We have plans for community art showings, a gala wine tasting and art exhibition, educational projects—"

"Okay, you've made your point. Now, why the distress call?"

"It's—it's about Barry and me. I need your help."

"Uh-oh. What's going on?"

"It seems I'm not Barry's golden girl anymore. He's bored, he's restless, and he's distant. Oh, not all the time, of course, but his attitude toward me has changed." Another deep sigh. "I'd appreciate some sisterly advice."

"Are you available in the next hour or so?"

"Absolutely."

"Your place or mine?"

"I'd say come here, but Gracie's cleaning up the mess, as we speak, from Barry's birthday party, and I'm not sure when Barry will return from golf."

"Two good reasons why you should come to my place. Oh! I just had a brilliant thought about something that might bring you two closer together."

"I'm on my way."

The grand piano positioned just inside the entrance to her sister's apartment struck Kim as ostentatious in an otherwise elegant great room. Couches arranged for intimate conversation or for entertaining on a grander scale were backed by lighted recessed shelves that showcased objects d'Art–most prominently, a huge ceramic plate, a Grecian urn, a carved Chinese Buddha. A wall of glass invited a view of the terrace and cityscape.

Had it occurred to Dana to require visitors to remove shoes as they navigated a sea of white carpeting? Apparently not.

White on white, Kim mused as she settled onto a brocade couch, waiting for her sister to return from the kitchen. It wasn't an entirely vanilla world; relief came in the form of dusky blue accent pillows, with chairs upholstered in color combinations of blue and gold.

What did this room bring to mind? Ah. The posh Presidio Room in the Hotel San Francisco where wall-to-wall martini drinkers swooned over piano renditions of Cole Porter or Gershwin. Too bad no one here played the piano.

"Here we are." Dana handed an iced tea to Kim and in the other hand, held another Coke for herself.

"I thought you were weaning yourself off Coke, or have you cut back?" Kim asked as Dana sat down in the chair opposite the couch.

"I gave it some thought, but I guess I like being wired."

"It amazes me how much you and Barry have in common."

"He's addicted to Coke?"

Kim decided to ignore the question. "Except for your green eyes, you and Barry could be brother and sister. You're both magazine cover gorgeous, have the same dark hair and sculptured features, not to mention great sex appeal. You're alike in other ways, too–restless, edgy, and energetic. It's no wonder you two clash. You're too much alike." She fell silent, put off by something in Dana's expression. Was it anger?

Dana stared at her over the rim of her raised glass. "Can we move on?"

"Of course. Tell me about this brilliant thought of yours that might bring Barry and me closer."

Dana set down her drink. "We'll get there. First I want to know what's going on with you and Barry."

"Where to begin? Okay. Barry's not the man I married. He used to be so affectionate, so caring. Our sex life was incredible."

"And now?"

"The sex part is still okay; at times he can be quite loving. But he can also be sharp or impatient with me. What I hate the most is that it's never just the two of us anymore. We're always with another couple or with a group, whether at the theater or eating out. I've tried to pin him down, to hold a serious discussion, but he's always on the run. It's obvious we're drifting apart."

"Is he cheating?"

"I didn't think so before last night. Now I have this really bad feeling." Kim concentrated on sipping her iced tea, and then pushed it aside. "Let me tell you about last night." She left nothing out, including his indifference at bedtime. "Oh, and what really hurt was that he made light of the broken ballerina."

Dana remained silent, as if lost in thought.

"What do you think? Did I overreact?"

"You were angry last night. Justifiably so. How do you feel now, at this very moment?"

"I don't want to lose him. What I felt for Barry in the beginning hasn't died. I'm still crazy about him."

"Even when he treats you like shit?"

"Oh, come on, Dana, I'm not a doormat. I wouldn't put up with abuse. Just tell me what to do." She folded her hands onto her lap and smiled. "Short of breast enhancement, that is. I draw the line at that. It looks good on you, but it's not for me."

"Thanks. My Botox is scheduled for next week. But back to you. As you know, I don't beat around the bush. Bottom line…Barry is not a nice man."

"Well, consider this. From what I can tell, Barry doesn't think you're a nice woman. Which brings up another subject: the antagonism between you and my husband. Was your falling out really about a business deal gone sour? Is there really nothing more to it?"

"You're referring to my jewelry business? That he reneged on a business agreement and I mislead him? That was our cover story. But yes, there is more to it." She stood. "More iced tea? No? I think I'm ready for another Coke." With a bouncy stride she was off to the kitchen.

Kim reached for her drink, and then sank down into the couch, feeling a bit queasy. *What did Dana mean by there is more to it,* Kim asked herself? *And why did she bring up Barry's opinion of Dana? Her sister did not take well to criticism.*

It seemed like only seconds before Dana was back. This time she hadn't bothered with a glass. She took a sip from the can and then set it down hard. "Let me make this short and simple," she said. "Barry and I had an affair. Kyle found out and filed for divorce. Barry dumped me." Her hand shook as she raised the can to her lips.

Kim felt her heart beat faster, her vision began to blur. "This affair with Barry—"

"Was before you were married."

"But while we were dating?"

Dana shrugged. "I suppose so. But not at the time I introduced you to Barry." She stared at the floor for a moment, and then came over to Kim's side to squeeze her hand. "Look, I'm sorry. I never should have told you about Barry and me. What's past is past."

Kim jerked her hand back from Dana and stood. "I can't believe this. My own sister—" She swallowed a sob and grabbed her purse. "I'm outta here." She stomped quickly to the door, but Dana was faster, blocking her sister's exit as she thrust herself between Kim and the door.

Kim gasped. "What are you doing?"

"Kimmy, don't go. Please don't go."

Kimmy? The childhood name gave her pause. As did Dana's pleading tone.

"Kimmy, listen to me. Who can we call family? Our parents are gone, our few relatives are scattered God knows where. We're all we've got. We *are* our family: you and me. Of course, we've had our differences. What sisters haven't? But we've always been there for each other." She paused. "Right, Kim?"

"Of course. But what does that have to do with you and Barry? Damn it, Dana. You *slept* with my *husband*."

"Barry was *not* your husband at that time, Kim."

"Well, that just makes it fine and dandy."

"Our affair was a mere dalliance. *You* were the woman he married."

Kim couldn't tell if Dana's wistful tone was play acting or for real. The hurt she felt over Dana's betrayal was palpable, like a kick in the ribs or in the gut. Yet what about Barry? After all, it takes two to tango.

"Okay. Okay," Kim said. "You told me you had something in mind that could bring Barry and me closer."

Kim and Dana resumed their seats in the great room and Dana struck a contemplative pose. "You may not want to hear this," she said, "but I think Barry likes the challenge of molding young, impressionable women into his vision of what they should become: smartly dressed, sophisticated, knowledgeable about art and fine wines, good restaurants, etc., etc."

Kim rotated her shoulders. "And when he's completed his objective?" She paused. "Never mind. You've given me a lot to think about. In the meantime, can we get back to what, if anything, I should do?"

"First of all, toughen up. Barry may thirst for young vulnerable women, but he's getting older. He isn't the hot shot he once was. Show him you're strong and not crumbling over his wayward behavior.

"How to accomplish this? Obviously, you have this big thing for Barry chemistry-wise, so you're motivated. Secondly, be practical. We both grew up in modest circumstances. Look at our lives now. Do we want to return to the old days?"

"I really hadn't considered that."

"Another thing to think about: we've both had failed first marriages. You want to try for marriage number three? I think not." She paused to let Kim let her message sink in. "Now, on the positive side, I may have the solution to your problems with Mr. Bored and Restless. How about a romantic get-away?"

"I'd certainly be willing."

"Jasper and I own a condo in Kona on the big island of Hawaii. It's elegant, intimate, and right on the ocean. You never hear your neighbors–only the crashing of waves on the rocks below."

"I'd love it, but Barry isn't a big fan of nature's beauty. Unless, of course, it's star studded Malibu."

"Not a problem. In walking distance from the condo, I can name a dozen restaurants and shops, everything from funky and casual to posh with stellar ocean views.

"Now Barry doesn't have to know I'm behind this caper. You belong to several women's groups. Tell him you won the trip at a fund-raiser silent auction."

Kim nodded. "That sounds plausible."

"You'll need to make the trip fairly soon because another couple will arrive at the condo a day or two before their anniversary on July 15."

Eyes narrowed, Dana hesitated for a moment, and then said, "Do you remember Beatrice and Frank Devlin?"

"The names ring a bell."

"You've met them. Bea teaches or used to teach math at the community college. I brought you along to one of the social gatherings they held in their home for a select group of students."

"I can't quite picture her."

"Plump, soft all over, short salt and pepper hair, pert nose, wears glasses."

"Ah, yes. I remember now. And Frank, he was a sturdy type, tanned, weather beaten skin, smiled a lot. Wait a minute, Dana. Didn't you have a serious falling out with Bea?"

"I thought she almost ruined my life."

"I'm not connecting the dots."

"Despite the circumstances–and I don't want to dredge up the ugly stuff–I was hurtful, obnoxious, a real brat. Having said that, I still harbor a lot of resentment. But they're getting on in years, and I don't know how much longer we'll keep the condo, so I thought it would be a treat for them to enjoy a week in Kona. A lot of owners donate a week through silent auctions within charitable organizations.

"For reasons not clear to me, maybe out of curiosity? I've kept up with them, though we've not spoken or gotten together. At any rate, I knew that Frank was a member of the Elks in Tustin, where they live. For the organization's recent big fling, I volunteered a stay at our condo as part of their silent auction. I persuaded one of the Brothers to see to it the Devlins won by any means possible.

"Manipulate the sign-up sheet, I suggested, or add an anonymous donor in the Devlin's name. In turn, I made a substantial donation to the group."

"I take it the Devlins are unaware of your part in all this?"

"My stipulation was that this arrangement remain hush hush."

"Oh, Dana, what can I say? Your generosity to me and to this other couple is beyond measure."

"I like giving to others. Also, I find a certain selfish satisfaction in making up for past wrongs. Bea and Frank deserve the best."

Kim nodded in response, but the hard look in her sister's eyes didn't jibe with the sentiments she'd expressed.

Suddenly, Dana was on her feet. "Come on, Kim. Let's sit on the terrace for awhile. It's gorgeous out there."

Lagging behind her sister, Kim glanced at the piano. The skylight above showered sunbeams onto the raised lid, bringing the instrument into harmony with the luminosity of its surroundings.

It was an auspicious sign, Kim decided as she headed outside. It was time to banish gloom and embrace hope. No, make that certainty. In no time, she and Barry would be back on track. She felt it. She knew it.

After seeing Kim out, Dana returned to the terrace to bask in the sunshine and to reflect on her sister's visit. The woman was definitely in denial: her marriage was headed to the dump.

Of course, she wanted the best for her sister, but it was hard to quash impish thoughts that surfaced: that in the most secret recesses of her mind, she was pleased Kim and Barry were experiencing marital problems.

That damn Barry. He was a supercilious, manipulative, devious man, addicted to women. And for awhile, she'd been addicted to him–so much so, she would have dumped Kyle in a heartbeat if Barry had so much as beckoned. Instead, she had lost both men.

Dana wondered how Barry was doing health-wise. Not that she cared, but the heart murmur he revealed to her when they were together was nothing to fool around with, especially combined with cocaine use. If he had confided in her, surely he had confided in his wife. But Kim never mentioned a heart problem or any kind of drug use.

She shivered as clouds blanketed the sun. The wind was picking up as well, whipping the corners of the cloth that covered the patio table. Her thoughts switched to Jasper and the time difference in Australia, to the cockeyed seasons. Mainly, she thought about her remaining time in the U.S. "So much left to accomplish," she murmured.

A sudden warmth signaled the resurgence of the sun, along with light breezes that now prevailed over wind gusts. But she could not sit a moment longer.

Back in the great room, Dana wondered how she would spend the rest of the afternoon and evening. She didn't expect to hear from

Jasper until next week, and she hadn't planned to return to her jewelry shop until Monday. She'd made tentative plans to join a friend for a movie and dinner, but that wasn't until later.

Ah, she had it. A brisk walk down Wilshire Boulevard would energize her. But first, why not a detour to the offices at the far end of the lobby? Mark Hampton's office, specifically.

Her excuse for barging in? Advice for her dear sister's troubled marriage. And if she happened to bump into Susan Connelly? How delicious that would be.

Chapter Three

Dr. Mark Hampton shifted in his armchair and glanced at his watch. The hour was almost up. He looked at the notepad lying dormant in his lap.

Susan Connelly, perched on the edge of the sofa across from him, seemed transfixed by the box of tissues on the table that established doctor/patient boundaries.

One more try. "Susan. Tell me what you're thinking. Now. At this very moment."

Silence. She was imbedded in the catacombs of her misery, in a dark place that reeked of despair.

And then she stirred. "I shouldn't be here. I hate that I'm here." Small voice, shoulders hunched.

He picked up his notepad. "Can you tell me why you feel this way?"

She straightened and looked Mark in the eye. "I've always been self-reliant. I detest people who snivel and whine, who grouse but don't have the guts to take a stand."

"The whiners and the wimps seldom seek help. You've taken a positive step."

"It scares me that I have trouble concentrating, that I can't stay focused."

"You've admitted that you're in distress. Now we'll work to search out the root of the problem."

"What *problem*? I shouldn't *have* problems!" Button brown eyes, teary but contained, fastened on him.

"And why is that?"

"I told you my background, Dr. Hampton. Growing up, I had all the advantages. I'm a university graduate; I married a professional, have a lovely home, a beautiful daughter, more friends than I can keep up with. Oh. And of course, a happy marriage. I could recite a laundry list of my family's accomplishments."

"And yet, you quit your job," he looked at his notes, "stepped down as Regional Director for Campfire Girls, and dropped your commitment as volunteer receptionist at the hospital."

"It's the same people, over and over who volunteer, including myself, and I'm burned out. Besides, I could perform those duties in my sleep." She fiddled with a strand of hair, sweeping it behind her ear. "As for my job, it's trendy among my set to make the cut as a dental hygienist. Most of us don't need to work, but at least we have an answer to 'What do you do?' In any case, I don't consider that vocation much of a career."

"You'd have a number of dissenters, I'm afraid."

"I aspired to loftier ambitions. I thought of becoming a pharmacist or a medical researcher."

"It's never too late."

She bowed her head. "I don't sleep well; I'm tired all the time, I count my blessings and end up in tears."

Her voice was thin, muted in tone, and Mark had to struggle to hear her last sentence.

"Help is on the way, Susan. We'll work together to brighten your life." He rose. "If possible, I'd like to see you next week."

"Your Pasadena office would be closer to home."

"By all means." He pointed to the outer office. "You can see Dolores about setting up an appointment."

He walked beside her to the door, then ushered her out with a reassuring pat on her shoulder, all part of the protocol.

For the first time since she'd started therapy, Susan smiled as she said goodbye.

With Susan's chart in hand, Mark settled in at his desk. He studied the paper work she'd filled out at their first session. No serious medical problems, except for asthma (several acute attacks in the past two years) and a propensity for claustrophobia.

He scribbled some notes from today's session, underlining her comment regarding a happy marriage; then, as was his custom after a second meeting, penned a detailed physical description.

Patient: 42 years old. Square shaped face, slight sagging under chin. Broad forehead, medium length brown hair, small brown eyes, thin lips, clear, rosy complexion, stocky build. He'd also noted shapely legs and generous breasts. In all, she appeared heavier than what she'd recorded as her weight.

Mark leaned back in his chair and stretched. Despite a shaky start and her initial insistence to see him away from her home turf, he had a good feeling about this case; so much so, he was 99% certain he could help Susan Connelly come out of her depression. He pictured a smiling, alert woman with an unfaltering step. Add a more pleasant disposition as well.

That was enough work for a Saturday. He shrugged into his jacket and stepped into the waiting room.

"You just missed her," Dolores said. "A woman. Peeked in, asking for you, then said not to bother." Dolores gave him a knowing look, eyebrows arched. "A real babe, Dr. Hampton."

Who on earth? Mark wondered as he left his office. And then he caught sight of the woman from the mail room. Dana…James? Was it James? He thought so.

He picked up his pace and was close enough to the doors to observe that once out of the building, Dana had turned right. As he exited through the revolving doors and out into the sunshine, his progress was slowed as he dodged package-laden shoppers, two small children prancing on either side of a harried looking woman, and maneuvered around a group of teenagers, five abreast, who held dominion over the sidewalk.

Dressed all in white, Dana was easy to track. He marveled at how she managed her fast clip in strappy three inch heels. She appeared oblivious to the heads that swiveled in her direction. "Dana!" he called out.

She stopped, looked back, and then turned, her eyes widening in recognition. "Or should I say Ms. James?" he asked, now at her side.

She smiled. "Dana will do just fine."

He could see confusion in her face and quickly explained he'd spotted her in the lobby, then on impulse decided to catch up with her. "Maybe we should step over to the side," he said, guiding her with his hand on her elbow away from the advancing band of teenagers.

"Think they own the world," she said. "Enjoy it while you can, darlings," she called out, and then clamped a hand over her mouth. "Oh, dear, what must you think? Am I fodder for analysis?"

She was stunning, the green of her eyes mesmerizing. "What I think," he said, "is if you're free, we might go to lunch," he gestured, "away from the madding crowd?"

She hesitated only a second. "Are you familiar with La Casita around the corner? The patio is charming, the fajitas are scrumptious."

Her ready acceptance pleased him, but he thought he'd caught, though fleeting, a calculating look that preceded her radiant smile. Or was he being overly analytic? In any case, he was more than willing to take the chance.

Their table beneath a shade tree featured miniature Mexican flags and green and red napkins on placemats that depicted a range of colorful scenes, from elaborately costumed Mariachi musicians to bougainvillea draped casas overlooking a cobblestone street.

The soft singing of "La Paloma" by a young man accompanying himself on the guitar made for the perfect background music. Dana raised her margarita in a toast to her companion, who raised his martini, in turn.

"What a lovely way to spend an afternoon," Dana said, taking a sip of her drink.

Mark nodded. "I couldn't agree more. I'm curious, though. Was it you who stopped by my office? From my receptionist's description—"

"I confess. It was me. I was just curious… when you mentioned seeing a patient, I decided to check out what medical services you offered. Now that I know you're a psychologist, I–well, I hesitate to bring this matter up…"

Mark sipped his martini. "You can't stop now. Please, go on."

"Someone I'm close to is going through a dreadful time in her marriage. I wondered if marital counseling was part of your practice."

As she spoke, he felt his face transform from flirtatious to professional. His concerned clinician expression.

"I certainly do provide marital counseling, so if you, I mean if your friend would like to set up an appointment—"

"Whoa, stop right there. I swear I'm not hiding behind a fake friend. I'm talking about my sister. I put in an emotional morning with her, and it's obvious she needs professional help."

He handed her his card.

"Oh, thank you," she said, reading the business card.

Mark signaled the waiter. "I'm going to order another martini. Would you care for a re-fill?"

"Not just yet. So, tell me, do you always act on impulse?"

"Only in pursuit of something or someone irresistible."

"Does Mrs. Hampton fit that category?"

"If by Mrs. Hampton you mean my mother, I suppose my father thought so." Mark spread his hands. "As for me, I guess I've been so busy fixing other people's problems, I haven't made the effort to follow through on my own relationships."

His gaze fell on her rings. "Tell me about Mr. James."

Dana was obviously taken aback. Mark had been a bit more to the point than she had. She filled him in on her husband's background and business, adding that presently he was in Australia. "Jasper wants us to move to Sydney."

Mark frowned. "How do you feel about that?"

"I have mixed feelings." She paused as the waiter placed Mark's drink before him. "It's a big step, of course, but once Jasper makes up his mind, he doesn't welcome an opposing point of view."

Mark raised his glass to her. "I don't even know you, but I think I would miss you."

"This is crazy," Dana said, "but I was thinking the same about you."

He smiled in response, and as they engaged in conversation, Mark gave himself a mental pat on the back. The woman had definitely been worth pursuing.

"Incidentally," Dana said, "I almost ran into someone I know in our lobby this morning. I say 'almost' because as she walked past me, she seemed in a bit of a fog. I even called Susan by name, but she didn't respond. Being the snoop that I am, I tailed her. It turned out she was headed for your office."

"So you and Mrs. Connelly are friends?"

"We go back a ways, yes, but I wouldn't call us friends. We—well, this is not the time to go into that."

Mark was bursting with curiosity, yet it would not be ethical on his part to press for details. However, Dana offered one more tidbit.

"Speaking of Susan, I don't know if you're into politics, but Susan's name often appears in the papers, associated with Republican causes. In fact, she's quite well-known in Republican circles, and about as far right as you can get. I wouldn't call her a poster girl for the downtrodden."

Though Mark was disappointed that Dana had not been more forthcoming about Susan, he gave her a direct look and a warm smile. "Very interesting." He held her gaze for a moment, and then said, "I think it's time we looked at the menu. Now may I buy you another margarita?" At her nod, he said, "Good. Maybe I'll order another martini. Celebrate the season and my good fortune for sharing lunch with the beautiful Dana James."

She rewarded him with an enigmatic smile. And as he ordered their drinks, Mark sensed that until Dana moved to Australia, getting to know this lovely lady would bring more rewards than a mere smile.

Barry could have called. Damn. It was well past the cocktail hour now; the clock was the enemy, grinding into overtime, eroding Kim's confidence and making a mockery of the sense of optimism that had infused her earlier in the day. The question was sickeningly familiar: Where was Barry?

He'd been in good spirits when he returned from golf, pleased with his performance, having tallied the lowest score of his foursome. A quick shower and he was on his way out again, this time to the office to catch up on paper work. He promised to return no later than six.

At 6:45 Kim had called his office, but had gotten no answer. It was now 7:15, and she returned to her lookout perch by the window, vacillating between worry and anger.

They had not discussed dinner plans, though it was customary for them to dine out on Saturdays. She could only hope he would opt for casual over upscale.

Another five minutes that seemed like fifty, and then she breathed a sigh of relief as she caught the glint of sunlight on champagne as the Lexus wound its way up the street. What followed was the reassuring crunch of the garage door opening, and then closing.

She met him in the kitchen as he entered through the garage carrying a grocery bag.

"Hi, baby, I know I'm late. I did try to call you, but the line was busy. Rather than wait around, I decided to hightail it home. Unfortunately, Sunset Boulevard was the usual Saturday evening stop and go."

"I thought you planned to be home by six."

"I'll explain later. First things first. I stopped at the grocery at Vermont and Franklin to pick up some steaks. After the hoopla of last night, I thought we'd enjoy an evening at home. You know, have a couple of drinks on the patio, bring out the barbeque, toss a green salad."

Kim reached for the bag. "I'll put the steaks in the fridge."

While she did so, Barry came up behind her and wrapped his arms around her waist. "I thought you'd be pleased," he breathed into her ear.

She turned, and then stepped away from him. "I am pleased we're staying home, that it's just the two of us for a change. But I was worried and upset. Couldn't you have called me on your cell phone?"

"I didn't have it with me." He stared at the floor for a moment before looking up. A shrug, a rueful smile: that was Barry.

It was still light out when they settled on the patio for cocktails. Kim had provided an assortment of cheeses and crackers. After Barry placed their drinks on the table, scotch and water for him, vodka and tonic for her, he stood behind her chair and gently massaged away the tightness in her shoulders, and then kissed the back of her neck.

It was a sweet moment; his actions imbued her with the sense of well being that marked the high point of her visit with Dana. Now she listened with an open mind to Barry's explanation of his tardiness.

"—and so, without boring you with all the grubby details, one phone call led to another, with everyone claiming greatest urgency, and with me working my tail off to clarify this situation, patch up that misunderstanding, mollify him, her, them." He raised his hands. "I simply lost track of the time."

She'd made a mental note that Barry never used the word "sorry", but then, what man did? "I guess you can't help it if you're good at your job." She paused. "And now that we've gotten that out of the way, I have a surprise for you."

His expression turned wary. Was he afraid she would herald the news of impending fatherhood? "It's a nice surprise," she said, "that I thought I'd save for the day after your birthday. Remember I mentioned the fund raiser last week for Women's Forum? Well–ta-da! I won the grand prize in the silent auction. We're about to be whisked off to Hawaii for a one week stay at a condo in Kona, on the big island."

He set down his drink. "That's all very extraordinary Kim, but you can't imagine my workload. I have meetings with clients, a special project in the works, a business trip coming up."

"Barry, listen to me. You're not a minion who exists to please the boss. You *are* the boss. Give yourself some time off. We could take four or five days instead of a week. We could also include the 4th of July weekend. That's not a happening time in the workplace."

She was not encouraged by his obdurate stance–the tightened facial muscles, creased brow, and lack of eye contact. She held her tongue, seeking inspiration from a higher source, but what could she say? Threats and ultimatums were out of the question.

Barry sipped his drink for a moment or two before gently setting down his glass, his expression more open. "As I think about it, the time around the 4th could work out, and the idea is appealing." He nodded. "Let's do it. Besides, you deserve a break."

"Oh, sweetheart, you won't regret it. From what I've heard, the locale is gorgeous and the place is filled with restaurants and shops."

As she started to reach for him, he pushed back his chair. "Let's have another drink while we map out the details. Oh. Before I forget, I talked to George today. He was surprised you hadn't given his message to me."

"I surprised myself, too. But I guess I had other things on my mind. Like Felicia. Like the broken sculpture. Enough said?"

He smiled. "No need to spell it out."

Before he turned to go back inside, he held her gaze for a moment. He looked at her with affection and respect. Glory be, they were back on track!

Mark had turned down a dinner invitation from a colleague, pleading a previous commitment. The truth was he felt the need for a quiet evening at home. In the past week, he had played poker, attended the theater and dined out twice with friends. Also, he wanted to update himself on pharmaceuticals for bi-polar disease, research he had planned to pursue this afternoon.

His home in La Canada Flintridge was minutes away from his Pasadena office but seemed a world apart. It was now mid-evening, and as he relaxed on his deck, enjoying brandy and a cigar, he congratulated himself yet again on his choice of location. As much as he enjoyed the company of friends, this wooded area with sunlight-dappled trees that bordered slowly moving streams provided his sanctuary; it was a place for reflection.

More than once, he'd questioned if it was his destiny to share this space—or any space—with a woman on a permanent basis.

Thus far, he enjoyed life being single.

Still, he adored women and considered himself a romantic at heart. Too bad he had no one in his life at present. Dana James came to mind. He pictured her—a sensuous patchwork of velvet and silk, laced with diamonds and edged with attitude. Whimsy aside, the woman was married and soon, he imagined, would be trading diamonds for opals from Down Under. Of course, one's marital status had not deterred him in the past, nor did he think a woman like Dana placed a great deal of importance on fidelity.

In any event, consistent with his musings at lunch, she was well worth a try. To her obvious attributes, he could add playfulness, a sense of humor and lack of coyness. And yet, another plus: it appeared Dana might provide valuable insights into the troubled world of Susan Connelly. If only he could figure out a way to probe Dana for information without revealing Susan's state of health.

He'd take it a step at a time. First, he would call Dana in a day or two to invite her out to dinner. Next, he might come up with tickets to a musical or sports event. Maybe even prepare a dinner at home.

He could only hope that in the time left, they might forge a loving relationship. And somewhere down the line, he_could only imagine the joy of making love to this very desirable woman.

Best of all, they would enjoy the moment. No regrets.

No strings attached.

The lights in the great room were dimmed like the houselights in a theater, enabling Dana, sitting at the piano, to conjure up a scene in her mind. She pictured a hushed and reverent audience, and then wild applause interspersed with shouts of praise as she concluded her selection. She would finish by rising from the piano in her shimmering emerald green gown. She would glide toward the footlights to acknowledge her audience and accept a huge bouquet of roses from a devoted fan.

She held the image for a moment, and then thumped the keys, dissonance edging out fantasy. "Not in this life, baby."

She rose from the piano leaving a half-finished Coke, and drifted aimlessly about the room, coming to a stop at the doors leading to the terrace. Here was the perfect setting where one could tower above the masses. She pictured Eva Peron, a benevolent presence before adoring crowds. She pictured herself. Queen Dana? Pope Dana? She gave a little snort and entered the terrace.

The night was balmy, and as Dana stood at the terrace railing, reality took ahold of her grandiose fantasies to the tune of horns and Saturday night hullabaloo, backed by a profusion of city lights and bawdy neon.

She ached to be out there, standing out from the pack, acclaimed for her star quality. She might have made it, damn it, had Bea Devlin not pulled the plug on her drama scholarship.

Before she'd settled on merchandising as a career, she'd made a half-hearted attempt at acting lessons to improve her chances in TV and movie auditions. She'd been adequate if not great. Mainly, she lacked the wherewithal to stick with it, to sacrifice for her craft.

Why play the part of drudge waitress at a Denny's or similar venues when she could be wined and dined in style? If nothing else, she knew she stood out as a woman.

What a waste, not to have a man by her side. She had Jasper, of course. But Mark Hampton would do in his place. Her dinner out with Jill from the unit above hers wasn't nearly as much fun as lunch with the therapist. He wasn't the kind of man she typically would have chosen, but maybe it was time to switch to outgoing and relaxed over intense and guarded. As she moved from railing to chair, she replayed their afternoon together, remembering the easy camaraderie, the delectable male-female connection. But other considerations eclipsed pleasure for pleasure's sake. She wanted information about Susan–her mental health, the state of her marriage. To think: this self-satisfied, condescending excuse for a woman teetered, she hoped, on the brink of something really nasty. Mark, on the other hand, wanted her input on the patient. He also wanted her, she was sure.

She pictured intimate dinners where she'd reveal information, but only enough to perk his interest. This rationing of information would lure him back for more. At the same time, with the aid of martinis and wine, she would charm Mark into divulging all. And the most enticing strategy of all? Pillow talk. If it came to that.

The bonus in all her scheming? She found Mark extremely attractive and he was a genuinely nice man. That they both had agendas only enriched the game of seduction.

In retrospect, her ploy to sound him out regarding her sister's crumbling marriage seemed contrived and weak. But it had worked. She also had his card that in good faith she was supposed to hand over to Kim.

She might or might not dispose of it. The only certainty was that Kim would never see it. Why give Kim the card when she was not going to need it.

Chapter Four

It didn't surprise Mark that the doorbell to Dana's apartment chimed a mellow octave below standard tones. He anticipated stepping into a showcase of elegance. And he wasn't disappointed.

Following a casual get together at a bistro on Sunset Boulevard, they'd wined and dined at more upscale establishments. Tonight, however, he would dine with Dana in her home—a move Mark viewed as a giant step forward.

Dana still hadn't come to the door so he rang again, pushing harder this time, and then heard, "I'm coming, I'm coming."

The door swung open. "I'm sorry I took so long. I was on the phone with my sister. Please come in. Oh! Look what you've brought. How did you know orchids are my favorite?"

He handed her the plant, and while she marveled at the petals—variegated pink and purple, with unique gold and white centers—he simply stared. She wore what he supposed was a hostess gown of sea foam green, deeply low cut in front, with sheer, full length sleeves. Her perfume, spicy but not overpowering, had Dana's signature. Who was out to seduce whom?

"I'll set them next to where we're dining so we can enjoy a double feast of the senses." After carefully placing the flowers near the table, she gave him a sidelong look. "You're staring at me."

"You look like a medieval princess, awaiting the knight who has won the right to claim you, fair maiden. God, you're beautiful."

She giggled. "And you are a romantic. Thank you for the kind words and the lovely description. But maiden I am not.

"Oh, Mark, you're so sweet. Let's have cocktails outside. The martinis are already poured."

When they were settled on the terrace, Dana said, "You'll be glad to know the catering service I'm using tonight is renowned for its bartending skills. Cheers!"

They clinked glasses and sipped. "Excellent," Mark said. He gestured outward. "I didn't expect such a spacious terrace. And your apartment is lovely. I'd say it suits you very well, though I hardly expected a hovel."

"I don't do hovels." She paused. "You're right that I'm in a place that suits me. I've loved living here, and I hate having to give it up."

Interesting, he observed, that her expression mirrored defiance over sadness. "I've heard of bi-coastal relationships, but Sydney to Los Angeles is a bit of a stretch."

Her smile was a mere flicker. "Indeed. On a happier note, my sister and her husband are off to Hawaii tomorrow."

"Good for them. So their situation is not as dire as you thought."

"Hope springs you-know-what, but I think it's a stopgap, at best. The last hurrah. At least on his part."

Mark shook his head. "Their timing might be questionable. It's the height of tourist season, and with the Fourth of July around the corner, it could be a mob scene."

"I know. I'm not looking forward to the crowds."

Mark raised his eyebrows, prompting Dana to explain, "Don't get the wrong idea. I'm not following them to Hawaii to act as a referee or love coach. It so happens the day after they leave home, I fly to Honolulu on business. They'll be in Kona, but I'm only a short flight away if Kim needs me."

She looked thoughtful. "I did give Kim your card. If, as I suspect, their break-up is imminent, I hope she contacts you."

"You seem so sure that the marriage is over."

"Her husband Barry is a snake, an egotistical, manipulating jerk. My sister knows this all too well, but she's smitten beyond smitten with the creep."

"Would you like another card for yourself? Maybe I can defang the man." He paused. "Sorry. I don't mean to make light of a difficult situation."

"And I don't mean to bore you with the kinds of problems you deal with every day." She indicated his glass. "I think you're ready for another martini. Sit tight. I'll bring out the pitcher."

Dana had set the stage: their table graced with fine bone china and crystal goblets that emitted a soft diamond radiance by candlelight. Jazz piano music in the background—Duke Ellington, Stan Kenton and others—pumped spice into the elegant setting.

Her menu consisted of sherry flavored crab bisque, followed by blue cheese and pears on greens, sprinkled with almond slivers. Duck a l'Orange was the entrée with crème brûlée for desert. And lastly, of course, an after dinner drink.

When they'd finished the meal Dana said, "Come, let's sit on the couch. What's your pleasure?"

One of the staff from the catering service served their brandies within minutes. Wine with dinner was a pricey 2004 Sonoma Coast Vineyards Pinot Noir–his favorite, she'd learned. He'd consumed three—or four?—martinis to her two, and she'd lost track of how many re-fills of wine, but his hazel eyes flecked with gold were clear, and except for expansiveness in speech and gesture, he appeared to be physically in control.

Still, with all that booze, plus a little help from St. Remy Napoleon Brandy, Dana was counting on getting Mark to open up about Susan.

He pounced first, asking if she knew Susan's husband, Ted Connelly.

"We've talked briefly at a couple of charity events."

"How would you describe him?"

"Are Susan and Ted having problems?"

"You know I can't talk about that with you."

"I can provide a clearer picture for you if you choose to comment discreetly." She moved in closer to take his hand. "Romance bloomed between them through the auspices of Young Republican related activities."

"Is he as deeply into politics as Susan?"

"That was not my impression. Ted struck me as Mr. Nice Guy. Maybe a little shy. I suppose you know he's a CPA."

Mark nodded. "Tell me more."

"You tell me. Are they having political differences?"

"It's not a central issue. So many factors can cause a rift. People change, outgrow one another. Marriages become stale. A partner suffers from depression."

He spoke in generalities. Or maybe not. Dana made a mental note of key words: rift, stale, depression.

Mark took a sip of his brandy. "You mentioned you and Susan weren't exactly friends. I'd like to hear about that."

"Maybe another time?" She moved in closer to him, her tone inviting, intimate.

He took the hint.

Mark's touch was gentle but commanding, his kisses sweet and enduring; now growing more passionate. She felt the thumping of his heart as he pulled her against him, as he caressed her breasts. His excitement was contagious, drawing her deeply into a warm center of sheer sensuousness.

It was time to stop. Gently, she pushed him away. "I want you Mark Hampton, but it can't be tonight. I have an early morning meeting, a ton of things to take care of before my trip. May we get together when I return from Hawaii?"

"Yes, of course." His expression conveyed a sense of amusement. As befitted her opponent—or ally? In the love game—a fellow player.

He held out his arms. "A goodbye hug, okay?" When they drew apart, he pulled a comb out of his back pocket and then rose to retrieve his jacket.

Dana gave a soft laugh. "Now that you're neat and tidy, I should make some repairs."

"Nonsense. You're perfect as is." Mark took her hand as they stood together at the door. "When you're back, I want to plan a dinner for you at my place. Mind you, you'll have to substitute a deck for a terrace, with me in the kitchen."

"I'll bet you're a first-rate cook. I can't wait."

"Tonight was incredible. You're incredible." He leaned down to kiss her lightly on the lips. "Good night. Have a safe trip."

She called out his name before he was out the door. His look of expectancy when he turned back was almost laughable.

Dana spoke softly, sweetly. "I'm thinking of asking Jasper for a divorce."

She'd caught him off guard, though only for a minute. "I'll be interested to hear more on that subject." He kept his tone light, smiled, then turned to leave.

A bombshell, for sure, Dana thought as she shut and locked the door. She leisurely walked over to admire her orchids.

Had she caught a hint of wariness in his expression? For all his attentiveness and extravagant compliments, the man was no shoo-in. Call him... elusive. Call her interested.

She loved a challenge.

"I think we're starting our descent." Kim gave Barry a little poke and then reached across him to close his magazine. "Sweetheart, you have to look out the window. The blues and greens of the waters are jewel-like, so clear and vibrant."

"I've seen it before."

They were seated in first class, on a direct flight from Los Angeles to Kona. Barry had been taciturn during much of the trip, as if preoccupied, and over lunch, Kim had labored to keep the conversation flowing.

Now she wondered: Was he so jaded he'd lost touch with nature's gifts? Or was he unable (or unwilling) to make the transition from work to play? Maybe he needed a nudge.

She moved in close to him, their shoulders touching, her words meant for his ears alone. "All right, my darling, it's time to embrace the island spirit. Now picture in your mind's eye following the scent of hibiscus to a sun drenched lanai, cooled by trade winds—"

"Don't forget falling asleep to the gentle lapping of the waves. Kim, for heaven's sake, you sound like a travel brochure or the first paragraph of 'How I Spent My Summer Vacation'."

"It wouldn't hurt you to show a little enthusiasm."

"I haven't? Well, darn me, anyway." He smiled. "You don't have to convince me, honey. I'm sure it's going to be a memorable few days."

They were close to landing and Kim rested her head on his shoulder. "I'm glad you've decided to come to the party."

"I wouldn't miss it," he said.

She raised her head to stare out the window. Though his words were reassuring, his tone reflected otherwise, as if he expected to witness rather than participate in their time together in Hawaii.

She grabbed his hand as the plane hit the tarmac, as her stomach muscles tightened and her body went rigid, reacting to the reverse thrust of the jet engines.

Barry slid his arm around her shoulder and gave her a squeeze. "It's okay, baby, we're down, we're safe."

Together and safe. It was all she could ask for. And yet, she tasted grit, envisioned ashes obliterating light. *Ashes, ashes, we all fall down.* The nursery tune jangled in her head in a mawkish duet with the Hawaiian music that was now playing throughout the cabin. *Welcome to paradise.*

Driving from the airport in their rental car, Kim dismissed her sense of foreboding as dramatic conjecture, honed by her fear of flying.

By the time they got to the condo, she was feeling far more upbeat.

She and Barry stood at the glass doors that opened onto their lanai. "All you can see is ocean," Kim said. "It's like being on a cruise ship. I can tell I'm going to love this."

Kim followed Barry outside where he stood at the railing. "From here you can see the rocks below."

Kim nodded. *Gentle lapping of waves, my foot*, she thought. The surf pounding against the rocks sounded like an avalanche. "I could stay here all day, but I vote we go back inside and explore the rest of this place."

The living room was spacious enough to include a large off-white sofa, fronted by a circular glass coffee table rimmed in gold leaf. The accompanying chairs were cushioned in a sunset after-glow of soft peach and saffron, the legs exhibiting a delicate leafy cross pattern. Nothing tacky or drowning in bamboo, thanks to big sister Dana.

As Kim entered the dining area, the credenza against the opposite wall, complete with two silk orchid flower arrangements, caught her attention. The flowers were in porcelain vases, accented by leaves of gold cascading down the sides. The majesty and magnitude of this grouping declared it a shrine in homage to the portrait centered above the arrangements.

Dana stared out at Kim: the intense green of her eyes, the cloud of dark hair framing a creamy complexion, dewy pink lips slightly parted. Kim moved in for a closer look. The raised chin and tilted head might have been construed as haughty, but were countered by the impish expression in Dana's eyes. Someone had caught the essence of her sister.

The slamming of a cupboard door reminded Kim that while Barry was now investigating the kitchen, he could be at her side in seconds. The picture had to go.

Most of the space inside the credenza was filled except for one drawer with only linens and plenty of room to spare. She grabbed the portrait and in her haste knocked it against one of the vases.

Shit. The glass had cracked and there would be hell to pay. Quickly she shoved the damn thing into the drawer. Glass could be replaced; Barry's trust could not. God only knew what would happen if Barry had been the one to discover the portrait. How could she explain her duplicity?

On their third day in Kona, Barry, God love him, had thrown off the cloak of business related angst to don shorts and shirts that conveyed the Aloha Spirit. Well, almost. Kim still thought of her husband as a fish out of water, but a sense of calm had settled over her. They were close, loving, having fun. Just the two of them.

The closest beach, a fifteen minute drive south of their condo, was crowded with tourists and locals, but not to the point of close encounters with flying sand or bouncing beach balls. Most of the kids played in the water, and their shouts and squeals were a mere footnote to the hiss of billowing waves.

"What are you thinking?" Barry asked. They had placed beach towels on the sand and lay side by side, holding hands. The paperback books each had brought remained untouched.

"That maybe this bliss is too much of a good thing. I much prefer bronzed over lobster red."

"Time for a swim?"

"In a minute. I was also thinking about Dana's call this morning."

"I'm surprised she knew where to reach you."

"I talked to her before we left home, told her about winning the big prize. It's really a coincidence we're both in Hawaii at the same time."

"But not on the same island," he said, sounding relieved. "What is she doing in Honolulu anyway?"

"Checking on some property she and Jasper own." With her foot Kim flicked a little sand onto Barry's ankle. "Don't be so hard on her. She knows the area and when I mentioned we planned to spend the morning sunning and swimming, she suggested this beach."

"She also made another suggestion." Kim sat up and pointed to the right, "See that terraced restaurant? According to Dana, they have it all: ocean view, superb food and spectacular sunsets."

Barry raised himself to a sitting position, his frown an indication of–what? That Dana was up to no good? He shaded his eyes, staring in the direction of the restaurant.

"What do you think? If you'd rather not—"

"It's a great idea, Kim. Let's go there tonight."

When he turned back to her, his smile was beguiling, the warmth of his gaze intimating that special, and private place known only to them. For Kim, this moment shut out the world, softened the sun's rays, and silenced all sound. "Ready for that swim, now?" he asked.

It wasn't a question; it was a caress, and Kim had to catch her breath as waves of desire swept over her. "We can always swim later," she said.

"Later is better." He held out his hand. "Let's head back to the condo."

Kim sat at her dressing table in an afterglow of sweet gratification. Making love in the afternoon had always smacked of indulgence in their busy lives. She relished replaying the past several hours when, after the first urgent coupling, they had played their bodies like a musical instrument–stretching a tender legato phrase into a pulsating rhythmic journey that soared into mindless abandonment.

It was Dana who had brought Barry into her life, and now thanks to big sister's generosity and intuitive wisdom, Barry would remain in her life.

Kim smiled at her reflection and then gave a start as she glimpsed her husband standing in the doorway. Still smiling, she rose to join him, but then hesitated. “Barry? You look so solemn. Are you okay?”

“Why wouldn’t I be?” The gruffness in his tone was unsettling.

“I’m sorry. I guess in the fading light—”

He relaxed his stance and held out his arms. “Come here, you.”

“Now that’s more like it,” she said, snuggling in his embrace. “Ready for another round?”

He laughed. “Tempting as it may be, I think we’d better go to dinner. We’ve skipped lunch, you do realize that. And that makes Barry a grouchy boy.”

She rose on tiptoe to kiss him lightly on the lips. “I’m all set with makeup and hair. Just need to exchange this robe for my black and white strapless sundress. Oh, and if you were expecting preppy, you’ll just have to settle for sexy. Five minutes and we’re out of here!”

At the restaurant, they sat on a terrace illuminated by torch light. The gentle breezes carried the scent of gardenias and mimosa, and the ocean played a steady beat for the setting sun.

Even as darkness neared, Kim still felt the sun’s radiance, the glowing warmth that covered her cheeks and caused a tingling in her arms and shoulders. She took a sip of her Mai Tai, and then sat back as the server removed their plates.

“I wouldn’t change this day for the world,” Kim said.

Barry nodded. “I hoped—that is, wanted today to be perfect.”

These were words she wanted to hear. Yet, his quietness throughout the meal, his sober expression now, gave her pause. Something was eating at him. Dare she risk another testy response? She leaned forward, “Barry, I asked you before. Is everything all right? Are you feeling okay?”

When he didn’t answer, she tried again. “It’s obvious something is bothering you. Whatever it is, please tell me. We’ll work it out together, find a solution.”

“Kim, it’s not my job; it’s not my health. I want a divorce.”

"Why? Because I'm a hottie, too much for you between the sheets? Barry, come on, this is not funny or clever."

"I am not joking." His tone was flat, and he stared past her avoiding eye contact.

"What is this about? Not wanting to move to Malibu? Not dressing glamorously? Offending George Anderson?"

"You seem to be taking this lightly enough, which is a relief."

"Lightly?" She had to moisten her lips. She felt like she was talking through a wad of cotton. "I assure you I take very seriously the prospect of going through a shitty divorce." She sat back in her chair, focusing on the man who was her mate, her lover, who now said he no longer wanted her. "You can't be serious. What about this afternoon?"

"You've always been a fantastic bed partner. You're lovely in so many ways, Kim, but I simply don't want to be married."

This was not some sadistic joke. He was making it plain he wanted her out of his life. "I can't sit here." She grabbed her bag with a swooping motion as she rose, and in the process, knocked over her Mai Tai which spilled across the tablecloth and onto the floor.

Barry stood up but kept his voice low. "Kim, sit down. We have to talk."

"Screw you!" Heads turned and their waiter hurried toward them, his face cringing with concern.

Kim felt Mai Tai on her sandaled feet as she worked her way around tables of romantic twosomes and merry multiples of four, six and eight. It was an endless journey that should have been a blur but was etched in her mind. How could people be eating, drinking, smiling and laughing while she teetered at the edge of this untroubled world into an abyss of darkness and despair?

Barry caught up with her in the parking lot just as the valet brought their car. "Why didn't you wait for me? People were staring."

"Go to hell."

"Get in the car. Please."

She did as he requested, her legs moving stiffly, her breathing labored. She'd only come from inside the restaurant but she felt as if she'd run a marathon.

The drive back to the condo felt, to Kim, like forever. Her throat hurt from trying to hold back sobs. Finally Barry broke the silence with words to the effect that she needed to be reasonable, that she should try to view this whole scenario from his perspective.

"Also," he said, "we need to work out travel arrangements for the trip home and discuss matters pertaining to the division of property and so on."

So business-like. So sure of himself. Food and drink churned in Kim's stomach, leaving a sour taste in her mouth. So he didn't want to be married. Why? And how dare he degrade their marriage into the likeness of a scenario.

They had reached the access road that led to the parking garage and as Barry drove into their assigned space, Kim placed a firm hand on his arm. "I'm not leaving this car until I get some answers. Are you having an affair?"

"Not really."

"Not really? Either you are or you're not."

"I've—I've been with someone a couple of times."

"Felicia?"

He nodded.

His nod was a knife, cutting into rawness. "The woman you said meant nothing to you." She spaced her words as if she were spitting out stones. Then suddenly she felt the heat in her cheeks. "The Saturday you returned from golf, then said you were going to the office. You were with Felicia, weren't you?"

He bowed his head. Silence.

"Lies, lies, lies!" She couldn't breathe, needed air. She grabbed the door handle and stumbled out of the car. In the dim light and in her haste to escape, she banged into the pole that separated the parking spaces and went down hard on one knee.

Barry was out of the car, then kneeling at her side. "Kim, let me help you."

"Bastard! Get away from me; don't touch me."

Footsteps echoed in the garage, now speeding up as a man ran toward them. "Hey, what's going on here? Miss, are you all right? Did he hurt you?"

She recognized Tony, the handyman for the units. "Hurt? Yes, but not what you're thinking."

Barry straightened. "I'm her husband. She fell, and it was an accident. I need to get her upstairs."

"My husband? What a joke." Her laugh broke off into a sob.

Tony was a slight man, but his determined stance, the thrust of his jaw signaled "Don't mess with me. Look miss, if this man has hurt you, if you're afraid to go with him, we'll take care of it now."

"Thank you. I know you mean well, but he's right. My fall was an accident."

Doubt clouded his expression. "If you say so." He opened his mouth, but then clamped his lips shut. He turned away, walking slowly out of the garage, pausing once to look back.

"Kim, don't fight me. You're going to be in trouble if we don't ice that knee."

She was too shaken, too tired to protest, and when they were back in their unit, she allowed him to settle her onto the sofa with an icepack on her knee.

He also brought a brandy for her and one for himself.

"What, no scotch tonight?"

"Later," he said.

God, how cozy was this, the loving husband ministering to his injured wife. Except—she felt her face awash in tears.

"Kim, I know how difficult this is for both of us."

"Is that what you told wife number one and wife number two?"

"Let's not get sidetracked, or if you insist on delving into the past, wasn't it you who broke it off with Kevin?"

"Our decision to part was mutual. Kevin was a failed artist who needed–forgive the cliché–to find himself." She sucked in her breath. "Jesus, Barry, I don't want to talk about Kevin. I want to talk about us. Why do you want a divorce?"

"For one thing, what do we really have in common? Not much."

"I've tried to please you."

"I'm aware of that, but you've only been kidding yourself, trying to be something you're not."

"Glamorous? Witty? In the know?"

"Think about it. Have you really enjoyed moving in my circles? Wouldn't you prefer a more wholesome, family-oriented life? And what about children? You know that's not an option for me."

"But we were so happy in the beginning. What about the passion we share for art?"

"For you, art is a passion; for me it's a business investment. As for our beginnings, I took great pleasure in introducing you to a richer, more sophisticated way of life, of watching you mature into the lovely woman you've become. Now I feel it's time for both of us to move on."

"I can't believe this. Dana was right about you."

"Dana?" He laughed. "Let me tell you about your sister."

"Don't go there, Barry."

"All right. So Dana made ugly about me. We'll leave it at that."

"Essentially, she said you thrive on doing make-overs of young, vulnerable women. Which is certainly not applicable to Felicia."

"Drop it, Kim. We have far more important matters to discuss." He drained his glass. "But not tonight. I'm going down to the pool."

By way of the kitchen, of course. Kim swung her legs over the sofa and stepped down. It hurt to walk, but the fact that she could walk was encouraging.

"I don't think anything's broken," she said as she limped into the kitchen carrying her glass.

Barry frowned. "You probably should continue icing your knee."

She nodded and held out her glass. "I'll have another brandy."

Back in the living room, Kim eased into the chair where Barry had been sitting. She reached for the icepack, and then tasted her drink, welcoming the numbness that was beginning to settle over her. And when this anesthetic wore off? Somehow she'd deal with the pain, the disillusionment. For now, fatigue was her best friend.

Had she nodded off for a minute? If so, a noise had awakened her. Kim looked up to see Barry at the door, Drambuie in hand.

"I'm on my way to the pool," he said. "Are you all right?"

His expression of concern brought on a surge of hope.

"Barry. Are you sure this is what you want? Are you absolutely sure?"

His expression hardened, his mouth stretching into a thin line. "We're over, Kim. That's it." He shut the door behind him.

Chapter Five

Kim had fallen asleep for only a short while before waking in her chair, slumped over. Her empty brandy glass was precariously close to the edge of the coffee table. Her head ached, her knee throbbed, and the room was chilly. She wondered how long she'd been asleep.

She examined her knee. Though bruised and a bit swollen, it didn't appear she'd sustained major damage. Still, she'd check in at a clinic in the morning just to be sure.

Oh God. Tomorrow. And the day after that. Her world had crashed; her future had turned bleak. The shock, the hurt, Barry's callous treatment of her was unforgiveable. And what about the indignity of being dumped, the realization that her husband had lied, cheated and was impervious to her feelings?

She could focus on his flaws, his cruelty. But the question remained: How do you mend a broken heart? *Maybe you can't*, Dana's voice scolded in her head, *not if you're a wimp and have no pride*.

So life sucks. Tomorrow she'd be on a plane headed home. And oh, how she wanted out of paradise. At this point, hell seemed more inviting.

But first things first. She had no choice but to confront Barry. Onward to reclaim the bedroom.

No light seeped through the bottom of the door; no soft music raised a red flag. She wouldn't encounter sexual shenanigans in the guise of so-called dancing, as she had before.

Kim took a deep breath and opened the door. To her surprise the room was empty. She turned on the light for a better look. The bedroom appeared as they'd left it, tidied but not completely in order. Had Barry gone to a hotel? That seemed unlikely, since his toiletries and night clothes remained neatly in place.

He'd left for the pool around 10:30. It was now 11:45 and way too late for routine-oriented Barry. On the other hand, she couldn't picture him lounging in a bar or traipsing around town in his swim trunks. Maybe it was her addled state of mind, but she couldn't conjure up a reasonable explanation for his absence. Nor could she settle in for the night not knowing where he was.

Walking slowly and stiffly, Kim made her way to the elevator for the five story descent. Fortunately, the pool was close by, located off a walkway between the condos and the garage and adjacent to a grassy area where tenants could lie out on beach chairs.

Even before the doors opened on the ground floor, she could hear raised voices and excited chatter. Out of the elevator now, she blinked against a frenzied jumble of blues and reds flashing from emergency vehicles parked along the access road. What on earth?

Was Barry among the spectators? Pressing on, heart hammering in her chest, Kim tried not to get distracted from looking for Barry at the pool.

People were gathered in small groups, their attention glued to medical personnel bent over a figure lying prone on the ground. Again, she tasted grit. "What's going on? What's happened?" Kim asked, her voice sounding splintered, cracked.

A woman turned to her, shaking her head. "Some kids came out for a swim and found a man lying face down in the pool. Poor guy probably suffered a heart attack."

Rooted in place, Kim watched as the medics surrounded the man, positioning him on the stretcher. Just before they covered him, head to toe with a sheet, she caught a glimpse of his face: *oh, God.*

"Oh, my God. No, no. Oh, no!" she cried out.

The Drambuie glass at the side of the pool was the last thing to catch her eye before everything went black.

Noise, confusion, her own voice thin and distraught echoed in her ears as Kim came to and allowed herself to be led by a male bystander to a lounge chair in the grassy area. "Here we are, miss. Can I get you anything?"

"Thank you, no." Her voice, a whisper, was eclipsed by the strident female tones of a woman explaining to a policewoman, "She was out but seconds and when she opened her eyes, she kept saying, 'It's my husband, it's my husband' over and over."

The policewoman, now at Kim's side, knelt down, resting on her haunches, and established eye contact. She spoke softly. "I'm very sorry, ma'am, but if the decedent is your husband, we need you to make the identification." She straightened and looked around. "Do you have a relative or friend here to accompany you?"

"Not here, no, but my sister is in Honolulu." Kim attempted to raise herself from the chair, but then fell back. "I need my sister. I need her here now. Please. You have to let me call Dana."

"We'll assist you in reaching your sister, and then you need to come with us. When we bring you back to your unit, we'll want to make sure you're okay, maybe find someone to stay with you."

"I'd be willing." It was the woman Kim had spoken to earlier, the same woman who had commented on her condition.

Kim shook her head. "You're very kind, but I'll be all right."

"You're sure?" Her dubious tone was at odds with the excitement in her eyes.

"Yes, I'm sure." She wasn't looking for a baby sitter, for God's sake. She wanted Dana!

Dana did her best to console a distraught Kim after receiving the call about Barry's death. "Hang on 'til I get there. I'll take the first flight out tomorrow morning," she assured Kim. What Dana did not reveal was that she was not in Honolulu, but in Kona at a hotel only minutes away from the condo.

After talking to Kim, it was difficult for Dana to settle down for the rest of the night. Aside from keeping her from sleep, the heart wrenching but dreary double plague of divorce and death recited by Kim had tested her endurance. Poor Kim. And poor, weary Dana.

Dana knew her sister would have to submit to questioning by the police, but at least the interview was taking place now in the condo at a decent hour and not in a sterile interrogation room.

Dana and Kim were seated on the sofa, while Police Detective Chang had settled on the ornate chair closest to Kim. The room, like a movie set, was dressed to perfection: the sun's rays creating rainbows across the carpet, the view of the lanai with its blue lounge chairs, all set to the sound of the crashing surf.

For Dana the setting was an enticing distraction. *Not so for Kim,* she thought. Her sister looked like a disaster refugee, her hair lank and dull, the bruising beneath her eyes tinting them an unnatural sea green. Couldn't she have put on some lipstick, for heaven's sake? Dana turned away in disgust, and then decided she'd better pay attention. Chang was speaking.

"Mrs. Williams, you've stated it was customary for your husband to prepare a nightcap when he took his evening swim. His glass turned up at the side of the pool but contained pool water, which suggests he had rescued it after it had fallen or been dropped into the water. Was he inebriated when he left for his swim?"

"We'd had a couple of drinks at dinner and a brandy when we arrived home. Nothing out of the ordinary."

"Tell me about his medications."

"There's not much to tell. Barry took a pill for slightly elevated blood pressure. We seldom discussed his health. I just assumed it was good."

Dana crossed, and then uncrossed her legs. "Kim, forgive me, but I don't think you're aware of the total picture. Detective Chang, I knew Barry Williams before he and my sister married. He confided he had a heart murmur, and I know for a fact he was into nose candy." Responding to Kim's confused look, she said, "Cocaine, Kim. He sniffed cocaine."

"Dana, for heaven's sake, I've been his wife for five years. He never mentioned a heart condition, and he was not a user." She sighed. "At least not around me."

Dana shrugged. "I'm just telling you what I know."

The detective looked up from his notes. "Mrs. Williams, cocaine use can be deadly. It increases heart rate and blood pressure. Any amount can induce a heart attack or seizure. Also, the drug is particularly dangerous if used with alcohol."

Kim shook her head. "I can't conceive of Barry on cocaine."

Dana struggled to keep a straight face while mentally rolling her eyes.

The interview was over. "For now," Chang stated, stressing the now. And, of course, he would inform Mrs. Williams as to the medical examiner's report.

"Oh," Chang said, as he and Kim stood at the door. "One more question. Was Mr. Williams upset or agitated when he left for the pool?"

"He was fine. I, on the other hand, was—well, numb."

A twitch at the side of the detective's mouth betrayed his impassiveness. "How so?"

"At dinner my husband asked me for a divorce."

"I'm sorry, Mrs. Williams." He paused. "It would appear you had a really bad day." He nodded, and then let himself out.

Dana tossed aside the magazine she'd been thumbing through, and stifled a laugh. "Finally, the man shows a little personality. But for heaven's sake, Kim, why would you bring up the divorce?"

Kim winced as she sat down next to Dana. "Why not?"

"Because it complicates matters."

"Oh. I see. The revenge factor. Hubby asks wifey for a divorce, so the enraged wife mixes a lethal cocktail and in so doing, big, bad husband is poisoned or falls asleep and drowns."

"Sardonic humor is not your strong suit. But seriously, if there's any indication of foul play, the information you gave Chang establishes a motive."

"Oh, come on, Dana, you're being overly dramatic. I brought up the divorce because of my actions at the restaurant and in the parking garage. The handyman or other witnesses could come forward and report my—my rather deplorable behavior. I don't want to give the impression I've got something to hide."

"Got it. Now I have a suggestion for you. Take a nice, long nap. If you need a sleeping pill—okay, you're shaking your head. But for God's sake put Barry out of your mind. If he hadn't died, you'd have lost him anyway." She gave Kim a sidelong look. "Sorry, I know that sounds heartless, but as Mom used to say, the truth is the truth."

Kim reached for her hand. "You can't imagine what it means to me to have you here. Without you, I—" She choked, overcome, as the tears flowed.

"It's okay, sweetie, you'll get through this. I'll walk with you to the bedroom. You need to rest your knee and most importantly, you need sleep."

When she'd settled Kim in bed, Dana said, "Mind if I help

myself to a Coke to take back to my hotel? I'll be back here at sixish, and we'll go to dinner."

Kim responded with a wisp of a smile. "Dana and her Cokes. I guess the world is back on its axis. I guess I'm going to survive after all."

"You bet." Dana shut the bedroom door and took a deep breath. She made a bee-line for the dining room table to retrieve her oversized bag, marched into the kitchen, and set the bag on the counter. She scanned the bottles of booze–scotch, gin, vodka, brandy and Drambuie–lined up like good little soldiers at the far end of the counter. *Barry, the neatnick*, she thought as she reached into her bag for gloves.

When she'd slipped them on, she glanced toward the bedroom where all was quiet, then brought out the bottle of partially filled Drambuie. "Time to trade places, just like before, when they were at the beach," she whispered, making the substitution. *You can thank me, dear, dead Barry for one final fine day.*

The bottle she removed from the counter now rested at the bottom of her bag. But its stay would be brief. Destiny called for it to head out to sea or meet its fate smashed to bits on the rocks.

Dana remembered to grab that Coke she'd asked Kim about and then started for the door, only to stop as it occurred to her something was radically wrong.

She sucked in her breath. Her portrait was missing. Where in the hell was her portrait?

Kim awoke at 4:30, sweaty, dry mouthed and thirsty, as if she'd been on a bender. A glance in the mirror confirmed that she looked as bad as she felt.

A shower restored her energy and brought forth a semblance of the old Kim. Now as she sat once again at her dressing table, she envisioned Barry as he'd stood in the shadows, his expression somber, his tone curt. Most men hated scenes. Maybe even Barry had to steel himself to confront her at dinner.

But why play out the scene at dinner? To satisfy his urge for high drama? Or had he assumed that in public she'd maintain her poise and decorum. Surprise, surprise if he'd assumed the latter.

She jumped at the sound of the phone.

It was Detective Chang.

"Mrs. Williams? I have the medical examiner's preliminary report."

"Yes? Please go on."

"In all probability, your husband died of heart failure."

"I see." So Dana was right.

"There's more. Several witnesses – a restaurant server, the parking attendant and the handyman for your units–have come forward to report that you and your husband were fighting, that you appeared to be in a highly emotional state."

"It's true. I did make a scene at the restaurant, and I'm sure Tony told you what occurred in the garage. I can't imagine what the parking attendant had to say."

"That you and your husband had words."

"Yes. I told him to go to hell."

"I appreciate your honesty. When do you plan to fly home?"

"As soon as possible. Tomorrow, hopefully."

"You might have to defer your departure by a day or so for paperwork and so forth." He paused. "Thank you for being forthcoming with me. Let's see. We do know where to reach you in Los Angeles, should that be necessary, and we do have your e-mail address. In the meantime, please accept my condolences for your loss." The line went dead.

"You were right about Barry having a heart problem," Kim said as soon as Dana arrived. "The medical examiner's preliminary report states the cause of death as heart failure." She thought her statements would elicit a smug smile or caustic comment, but her sister seemed preoccupied.

"Dana? Did you hear what I said? Look, could we sit for a minute or two before we leave? I want to tell you about Detective Chang's phone call."

"We'll sit after you tell me what happened to my portrait."

"Oh, that. I stored it in the credenza. Remember, we agreed Barry shouldn't know you arranged for our being here, so naturally—"

"Since it hardly matters now, let's put it back where it belongs."

"I'm sorry if you're angry, but I didn't have a choice." Kim started to the credenza, but then hesitated. "Oh, God. You're not going to like this."

"Like what? Tell me." Dana was at her side.

Kim reached into the linen drawer and brought forth the portrait. "I'm so sorry, but in my haste to hide it from Barry, I cracked the glass. I'll gladly replace it and pay for it."

Dana took the picture from her, holding onto it as if it were a precious artifact, and then placed it between the porcelain vases. She stared at herself for a moment, and then turned to go into the living room, with Kim following.

This time Dana sat in a side chair, leaving Kim to go it alone on the sofa. "I'll take care of replacing the glass first thing in the morning. Now. What did Chang have to say?"

"He knows Barry and I were fighting." She described Chang's account of the witnesses' statements. "He also said I might be detained a day of two for paper work—and so forth."

"So?"

"How would you interpret 'and so forth'?"

"Have you heard of verbal crutches? How about 'stuff like that'; 'or something'; 'be that as it may'; 'and so forth'; I could go on."

"Okay, Dana. But he also mentioned he knew where to reach me in L.A. if necessary. What does that say to you?"

"It doesn't say anything. I suppose it's part of police protocol." She rose. "Why would you want to borrow trouble? Come on, let's catch the sunset over a drink and order mahi mahi. I know the perfect place!"

And she did. As the evening progressed, her sister had lightened up. Hooray. But Kim was uneasy. She felt in her gut something was amiss. What weren't the police telling her?

And another question: How might Bea and Frank Devlin react to staying in a place where a previous tenant's life had ended tragically? They probably wouldn't know. The name Barry Williams would not resonate with Dana's former math instructor and her blue collar husband, *How nice to celebrate an anniversary in that glorious setting*, Kim thought wistfully.

She reflected on the joy of those first days with Barry. Sadly, it was all a sham, an artfully staged, sugar-coated final act leading to a humiliating and crushing denouement.

At least she was spared the torment of watching Barry methodically gather up his belongings. Maybe he'd even gone so far as to rent an apartment for himself before the trip.

As if it mattered. Barry was returning home in a casket. At his services, friends and colleagues would approach the bereft widow with doleful expressions and murmured condolences. Despite his heartlessness, she didn't want him dead.

Kim pictured the night of the birthday party when she'd lain next to Barry, hurt and angered by his indifference. A chill now coursed through her as she remembered thinking she'd rather see him dead than in the arms of another woman.

Had the thought given birth to the deed?

Aloha!

Family, Friends and Neighbors
It's a luau at the Devlin's!

Bea and Frank will soon be off to celebrate
their 36th wedding anniversary in Hawaii.

Let's give them a big send-off!

Date: Saturday July 8
Time: 3:30 p.m.
Place: 450 Waverly Place–Tustin

RSVP: Elizabeth Devlin - (714) 6015-3269
Diane Jennings - (818) 8941-5607

Chapter Six

Bea could hear the ukulele from her recliner in the living room. The sound traveled clearly from the back patio where the luau was in full swing.

Their neighbor Joe's exuberant but uneven plucking of island melodies challenged her to sit straighter as the music energized her, sparking a sense of get-up-and-go that had been missing for some time.

As more gentle rhythms prevailed, Bea heeded the call to lean back, shut her eyes and waft into cinematic frames of pictorial delights. She pictured grass skirted hula dancers, their hands telling a story, swaying against a blazing sunset. When that sunset cooled, it transitioned into a spectacle of drum play and boys lighting torches, as with grace and agility they swept over the beach.

Bea smiled as Joe segued into "The Hawaiian War Chant." A jungle scene? Warriors?

"Mom!" Bea started, and her image shattered.

"Why aren't you outside with the others?" Elizabeth stood over her, the premature lines in her daughter's forehead locked in what seemed to be a perpetual frown.

"It was getting a little breezy for me so I came inside." She focused on the little apostrophes that formed at the corners of Elizabeth's pinched lips. "What is it, dear? What's wrong?"

"Your eyes were closed. I wondered if you were all right."

"I'm fine. Blame the music. I was painting pretty pictures in my head."

The frown remained. "You've had a long day. I think you should—"

"Hush. I hear your dad coming."

It was not only Frank, but Diane and the two grandchildren.

Diane swooped in on them. "Hi, you two. Taking a break from the festivities? Norm is still bartending, but the children are getting cranky, so I thought a change of scene would settle them down." She plopped onto the couch. "Timmy," she said to the four year old, "you sit next to Mommy. Brian—"

"I want to sit by Grandpa! He's telling us a story."

"Six is not too old to sit on my lap." Frank took the armchair, a companion to Bea's recliner, and smiled as the boy came to him. He looked up at Elizabeth. "Honey, you did a great job with the party. Now it's time to relax. Sit down, for goodness sakes. Or go outside and have a beer."

Diane snickered and Bea chuckled. Elizabeth with a beer? "Dad's right," Bea said. "Why don't you join your sister? I'll bet it's been awhile since you two have had a good chat." *And stop hovering over me*, Bea wanted to plead as Elizabeth left her side.

"I was telling the boys about the triathlon that takes place in Kona in October," Frank said.

Bea nodded. "What they call the Ironman competition. It consists of running, biking and swimming."

Frank's eyes, a deep blue against tanned skin, took on a sparkle. "It's the granddaddy of all athletic competitions. Talk about training. It was the toughest thing I've ever done in my life. I've always been a good swimmer but man, it's endurance that counts in a six mile swim."

Brian's eyes had become huge. "Gosh, you did all that?"

"There's more. When you bike, it takes hours and hours of practice, say for a 260 mile ride. But running was the hardest." He whistled. "Was it ever grueling training for a 52-mile run."

The girls had stopped talking and listened as Frank continued. Diane pulled at a blond strand, her eyes–Frank's eyes–showing a glint of deviltry. Elizabeth was not amused.

"Did you win?" Brian asked.

"I qualified, but I couldn't compete. My company called me into work on a particularly thorny problem that required my engineering know-how."

Bea couldn't look at Elizabeth. So her father was a mechanic. So he exaggerated, stretched the facts. And now in his fantasy world pictured himself a triathlon contender.

Elizabeth was on her feet. "Dad, that's enough. We need to get back to our guests."

Diane had risen, too, after admonishing Timmy who had started to whine. "It's 7:30. Come on, boys, let's grab Daddy and head on home. I think the party's about over."

As if on cue, the remaining guests now filed into the house, and amidst hugs, kisses, and good wishes, Bea felt love and gratitude toward her friends for their outpouring of warmth and generosity.

Elizabeth was the last to leave. "I'll walk with you to your car," Bea said.

They ambled out wood paneled doors, a contrast to the brick façade of this ranch style house, then down the short concrete walk that led to the street.

Bea placed a firm hand on Elizabeth's arm. "The *Bird of Paradise* cuttings. I forgot to give them to you."

"I'll walk over tomorrow and pick them up. The exercise will do me good." She cast a discerning eye on the small front lawn. "The Lilly of the Nile is doing well, but I wish you'd get rid of the hydrangea. I've always thought it was an ugly plant."

"It's not my favorite either. Maybe I can talk your dad into doing some digging tomorrow."

"You do that. Then Dad can add landscape architect to his list of accomplishments."

"Elizabeth—"

"Sorry. But to be training for the triathlon?" She laughed, and then shrugged. "I should be used to his embellishments."

"Deep down, he realizes people doubt him but on the upside, he's popular with just about everyone."

"Right." A frown replaced her smile. "When are you going to tell Dad?"

"I'll know when the time is right."

Elizabeth's expression had softened. "Do you honestly think this is a good time to go off to Hawaii?"

"Yes," Bea said emphatically. "It's exactly what I need."

"I can't help it if I worry about you."

"And I worry about you, Elizabeth. You're only thirty-four years old and already burned out. Of course, it's no wonder with that job of yours."

"It's a career, Mom, and a good one." She paused. "Okay, I think we've both said enough. Gotta go. I'll see you tomorrow."

After their goodnight hug, Bea waved her daughter off, and then returned to Frank.

He was sitting in his TV chair in the den, gazing at a blank screen.

"No sports events?" she asked, settling on the sofa that also folded out into a bed. He rose, a little stiff from sitting, removed the toothpick from his mouth and sat down next to her. Despite his paunch and his increasing baldness, he was still a good looking man to Bea.

"The Dodgers play the San Diego Padres–but I'll get to that later." He looked at her and squeezed her hand. "Wasn't it great to have Timmy and Brian with us today? Now if only we could get Elizabeth hitched and having kids, our life would be complete."

Bea nodded. "She's smart and pretty and would make a devoted wife. She'd also be a caring mother."

"Elizabeth reminds me of you when we met. She has your round face and cute nose. And she's – what do they call it – pleasingly plump?"

Bea laughed. "Just so long as it stays pleasingly. But on a serious note, I do think our daughter is too assertive, too controlling around men. Diane's noticed it too. Do you think she should talk to Elizabeth, tell her to soften up a bit?"

"You would have to decide that. But I will say she doesn't cut people a lot of slack."

"What do you mean?"

"I know I carry on at times, and I know Elizabeth isn't impressed with my stories, but why can't she accept me for who I am? It's like she's always judging me or is embarrassed to be around me."

"Now, honey, I wouldn't go that far. True, she's judgmental, but she also sees you as a warm, kind and loving dad.

"But let's not dwell on that. Focus on the good stuff. People like to be with you. And best of all, you're my hero."

"And you're everything to me. I don't know what I'd do without you."

Bea leaned over to kiss him, and then broke away when the phone rang. "You watch your game. I'll take the call in the kitchen."

The caller, to Bea's surprise, was Diane.

"I'd forgotten to mention," Diane was saying, "that the boys would be thrilled to receive a little something from Hawaii."

"We'll bring back souvenirs for all the family."

"You want a suggestion for Elizabeth? Bring her a hunky surfer or a gorgeous island boy, someone to bring fun and games into her life. For once, I'd like to see her mouth curve upward. And how about if she could even slouch a little?"

"I think your sister may be burned out. She's seen too much abuse of children, women, elders. I know I could never be a social worker. If only she'd gone into teaching."

"What she needs is a good roll in the hay."

"Diane! For goodness sakes."

"Whoops. Sometimes I forget I'm talking to my mother."

Bea laughed. "Your remark was inappropriate." She paused. "But you may be right."

When they'd ended the conversation, Bea decided to sit on the patio awhile before joining Frank. The light was more silvery now than golden, the air still, everything neat and tidy, thanks to their kind guests who had disposed of paper plates and plastic glasses.

She thought about her husband. He hadn't always been so inventive, but how true it is that certain traits become more entrenched as one ages.

He was still her hero. Bea could picture their first meeting thirty-seven years ago as if it were today. She removed her glasses, blurring the present to bring the past into focus, as in a TV script.

Scene I

Beatrice Thompson, working over the summer as a bookkeeper for a construction site, sits at a desk in the cramped office, hunched over a sheet of figures relating to building specifications.

She sneezes from the mustiness of the room—or is it dust? A crane on the other side of the window blocks her view of the insipid sunshine barely making it out of Southern California's June gloom.

The door to the office opens with a creak and a man strides over to the desk. Bea looks up, annoyed at the interruption, but then fastens her gaze on his dark blond hair, deep blue eyes, and tanned but unlined skin.

"Hi!" he says. "You must be the new hire. The guys said to check out the cutie in the office. Had to see for myself. They were right." He extends his hand. "And you are?"

"Bea Thompson." She places her hand in his, and then quickly removes it. Actually, she finds his brashness appealing, his wide smile genuine, his confident stance not the least bit arrogant.

"Welcome to Courtland Construction. So, Bea, are you here for the long haul?"

"Only for the summer. In the fall I'll return to my regular job."

"Which is?"

"I teach high school mathematics and home economics."

She can tell he's impressed. "What do you do?" she asks.

"I'm a developer. Well, I'm aiming for that. Right now I'm in construction."

As they talk, Bea is drawn to this man with his beautiful smile and sunny disposition. She overlooks the occasional grammatical slip. When he returns at the end of the day, she accepts his invitation to dinner.

Scene II

Bea's mother—a gray entity in hair, skin, clothes, but steadfast in meeting life's challenges head on–marches up to Bea who sits at the dining room table, correcting math tests. "We need to talk," she announces.

"Sure, Mom." Bea looks up, feeling a tightening across her abdomen. Her mother does not look happy.

Not one for conversational foreplay, her mother gets right to the point. "You've been seeing this Frank person, for what? Six months? What's going on?"

Bea sets down the red pencil she's been using and looks her mother in the eye. "We're going to get married."

A gasp. "You're a college educated professional, and you're marrying a laborer?"

"I'm marrying a highly skilled worker. He just happens to work with his hands."

Her mother stands like a sentry, proudly erect, in this cheerless room in this cheerless house, shaking her head. And now that Bea thinks about it, she can see Elizabeth's resemblance to her grandmother.

In her effort to penetrate the icy wall between herself and her mother, Bea continues, "Frank is like a breath of fresh air. He makes me laugh; he makes me happy. We love each other. It's as simple as that."

All true. What she didn't tell her mother was that she suspected Frank was close to illiterate when it came to basic writing skills. Did it matter to her? Only a little. After all, she was a teacher; it was her job to impart information, to inspire others to achieve proficiency in the fundamentals and beyond. Frank would be a willing student, easy to teach.

Later, Bea wondered if Frank were dyslexic. They discussed that possibility, but Frank never seemed to have the time nor inclination to follow through with testing or seeking remedial help.

Leaving the past in the past, darkness now enveloped Bea like a cozy blanket. From within the house, a sports announcer's voice punctuated the quiet, and outside, garden lights edged the patio like a miniature cheering squad.

The Hawaii trip was a blessed distraction from her concerns and fears–a reprieve from whatever lay ahead. Kona augured unparalleled beauty, a colorful blend of nature's best in a timeless, uncomplicated world. Together, she and Frank would savor their every moment on the island.

She could hardly wait!

The office at the rear of the Melrose Art Gallery served as a workplace for Kim and Jenna to negotiate offers, set prices, and determine profits and losses. It was all business, but it was also a refuge, and on the day after services had been held for Barry, Kim was holed up in this untidy but familiar haven, grateful to avoid public scrutiny.

She cast aside phone messages and e-mails relating to Barry's passing and focused instead on a lithograph of a lovely young woman hanging on the wall. In a yellow gown, she lounged on a garden swing against a lush background of trees, and held a bouquet of flowers in pastel shades.

Kim yearned to reach out and touch the delicate clusters, to bury her face in the cool fragrant petals—a response unlike her instant aversion to the funereal displays that took center stage at Barry's service and the celebration of his life that followed.

At least, as the grieving widow, she was spared having to eulogize her late husband. That task fell to George Anderson and others from the firm to recite anecdotes of Barry's personal and professional achievements. The comments, more clever than heartfelt, drew more laughter than tears from those in attendance.

An only child, Barry's mother was deceased, and his father was unreachable since he'd moved to the island of Fiji. The agency was Barry's family; his mistress was a no-show.

Kim leaned back in her chair and closed her eyes. If only she, too, could flee to Fiji or to Provence to become the young woman in the lithograph. Let others dispose of Barry's clothes and possessions; let them shuffle through documents, papers, and deeds. And let them unravel the mysteries of financial transactions and business directives.

The problem was she could not breathe life into these nebulous beings she should have been counting on to solve the issues facing her. Help was out there, but she had no idea where to begin. She opened her eyes, sat up, and then reached for a tissue to dab at her eyes. What a mean, shitty world.

The soft rapping at the door, the sight of Jenna peering at her through a narrow opening, caused Kim to shift mental gears. Her friend looked like a child requesting permission to end a time-out. "You can come in. I'm not going to bite or bawl."

Jenna stepped into the office but remained standing. "I'm not even going to ask how you're doing. It must be pure hell, losing Barry."

Kim lowered her gaze. "Yes, I had it all, didn't I?" *For a time*, she thought.

Jenna cleared her throat and Kim looked up. "What?" she asked. Jenna twitched, eyes blinking rapidly as she fiddled with the buttons on her blouse.

"Jenna, what's going on?"

"You have a visitor. It's Kevin."

Kim opened, and then closed her mouth. She was speechless.

"Should I tell him to get lost?"

"No, of course not. But I think I'd better see him privately. Would you mind sending him back?"

"I'm on my way."

Her ex looked much the same as she'd remembered him eight years before at their tearful parting: curly brown hair, wide-set dark eyes, pale complexion. He was heavier now, and his face fuller.

Kim stood and then came around her desk with arms open to greet him.

They embraced for a long moment, and then Kim led him to the small couch against the opposite wall. "I am stunned beyond belief. You're the last person I expected to pop in. You look wonderful, Kevin. How are you doing?"

"All's well with me." He looked at her closely. "It's you I'm worried about. I read in the paper about your loss. I'm so very sorry, Kim. This must be a God awful time for you."

His soft tone, his expression of concern and his warmth enveloped her. She wanted more; she wanted to be embraced by Kevin's beautiful hands stroking away the hurt and anguish. She turned from him as she felt the tears come.

"What can I do? How can I help?"

"Are you free this evening?" She said this without thinking and placed her fingers over her mouth, taking in Kevin's startled expression.

He quickly recovered. "It just so happens that I am free. How about dinner? It's on me."

It was his tone, firm and reassuring, that brought Kim out of her despairing mood.

The Park Inn Restaurant on Los Feliz Boulevard was only minutes from Kim's home. The dark paneling, burgundy leather booths, subdued lighting and hush hush tone conspired along with discreet servers to endorse romantic trysts and stolen moments. If a bit of a cliché, the setting was perfect for a get-away with Kevin, who had always been in tune with her thoughts and moods.

"Tell me about your writing," Kim said. "Or did you decide to pursue painting full time?"

Kevin took a sip of his martini. "For now it's definitely the writing life."

Kevin held her attention, but so did the martini. What had happened to his penchant for wine, his disdain for hard liquor?

"My break-through," he said, "came when I was hired to write for the soaps. Have you seen *Balboa Island* or *Endless Love*?"

"No, but I've heard of them. You're writing for these shows?"

"Not anymore. I'm freelancing with articles, special features, and celebrity profiles. My biggest coup was an article on Hollywood celebs for *Vanity Fair*. Next comes the novel." He crossed his fingers.

"It sounds wonderful. But how did all this evolve?"

"Let's go back to the soaps. You've heard of Tom Winchell? His book was on the *New York Times* best seller list."

"Ah. For *Malice in the Middle East*?"

"Right. Back when I was hired for *Balboa Island*, Tom was head writer and took me under his wing. I guess you could say he was my mentor."

"Lucky you."

"Anyway, he saw my potential, and now I'm riding high, thanks to Tom. But enough about me. Tell me about you. Everything."

Maybe it was the ambience of a room that shut out the world and invited intimacy. Maybe it was Kevin. Or the wine. By the time they'd finished dinner, Kim had confided that her marriage had unraveled, then drifted into a cold and ugly void. She'd been cast aside like a worn, smelly sock.

Back at the house, Kim offered Kahlua on the rocks, Kevin's favorite after dinner drink, and poured a Cointreau for herself.

"I'm curious about your personal life." Kim said as they sat joined at the hip on the sofa. "Are you married, divorced, in a relationship?"

"I've been married only once. To you." Kevin slipped his arm around her shoulders. "Let's not talk about me, okay?" He nuzzled his cheek against hers. "I've missed you."

Kim drew away to look him in the eye. "Kevin, what are we doing? Where is this leading?"

"Where do you want it to go?"

"I don't know. Maybe if we gave it a chance, we could find our way back to each other. But on the other hand—"

"Let's not bring up emotional issues, the maybes or what ifs. Let's simply enjoy the moment."

He was talking like a philandering husband or a man on the make—this was not the Kevin she knew. Although, how would she know after an eight year gap? Then again, maybe she was more than a little shaky in the faith and trust department.

"Well," he said, breaking the silence. "You need your rest, and I should be on my way." He withdrew his arm from around her shoulders and got to his feet. "I'm glad we could get together. It was great being with you. I'm just sorry for what you've been through."

Kim stood up to join him. "Kevin, I can't thank you enough for your kindness, for your willingness to sit through a real life soap opera."

"Hey, I can do you one better. I'll stay long enough to tuck you into bed. And if you'd like, I'll rub your back and send you off to sweet dreams."

"I remember your back rubs. Who could resist?"

Kim awoke with the light of morning, having forgotten to close the drapes. The acacia tree that shaded the bedroom shone through windows, framed by the sun's early rays.

She stretched, and then breathed deeply, inhaling the promise of a day full of delights, releasing tension that was nonexistent. Quietly, Kim slipped into her robe and slippers, leaving Kevin snoring softly as he sprawled on Barry's side of the bed.

In the bathroom her sense of joy diminished as her reflection sent her spilling into a vortex of uneasiness. How could she have let Kevin into her bed? Was she crazy? So needy that next she'd be putting the moves on George Anderson?

Hardly. She looked at herself and smiled, giggled even. What happened, happened. Or to put it more succinctly: blame it on the back rub!

Kim took a closer look at herself. Her eyes were bright, her skin glowed, and her face was serene. She could almost hear what Dana would likely say, "Well, sis. Good sex will do it every time."

And nobody knows that better than Dana, Kim thought later as she sat at the kitchen table sipping coffee. But acts incur consequences. So where would life's little journey take her next? Did she want Kevin back in her life? A small voice from within whispered "maybe."

She didn't hear Kevin enter the kitchen and was startled when he appeared at her side. "You seem lost in thought," he said.

"Oh! Good morning. I can't recall ever seeing you up as early as seven. Take a seat. I'll pour you some coffee."

He smiled. "You remembered I'm not a morning person. Or, I wasn't back then."

As self-absorbed as Kim had been the day before, she hadn't paid close attention to Kevin's attire. Now in the bright daylight, she noted he was neatly turned out in a blue Armani shirt and pressed tan slacks—a giant step up from his days of rolled up sleeves and an un-tucked shirt over cut-off jeans. He hadn't shaved, but the shadow of facial hair lent a reassuring degree of masculinity to his fashion perfect appearance.

"Here you go," Kim said, pouring his coffee and setting a container of sugar cubes by his cup.

"Thanks, but I take my coffee black now."

"I do remember breakfast was your favorite meal. I can fix eggs, any style, or pancakes. I also have bacon and sausage on hand."

"Kim, please sit down. I can stay only for coffee."

"Sure." She returned to her seat. "But what's the hurry?"

"Tom is being interviewed by 'First Edition' this morning, and I promised to accompany him to the shoot."

She stared at him. "Kevin, I don't even know where you live. When we separated, you decided Santa Barbara was your sanctuary. I assume you're living in L.A. now?"

"Tom and I have a place in the Hollywood Hills."

"How nice that you have a famous roommate." She raised her cup to her lips. "And a live-in editor."

He looked down at his manicured nails. "Actually," he paused, "partner would be more accurate."

Kim choked on her coffee and set down her cup. "I'm confused. That is if you're saying what I think you mean?"

"That I'm bi-sexual?" He nodded. "Who knew? At least, I didn't know when we were together. But I felt like something was missing."

"Again. Lucky you. Not everyone can have it both ways."

"Now you're disgusted with me."

"I wouldn't call it that. I don't know how I feel. Shocked, dismayed, accepting?"

His doleful look, the long lashes blinking away tears brought her back to the end of their marriage; it felt like a re-enactment of a scene she'd just as soon bury. Take away the designer clothes, manicured nails, altered drinking habits and sleep patterns, and Kevin was still the man she'd married. And just as predictable.

For some insane reason, Kim found the absurdity of the situation laughable. She covered her mouth to muffle a sound that was half giggle, half snort. Kevin's troubled look–did he think she was crying?–set her off.

"I'm sorry," she said, between spasms of laughter, "I can't help it. You'd better go."

She couldn't make out his parting remarks, only the conciliatory tone, which she found even more hilarious. "Bye, Bye, Kevin," she murmured to the already closed door.

Finally, Kim caught her breath, wiped her eyes, and then reached for the phone.

Dana's sleepy voice responded on the eighth ring.

Chapter Seven

"You *slept* with *Kevin*?" Dana's mouth quivered in an attempt to contain her laughter. She'd gone over to Kim's after the conversation they'd had on the phone, and now the sisters were seated on the sofa in Kim's living room.

Kim shifted, distancing herself from Dana. "You find that amusing?" she asked. Kevin was long gone, and it was now late morning.

Dana's expression became veiled. "I find a lot of things amusing these days."

What was that supposed to mean, Kim wondered?

"Of course," Dana continued, "Kevin is an attractive man, but overly emotional. Dare I say—also a shade effeminate?"

"I'll have you know that Kevin is sheer poetry in bed. And on a grand scale."

Dana shaped her mouth into an "oh." "Well, in that case, go for it."

"Not in the cards. It turns out I have a rival, and it's not a woman."

"Oh, m'gawd. Tell me everything!"

When Kim completed her tale, Dana shook her head. "You poor kid. Let's examine your track record. From Kevin, the failed artist, you skid to Barry, the bastard, then flounder back to Kevin, who tops the scale for sensitive but confused.

"But don't despair. One of these days you'll get it right. At least you're in good financial shape. I assume Barry named you beneficiary on his accounts, the deed to the house, and so forth. With the divorce you could expect a settlement but now as his widow, you get it all. Nice, huh?"

"I suppose. I don't know. I've been such a blob, a vegetable. I just want it all to go away."

"It's not going away. And the sooner you talk to Barry's

attorney, the better. Then you can think about making investments, expanding your gallery, moving into a sexy condo, raising hell."

Kim laughed. "Be careful or you may cheer me up. But on a sober note, I suppose the first step is to contact Barry's lawyer."

"Also it wouldn't hurt to meet with a CPA. I know a good one, and I can give you his number. No, scratch that. Let me talk to Ted Connelly. Pave the way, so to speak?"

Dana's features had settled into complacency, her cat's smile seemed to Kim to be concealing something, but what? Kim decided not to pursue it; her sister was the voice of reason, and that's what counted.

She said as much to Dana.

"Big sister to the rescue, eh?" She gave Kim an appraising look. "You do seem a lot brighter now than when I arrived." She rose. "Well, I'd better get going."

"Some hostess I am. I didn't even offer you a Coke." Kim walked with Dana to the front door. "I'm surprised you're still in L.A. Didn't Jasper want you to look at properties in Sydney's outlying areas?"

"I told him I had more urgent concerns here."

"You can't neglect your husband on my account."

"I'm not going anywhere until you get on your feet." She paused. "Why the frown?"

"I don't doubt your good intentions, and I'm ever so grateful for your help."

"But?"

"I sense something's wrong." When Dana failed to respond, Kim said, "Why don't you stay for lunch or come back this evening. I'll fix dinner."

"You also want to fix me." Dana gave a little snort. "Maybe another time. Right now I need to get back to my shop. As for this evening, I have plans." Again the cat smile. "But call me anytime. Well, preferably not before ten in the morning.

"Speaking of time," Dana looked at her watch. "I have to remind myself it's three hours earlier in Hawaii–11:30 here, 8:30 there. So the Devlins probably aren't due in Kona until mid afternoon, Hawaiian time."

"I could comment, but why bother?"

"Oh, sweetie, I'm sorry to bring up Kona. I wasn't thinking. Or maybe I was thinking out loud."

"It's okay. You don't have to tiptoe around me."

"I'm going to tiptoe out of here before I erase the good that's come out of our visit. I'm not sure I'm up to making another house call."

She blew a kiss, and then breezed out the door and onto the circular driveway where she'd parked her Mercedes.

As always, Kim was grateful for Dana's help. But it was not like her sister to accommodate others over her own interests. So what was going on?

Dana's cryptic remark about finding a lot of things amusing puzzled Kim, but even more perplexing was her lack of reference to Jasper. *Was he in or out of the picture*, Kim wondered, returning Dana's wave as she sped off. Kim shook her head and shut the door. She'd bet big that Jasper's days were numbered.

Back in the kitchen, Kim found the sunlight pouring into the room, the cheery décor a mockery as the ghost of Barry and a wisp of Kevin hovered over her. Dana's comment about the Devlins in Kona brought it all back–the joyous anticipation of the rebirth of her marriage, followed by crushing hurt…followed by the horror of Barry's death.

Hawaii for Kim was now about as appetizing as the Black Plague meets the West Nile Virus.

Let the Devlins revel in Paradise.

Frank held Bea's hand and squinted against the brightness as they stood in line at the Honolulu airport, waiting to board their Aloha flight to Kona.

The lines at LAX had tried his patience, but once on the plane it was smooth sailing. Well, if you didn't count the fact that he'd felt like a huge stuffed bear in the middle of a three seat configuration. Bea, next to him in the aisle seat, had endured with good humor the little girl in the seat ahead of her who kept twisting her head to stare at Bea while making fish lips or crossing her eyes.

Frank could see Bea looked tired, maybe even a tad down. But no wonder, after having to trudge through all the security check points, and in this heat.

Ah. Finally their flight was ready to board. Still in line, they made their way out of the gate, and then traipsed across the tarmac, hurrying to keep up with the other passengers, only to face another line-up as they climbed the steps to enter the plane.

"After what they put us through, we need a vacation," Frank said, glowering, as they settled into their seats.

Bea patted his hand. "It's a short flight; then the fun begins."

"Fun" didn't materialize immediately upon landing. They had to compete with others for a spot at the luggage carousel, and then carry their bags across a busy intersection to wait for a shuttle to take them to the car rental lot.

Bea gave Frank a warm smile and a thumbs up as he drove the Chevy Impala out of the lot and onto the frontage road that would take them to the highway.

Frank shook his head. "I'm not trying to be a spoilsport, but my God, Bea, look around you. Have we landed on the moon?"

"It is a shocker how rocky the terrain is and, good heavens, so black. Not exactly the way we visualized Hawaii."

It got better. A lot better. Both were relieved that the village on the way to the condo was, on a smaller scale, like home. There was a supermarket, fast food outlets, hotels, shops and upscale restaurants, most paralleling the ocean.

Once inside the residential section, his wife perked up, her eyes luminous behind her glasses as she exclaimed over the lush foliage and brilliant bougainvillea. Each plumeria, banyan tree, and ginger plant was another exciting discovery.

The condo, luxurious beyond their expectations, was the icing on the cake. Bea was quick to comment on the furnishings that she described as colorful but tasteful, and the many decorative touches with their island flavor.

Frank wasn't keen about flying fish sculptures and furniture was furniture, but the rooms were bright and open and, he had to admit, like something you'd see in a magazine.

Only minutes after they'd arrived, the phone rang. "Who would be calling us?" Bea asked.

"Only one way to find out." Frank reached for the phone.

It was Elizabeth, and after a brief exchange, Frank handed the phone to Bea.

"What a surprise," Bea said. She frowned. "I'm fine. Well, of course a little tired after the long trip— I know. I know. Not to worry. Let me tell you about this condo. It's gorgeous."

Frank tuned out. Let his wife deal with their overprotective daughter. Being a devoted child was one thing, but when it came to her mother, Elizabeth was over the top. She treated her parents like they were kindergarteners, for crying out loud. "Mom, you look tired. You need to rest. Dad, watch your food intake. Think about your allergies." All said in a gentle but scolding tone.

Frank decided to explore the exterior. He stepped through sliding glass doors onto the balcony–correction, lanai–to the sound of waves churning against the rocks and moisture in the air.

He nodded his approval. He could picture Bea seated at one of the tables, sipping her morning coffee while he searched the ocean for dolphins, eels or darting fish. Or, even better, sacked out on one of the lounge chairs.

Curious as to what lay below on the far side of the lanai, Frank discovered tidal pools with sea turtles in residence. Damn, he should have become a marine biologist. Because he had the natural inclination, he could have been successful in that field. He pictured himself in diving gear, lowering into the sea, then charting his findings, maybe even lecturing at a university.

He bowed his head. It would never have happened. Never. Not for Frank Devlin. He remained there, then stretched his head backward to feel the sunshine hug his face, the warmth melting away layers of self-doubt.

What came to mind was his family. Despite Elizabeth's aggravating ways, he loved his daughter dearly. Ditto for Diane and her two little boys he'd give his life for.

As for Bea, how had he gotten so lucky to find a woman so smart and accomplished, someone who could live with his shortcomings? She was the love of his life, his anchor, his love through all eternity.

What he held close couldn't be bought in the marketplace or

earned with a college degree. He had everything a man could want, and for that he was truly blessed.

When Bea hung up the phone, she remained seated in one of the ornate and brightly colored chairs. A painting of a plantation style home hung on the wall directly across from her. Nestled among trees and curling vines, the house stood back from the main road, its frontage glistening from a recent rain. Bea could almost feel the humidity, the wetness under bare feet and stray drops licking at her arms and face.

A glance in the direction of the glass doors quelled her flights of fancy. Frank stood at the railing of the lanai. She stared at him, but then looked away as a sudden welling of tears blurred her image of him. He had to be told. But only after their anniversary.

She did feel tired, though she wouldn't admit this to Elizabeth. Tired but not in pain. And for the moment, her determination to delight in every phase of their stay in Hawaii was eclipsed by sadness.

She wished now she hadn't asked Elizabeth to accompany her to the oncologist's office for the biopsy results. Her daughter had been upbeat on the way to see the doctor, reminding her mother that after the lumpectomy in her right breast, followed by chemotherapy and radiation, she'd been cancer-free after the magical five-year marker.

The mass discovered in her left breast had turned out to be malignant–what they called a stage four–and very serious, indeed. The doctor had wanted to start aggressive chemotherapy treatment immediately, but Bea had questioned the outcome. The prognosis? Iffy.

With the trip only days away, Bea swore her daughter to secrecy. Nothing was to come in the way of the anniversary celebration—not until after the party and after the trip.

Bea still hadn't decided whether to opt for treatment or let nature take its course. Elizabeth was all for getting a second opinion and currently was searching the internet for in-depth information on cancer treatment.

Elizabeth's phone call had been made out of love and concern, but it had dampened Bea's mood; it brought up the specter of what lay ahead. What to do with an over-anxious daughter? She knew what Frank would say. "Don't answer the phone."

Her good humor returning, Bea decided that before making out her grocery list, she'd check the kitchen cupboard and refrigerator for food left behind by previous guests.

Earlier in her trek to the kitchen, she'd noticed a picture in the dining area of an attractive woman–possibly the owner of the condo? She stopped now to take a closer look and her heart stopped.

She was dimly aware Frank had come in from outside. Shaking off her shock, she found her voice. "Frank, you've got to come here!"

"What is it, hon?" He came quickly to her side, reacting to the urgency in her tone.

Bea pointed to the portrait. "Tell me who that is."

Frank rubbed his chin. "Quite a knockout, I'd say. She does look familiar. Wait a minute. Wasn't she in your math class when you were teaching at the community college? And didn't she come to our home a few times?"

"Right on all counts. Dana–can't remember her last name. She was enrolled in my advanced math class, and she and her younger sister attended a couple of student gatherings in our home."

Frank looked troubled. "And somewhere along the line, didn't you get a threatening letter from her?"

"More vicious than threatening. If this is the same person–" she shook her head. "Let's sit a minute." Bea led him to the sofa. "I'd like to refresh both our memories."

Bea took a deep breath. "Okay. I can picture an energetic, vibrant girl, an A student, or so I thought. She also seemed quite taken with me–all smiles, deferential, quick to agree with the teacher.

"It was all a sham. She was anything but sweetness and light. I overheard a conversation she had with a friend about her fellow students, and she came across as mean spirited, if not downright cruel."

Once again, Frank rubbed his chin. "I'm fuzzy about the details, but wasn't there something about cheating?"

"I caught her cheating on the final exam and as it turned out, she may have cheated all along. She had a thing going with the proctor who provided her the answers. Anyway, after he fessed up, I had to report them, and my, did things get ugly."

Bea paused. "Something I never told you. Dana came to me to plead her case. She said it was in my power to revoke the F grade, and that with at least a C+, she'd be granted her drama scholarship to UCLA.

"I refused; the proctor had hinted he'd helped on other occasions. Also, since the dean knew about her cheating, her chances for the scholarship were nil." Bea sighed. "She showed no remorse. Had she, I might have talked to the dean or," she raised a hand, "maybe not. But you do agree we're talking about the woman in the picture?"

"I'd say yes, though she looks a little different from the girl I remember."

Bea nodded. "No rough edges, perfect makeup, sophisticated pose." She smiled at Frank. "As coincidences go, it's huge. But if this is Dana's condo, the joke's on her. Wouldn't she have a fit if she knew who was sleeping in her bed?"

Bea chuckled at the thought, and then announced she needed to make out a grocery list.

The Devlins were in bed by nine–midnight on their time clock–exhausted but happy to be settled in.

At 3:30 in the morning, Bea awakened and resigned herself to the inevitable: sleep, if it came at all, would be at least two hours off. So she might as well plot the day's activities and review their many options for sightseeing and dining.

She'd planned as far as lunchtime when the thought of Dana entered her mind. Damn that woman, anyway. Bea sighed and turned on her side, away from her husband, as if her memories of that time would soil him.

Frank had remembered the letter but not its contents. She recalled it in its entirety, even after almost twenty years. The words had jumped off the page, characterizing Bea as a mean, smug, self-righteous bitch who had betrayed Dana and ruined her life. It went on and on, including Dana's closing malediction that Bea rot in hell.

The diatribe had alarmed and angered Bea, but it had also puzzled her. Had Dana no conception of wrongdoing? Was cheating her entitlement?

A few days before the cheating incident, Bea had stepped into the women's room across from her classroom. She had just entered a stall when a lively cortege of girls invaded the place, laughing and acting silly as they commented on makeup and hair styles.

The talk then turned to classes.

"Gotta go," someone said. "Devlin has a tizzy if someone comes in late."

Bea recognized Dana's voice.

Another voice: "Didn't you and Kim go to her home for some sort of meeting?"

Dana: "It was supposed to be a social gathering. Of course, we didn't dare smoke and God forbid anyone offer beer or peanuts. I gather if poor old Frank even looks at a peanut, he's wiped out. Anyway, Devlin should lose the husband. Talk about corny. God, he's pathetic."

Bea had stayed hidden until the girls left. Then she returned to the classroom and somehow made it through the period.

Dana's remarks had stung; they still hurt. Based on that hurt, had she been biased in her actions against Dana? She hadn't thought so then; she didn't think so now.

But a voice within her head cried out, *What if? What if you were hard on her on purpose?*

Bea turned back to Frank, to feel his reassuring warmth. To seek his comfort.

Dana snuggled her head onto Mark's shoulder as they lay in bed, resting from an especially athletic sexual encounter. Thinking back to their first time together, when she'd returned from Hawaii, she had been surprised by his agility. He'd been gentle, considerate and passionate, but not overly creative, which was fine by her.

Mark kissed her forehead, her eyes, and the bridge of her nose. "I want to devour you, my lovely Dana."

"Making love will do just fine." She kissed him back. "Tonight was extraordinary, Mark, but I like it simple as well."

"A little variety can heighten the experience."

"I agree. Just don't bring on the whips and chains."

He laughed. "That might tarnish my image as a family therapist."

Dana raised herself on one elbow to look into his eyes.

"How nice to have a lover who pleases his partner. The men I've known or married have not always had the patience or technique to satisfy me."

She had provided the perfect opening for him to question whether she had followed through in asking her husband for a divorce. When he didn't respond, she decided to let it go. "So what's next?" she asked.

Mark sat up and reached for his robe. "How about we relax for a bit? I'll bring us brandies." He got out of bed. "Then who knows?"

She'd go with pillow talk, but it had to be quid pro quo. Tonight she might tell him about her clashes with Susan since he obviously was dying to learn what had happened between them. But she would expect some insights about Susan from Mark in exchange.

Earlier, over cocktails, she'd related in agonizing detail what had befallen her sister.

"I'm stunned," Mark had responded. "I'm sorry about his death, but even after everything you told me about him, I wouldn't have thought the man could be so callous."

"I told you he was a snake. A vile, contemptible excuse for a man."

"What did he do to hurt you?"

"I— I don't understand the question. It's my sister we're talking about."

"True. But your anger and hostility toward your brother-in-law seem deeply rooted, as if on a more personal level."

Deny or confess? She decided to tell the truth–to a point. She admitted that she'd had a relationship with Barry before he and Kim were married, and that he'd been cruel and heartless in the manner in which he'd ended the affair. Mark didn't have to know she'd been married at the time, and that her husband had divorced her because of Barry.

Had she made a mistake in opening up about her affair with Barry? Surely she was justified in expressing her hatred and contempt toward the man. Maybe she'd said too much. Or maybe not. Part of the allure, the exhilaration of being with Mark, was in matching wits. As for her "confession", without doubt he'd heard worse in his practice.

Mark was coming with their brandies–and the bottle–which

meant he planned on a refill or two, a sign she took as favorable for an exchange of confidences.

But she decided it would not be tonight. It was impossible to concentrate on Susan when all she could think about were the Devlins.

Chapter Eight

Frank unlocked the door to the condo, and then, with a show of bravado, stepped back for Bea to enter first. "Here we go, my little Kona cutie, out of the squall and into the shelter."

Bea laughed as she preceded him inside. "How you exaggerate. What's coming down is more mist than rain, though I could do without the wind."

Frank was already on his way to the kitchen, and Bea followed, averting her gaze from the credenza where Dana's portrait presided.

"Two full days," Frank said, as he reached into the refrigerator for a beer, "and not one word from Elizabeth. Imagine that."

"We've been out a lot, especially today with our trip to the volcano."

Frank nodded, and then grinned. "Still, it wouldn't hurt to check under the bed."

"What, for Elizabeth?" Bea suppressed a giggle. "Frank, you're being bad."

"I know. I know." Using a bottle opener, he popped the cap from the bottle, and then took two glasses from the cabinet.

"Nothing for me," Bea said. "I'll wait 'til dinner. Why don't you bring your beer into the living room? We can discuss our dinner plans." When they were settled on the sofa, Bea reached for one of the magazine guides they'd picked up at the airport and turned to the dining-out suggestions. "At least we're all set for the big celebration tomorrow evening." She squeezed his hand.

"The sunset dinner cruise? Sounds romantic."

"Which it should be for our anniversary. But what about tonight? Any suggestions?" She peered at him. "Frank?" In a sudden transformation of mood, his features seemed to sag, his squint lines became more pronounced, his lips pressed together deeply, like a toothless person. "Honey, is something bothering you?"

He hesitated, and then said, "I guess so. You know I was kidding earlier about Elizabeth. But it's no joke the way she hovers over you, at least lately. Damn it, Bea, this concerns me. Are you two hiding something from me?"

Bea took a deep breath and then forced a smile. "She does cling a bit. Maybe it's a reflection of her work, in having to deal with older adults and fussing over them. When we get home, I'll encourage her to broaden her interests, to get out more."

"Get her off our backs, huh?" He said this with a smile that quickly faded. "You haven't answered my question."

"For goodness sakes, Frank, I can't imagine what you're implying. Let's get back to tonight." She turned once again to the restaurant listings. But she couldn't deny the grief she felt inside about Frank living without her; that sadness was like a cancer in itself, spreading unabated and gaining momentum. Disclosing her cancer would lighten her burden, but God knows what the news would do to Frank.

She felt her eyes tearing and busied herself scanning the open pages.

"Can't seem to make up my mind," she said. "Here, you take a look." She handed Frank the guide.

While he searched for his glasses, Bea filled the void. "We can always walk to the family buffet. It's just down the street. Or, if we take the car—" the ringing of the telephone startled her.

Frank flicked the guide against his leg, then sailed it onto the coffee table. He let out a deep sigh.

Bea sat very still, holding her breath, as if in so doing she could shut out the clamor, each ring like a death knell.

She found her voice. "We don't want to miss shopping at Hilo Hatties. Let's go there the day after tomorrow. All right with you?" She wasn't sure he'd heard her over the ringing and started to repeat the question. But then all was silent.

At his nod, she stood, and then glanced toward the glass doors that led to the lanai and beyond. The wind had stilled, and a rainbow arched across the sky, a colorful, silken canopy that contrasted with the darkened waters.

Bea felt an immediate lightness of being. This was a good sign, a beacon of hope. She smiled at Frank. "Shall we get ready for dinner?"

Dinner at 7:00 with Dana was Mark Hampton's fleeting but happy thought. His attention had not wavered from his patient who now related an upsetting dream, but his gaze did wander to the newly acquired painting that hung above the fireplace in his Pasadena office.

A rainy afternoon on the Left Bank in Paris was the backdrop to shops and cafés in a myriad of colors subdued by a wash of pale light that covered the canvas. The facades of buildings and street corner foliage appeared elongated as reflected in the glistening street. It pleased him that this misty exterior blended with the muted blues of his furnishings.

He was also pleased with Susan Connelly's progress.

"I'm beginning to understand myself better," Susan said after they'd finished discussing her dream. Today she wore a turquoise sleeveless top over white tailored pants—a giant leap from the business-like grays and navy blues she'd worn to previous sessions. "I can't believe how uptight I was—what was it, a month ago?"

Mark nodded. "You're certainly more open and relaxed now."

She looked pensive. "Because I trust you. Which means I can be honest. Still, baring one's soul has a downside, I suppose, in dredging up the yucky stuff." She sighed. "How can I put this?

"It's like I'm at a parade. A marching band, big and brassy, files by; bagpipes drone, horses clip-clop along, and I hear applause and laughter that sweeten the air. But it's all a tease because I'm sitting on a curb with people towering in front of me. I'm missing balloons, floats, strutting majorettes. I'm—I'm missing all the excitement."

"And how does that make you feel? Sad? Angry?"

"Maybe afraid. Because if the parade is passing me by, then I have to take a stand, make changes. I don't know if I can do that, or if I have the guts to reinvent myself.

"After all, I've led such a tidy life. Ted and I are the perfect couple, with the perfect child and perfect lifestyle."

She cracked a smile. "Wouldn't it be a kick in the pants if I ran away from home?"

"Where would you go?"

She pushed a strand of hair from her forehead. "I wouldn't. I'm talking nonsense. By the way, I like your new painting. I'll bet it's from the Galleria Lafayette. The one on Rodeo Drive?"

Mark laughed. "Only if I doubled my hourly fee."

"Where did you find it?"

"A friend recommended a gallery on Melrose Boulevard."

Her smile, really a smirk, and knowing look conveyed a sense of smugness that puzzled him. It was time to move on.

He glanced at his notes and then looked Susan in the eye. "You've seemed reluctant to talk in depth about your husband."

"Ted? I'm not sure there's much to say. He's a good man."

"How did you meet?"

"We both attended USC, but I knew him only casually on campus. Later, after graduation, we mixed at Young Republican meetings. And, eventually, we became a couple." She paused. "The truth? I wasn't wildly in love with Ted when we married, but I was flattered by his attentions–he is an attractive man–and impressed that he was established in his career. And, of course, we do come from similar backgrounds."

"How do you feel about Ted now?"

"Oh, I still care about him."

"But?"

"I can't always relate to his interests; in fact, we're worlds apart on some matters. He doesn't share my passion for politics, and that's disappointing to me." She studied the carpet for a moment or two, and then looked up. "There's more."

Mark nodded his encouragement.

"If Ted said this evening, 'Pack your bags, I'm taking you on a weekend whirl to Paris,' I'd say, 'Sure.' But it would be more of a hassle than sheer pleasure. Not that he'd be that spontaneous. With us, it's everything by the book.

"I wish, I really wish he'd speak up on personal issues. I'd like to know how he views our life together now, or five years from now, on what he wants from life. And it annoys me he won't take a stand on current events, politics, the economy. I'm thrown together with people in my political groups who breathe magnetism, who pursue goals. Ted just putt-putts along."

"Isn't it possible that Ted senses your dissatisfactions, your restiveness?"

"It's hard to tell because he's always there for me."

"Susan, I have a suggestion. Bring Ted to our next session. It's difficult for me to understand the dynamics of a marriage unless I meet and talk with both parties."

She frowned. "So that's when the shit hits the fan?"

"Not necessarily. What you tell me is confidential. However, I would like to assess your relationship from his point of view, as well as yours."

"Hmm. Well, all right." She rotated her shoulders and then glanced at her watch. "Looks like I'm on overtime."

She rose and Mark followed suit, but instead of moving toward the exit that led to the outer office, Susan stepped up to the painting over the fireplace, taking a moment or two to study it.

When she turned to Mark, the lift of her eyebrows, the tilt of her chin lent an air of superiority. "Do you mind if I say something personal?"

"Not at all."

"I saw you at Café-Grimaldi Thursday evening. You were with Dana Sterling. Oh, I forgot. It's Dana James now, isn't it?"

"You know Dana?" he asked, feigning surprise.

"We took some classes together at USC, but she didn't stick around long. It seems Dana wasn't university material. Some years later we ran into each other at several charity events. I've always suspected she wanted to break into my circle of friends, but," she made a face, "we have nothing at all in common. I did make noises to the effect that we should stay in touch because I didn't want to appear rude."

"And do you stay in touch?"

"I send her a yearly Christmas newsletter, but that's as far as it goes.

"It's the painting that got me started on Dana. Her sister, Kim, runs an art gallery on Melrose Boulevard, and so I made the connection."

"You seem to know a lot about Dana."

She shrugged. "Just how well do you know her?"

"Why do you ask?"

"I was surprised that someone with your status and background would show up with a person who's morally and socially beneath you. Dana may be a sexpot, but she's bad news. She comes on to every man she meets, including my goody-goody husband. And my, was he all aglow–or shall we say turned on by her attentions? The woman's cheap. She's a slut."

Mark held up his hand. "Stop this. Your purpose for seeing me is for us to work together to provide for your emotional well-being. And you have made excellent progress. If the hostility you profess toward Dana is part of the larger picture in our quest for solutions to your problems, then so be it. But character assassination doesn't solve anything."

"Okay, okay. I hear you." She paused. "I'll make an appointment to include Ted in my next visit." She started for the exit.

"Good."

Partly out the door, Susan turned back to him. "Sorry, Dr. Hampton. I was out of line." Her smile was that of a little girl placating Papa. "I won't mention Dana again." She closed the door gently behind her.

Sorry, my foot, Mark thought, as he gathered up her file and then shoved it into a drawer of his cabinet.

Susan was no longer the shadow of a woman who had crept to him like a forlorn puppy. She had metamorphosed into a snarling pit bull, at least when it came to Dana.

Given the circumstances, he could always take himself off the case. If he did so, his observations for his replacement would not be complete without a report of his meeting with Ted Connelly.

It was now 3:30 and his next patient was due at 4:00. Then he'd be free for the day, with plenty of time to go over his notes and freshen up for his evening with Dana.

Dana had been riding high, with hints and evasions regarding Susan Connelly. It was time to knock her off her steed. No more game playing. He wanted Dana's input on Susan. In return, he'd toss a few nuggets her way.

He sighed. Were Susan's comments about Dana the outpouring of a jealous, spiteful woman? Or did her allegations bear scrutiny?

Did he even care?

Mark was in for a surprise when he arrived at the penthouse to pick up Dana. She wore what he presumed were designer jeans, with a bright red shirt, tailored to emphasize her breasts and trim waist. She also clutched a serving spoon in one hand and an apron in the other. Obviously, there'd been a change in plans.

"Wow," he said, "don't you look cute."

She swooped forward to plant a kiss on his lips, and then backed away with a graceful bend of the knees. "We're eating in tonight, my love, minus the caterers." She waved the spoon. "So it looks like dinner will be a joint effort. Sound like fun? Anyway, I called Chasens and cancelled our reservation." Her words tumbled forth breathlessly.

"I think you're a chapter ahead of me. But okay, I guess this calls for ditching the jacket and tie."

"You do that, and then come back to the kitchen." She pivoted in red high heeled sandals and was out of sight in seconds.

Mark draped his jacket over the back of a chair, but took his time removing his tie as he gathered his thoughts. Today was full of surprises.

"You probably weren't expecting a small kitchen," Dana said, when he joined her. She paused to point to the bottles of Beefeater gin and vermouth, indicating he should make the drinks. "The size bothered me at first," she continued, "but the cupboards and drawers are a natural wood maple–none of that plastic crap–and check out the counters."

Creamy granite blended nicely with the maple. "Beautiful," he said. He looked up. "I never cared for recessed lighting because it can be dim, but in here I could just as well be standing under direct sunlight."

"Too bright in my opinion. I could have asked for different lighting to be installed, but why bother? Except for making breakfast, I'm rarely in the kitchen."

Ditto for the rest of the tenants, he figured. As he worked on the martinis, Mark kept one eye on Dana as she flitted about, putting the finishing touches on a green salad.

"You're in charge of grilling the burgers," Dana said. She placed the salad in the refrigerator and then slipped off her apron. "But I've taken care of the side dishes and you, my dear, are in for some treats. Papa's Deli on Fairfax has the best potato salad, kosher pickles, coleslaw, sauerkraut–you name it." She paused. "I see you're ready to pour. The glasses are chilling in the freezer. But let me take the cheese platter out to the terrace." In a whirl she was gone.

He stared at the place she'd occupied. Her energy had ignited a room that, without her exhibited all the personality of a kitchen display in a home improvement store.

My, is she ever wired tonight, Mark thought, as he carried their drinks to the terrace.

"There's no wind, so we can barbeque out here," Dana said as they settled into patio chairs, separated by a small round glass table.

Mark raised his glass. "Cheers," he said. "Now. Are you going to tell me what this is all about?"

"It's summertime. Who wants to sit in a stuffy, old restaurant?"

"You do. Usually."

"What's wrong with a picnic-style dinner?"

"Nothing. It's a great idea. I'm just curious as to why the change in plans."

She took a sip of her drink. "I realize it's spur of the moment. But I wanted a casual evening at home because I have to be up at dawn tomorrow morning." Her pause was dramatic.

"And where are you off to?"

"Australia to see Jasper. I had to pull some strings to set the trip in motion, but perseverance paid off, and my reservations were confirmed this morning."

"What's going on with you two?"

"Remember how I threw out the idea of getting a divorce?" He nodded.

"Would you be sad if I decided to stay with Jasper?"

"I'd miss you like crazy," he said, and he meant it.

"Good. Because I've made up my mind. I've decided to ask Jasper for a divorce."

Blithely said, Mark thought. And how, he wondered, would gaining her freedom impact their relationship? "Is Jasper aware of your intentions?" he asked.

"Surely, he suspects we're headed that way. Our long distance conversations have been strained and few and far between. He knows, too, how reluctant I am to move to Australia."

"I'm surprised you didn't cancel this evening."

"I thought about it, but if I were alone, I'd be pacing the floor and grinding my teeth. Besides, I like being with you."

"The feeling is mutual." He smiled briefly, and then stared into his drink. "It's been a tough day."

Dana put a square of havarti cheese on a cracker and leaned into him, brushing her breast against his arm as she held the cracker up to his mouth. When he'd taken a bite, she said, "Too bad you can't tell me about your day."

"Actually, I do want to bring up something that occurred with a patient. But first, I'll make us re-fills."

When he returned to the terrace, Dana stood at the railing, staring upward.

Mark put down their drinks, then joined her, placing his arm lightly around her shoulders.

"If I were to stay with Jasper," she said, "I'd be trading garish neon images for gazing at a night sky bright with the southern constellations." A hint of wistfulness softened her tone.

"Are you really sure you want this divorce?" Mark asked.

"Yes, I'm sure. In no way do I intend to live out my life with that pig-headed Aussie."

She gave him a little poke. "Let's get back to our drinks; I'm dying to hear about your patient." When they were seated, Mark spread camembert cheese over a water cracker and handed it to Dana. He fixed one for himself, and then turned to his martini.

Dana watched his every move. "You're stalling," she said.

"Okay. Here we go. Susan Connelly saw us having dinner at Café-Grimaldi."

"Oh, my, and did she comment on what a sweet couple we

make?" Dana asked in a little girl voice.

Mark laughed. "I wouldn't even call us that."

"I'm sure she searched in her bag of snide remarks for the nastiest pick."

"She seems to know a lot about you, and apparently the two of you had a falling out."

"Nothing quite so specific." Dana raised her glass, drank deeply, then set it down. "Wow, look at me. At the rate I'm going, it'll be a contest over which of us finishes the bottle first. Now, what did she say about me?"

"I'll tell you. But first I want to know what went on between you and Susan."

"All right. First some background. We became acquainted when I enrolled briefly at USC. We were in a few classes together and ended up as partners on some study projects. Not that she wanted to work with me, but she had no choice.

"At any rate, I tried to be friendly, to fit into her group of friends. And believe me, she was the queen bee of that circle. But I saw the looks that passed between her and others when I approached them. And I'd overhear them planning parties and organizing study groups that never included me."

Mark squeezed her hand. "Rejection is the granddaddy of all hurts."

She shrugged. "If you say so. Well. I didn't stay long at USC because I couldn't afford the tuition. Anyway, as fate would have it, Kyle, my first husband, was big on fund-raisers and charity events–as were the Connellys."

"So you reestablished your acquaintanceship?"

"I guess you could put it that way. At this point we were grown women, not college girls with middle school mentalities.

"The first couple of times we met, Susan seemed genuinely friendly, asking about Kyle, my family, our activities and so on. We exchanged phone numbers and after a decent interval, I called her and suggested we get together for dinner.

"She was cordial but vague. Said she'd call back, which she never did. The next time I ran into her, she was polite, but seemed in a hurry to catch up with a group of people she had no intention of introducing me to. Later I saw her on the dance floor. What a joke–swishing her fanny, about as graceful as an ox."

"You seem so intense about this, Dana. Where is it written that everyone has to love us? We can't make a connection with every person we meet."

"Mark, don't you get it? Susan Connelly purposefully shut me out, both in college and after I married Kyle. Apparently, we weren't educated or cultured enough to meet her arrogant, high and mighty, know-it-all standards. The woman is an overbearing snob and ugly to boot!"

"Whew. I guess you told me."

"Oh. And how does this grab you? She'll have nothing to do with me on a social level, but every damn year I get the Connelly's Christmas newsletter that practically bites me with boring details of their accomplishments. They don't get sick, they never have leaking roofs, cancelled flights, or deaths in the family. It's always about how blessed they are with good fortune, and may the heavens smile on you, the less endowed recipients as well. How incredibly smug can a person be?"

"Sometimes people try to come across as positive and successful when it's not all that great behind the scenes."

"Are you telling me the letter is a sham?"

"I wouldn't think so. But I could make a list of what I've accomplished in a given year, and yet it wouldn't reflect my inner life."

"I get your drift. Now tell me what that bitch said about me."

Mark made a mental note not to get on Dana's bad side; that is, if he wanted her in his life. "Susan said she was surprised to see us together because of a disparity in our personas."

"Plain English, please?"

"For whatever reasons, she couldn't picture us as a couple. She also brought up USC, then about running into you in later years. She felt the two of you had nothing in common."

"You know what that damn newsletter says? I, Susan, have it all–a stable marriage, a brilliant child, a thriving social life. Ain't it great? Isn't my life just P-diddly perfect?"

Mark chuckled. "When you put it that way, you've cut her down to size. So what's the fuss about?"

"I tell myself Susan lords it over me because she's jealous of my attributes, that I can attract men where she can't. I tell myself her snubs meant and mean nothing. And, obviously, if she's seeing you, the good ship Connelly is listing, if not sinking. But it doesn't matter. The thought of Susan Connelly makes me crazy!"

Mark stared at Dana, fascinated. Her features had hardened into mask-like severity. Her skin, in the fading light, looked ashen, her jewel-like eyes now murky with smoky undertones.

And then in an instant, her mouth curved into a half smile, and her expression softened. "I guess you wouldn't mind if I dropped my Wicked Witch of the West act?"

Mark took her hand. "I'm just sorry you're upset."

"Actually, I'm feeling better now. Maybe my ranting has resulted in—how would you put it—a catharsis?"

"Let's settle for that." Mark checked his watch. "Think I should heat up the grill?"

Dana kissed his cheek. "I'm ready to rumble."

Later at home, Mark poured himself a brandy, lit a cigar, and then stepped onto his deck. The night was bracing but pleasant, and all was quiet except for the cicadas buzzing in a never ending gab fest, shutting out the gentle ripple of water over rocks.

Mark decided to sit outside in his usual chair where he could reflect on the day's happenings.

Dana and Susan. How different could two women be? And yet, each by her actions and words had provided insight into the character of the other woman. He supposed their accusations were credible, if exaggerated. But most interestingly, it was the accuser who told him most about herself.

He still hadn't decided whether he should take himself off Susan's case; he would continue to see Dana.

Dana had lightened up after her outburst and preparing dinner together had been fun, their picnic meal delicious. They had cut short the evening by mutual agreement.

Mark concentrated now on his cigar and brandy, the sensuous

delights of rich taste and aroma. But Dana once again intruded his thoughts.

Something about that woman disturbed him. It wasn't her mood swings—then what was it? He had commented on her intensity in going after Susan. As he mulled this over, it occurred to him that Dana had exhibited the same fervor or passion in expressing her hatred for Barry Williams. Was this a personality quirk, or did it represent something more troubling, like a dark side he was reluctant to explore?

This is what he knew: Dana excited him, fed his imagination, and was a challenge as well. Could he tame her? Probably not. But whatever the future held for them, he did not envision his name on the list of Dana's discards.

It would not come to that.

Dana sipped her Coke from the can as she surveyed her kitchen.

It glistened–crumbless, stain free, and pristine on all counts, thanks to Mark. He'd been an able assistant throughout the evening and, to her relief, had not pressed to stay over.

She was glad to be alone, to take a few moments to gather her thoughts before bedtime. But who could think with that damn overhead light? She found the off switch, and then with Coke in hand sauntered into the great room.

The one place she wanted to avoid was her desk but in some perverse way, she was drawn to it. She stood behind her chair and stared at the long, white envelope mailed from Sydney, Australia.

A sudden feeling of light headedness prompted her to sit down. She sipped her Coke, choked on the liquid, and then with an unsteady hand set down the can. Hastily, as if handling something soiled, she used her fingertips to extract the one page letter from the envelope.

In his spidery handwriting, Jasper proclaimed their union had been one huge mistake, and that he saw no way to resolve their differences. Therefore, the only recourse was divorce. She would hear from his solicitor in a timely fashion. Blah, blah, blah.

Dana placed the letter that had been sitting on her desk for three days back in its envelope. Slowly, deliberately, she tore the envelope in half, then in quarters, and then tore it again and again until only scraps remained.

Of course, she would deal with the situation in her own way when the time was right. For now, she would consult her lawyer, and, she smiled, set up an appointment with Ted Connelly. She had already spoken to him about Kim, but that had been on the phone. She looked forward to meeting with him in person.

After her trip. To Hawaii.

Chapter Nine

Kim sat on the edge of her bed, submitting to the sleeplessness that plagued most of her nights. She stared at her digital clock. The numbers blipping on course toward early morning cast a soft blue sheen in the dark.

Was it just two days ago that Kevin had arrived at the gallery as the bearer of condolences? An unsettling interlude, indeed, but thank God she needn't gnash her teeth over should they or shouldn't they try again. What happened, happened. End of story.

She kneaded her forehead. Barry was another matter with still so many loose ends. She'd trashed his toiletries and personal items of no great value, given away his golf clubs and donated his clothes to Good Will.

Then yesterday, minutes after Dana had driven away, the phone rang. An expressionless male voice informed her that the condo Mr. Williams had leased in the Hollywood Hills was about to be put on the market for sale. Someone needed to clean out the closets and drawers and pick up any items left at the property.

ASAP, he'd added.

Kim pictured nighties and other feminine apparel in lustful contact with garments Barry had confiscated from home, the rest to follow when he'd moved permanently into his bachelor quarters.

Felicia's belongings were undoubtedly long gone. Still, Kim had half a mind to call the slut and insist she be the one to clear out Barry's things. Why not take them home as a souvenir? Better yet, start or add to a collection of keepsakes from dumped (or dead?) suitors.

Kim wondered, too, if Barry might have lived in proximity to Kevin. And if so, what a hoot.

Actually, the thought depressed her. She lay back down and turned away from the clock. If she couldn't sleep, at least she could rest.

Fat chance. Her whirling mind had dredged up the second phone call of the day from Dana in the late afternoon. How had the conversation played out? Something like this:

Dana: (Animated) Are you in for a surprise!

Kim: Really? Something wonderful, I hope?

Dana: For you, absolutely. For me? Well, yes, but with complications.

Kim: All right. If you want to play games, I'll go first. What's my surprise?

Dana: Big sister stays in L.A.

Kim: You've reached a compromise with Jasper?

Dana: I wouldn't call divorce a compromise.

Kim: Silence.

Dana: Kim?

Kim: I'm stunned. You're really going to ask Jasper for a divorce? Of course, I'm thrilled you're not moving to Australia, but my God, Dana, a divorce? Or to use your euphemism–complications?

Dana: (Soft laughter) I did say that, didn't I? There's more. Shortly after I left you this morning, I learned there'd been a cancelation on a flight to Sydney that leaves from LAX early tomorrow morning. So I'm off to confront Jasper.

Kim: I don't envy you. I wonder how he'll take the news?

Dana: If he were English, I'd say with a stiff upper lip. But in his case, I'll go with the Australian equivalent.

Kim: Let's hope so. Can I help in any way?

Dana: Thanks, but I'm good on my own. As for you, now that I'm staying, I can help you with any obstacles that come along. Okay, gotta go and get packing. Oh, one more thing. Call Ted Connelly. Here's his number.

Kim lay there with Dana's voice fading from her mind.

Totally awake now, she turned back toward the clock. Five a.m. She remembered her sister's instructions not to call before ten in the morning. Had Dana been up since four? Kim shuddered at the thought.

On the other hand, Dana had come across as spirited, motivated, and now that she thought about it, not the least bit distressed over what lay ahead for her and Jasper.

Another glance at the clock and Kim decided to make an agenda of the day's activities. She had to make a call to the CPA and, she made a face, remember to collect Barry's things from the condo.

She slipped out of bed and into her robe and started for the bathroom, only to detour to the small desk in the corner of the room. Though not under lock and key, this desk marked her territory, its contents for her eyes only. Private papers, correspondence, a packet of love notes from Barry–why had he even bothered?–and other personal items crowded the drawers, while a large calendar covered part of the desk. Kim sat down, switched on the lamp, and opened the calendar to the month of July. *Not much to look forward to*, she thought. But that would change. She would emulate Dana, get crackin', by golly, and tackle her to-do list.

She looked at the blank square with the number 15 printed in the upper corner. July 15th. Something about the date rang a bell. And then she remembered her sister had stressed that she and Barry schedule their stay in Kona posthaste because the Devlins would arrive some days before their anniversary on July 15. Oh, happy day. For them.

It seemed to Kim that the circle of light that fell on the calendar, illuminating month and day, was akin to a spotlight highlighting her own hapless existence. With a snap, she pulled the chain on the lamp, and then stood.

A sudden malaise had come over her, and she felt her eyes drooping shut. Back to bed? No. Purposefully, she moved to the picture window and opened the drapes.

Ah, better. Early morning light dusted the acacia tree a sedate green, threaded with tinges of gold. The night was giving way to grayish blue with a trace of the moon still visible, while light from a street lamp glowed faintly, as if set on dim.

Somber suited her mood and her pledge to push herself whithered quickly. But in her heart of hearts she wished she might change places with the Devlins. She would wake up to a cloudless, golden day filled with delightful promise. On her to-do list? First, and foremost, to celebrate a marriage powered by love and devotion.

Shutting out images she had no claim to, Kim turned away from the window.

Her sister had treated her and Barry to a romantic get-away. Outcome? Disastrous. Now, unbeknownst to the Devlins, Dana had insured them a celebration they'd likely never experience again. So good for them!

Kim choked back a sob. And good for the whole god dammed world!

A perfect morning in paradise. Frank ruminated on this observation as he devoured scrambled eggs and sausage on the lanai. The words came across as gushy, but hell, it was true. You couldn't complain about the weather, the view or–what was Bea's favorite word?–the ambience. He rolled his tongue over ambience, saying it aloud, liking the sound of it.

Frank inspected the large blueberry muffin, the only thing left on his plate. He was no longer hungry but not ready to quit either. Between bites and sips of coffee, he tipped his head back to absorb the sun's rays and then gazed at the horizon. Water and sky met seamlessly, lathed to exactness. And to think the day was just beginning.

With only a trace of guilt, he thought about his wife in the kitchen, cleaning up after them. Why hadn't he offered to help or take on the job himself? Maybe because the shock would be too much for Bea? Early on in their marriage Frank had declared the kitchen foreign territory, avoiding the maze of drawers, cupboards and cabinets containing kitchen tools and doodads outside his expertise.

But that would change. Retirement wasn't far off and when that day arrived, he'd conquer the kitchen. Who knows? In time he could become a master chef.

"Someone must be daydreaming." Bea stood beside him, coffee pot in hand. "More coffee, Frank?"

Surprised, he sat straighter. He hadn't heard the doors opening or Bea's steps over the sound of the surf. "Sure, honey. Why don't you join me?"

"I'll sit for a moment, have a half cup." She settled across from him and when she'd finished pouring their coffee, she looked up and smiled. "I'll bet you won't recognize the new me."

"I don't want a new you. I like you just the way you are."

"Oh, now honey, don't be a spoilsport. The makeover is part of the package. So whether you like it or not, I'm getting a facial, a manicure, my hair styled and maybe they'll even apply makeup." She peered at him over the rim of her glasses. "And I can hardly wait."

"Sounds like you'll be gone for the day."

"I was told four hours tops, but you never know. Anyway, I should be back by one thirty or two. And you'd better have that camera ready!"

Her mouth curved into an impish smile. "You're going to receive a treat too, Frank. You'll see."

With that, Bea was out of her chair. "I'd better be on my way. Oh." She paused at the sliding glass doors. "Be sure to answer the phone. I have a feeling the girls will be calling to wish us happy anniversary."

Frank returned her wave goodbye, resisting an urge to go after her to give her a hug. Instead, he filled his cup with more coffee. He might not approve of Bea's new hairdo, but he sure liked her sparkle, her get-up-and-go this morning. Amazing what a trip to the beauty parlor could do for a woman.

Gingerly, he smoothed back his thinning hair and sighed. If anyone could use a makeover, it was Frank Devlin. He didn't need a mirror to point out his receding hairline, his expanding belly. Bea, bless her heart, didn't seem to notice these changes. And she was just as pretty to him now as when they'd first met.

He wasn't strong on sentiment, but Bea had become more dear, more precious to him with every passing year. It was high time, he decided, to put these feelings into words. Soon, he promised himself. Soon.

Frank stretched his arms to the side to ease the stiffness in his torso. He decided he'd had enough sun for the morning; besides, he wasn't sure he could hear the phone from outside.

Sure enough, only minutes after he entered the condo, the call came through from Diane, highlighted by messages from his grandsons. Frank couldn't help but gloat. He'd take that call any day over a high-falutin' makeover.

No sooner was he off the phone, when the doorbell rang, two cheery chirps that brought him quickly to the door.

Frank blinked at the florid red Hawaiian shirt that blocked the view beyond his doorway. A stocky young man with a round smiling face, whose belly matched his own, held a large basket.

"Yep, this is the right address," the young man said after consulting his notes. He bowed. "George at your service." The basket was draped with a colorful lei of white flowers interlaced with small pink and purple blooms. Two doll-like figures, a bride and groom, dangled from its handles. The open part of the basket was covered with a filmy, white material in folds, decorated with sparkly pink and white wedding bells.

"I'll bet it's someone's anniversary," George said, his smile growing broader.

An awkward pause followed until Frank had the presence of mind to dig into his pocket for his billfold. All he had was a five, which George readily accepted as he handed over the basket and then made a speedy exit.

Frank wondered what this could be all about as he carried the basket inside and placed it on the coffee table in the living room.

Had their daughters conspired to order an anniversary gift as a surprise? Or was this the treat Bea promised? Whoever had sent the gift, Frank decided to wait for Bea to return so that they could explore the contents together.

And then he noticed an envelope taped to the side of the basket. He couldn't resist; he had to open it. The note read:

Dear One,

On our special day, I ordered sweets for my sweetheart. Look inside. You'll find two cakes. Which cake shall it be? Which cake would you choose to celebrate our anniversary? I suggest you sample a slice from each selection. Then you decide! Have fun. Enjoy. See you soon.

He smiled. So it was Bea, after all. But only one slice? Well, Bea had been nagging him about cutting back. Whatever his choice, they sure as hell weren't going to let the other cake go to waste.

Carefully, he pushed aside the material that covered the basket to look inside. Placed one on top of the other were two medium sized see-through containers. Chocolate cake, his favorite was on top. He examined the one below for color and texture. A carrot cake? Possibly, but he'd have to taste it to be sure. So on to the kitchen.

After Frank cut himself a good-sized portion from each cake, he carried his plate and a bottled Coke to the lanai and took his place at the table, looking forward to the free entertainment.

Since they'd arrived, he had followed the course of water skiers, marveled at the precision strokes executed by competing oarsmen in canoes, or stared in fascination at parasailers soaring over the water. Today an added attraction tickled his fancy: a large cruise ship was anchored in position for tenders to carry passengers to the island.

Frank pictured himself standing in a raggedly line with people jostling each other to be first to board the tender. They would buck their way across the water, with ocean spray drenching him from where he sat in the open area with other macho types.

And for what? To comb the flea markets and souvenir shops? To dodge the shills bugging tourists to sign up for this or that?

No way. He'd marked his own bit of paradise right here on the lanai with no one to pester him. He imagined posting a sign: Frank's Party. Private: Keep Out!

Frank's party began with the chocolate cake, of course. He took a bite, allowed the moist, sweet texture to linger on his tongue, and then chewed and swallowed. Oh, baby, without a doubt, this was it. Why even bother tasting the other sample?

On second thought, he owed it to Bea to compare the two cakes. And besides, he was curious to try this grainy, beige colored concoction with white frosting.

So down to business. Like a wine taster, Frank brought a forkful of cake to his nostrils to inhale the aroma. It reminded him of something...He scratched his head. Something familiar, but he couldn't put his finger on it.

Not only did it look good, it tasted good. He took another bite, then another, but still couldn't identify the flavor.

He stared out at a tender discharging passengers as he enjoyed another taste. And then something seemed peculiar; something was off. Was it his imagination or did he feel a tingling sensation on his lips and tongue? It seemed to be bleeding into his throat as well. He reached for his Coke then set it down, suddenly light headed.

Whoa, there. Maybe he needed to get out of the sun. Time for more fluid. Once again Frank reached for his Coke. He brought the bottle to his lips and took a swig, only to have the liquid spill onto his chin. It didn't take but a moment for him to realize his lips felt swollen–he raised a hand to his cheeks–as did his face. Worse, now his throat hurt and he was having trouble swallowing.

Blame the cake! Peanuts or peanut oil in the cake had brought on these reactions. He stood and grasped the edge of the table, feeling faint. "Come on, Devlin, inside, inside," he urged himself. Bea would never have ordered anything with peanuts. How had this happened? He could die, for Christ's sake.

His breathing shallow, Frank made it into the condo. Epi Pen…Epi Pen. He knew the medication was somewhere in the bedroom or bathroom. They carried it with them everywhere. Had to find the damn thing and inject it now.

Oh, God, the phone was ringing. No time for that. Unless it was Bea? She'd tell him where to look and then call an ambulance.

He picked up the receiver, aware of a female voice and then turned up the volume. Elizabeth? He tried to answer but couldn't catch his breath. He pressed his throat, as if to force out the words, then gave up. Besides, everything around him seemed distorted.

The receiver fell out of his hand and Frank dropped to his knees. He tilted his head backward, gasping for breath. Oh, God, if only he could summon the strength to crawl to wherever it was he needed to be. If only Bea were here. If only, if only, echoed in his mind like a hollow, endless dirge.

His knees gave way, and he lay on the floor in a fetal position, a sensation of cold glutting his pores as the light began to fade. He was drowning, drowning…

Frank embraced the cold and the darkness.

Chapter Ten

Elizabeth stared at her phone in disbelief. Heavy breathing? She pressed the receiver hard against her ear. Nothing, not a sound. She pushed aside papers strewn over her desk to retrieve the Kona phone number her mother had jotted down, and that in turn Elizabeth had recorded in her address book.

The numbers corresponded. Surely, she hadn't misdialed. Someone, her mother or father had lifted the receiver. She'd hang up, try again.

Shoot, a busy signal. Several times she'd called her parents but had reached them only once. And now this.

With a heavy hand, Elizabeth rearranged papers on her desk to secure the half-finished report that she'd promised her supervisor in the morning. She snapped open the folder and read the first page, then read again. She reached for the phone. Still a busy signal. Who could they be talking to?

On her feet now, Elizabeth started for the kitchen, only to stop halfway to examine the plant she'd bought yesterday at Wal-Mart. Leaves spilled over the ash colored container that squatted on an end table adjacent to the sofa. Azalea blossoms and buds crowded in bunch-like clusters as if struggling for space within the thicket of green.

In the store—maybe it was the lighting—the leaves glistened an emerald green, providing an aesthetic counterpoint to variegated pinks, both bold and pearly. She hadn't set out to buy a plant, but in passing through the garden section on her way to household cleaners, had impulsively placed the shrub in her basket.

A big fat mistake, Elizabeth decided. Delicate pinks made a wimpy accessory to no-nonsense beiges and browns that dominated the furnishings of her apartment. She'd give the plant to her mother.

Because she couldn't remember why she'd been on her way to the kitchen in the first place, Elizabeth returned to her desk. She'd finish her report, then go for a walk or make some work-related phone calls.

The sound she made was half way between a cough and a

snicker. Now that was an ass-brained idea. Leave the house or tie up the phone? No way. Not until she talked to her parents.

Another try–still a busy signal. Okay. Enough. Elizabeth delved into her work, pausing only when her miniature grandfather clock–a gift from her maternal grandmother–chimed five mellow but decisive strokes, reminding her that despite her anxieties over reaching her parents, the hours had flown by. Soon, she would be thinking about what to fix for dinner, while her parents were undoubtedly still full from lunch.

Elizabeth rubbed her eyes, stretched, and then resolutely turned from the phone to fasten her gaze on the clock that adorned the mantel of her fake fireplace. The elegant simplicity of design, the burnished wood, the even swing of the pendulum spoke to her of a more formal and disciplined era.

This symbol of rectitude and steadfastness brought to mind her grandmother whose values she could relate to and who, if she were alive, would surely praise Elizabeth for her tenacity and perseverance in providing guidance and help to the disadvantaged.

For Elizabeth the clock represented a kinder, more genteel world. She closed her eyes and not for the first time imagined herself in a time warp where life moved at a slower pace, where common courtesy prevailed over boorishness and disrespect.

The jangling of the phone broke into her reverie.

"Hello." She paused. "Hello?" She waited, and then someone broke the connection. Damn nuisance call, she thought. But at least this aggravation had pulled her back into the real world. So why not bring on another aggravation, she determined, as she set down her pen and picked up the phone.

No busy signal this time. Elizabeth tapped her foot in double time. *Why weren't they answering?* She had decided to wait ten rings, but on the sixth, someone picked up. The voice was male, somber, and not her father.

"Hello?" She hesitated. "I wonder if I have a wrong number. This is Elizabeth Devlin, and I'm trying to reach Bea or Frank Devlin."

"Uh, please, would you hold on? I have to check on something."

Voices in the background, a long pause. Elizabeth felt as if rust had corroded the insides of her mouth. She wanted to know what was going on and who was the man who had answered the phone? She pressed her lips together to stop their trembling and tears began forming. She knew it. Without a doubt, something had happened to her mother, something connected to her illness. Maybe she had collapsed, or contracted a life threatening virus because of her weakened immune system. Oh, God, what if her mother had been in an accident. And where was her father?

Why, oh why, had they insisted on taking this trip? Why?

"Elizabeth?" It was her mother; she sounded weak and old.

"Mom, what's going on? Are you okay?"

"Elizabeth, it's your father. He's suffered anaphylactic shock."

"I don't understand."

"It's when the airways become clogged and you can't breathe." Her voice was teary but now stronger than when she'd come to the phone. "He ate something that had peanuts in it and—and—I'm shaking so, I—."

"But he has his medication. You brought it, didn't you? He's in the hospital, right? Mom talk to me."

"I'm sorry, sweetheart, but your father didn't make it. I tried to call you a few minutes ago—" she broke into a sob.

"How could this have happened? Mom. Mom. Are you there? Tell me how this happened."

"A bizarre mix-up in a delivery of cakes, of all things—" her voice faded as if she'd turned away from the phone.

A male voice, sturdy but kind, came on the line. "Elizabeth? Hi, this is Dr. Reed. I've given your mother a sedative, and now I think she should rest."

"Yes, yes, of course." Her words came out high pitched and strained, bringing on a ringing in her ears.

"Doctor?" Elizabeth lowered her tone. Falling apart was not an option. Not now. She spoke slowly, spacing her words. "Please tell my mother I'll take the next flight out to be with her. Tell her I'll call my sister. Tell her—just tell her to hang on and that I love her."

She didn't wait for the doctor's response. She was trying too hard to steady her hands in order to put the receiver back in place.

This could not be happening. Her father's death did not fit into her plan of seeing to all of his needs should, God forbid, cancer take her mother.

Now he was gone, and she hadn't even said goodbye, hadn't told him how much she loved him. Tears came in a rush, and she sobbed uncontrollably, blubbering like a baby. But the outburst was short lived when she thought of her mother, heartbroken and alone, miles from home.

She wiped away her tears and turned to her computer to search for flight information. And then a jarring thought brought her to a halt. How could her father have been so careless as to ingest something toxic to his body? How could he justify taking such a chance? Didn't he care about himself, his family? Was he just being stupid, for God's sake? She focused on the anger and let it build into a rage that, in turn, would galvanize her into taking action.

Elizabeth ignored the grandfather clock chiming the half hour as she picked up the phone. She had work to do: Call Diane, then book her flight. Sentiment, she could do without.

"Mrs. James! What a surprise." Heidi McGowan, manager of Kailua Condos, came from behind her desk to greet Dana, her broad smile now faltering. "I guess you've heard."

Dana shook her head. "I happened to drive by yesterday and saw emergency vehicles. Was someone hurt?"

"Oh, gosh." Heidi ran her hands over her hips, smoothing nonexistent wrinkles. She wore a pink and white muumuu, splashed with oversized magenta flowers—which did little to minimize her ample proportions. Her frown accentuated her middle-age sag. "Wouldn't you like to sit down?" She pointed to the love seat positioned to the left of the entry way.

"I stopped by only for a minute," Dana said, forcing a smile as she mentally prodded the woman to get on with it. "As an owner, I thought I'd better make sure a gas or water leak hadn't damaged the units."

"Oh, my." Heidi said. "If only it'd been a gas or water leak. Well, maybe that's not so good either." She seemed near tears. "What happened is that one of the persons staying in your unit died."

"Died?" Dana stared hard at the woman. "Jesus," she muttered, backing away from Heidi to lower herself onto the love seat.

"Oh, it's so sad. Such a lovely couple. They were here to celebrate their anniversary and then when Mrs. Devlin was out running errands or something, these cakes arrived and—"

Dana tuned out. She not only knew the circumstances, she'd set them in motion, careful to create as much confusion as possible.

Step one: After replacing the glass for her portrait, Dana had stopped at Miss Lilani's Confectionary Shop. Wearing a head scarf, tinted glasses and her face devoid of makeup, she'd paid cash for the anniversary basket to be delivered on July 15th.

Step two: Dana had utilized her acting skills, playing the role of caterer, with a call to the office here at the condos on Heidi's day off. The assistant, Jeremy, was a droopy-eyed young man of few words who would smile inexplicably or nod as if reacting to inner voices. Though he gave Dana the creeps, he was affable enough and, most importantly, not prone to asking questions.

She had lowered her voice and spoke in a southern accent.

"Is this Jeremy? I'm callin' from Miz–mumble, mumble–Confectionary Shop. It seems there's some confusion? We're supposed to deliver an anniversary basket to a party named Devereaux or Devin. Do y'all have either party registered at this time?"

"Umm. Gee, I don't know. Let me check."

Dana had waited patiently. She had already checked to made sure that no one by the name of Devereaux was listed at Kailua Condos. She'd also learned that an order had been placed a week earlier at the same confectionary shop for cakes to be sent to the hotel next door for a Mr. and Mrs. Devereaux who were celebrating their 25th wedding anniversary. Conveniently, they had checked out several days ago.

"Ma'am? I can't find the name Dever – umm, whatever it is, but we do have Mr. and Mrs. Devlin registered."

"Oh, Dev<u>lin</u>. Okay. That's gotta be it. I hope. Thanks and y'all take care."

"Glad to help. Have a nice day."

Dana shuddered, remembering his words. Frank Devlin did not have a nice day.

"Mrs. James?" The words ruptured the silence, Heidi's recitation apparently at an end. How long had she stood there with that aggrieved expression on her face? It wasn't like Dana had requested all the gory details.

"Are you okay?" Heidi asked. "I know this is all very upsetting. Fortunately for Mrs. Devlin, one of her daughters is with her now."

Dana rose. "I'm glad to hear that. Maybe you could look in on them? I'd offer, but I have a business appointment and then a plane to catch, so I'll be on my way."

She swept out the door, only to stop as Heidi called to her. "Mrs. James, it just occurred to me that two people who've recently stayed in your unit have died." Her stance, her expression mimicked that of a disapproving school marm.

Dana stepped back into the doorway. "Well," she said, "it would appear the angel of death hovers over these premises. I wonder who will be next?" She smiled sweetly and turned on her heel, leaving Heidi with a dropped jaw, her eyes widening in consternation.

Once outside, Dana paused to catch her breath, to slow her heart rate. She hadn't set out to kill the man, for God's sake, only to inflict pain and suffering. Not that she held Bea's husband accountable for sabotaging her acting career, ruining her reputation and humiliating her beyond belief, but his torment was to be the instrument of revenge for Bea's treachery.

Now Frank Devlin had made the ultimate sacrifice. Well, so be it. Frank was old, useless and probably an embarrassment to his family. As for Bea, payback was long overdue.

With renewed energy, Dana strode to her car. Her so-called business meeting was a fabrication, an excuse to get away. She did have a plane to board in the morning, but it was to L.A. She'd make it a point to fly to Australia to meet with her dear, darling husband in a month or two. However, not until she'd completed her business at home.

Dana settled into her rented Mercedes. She flipped open the visor mirror to adjust her dark glasses and noted an Asian man entering the lobby of the Kailua. Though she'd only caught a glimpse of him, he looked vaguely familiar. But then, most Asian men looked alike to her.

Bea sensed Detective Chang would soon wrap up his interview.

What more was there for her to say? She had explained the circumstances of her being out in the morning, the tragic mix-up in the delivery of cakes and her frantic call to 911.

Now she was weary beyond weary and for once would welcome Elizabeth's intervention. Her daughter, however, seemed strangely unfocused as she sat just inches away on the sofa, her gaze drifting to the lanai where her father had enjoyed his last precious moments.

The detective rose and Bea stood along with him, ready to escort him to the door. "One more thing," she said. "I'm sure my husband didn't suspect anything was amiss when the cakes were delivered. I had promised him a treat. I'd thought—well I'd thought I might pick up something from the salon, men's lotion, or–" her voice broke. "Sorry."

"My apologies," Chang said. "I shouldn't have bothered you, but because someone who recently stayed in this same unit died under tragic circumstances, we needed a clear picture of what happened." He gave a small shake of his head and pursed his lips as if confounded by these occurrences.

He started for the door, but then stopped. "One moment, please." Abruptly, he turned back to stand before Dana's portrait. "Do you know this woman?"

At his question, Elizabeth came quickly to stand by her mother. "Dana was in my mother's math class at Tustin Community College."

Bea nodded. "Of course, this was some years ago. We did not stay in touch. In fact, we had a serious falling out. I was flabbergasted when I came upon Dana's picture. We had won a week's stay in Kona at a silent auction held at Frank's Elk's lodge. We never dreamed the designated place would turn out to be Dana's condo."

Chang chewed on the tip of his index finger. "So she didn't know you and your husband were staying in her unit?"

Elizabeth gave a little snort. "She'd probably have thrown them out. Dana was really pissed–sorry Mom–over failing the math class and forfeiting her drama scholarship to UCLA. But she was a cheat and God knows what else."

"Now, honey, you don't need to bring all that up. It was a long time ago."

Chang moved slowly to the door, his expression thoughtful. "I've met the woman in the portrait. And her sister. In fact," he said, pointing to the portrait, "I thought I caught a glimpse of her a little while ago outside the lobby—"

"Dana? Here?" Bea asked, her voice cracking.

Chang shrugged. "Possibly a look-alike. If you'll forgive me, I sometimes have trouble distinguishing one Caucasian woman from another." He bowed his head. "Thank you for your time."

"Well," Elizabeth said, after the detective had left, "that was interesting, if strange."

"I suppose so. At least, he provided a little distraction from—" without warning, Bea felt a surge of tears coming on.

Elizabeth took her hand. "Let's go to the kitchen. I think we both could do with a cup of tea. Oh. What about lunch?"

"Nothing for me." Bea sat at the kitchen table, allowing her daughter to take over. Earlier, Elizabeth had seemed so detached, but at the mention of Dana she had sprung to life. Was there something about Dana that intrigued her? Bea remembered when Dana had come to their home. Elizabeth, still in high school, had seemed enthralled with Dana, hardly taking her eyes off the young woman. But Dana attracted attention, whether for good or bad.

Elizabeth came back with their tea and then took a seat across from Bea, who smiled at her daughter. Elizabeth excelled at being in charge, a trait Bea was beginning to appreciate more and more.

"Diane wanted to fly out with me," Elizabeth said, as she spooned sugar into her tea," but I convinced her it wouldn't be practical to leave the children and so on. But she's offered to make arrangements for the burial and memorial service."

"I know. She called immediately after she'd heard from you. She took your father's death very hard. Well, I guess we were both quite emotional. But, anyway we finally got to the part about bringing your father home. I told her he would have wanted a simple service."

Elizabeth nodded and patted her mother's hand. Neither seemed inclined to speak, and Bea was grateful for the silence, savoring the quiet, the time for reflection.

And then reflection turned on her to give birth to a torrent of anguish. Bea's hand shook as she set her cup down. "God forgive me," she said, "but as terrible as all this has been, maybe your father's death was a blessing. How would Frank have survived without me? How would he have coped—"

Elizabeth's spoon fell from her hand and onto the floor, the clatter cutting off her mother's words.

"You think it's for the best that he died? How can you say that? How dare you say such a thing?"

"Elizabeth, calm down. Except for my children, I've never loved anyone as much as your father. His death was hideous, and I'll carry that vision with me for the rest of my life. And my God, no, I didn't want him to die. I wanted him by my side for as long as I have left.

"But tell me. How would he have coped with my illness, let alone with my death?"

"He would have had Diane and me. Don't we count?"

Bea looked down at the tea she'd barely tasted. She fiddled with her spoon, and then pushed it firmly to the side. "I want you to listen to me. As you know, your father didn't always live in the real world. And I was conflicted throughout our marriage as to whether I should try harder to encourage him to give up his fantasies so he could come to terms with himself.

"But mostly, I covered for him, though I guess enabler is the term that's used now. Right or wrong, I'm glad I let him get away with his exaggerations. He knew people doubted his word, but for the moment he could feel good about himself. Besides, he wasn't hurting anyone."

"Except himself."

"You see? Despite your intentions, you and Diane would have ended up chipping away at his self-esteem. Possibly, with tragic results."

"I don't want to hear this."

"Then let's talk about you. Had your father survived me, I'm sure you'd have been a loving and devoted daughter. But at what cost to your personal life?"

"On the one hand I'm a loving and devoted daughter, while on the other hand I'm destroying his self-esteem?"

"I guess that didn't come out right." Bea rubbed her forehead. "Well, it's so damned complicated. But we were talking about you. So let's stay with the present and discard the what ifs.

"I'm going to speak frankly, Elizabeth. I'm proud of your accomplishments and your devotion to me and your father. But at this stage of your life you should be getting out more, dating, traveling, and learning a new skill. Getting a life, as the saying goes. Your father felt the same way."

Elizabeth bowed her head for a moment, and then hastened from the table, taking her cup and saucer to the sink. She vigorously rinsed her dishes, and then turned to face her mother. "At least there's one less person now to lose sleep over me." She took in her breath and raised her hands. "I'm sorry. I'm sorry. I shouldn't have said that."

"We're both upset, and I provoked you."

"I made a stupid remark. That said, would you please hear me out?" Responding to Bea's nod she continued, "It's important for you to understand that I really enjoy my work. Yes, my case load is heavy but not intolerable; best of all, I'm never bored. I counsel people in situations that range from freaky to deplorable to heartwarming.

"And the job doesn't consist solely of gathering data and making phone calls. In interviews I interpret body language, nuances in facial expression, and speech as a test of credibility."

"But isn't it depressing to be exposed to so much misery?"

"It's not all peaches and cream, but my goal is to lessen the misery of these folks and, of course, to cull out the baddies from those in need. We can't have people screwing the system."

Elizabeth returned to the table, standing with her hands clasping the back of her chair. "I do have a personal agenda of sorts: be on the lookout for eligible men, knock off a few pounds, study Spanish or join a political group. But my first priority is you."

"Elizabeth, for heaven's sake—"

"Mom, shouldn't you be resting? You need to conserve your strength. In the meantime, I'm going out for a while. I want to check on something." She came around to plant a kiss on Bea's cheek and then stepped back with a smile. "You know what? Playing detective is fun."

Did she say detective? Bea wondered as her daughter left the room. She sat for a moment, reflecting on Elizabeth's words, then pushed back her chair and stood. What came to mind was Elizabeth as a bossy little girl, giving orders to Diane and other children.

"So what's changed?" Bea muttered as she made her way to the bedroom.

Heidi looked up from her desk. "Well, I've certainly had a stream of visitors today. Oh" she said, standing, "you're Miss Devlin."

Elizabeth took in her sorrowful look. Maybe fake; maybe not. "Could I speak with you for a moment?"

"Of course. Please—" She motioned to the chair in front of her desk and waited for Elizabeth to take a seat before sitting back down herself. "Please accept my deepest sympathy for your loss."

Eyes cast downward, Elizabeth nodded and then looked up and directly into Heidi's eyes in a no-nonsense stare, a technique she'd perfected in interviews with clients. "I have some questions, if you don't mind. Were you here when the cakes were delivered to my father?"

"I—," Heidi pursed her lips, "directed the delivery guy to your parent's unit."

"How did you know the delivery was for my father? I didn't see a name on the basket."

"Well, George, the delivery man, came to the office with instructions to deliver the basket to a Mr. Devin. I said, 'You mean Devlin.' Anyway, it was all a horrendous mistake. The cakes were supposed to be delivered to a party named Devereaux or Devin. As it turns out, the Devereaux party received their basket a week ago at the hotel next door, so why they were still on the list, I don't know.

"As for the name Devin, my assistant talked with a caterer who thought the Devins were registered here." She shook her head. "What a mess."

"So somebody made a mistake–the confectionary shop, the caterer, the hotel?" *And what about the note inside the basket*, Elizabeth wondered.

"A mistake, big time. But I'm sure detective Chang will get to the bottom of the mix-up."

The words "ah-so" sprang to Elizabeth's lips, but she quelled them in time to utter a soft, "Oh? He talked to you, too?"

Heidi nodded. "I think we'd all agree someone should pay for his or her carelessness."

"You'd better believe it," Elizabeth said under her breath. She stood. "Thank you, Ms. McGowan. I'd better get back to my mother."

At the door, Elizabeth paused. “By any chance, did the owner of the unit we’re staying in show up today?”

Heidi sniffed, her brows knitting in disapproval. “Yes. She stopped by briefly.”

“Just wondering,” Elizabeth said, exiting quickly before the question *why?* could form on Heidi’s lips.

As Elizabeth crossed the lobby, she noted plant and flower arrangements that brightened the interior and reminded her of her pathetic plant at home. Obviously, she didn’t have her mother’s green thumb. So be it. What excited her were ideas, not bug infested frippery. Plant the seed of a thought, nurture it, and watch it grow.

She carried in her mind the events and conversations of the last twenty-four hours. And when these seeds of thought burst forth? She would weed out conjecture and speculation from the garden of contemplation to arrive at the truth.

She owed it to her father. And to her dying mother.

Hawaii Calls!

Attention all Pasadena Republican Patriots:
Come join other California Patriot Chapters
in Honolulu, Hawaii for our third annual
summer conference.

Date: August 25th - 28th
Place: Gardenias 5 Star Seaside Resort

We promise fun in the sun, surprise celebrity
speakers, plus workshops to aid us in setting
the fall agenda. Details to follow:

Mahalo!
P.S. Space is limited.
Reserve through your chapter, ASAP

Chapter Eleven

Becky Childers, two years out of college with a BA in Theater Arts, considered her receptionist position with the Ted Connelly Certified Public Accountant Firm as temporary. After all, she had to eat and pay rent until the soaps beckoned or a forensics crime series cast her in a show—hopefully as a live character.

In the meantime, she had to endure Mr. Connelly's dry-as-dust clientele. Actually, she liked and respected her boss, and maybe had the tiniest crush on him… More than once she'd thanked her lucky stars she answered to Mr. C. and not his battle-ax wife.

Speak of the devil, Becky thought, watching as Mrs. Connelly marched into the waiting room, leading an invisible regiment. The woman was smiling, as she approached. "Mrs. Connelly, hi. What can I do for you?"

"Becky, don't you look fresh and pretty today. I suppose my husband's with a client?"

"Yes, but not for long. He has another client scheduled shortly."

"Well, this can't wait." She waved what looked like a brightly worded invitation in the air. "I need to look at Mr. Connelly's calendar for the month of August. *Now*. Please."

"Of course." She opened the appointment book to the month of August and placed it in front of Mrs. Connelly. "These two pages outline his agenda for August." Becky looked up to see an attractive blonde woman enter the waiting room. "I'll be with you in a minute," she called out.

Apparently, Becky's shift in attention hadn't sat well with Mrs. C., if the frown and tightening of her mouth were any indication. *Tough*, Becky wanted to say. Instead, she smiled. "How does it look?"

"I'm sure Ted can reschedule the appointments for August 25 - 28. Besides, I don't see his honor, the mayor, or the governor listed." She smiled thinly at her joke, and then leaned closer to Becky, lowering her voice. "It's imperative I confer with my husband about attending a conference in Hawaii, so I'll scoot inside for a couple of minutes before he takes his next appointment."

Becky nodded, containing her smile as Mrs. C. moved briskly to plop into a chair farthest from the newcomer.

"May I help you?" Becky asked the blonde woman who was now approaching the sign-in area.

"I'm Kim Williams. I have an 11:30 appointment." She checked her watch. "I guess I'm a little early."

"Please take a seat. Mr. Connelly will be with you soon."

Becky watched in surprise as Mrs. C. switched chairs to sit next to Mrs. Williams.

"Did I hear you say you were Kim Williams?" Mrs. C. was asking.

"Yes." A pause. "Have we met before?"

"Briefly, I think, at your gallery on Melrose."

"Really?" She smiled. "Well, I hope you found a painting that you couldn't resist."

"I was just browsing."

"We're always pleased to have people take a look at our collections. If you visit us again, I'd be happy to assist you. I can give you my card."

"That won't be necessary. I'm seldom in your neighborhood."

Nor would I even think of returning, Becky having noticed the disdain in Mrs. Connelly's voice, mimicked under her breath.

"I'm Susan Connelly. Does the name ring a bell?"

Becky wondered at Mrs. C.'s self-satisfied smirk.

As for Kim Williams, her expression had changed from annoyed to wary.

This might get interesting, Becky thought, watching them out of the corner of her eye.

"My sister has mentioned you."

"Your sister. Dana. We do go back a few years."

"So I understand."

"Of course, we lead such different lives. I'm sure Dana would find our family life boring and unglamorous."

"Then why send her a yearly newsletter touting your family's wondrous accomplishments?"

"She's mentioned my Christmas letters? What else has Dana confided about me? Care to comment?"

"I don't care to continue with this conversation."

"Aw, that's too bad. Dana James can be a scintillating topic of conversation."

"What is that supposed to mean?"

"I'm sure I don't have to explain." Again, the smirk.

"Look, I don't know you; I don't want to know you, so cut the crap."

Becky strangled her laugh into a cough as she waited for Mrs. C's response. But just then the door opened, and a conservatively attired older gentleman strode out of the office, nodded to Becky, and then left the waiting room.

Immediately, Mrs. C. stood and made a dash for the office, slamming the door behind her.

Becky took in Mrs. Williams startled expression. "She promised she'd only be a minute or two, that it was urgent she speak to her husband."

"I see." The blonde woman made a face. "I'm sorry for that rude exchange."

Becky shrugged. "It happens." To herself she added, *yeah, and to think we were cut off just when it was gettin'good.*

"Believe me," Becky said, "I wasn't eavesdropping on your conversation, but did I hear the name Dana James?"

Mrs. Williams nodded. "My sister."

"How about that? A family affair."

"Excuse me?"

"Your sister was here yesterday."

"That can't be. Dana is in Australia."

Becky turned the page of the appointment calendar to the previous day. "Dana James at 11:30. And she signed in."

"But—"

The door to the office burst open, and Mrs. C., ignoring the other woman, smiled at Becky, gave her an A-ok sign, and then breezed out of the waiting room.

Becky came around from behind the counter. "Mrs. Williams?" She opened the door to the office. "Mr. Connelly will see you now."

Becky could hear her own voice, bright and perky, as she stood tall in contrast to Mrs. Williams' cheerless demeanor. No smile, no thank you from this lady. But that was okay. In Williams versus Connelly, the former had flattened the latter.

And that made Becky's day.

Ted Connelly's warm greeting eased Kim's tensions. He directed her to a pale blue cushioned chair across the cream carpeting from his desk, and then sat down in a matching chair. A glass table separated the two of them on which Ted had placed a large notebook, and Kim had set two folders with the information he'd requested.

The CPA's easy-going manner made it easy for Kim to relax. And it didn't hurt that he was very attractive, another quality Kim appreciated in her acquaintances. It was obvious that Ted Connelly took good care of himself—tall and slender with a well-proportioned build—with the exception of a slight leathery cast to his skin and the fine lines on his forehead and around his eyes which suggested a fondness for the sun. His hair, brown tinged with gray, was close cropped, his eyes a striking true blue.

"Thank you," he smiled, "for bringing the material I requested."

"I didn't think I was up to it, but my lawyer was very helpful."

"May I?" He reached for the folders.

Kim watched as he studied the contents and then reached for his notebook. She felt detached, as if aimlessly she'd wandered onto a stage set where a man sat at a table, making notations below a series of charts.

But then a painting on the wall behind Mr. Connelly's desk caught her attention. A sailboat, its pearly white sails broken up into soft patches, appeared lopsided, in contention with an unforgiving sea of blue-gray watery tones deepening into swatches of black. The sky was a crazy quilt pattern of mismatched shapes and colors: fiery balls of light in combat with ponderous black clouds, while peachy corals hugged the horizon.

Kim turned to the CPA. "Your painting evokes a primitive feel, but falls short of 'Abstract expressionism'."

He looked up and grinned. "I don't know that term; I was just fascinated by the contrasting colors and the feeling of the piece." He paused. "I suppose I'm taken by the grace and mettle of a boat countering the challenges of the sea. Ah, but now I remember. Dana told me you run an art gallery."

Kim noticed how his face lighted up, his eyes sparkled when he brought Dana into the conversation. "Speaking of Dana, your receptionist mentioned my sister was here yesterday."

"Yes, Dana wanted to give me the background on your situation, and I guess it's no secret she'll be availing herself of my services as well."

Kim closed her eyes in disbelief and then opened them, unable to hide her surprise. "Wow. Something's haywire. My sister's supposed to be in Australia. But," she made a palms-down gesture, "that's not your concern, Mr. Connelly. I'm here for financial advice, not detective services."

He smiled. "I'm not one to stand on ceremony. Mind if we continue on a first name basis?"

That was fine with Kim. As Ted laid out the facts, figures and recommendations, she listened as closely as she could, taking in the information, but at some point, he lost her.

She must have reflected as much in her expression. "Am I going too fast for you?" Ted asked.

Kim shrugged. She wanted to respond to his question, but the words wouldn't come out. In her purse she found a tissue to stem the tears that threatened to erupt.

He smiled wryly. "Sometimes I a need time-out, too. Can I get you a glass of water?"

She shook her head. What I'd like, her brain messaged, would be to fall into your arms, to be held, stroked, comforted.

The thought was so incongruous, she involuntarily let out a half giggle, half hic-cup. "No meltdowns on the agenda today," she said, "and no, you're not going too fast for me. I simply lost my focus. I haven't been sleeping well, and I can't seem to lift myself out of the doldrums."

Kim lowered her chin and raised her eyes. "I can't believe I've unloaded on you."

"I've heard far worse. As you might suspect, I counsel a lot of troubled souls, though mostly pertaining to business crises. At any rate, I like to think of myself as more than a numbers cruncher. So. We can continue this discussion another time. You are in good financial shape; we just need to cover a few more points."

She rose. "Why don't you e-mail me your recommendations. I'll study them and then make another appointment to finalize the details."

"Kim, would you mind staying for another minute or two?"

When she was seated, he said, "I'm going to make a suggestion. I may be way out of line, but someone in my family was going through a tough time and finally decided she needed professional help. I say 'was' because thanks to her therapist, she's shown great improvement. My point is that you can't always go it alone."

He got up and walked over to his desk. "I can give you the name of her therapist; better yet, I have his card. Or should I just shut up?"

"By no means. I'm tired of being tired. And cranky." Kim examined the card Ted had handed her. "Dr. Mark Hampton. Hmm. Nice name. Can't tell you why, but I'm getting good vibes about this man." She smiled. "Thanks. I promise to do better at our next appointment."

On the drive home, Kim mulled over whether she really needed to see a therapist. It would be costly. But what the heck, she was financially secure, so why not get professional help? The thought cheered her.

Then another thought surfaced. Why not tell Dana about this supposedly wonderful therapist? Surely, she, too, could benefit from Dr. Mark Hampton's expertise.

But first she had to track down that sister of hers and find out what the hell was going on.

Dana answered Kim's call on the first ring, and yes, she owed Kim an explanation. So why not make it a lunch affair and meet at La Casita around the corner from where Dana lived?

Kim didn't need persuading.

Seated in La Casita's outdoor patio, Kim breathed in the scent of citrus and observed the shifting sun spread pools of light on the surrounding tables. Soft guitar music in the background whispered of sensuous delights that sweetened her mood. If only for the moment.

"Talk about an oasis in the middle of bedlam," Kim said to Dana, "have you been to this restaurant before?"

"Oh, yes," Dana paused. "You've probably guessed I'm seeing someone?"

"I'd figured as much."

"The day this man and I met, we came to lunch here."

"Lucky you. The placemats alone are worth a visit; in fact, I could make a habit of coming here. But don't count on my being distracted by your new love affair. I still want to know—"

"My dirty little secrets? Oh, wait. Here come our margaritas. So, a toast to brighter and better days ahead."

They clinked glasses, tasted their drinks, and then Kim set down her glass. "What dirty little secrets?"

"Teasing. Only teasing. You want to know why I'm here and not in Australia. Right? Let's go back a bit. I did call Jasper to let him know I was coming to Australia; however, I didn't bring up the subject of divorce.

"Now to digress for a moment. You may remember Jasper and I own property in Hawaii?"

Kim nodded. "That you checked on when Barry and I were in Kona."

"At that time I wasn't able to finalize the sale of the property, so Jasper suggested I make a stop-over in Hawaii to attend to business and to break up the trip, which I was able to arrange."

Dana paused to sip her drink, and then continued. "Now for the hard part. I called Jasper from Honolulu to tell him the property was now on the market." She sighed. "I could tell he'd had a few drinks. He started carrying on about how beautiful I was, how much he adored me. And then he got graphic—actually, disgusting, about what we were going to do with each other in bed. Given the circumstances, I couldn't leave it at that. I told him gently bed wasn't going to happen; not then, not ever."

Kim gasped. "I guess that's one way to jolt a person into sobriety."

"I'd braced myself for pleas to stay with him, that he couldn't live without me—that sort of thing. Instead, he got really filthy with his language. In the end, I canceled Australia and told him he'd be hearing from my lawyer, to which he replied that I'd be hearing from his solicitor, blah, blah, blah."

"And I always thought Jasper was such a decent man." Kim waited for a reply, but Dana appeared lost in thought. Then again, maybe she didn't care to hear how decent Jasper was. Kim reached for her menu.

"How did your meeting with Ted Connelly go?" Dana asked.

Kim set down her menu, relieved to be on safer ground. "He's good; in fact I doubt I could find a more qualified CPA. Better yet, I felt comfortable with him. He's attractive, likable, attentive and, I would guess, dependable."

"Sounds like a resumé for Mr. Right."

"You may be on to something. Why couldn't I have met someone like him instead of Barry?"

Dana sipped her drink, and then set her glass down hard. "The question is, how he could have ended up with a drag like Susan?"

"Oh. You want the latest on Susan? Today when I arrived for my appointment, she was in the waiting room, at the counter in a flap over a trip. I think I heard Hawaii mentioned. Something about a conference there."

Dana smiled. "How about that? Most interesting." She signaled the waitress. "I'm going to order another margarita. One for you, too?"

Kim almost said no, but then relented. She knew Dana would grill her about Susan. A little Dutch courage would make the interrogation a bit less painful.

While they enjoyed their second margarita, Kim described the exchange between herself and Susan. When she finished, Dana merely shrugged. "She's pathetic, not worth a pile of—uh, dung." She gave Kim an appraising look. "Too bad you and Ted didn't meet somewhere along the line."

"I don't know about me, but when I mentioned your name, Ted Connelly lighted up like a boy in a spin over his first crush."

Dana smiled as she opened her menu. "Ted and I have talked a few times at charity events. And yes, I would say he was drawn to me, to put it politely. Now. Shall we order?"

As lunch drew to a close, Kim ordered coffee, which Dana passed on. Who needed coffee, with a refrigerator stocked full of Cokes?

"I'm glad we came here," Kim said as they waited for the bill. "It was a good call, all around." She squeezed her sister's hand. "You're always there for me when I need a boost. I can't tell you what that means to me."

"You did seem uptight at the beginning of lunch."

"I didn't want to harp on myself, but I can tell you now, I wasn't at my best today during my consultation with Ted." She quickly added, "It was his idea we use first names. Anyway, I had trouble focusing and got a little rattled.

"But Ted was very understanding—" she hesitated, "to the point of telling me about a therapist who, I guess, is successful in working with people like me who've become, well, disenchanted with life."

Kim noted Dana's veiled expression but decided to press on. "I'm seriously considering getting professional help. I thought you might be interested too."

"Me? I'm perfectly fine." Her eyes had narrowed. "Just who is this therapist?"

"I have his card. Here. See for yourself."

Dana burst out laughing and then, gave a lady-like snort. "I thought so," she said.

"What? What are you saying?"

"First of all, I would encourage you to see a therapist. And this man is good."

"You know of him?"

"You might say that. Let's say I know him in the biblical sense."

Kim was beginning to wonder if the margaritas had gotten to Dana. Or more likely, to herself?

"You look confused, Kim. Well, don't be, darling. Mark is the man I'm seeing. Is he good? Yes, especially in bed. Oops, here's the check." She grabbed it. "My treat."

Kim didn't argue. Talk about dirty little secrets? All she could utter was, "Holy crap."

Ted Connelly didn't always use his study for work-related purposes, though he supposed Susan pictured him pouring over tables and graphs on the evenings he chose to retreat upstairs. More often, at least lately, he listened to his jazz recordings, keeping the volume soft, or studied his sailing manuals.

Tonight he sat at his desk before an open ledger partially concealed by a catalog of sailing vessels with descriptions and prices.

Immersed in his reading, he blocked out the sound of approaching footsteps. Two sharp raps on his door brought him to attention. "Come in," he said, placing his hand over the catalog.

Susan was smiling as she entered the room. "Mind if we have a chat?" She didn't wait for an answer, seating herself on the sofa across from his desk.

"You're on," he said, returning her smile.

She fanned her face, her smile folding into a grimace.

"It's stuffy in here."

"Should you have a talk with the new housekeeper?"

"Nadia is fine. And I didn't say dirty; I said stuffy."

Her gaze swept the room. "I'm sure we both recognize the problem. Your desk is too big for the room, your shelves overpowering, there's hardly space for the computer, and the furniture seems squished together."

He shrugged. "You've mentioned feeling claustrophobic in here."

"All this closeness doesn't bother you?"

"I prefer cozy. Besides, I don't have to reach or walk very far for anything."

Her smile was coy. "When are you going to let me redecorate? Too much brown is depressing."

"Honey, I know you mean well, but I'm happy with the status quo."

"Your office at work is light, airy, and beautifully appointed, though I could do without that painting. My point is, how can you be comfortable with two such opposing types of décor?"

"Damned if I know. Maybe we should ask your therapist. Remember, we meet with him tomorrow."

She raised her eyebrows. "That should be interesting. Well. What I came in to talk about is Hawaii."

He gave her an encouraging nod. "Yes?"

"Aren't you excited about the trip?"

"I'd rather go for fun and relaxation, just us and Caitlin."

"Caitlin will still be in summer camp at the time of the conference, which makes it convenient for us to get away. We'll plan something for the three of us another time.

"Now about the conference. I'll probably be asked to head a committee. You can join my group, attend workshops of your choosing or, better yet, volunteer to lead a workshop."

"I don't know anything about the topics under consideration."

"I can help you with that. Also, we'll be receiving materials before the trip."

"Wouldn't it be enough to attend the workshops?"

"Of course." She stared at the ceiling, and then studied her nails.

"Susan, you know for the most part I share your political convictions. But I'm just not a rah-rah kind of person."

"No." Her gaze bore into him. "You don't raise your voice. You're content to stand on the sidelines, to make yourself invisible. Damn it, Ted, you have a brain, so why can't you come up with ideas, lead a discussion, contribute, for God sakes?"

He bowed his head for a moment and then looked up to return Susan's gaze. "I think you'd be happier if you went to the conference without me. I'd just be underfoot."

"But you don't have to play that role." She rose. "Oh, let's drop this for now. And no, I am not going to Hawaii without you."

She turned to leave, hesitated, and then sauntered up to his desk. "What have we here?" she asked, her gaze falling on the catalog.

He quickly placed the booklet inside the top drawer of his desk. "Just some information about sailboats." The silence settled on them, replacing their opposing views with a new uneasiness between them.

Susan fingered her throat and then sat back down on the sofa. "I'm feeling a little short of breath."

"I'm sorry. I can bring in the floor fan."

She coughed. "No need. I don't think it's the room. I may be having a delayed reaction to a minor altercation between Kim Williams and myself when we sat in your waiting room."

"Good heavens. You want to tell me about it?"

"I can see you're amused. Well, it was really nothing, not worth going into detail. But the woman was rude. And vulgar."

"Kim Williams? You can't be serious."

Susan shrugged. "I take it you have a different impression of her."

"She struck me as courteous, attentive, and cooperative." He didn't add troubled.

He thought for a moment. "You know, it amazes me how different two sisters could be physically and, I suppose, in personality."

"I'm not following you."

"Kim Williams is blond, fair skinned, conventional, I'm guessing. While her sister Dana is dark-haired, and well they're just different," he finished, reacting to Susan's hardened expression.

"You remember that much about Dana?"

"She was in to see me yesterday. She wanted to give me some background on Kim, who was recently widowed. But primarily she came in for assistance regarding her own finances. Dana's going through a divorce, and—"

"Ted, how could you? You know I detest that woman." She broke off in a spasm of coughing.

"This has nothing to do with you," he said, raising his voice. "She needs help from a CPA. Period." Susan was still coughing. Had she heard a single word? Good God, now she was wheezing.

"I'm feeling," she said between breaths, "a tightness in my chest."

"Come on, Susan, let's get you downstairs. You need to use your bronchodilator, and then I'll get you settled in bed."

As Ted assisted his wife out of the room, his gaze swiped the sofa where he would bunk down for the night.

Was it always going to be like this? Was it ordained he exist in a continuum of self-denial?

God help him, but maybe not. He visualized Dana during their last encounter—her vitality and glow, her jewel-like eyes. Something in the warmth of her gaze hinted of what?

He banished the image, but then decided to allow it to steal back into his consciousness. And to linger.

Chapter Twelve

Soft spoken, sincere, well groomed—these were the things racing through Mark Hampton's mind as he chatted with Ted Connelly. Not that he planned to compile a profile on the man—not for a one time visit—but after years in practice, physical and personality traits automatically fell into clear-cut categories, even as he met with a patient for the first time.

Ted leaned forward in his chair. "I didn't tell Susan I decided to see you without her. She was better this morning, and I didn't want to risk a relapse if the idea didn't sit well with her." He raised a hand. "Of course, I don't intend to keep this visit a secret."

"From Susan's medical history, I know she's experienced several serious asthma attacks in the last couple of years. Is she especially sensitive to environmental issues? We've been on smog alert the last couple of days, at least here in Pasadena."

"Smog could be a contributing factor," Ted said, "but I'd lay the cause to emotional distress."

Mark nodded, his expression, he hoped, prompting further details.

"Susan mentioned a minor altercation—her words—with a client in my waiting room. But she didn't seem too upset over the incident.

"But then I let it slip that an acquaintance of ours—actually, someone Susan knew in college, and the sister to the woman in the waiting room—is seeing me professionally. My wife can't stand this woman, and I do believe this information triggered her attack."

"Apparently, it was enough to make your wife ill. As Susan's therapist, I'd like to know why you're seeing this woman would generate such a strong reaction."

Ted shook his head, his smile apologetic. "Susan got it into her mind that Dana—sorry," he reddened, "I guess I shouldn't use names. Anyway, that this woman is not of our class, that she lacks refinement, education, is no better than trash."

Oh, my, so it is Dana we're talking about. And the infamous

volatile twosome: Susan and Dana. Okay, let's have Ted's point of view on this epic drama. "But why would Susan show such antipathy to a person she feels superior to?"

"You have to understand that my wife has many fine attributes. When we met, I was attracted to her fresh good looks, her bright personality, and her intelligence." He paused. "Dana, on the other hand, exudes sex appeal, glamour and enough charisma to light up a mansion. To be blunt, Susan belittles these qualities. She equates sex appeal, for example, with shallowness or worse, being a slut."

"Have you given Susan any reason to be jealous of Dana?"

"Absolutely not." Ted's smile was sheepish. "Though I have to admit I am attracted to the woman. Not," he added hastily, "that I'd ever act on this feeling."

Mark broke eye contact with Ted to make a note, while the lyrics, "Getting to know you, getting to know all about you" tripped through his head. He judged Ted a man of principle, yet what if Dana were to beckon?

Mark cleared his throat. "Because of Susan's hostility toward Dana, I'm guessing that Dana, at one time or another, turned her charms on you?"

Ted appeared to suppress a smile. "Oh, well, maybe in a mildly flirtatious way."

And you loved every moment of it, Mark concluded. He gave Ted a straightforward look. "Shall we move on?"

Ted nodded. "I understand you wanted to meet Susan's husband to round out the marital picture."

"That was the idea. Obviously, I can't observe how you and Susan interact, but the fact that you're sitting across from me suggests you may have some issues to bring up?"

"I don't know what Susan has confided to you about me, but I can guess enthusiasm, drive and outgoingness are not qualities she ascribes to me."

Well, well. A hint of bitterness?

"I don't mean to paint a bleak picture of our relationship. We get along for the most part, and we have a beautiful eight year old daughter, Caitlin. Susan's always been active whether in working part time or in volunteering—that is, until her breakdown, her depression. Now it would appear life's once again on an upswing for her."

"And for you?"

"Sometimes—well, sometimes I feel a third party has invaded our marriage. Namely, politics. What has sustained Susan through good and bad is her involvement in Republican causes. She's passionate in her support of our local group. And by that, I mean she serves on the board, chairs committees, heads membership drives."

"Do you share her convictions?"

"Basically; in fact, I'm a member in good standing of our local chapter. And I do admire Susan for acting on her beliefs. But I just can't get all steamed up about taking on a leadership position. This bothers Susan. Case in point, in August we'll be attending a conference in Hawaii that will bring together various California chapters of the organization. Susan is disturbed over my unwillingness to chair a committee. She berates me for not speaking up on the issues, for not taking on a leadership role."

"Outside of work, Ted, what are your passions? Or does work define your life?"

"Work matters. On the other hand, I can list playing tennis and golf, attending concerts, biking, heading for the beach and mountains, not to mention carrying out social obligations."

"Sounds like you've got some well-rounded interests. So is this chasm between you and Susan regarding politics your only bone of contention? Any conflicts over parenting?"

"We've seldom had disagreements over raising our daughter. I'd say we're damn fine parents."

Mark nodded. "A huge plus in any marriage. But to return to my first question, can you name other raw spots in your relationship?"

"Do you mind if I stand? I'm feeling a little stiff."

"By all means," Mark said.

Ted got to his feet. He rotated his shoulders, and stretched out his arms, while breathing deeply.

"Why don't we take a break? Better yet—" Mark rose and walked to the left of the fireplace to open the drapes along the back wall. "We can talk out here on my small terrace—if you'd like to continue our session. You're still on the clock."

"It's not that I'm claustrophobic—that's Susan's misfortune—but I am feeling restless. Outside sounds good."

Mark opened the sliding glass door, and then turned to allow Ted to precede him onto the terrace, but the CPA now stood before the painting of the Left Bank street scene, gazing at it intently. *What's really going on with this guy*, Mark wondered?

"Sorry," Ted said, joining Mark. "I like your painting. It—well, it draws me into a place of contemplation and quiet. And I feel a kind of wistfulness settling over me—I suppose it's brought on by the rain, the deserted street. In any event, I find the scene strangely comforting."

"How interesting," Mark said. He sat on one of the two cushioned patio chairs, fronted by a low, wood textured table that bore several circular coffee mugs stains.

Ted stood at the terrace wall, facing Mark. "I recently purchased a painting for my office of a sailboat in a storm at sea. The scene is far from comforting, but it grabs the imagination."

"Do you sail?"

"Ah." Ted clasped his hands as if Mark had hit a nerve. He moved slowly to sit down next to the therapist. "It's been a life-long dream."

"What's holding you back?"

"First it was my father. He dismissed the idea. Said I should go out for basketball because of my height and build, but I didn't make the cut. Later he focused on my getting a law degree and joining his firm. But that's another story."

"The obvious question is what's holding you back now?"

"Susan is not thrilled with the idea. She has no interest in the sport. It's an expensive hobby and time consuming. You've seen the attention and care sailboat owners devote to their craft?"

"Part of the pleasure, I suppose."

"So I do understand Susan's objections over getting a sailboat," Ted said.

"You understand, but the fact you're not doing it is frustrating as hell, right?"

Ted laughed. "You called it." He lowered his gaze to his hand, twisting his wedding ring. "Since I'm letting it all hang out, I might as well confess—" he looked up at Mark, "that I'd love to take up a musical instrument–sax or clarinet—and get involved with a jazz group." He held up his hand. "Please don't ask 'why not?'"

"I'm sitting this one out."

"Jeez. Hearing myself out loud like this; it sounds like all I do is whine."

"Has the C word, compromise, ever entered your conversation with Susan?"

"At one time we presented our cases. Now you can see why it wasn't in me to become a lawyer." Ted grinned at his own joke.

"Let's go back to the idea of compromise. How about this: You agree to take a more active role in her political activities. In turn, Susan gives you permission to look seriously into sailing or music."

"I guess it's worth another try."

In the silence that followed, Mark could sense defeat on Ted's part. Too bad.

Both men stood. Ted held out his hand. "I'm glad you agreed to see me alone. Our conversation has given me some perspective on where I am and where I'm going."

Mark raised mental eyebrows and revised his impression of a capitulating Ted Connelly. Would the grit of self-determination infiltrate the golden corridors of refinement? Maybe the man was ready to take a stand after all.

Back in the office, Ted turned to Mark. "I want to thank you for an outstanding job in bringing Susan out of her depression. She's her old self again," he winced, "and then some."

Ted was smiling when he left the office.

Ted was also smiling when later in the afternoon he ushered Dana into his office. His 4:30 appointment had canceled, and Becky had left for the day.

"I apologize for bursting in on you. I had a question concerning a joint bank account with Jasper, and I figured you might be available at this hour." Dana patted her chest as if calming a rapid heartbeat, the result of rushing about. "Also," she smiled, "I've been known to act on impulse."

"My pleasure," Ted said. "Come, sit down. Let's talk."

Dana knew from her previous visits which side of the table was for the client. As she settled in, she congratulated herself on carefully choosing the white cotton sleeveless dress (to hell with impulsiveness) that fit her like a glove, and her jade jewelry—earrings and necklace—which called attention to the deep green of her eyes. Ted was hooked.

Well, maybe not totally. She had observed him eying what looked like a brochure—something to do with watercraft? *My God, how boring,* she thought. It lay on top of the ever present reference notebook.

"That's impressive," Dana said, pointing to the cover and trying to sound knowledgeable. "What a handsome boat."

"I agree, but that model is a little out of my league, or should I say pocketbook."

"Are you thinking of buying a boat?"

"A couple of hours ago I would have said no. Now I'm at least considering the possibility."

"Are you familiar with Boat Works in Marina del Rey?"

"I've heard the name."

"I have a friend—he lives in our building on Wilshire–who brokers sales at the marina. Anyway, it might be fun to take a ride out there for a look-see. I could introduce you to Larry."

"Uh–when? You don't mean now?"

"Why not?"

"You came to me with a question about an account."

"I think it's a fairly simple matter. We could talk about it on the way to the marina. I would need to cancel a dinner engagement, but that shouldn't be a problem."

Dana took in Ted's varying expressions of hesitancy, doubt, more hesitancy, and finally, surrender. The man would not do well at poker.

"As it turns out," Ted said, "my wife is scheduled for a dinner meeting in Orange County. Which means I'm on my own for the evening. *If* she can make it." He told her about Susan's bout with asthma.

"However, she seemed fine when I talked to her about an hour ago. Let me check to be sure." He went to his desk and dialed the phone.

Dana heard, "Uh huh, uh huh, that's good. I'm glad you're okay. Well, have a nice evening. See you about nine? Okay. Bye, bye."

That was short and not so sweet, Dana thought, feeling a surge of boldness. She fastened her gaze on Ted–first his eyes, then a languorous drift to his lips.

She rose. "I take it we're all set?"

"I'll be happy to drive if you navigate."

"Deal. Oh, would you mind if I waited for you in the other room? I need to make a quick call on my cell phone."

"Go right ahead. I need to clear my desk and then I'll join you in a few minutes."

In the waiting room, Dana put in a call to Mark. Could they put off their dinner date until tomorrow evening? She'd received an unexpected call from a wholesaler in the jewelry business. He would only be in town for a short time and asked if she could pick him up at the airport. Not that she liked the idea, but she knew of his reputation, and it would be a coup for her to display his line of jewelry.

When Dana ended the call, she felt renewed energy, a heady feeling of purpose. Mark had been compliant but, of course, disappointed the evening had been canceled. Or so he implied. Unlike other men in her life, Mark was not an easy read. She knew he valued his independence; on the other hand, he was captivated by her and she by him. Where they were headed, God only knew.

For now, though, she would work her wiles to effect a shift in the status quo. The result? Mark's need for her would outweigh his free-wheeling ways.

But for now, another "project" was in the works: Ted Connelly. Dana glanced at his closed door and felt a quiver of anticipation. Let the games begin.

As it turned out, Larry was vacationing in Lake Tahoe. "He'll be back next week," Dana said to Ted, after conferring with one of Larry's colleagues. "Let me talk to him before you look seriously. In the meantime, why don't we stroll by the marina? You can get an idea of style and size."

With the walk completed, it seemed a shame to end an evening that had barely begun. Dana gestured to the restaurant that overlooked the marina. "The terrace offers a lovely view. Care to stop for a drink?"

Sunset colors hovered low on the horizon but golden-apricot hues would emerge to create an afterglow, softening the transition from daylight to nightfall. Who could resist?

Apparently, not Ted. Without equivocating, he jumped at the idea, and then insisted they stay for dinner as well.

Later, when Ted drove them from the marina to his office where Dana was to pick up her car, she sensed a reticence on his part, as if he were retreating from the spontaneity of their visit to the marina. It was back to business. Back to the advisor-client relationship.

Dana knew better. When they were ready to go their separate ways, she reminded Ted that she or Larry would be in touch when Larry returned from the lake.

What Dana interpreted from Ted's expression was an unexpressed "Oh", as in "Wait a minute." After a pause he said, "I would rather hear from you."

"And you shall," Dana said.

Chapter Thirteen

Elizabeth paced the small waiting room area outside Detective Robert Chang's office at the Kailua Police Headquarters.

Her mother's words rang in her ears: "Why do we have to bring up ancient history? Why so many questions?"

"Mom, it's important." She tried to be gentle. "Just tell me what happened between you and Dana when she took your class."

"The letter?"

"That in particular."

"You know the facts."

"I want to know every detail."

"Why? How can this possibly matter?"

"I may be on to something—well, never mind. Humor me this one time?"

And so Bea recited the events leading up to Dana's acrimonious letter, adding that it was in everyone's best interest for bones of contention to remain buried.

Heidi McGowan had been more accommodating. When Elizabeth returned to the manager's office with questions, Heidi was at her desk. Her body tense, she spit out the horrific details of a man lying dead in the Kailua Condos' swimming pool. "Adding to the mix," she said, her eyes glittering, "guess who turned out to be the bereaved widow? None other than the unit owner's sister."

"Kim Williams?"

The gleam in Heidi's eyes had flattened. "You seem to know a lot about this family."

"At one time, Dana and Kim were guests in my parent's home." Elizabeth inched forward in her chair. "We're both professional women," she said, "and I can tell you're an astute judge of character."

"You're referring to Mrs. James and Mrs. Williams?" Heidi

shrugged. "Unless I know or sense someone's up to no good, I pretty much take a person at face value."

"Okay, but as a manager, I'm sure you're very aware of what goes on around here."

"You bet I am."

"Are you aware of anything unusual that occurred before or after the discovery of Mr. Williams' body?"

Elizabeth knew she was on shaky ground. After all, the manager might clam up, questioning Elizabeth's right to interrogate her. But Heidi, her expression ranging from concern to consternation, had launched into a fervid account of the couple's behavior at the restaurant and in the garage before Mr. Williams' tragic death. "Word does get around," she sniffed.

"You haven't mentioned Dana," Elizabeth said.

"Well, let's see. Dana, Mrs. James, that is, came to be with Mrs. Williams after her husband's death."

"She flew to her sister's side from Los Angeles?"

"Oh, no. I understand Mrs. James was in Honolulu on business and rushed here to support her sister."

"I see. And you told me earlier Mrs. James was in Kona when my father died."

"Your point?"

"I'm not sure." Elizabeth pursed her lips as if at a loss for words. "As I said before, I'm convinced you're a good judge of character. I'd like your impression of Dana James."

Heidi had leaned back in her chair, her expression bordering on amusement. "I don't know what you're up to, Ms. Devlin, but you can stop buttering me up."

Elizabeth needed a different approach. She made a show of maintaining eye contact with Heidi. "I see I've met my match." She stood. "Thank you. I'll not bother you again."

Elizabeth was almost out the door when she heard, "I know her kind."

Elizabeth had turned to stare at Heidi. The manager, no longer buttressed by her desk, appeared now larger-than-life in an eye scorching yellow and lime green muumuu. When they were inches apart, Heidi had said, "Dana James has the super inflated ego of a tired old bag who thinks she's hot stuff. She's a phony and a liar. What can I say? She's a bitch."

Wow. Elizabeth stepped back from Heidi, distancing herself from this dragon belching venom.

Hands on hips, Heidi had taken on a defiant stance. "You did ask for my impression of Dana James?"

"I did. And thank you for your honest input." Polite, parting words that contrasted to what she had been thinking: That it takes one to know one.

Elizabeth smiled, picturing Dana and Heidi in a past lifetime, brandishing epées as they fought a duel to the death. One of them would take the fall. Her pick? Hmm. Too close to call. And then she sobered as Detective Chang invited her into his office.

The room reflected Chang's personality. Why bother with knick knacks, plants, paintings or photos? Serious business required only a desk, a table that held a computer, and two filing cabinets.

When they were both seated, the detective behind his desk and Elizabeth facing him, Chang said, "You stated on the phone, Miss Devlin, that you needed to see me before you returned home. That's tomorrow?" He tilted his head. "Once again, my condolences."

"Thank you, and yes, we leave tomorrow, so I'm glad you could fit me in." She found herself staring at him. He seemed more—what? More human? Certainly less robotic than he'd been before.

Then why did she feel flustered? Lord knows, she'd had plenty of dealings with the police, doctors and lawyers on behalf of her clients. She straightened, mindful of her posture, giving herself a mental thumbs up as well.

"I'm confused about the chain of events that led to my father's death. In particular, the mix-up in cake orders, the names of the people involved. And who is this caterer who called the Kailua Condos about an anniversary order? The manager was off duty for the day, and I understand her replacement was vague about the details. And not exactly big in the brains department."

Chang nodded. "I share your concerns. We're looking into the situation but as yet we've not come up with any answers. It may be the mix-up was a tragic mistake. Period."

"Or a deliberate attempt to set up a confusing chain of circumstances?"

"For what purpose?"

"To do harm."

"Would you care to elaborate?"

"The owner of the condo, Dana James, is a vindictive woman." She described Dana's fury over being denied a scholarship, her lack of remorse over cheating, and the letter to her mother.

"And what about Kim Williams' husband?" Elizabeth continued. "I understand he died of heart failure under bizarre circumstances. And at a relatively young age. I assume you questioned Mrs. Williams. After all, she and her husband had been fighting that evening before he died. But to take it a step farther, what if Dana James somehow figured into the equation?"

"I understand your hostility toward Mrs. James, but—"

"No, please. Hear me out. Just what was Dana's relationship with her brother-in-law? Remember, two people staying in Dana's unit died. And we know she was in Hawaii before and after each death."

Chang raised his hand. "Miss Devlin, you don't have to lecture me." The suggestion of a smile softened his expression. He made a quick note and then gave her a quizzical look. "Just what is it you do for a living?"

"I'm a social worker."

"Most impressive." His expression deadpan, Chang said, "If social work should become tiresome, I'm sure I could find a place for you on my staff." He stood and held out his hand.

The meeting was over and for once, Elizabeth was speechless. She shook his hand and muttered, "Thank you."

"Oh, and Miss Devlin, I will give serious consideration to the information you've given me."

"I appreciate that. I was afraid you'd laugh at my concerns or think I was a troublemaker."

Chang waved his hand in dismissal of the idea. He looked down at some papers on his desk. "Let's see. I have your address in Tustin,

California." He paused to study the information and then looked up at Elizabeth, giving her a broad smile. "Perhaps we'll meet again?"

When he smiled, he looked young. Even cute. She felt her cheeks flame. "Perhaps," she shot back, then turned and made a hasty exit.

A smile, Dana thought, conveyed a lot about a person's mood. At this moment, as she and Mark sat on her terrace with a pre-dinner drink, Mark's smile, as they clinked glasses, was tight and unconvincing.

"What's up?" Dana asked. "Did you have a bad day, darling? Oh, but gosh darn it, rules are rules so you can't tell me about it."

He chuckled. "I didn't realize it was so obvious."

"You're not answering my question."

"I can tell you I met with Susan Connelly for the last time today. Dr. David Baker, a colleague, will see her on a follow-up basis. She wasn't too pleased, but the only alternative would be for us to stop seeing each other."

"I'm that much of a threat to her?"

Mark shrugged. "It's just better this way."

"Goody. Now you can reveal all the grubby details about Susan's boring life and her self-righteous stance on politics and religion, plus all other forbidden subjects."

Again, the tight smile. "That's not how it works."

"I know, Mark. Just pulling your chain. So, another drink before we head out to dinner?"

"I'm fine. Trying to cut back a bit. Incidentally, your sister came to see me today. She mentioned it was Ted Connelly who suggested she contact me. Also, he'd given her my card." Mark gave her a questioning look. "Didn't you say you'd given your sister my card?"

"I did pass your card on to Kim. But that was before Barry died. She didn't comment one way or another, so I assumed she wasn't interested in seeking professional help." She paused. "Why that look on your face? You don't believe me?"

He patted her hand. "Take it easy, sweetheart."

What was with him? She was not thrilled about how the evening was going. "In any case," Dana said, "I'm glad Kim is seeing you. Poor thing can't get it together. She's really in the dumps." She decided to drop it, sensing Mark didn't want to pursue this topic.

She sighed. "I guess Kim and I are a sorry pair. I told you how that asshole of a husband of mine talked to me. Good riddance, right?"

"Right."

"Not exactly a rousing response."

"I'm sorry, Dana. I think I'll have that second drink, after all. Don't move," he said as he got to his feet. "I'll take care of it."

Dana followed him with her gaze as he left the terrace. Speaking of assholes–drinking her liquor, traipsing through her home as if he owned the place. What happened to the fawning romantic, serenading her with overwrought vocabulary? Could he be taking her for granted? No way. And yet, if so—she felt a tightening in her chest–how had she tripped up? *Think, Dana, think.*

She took a deep breath, and then slowly exhaled, chasing away panic. *Don't analyze*, she told herself. *Use your senses; go with your gut feelings.*

When Mark returned, she played nice, assuming the role of lady-love, catering to him with gestures and admiring glances. It worked. His smiles were warm and his hands caressed her shoulders while he planted soft kisses on the back of her neck.

Another minute and they'd be in bed. But what the heck, so be it. And then she heard the phone.

"I'd better get that," Dana said. "Be back in a minute." *Perfect timing*, she thought as she hurried inside. Bed could wait.

To her surprise and delight, it was Ted Connelly. "Uh, Dana? Hi. I'm sorry to bother you, but it seems we have a mix up in our scheduling. Would it be possible for you to come in tomorrow at 11:30 rather than at 10:00?"

"That's even better for me," Dana said, thinking it strange the call had not come earlier from his receptionist. "My assistant arrives at eleven, which means the shop can stay open without me."

"Great. Thank you. I'll see you then."

In the absence of a dial tone, Dana wondered if Ted had set down the phone, forgetting to hang up. "Ted? Are you there?"

"Sorry. I was thinking–that is, I'm wondering if we might grab a bite to eat after your appointment. I'd like to show you a catalogue I've received with a very comprehensive listing of sailing vessels. You'd get an idea of what I'm looking for, so when you talk to Larry—"

"A terrific idea, Ted. It pays to do your homework."

"Absolutely. I don't like to act on impulse when I'm making a decision that will affect my life. And my bank account."

But you already have, Dana thought. And never mind where we go from here. I will lead the way.

When Dana returned to Mark, she knew she was glowing with confidence. She sat and then raised her glass. "Cheers again."

"What are we toasting?" Mark asked. "A phone call from a secret admirer?" His tone was jocular, but his eyes hinted at uncertainty.

"I'll never tell." She leaned over to kiss his cheek. "Well. It would appear we have just enough time to make our dinner reservation."

"Too bad we can't stay here and order in."

She would not make it easy for him. "I think I'm ready to go to dinner." She leaned into him and lowering her tone into seductive range, said, "If you're a good boy, Mark, who knows how the evening will turn out."

It was no surprise to Dana that Mark was at his most charming. Later, after they'd made love, Dana, tingling in the afterglow and feeling warm and cherished as Mark held her, sensed they had taken a step forward in their relationship. No, make that a leap forward.

"Isn't this nice," she purred. "If I were your girl, we could count on this night as a regular feature."

"A super feature for sure." He kissed her square on the lips and the turned away onto his side. "Goodnight, my darling."

Dana lay very still, hands clenched. What the hell kind of response was that? Hurtful, that's what. Fair maiden, my foot. Try keeper of the slops. On the other hand, if she crooked her little finger, Ted Connelly would race to her side, only to fall at her feet in a blubbering heap of desire.

She giggled in spite of herself at these images. Dana, the drama queen. Oh, well, she'd known Mark was not an easy conquest. Setbacks happen; she knew this. It was only a matter of time before he brought up the subject of marriage.

Dana studied the outline of his body under the covers. Just a big lump of a man, but oh, so desirable, and her best lover ever. *Only a matter of time....*

And then like a jolt, her mind wondered to what ifs: What if Mark chose to carry on their affair with no thought of commitment, engaging in an endless, open-ended relationship? Worse, what if he, not she, walked away?

She did not take well to rejection. Others had learned the hard way that betraying Dana James was not without consequences—serious consequences. There was no easy way out with her. She likened herself to a graceful panther: sleek and beautiful but fierce and dangerous. Her victims had no idea the pain she could inflict. Be careful, Mark.

So, what's it to be, my darling? Pain or pleasure? You decide. She snuggled in next to him. Mark would determine his own fate.

Ted Connelly studied his wife, noting her grim expression as she worked at the desk in their den. Seated on the couch across from her, he couldn't make out what she'd been writing in her notebook, though he supposed she was outlining her presentation for the conference. But why did she look so glum?

He placed the book he'd been reading, a biography of Theodore Roosevelt, on the end table next to the couch. God forbid her illness had resurfaced. "Susan?" He kept his tone light. "Don't you think it's time for bed? You've put in a lot of time on whatever it is you're working on."

"Time wasted," she said, turning to him.

"What's the problem?"

"I can't concentrate"

Oh, hell, he thought. *This could be bad.*

Ted patted the seat next to him on the couch. "Why don't you sit here so we can talk?"

Reluctantly, it seemed, she traded the desk for the couch. "I'm just so damned upset," she said, avoiding eye contact.

"Susan, honey, look at me. Tell me why you're upset."

"Mark Hampton dumped me. I'll be seeing another doctor."

"I'm surprised. But you're doing so well, I assume you'll need only a couple of follow-up sessions."

"That bitch Dana is responsible." She gave him a scathing look. "Stop frowning. You think I'm blathering on about nothing?"

"I don't get the connection."

"Well, let me spell it out. The night we had dinner at Café-Grimaldi, I spotted Dana and Dr. Hampton in a corner booth. She was all over him."

Ted moistened his lips. "I don't recall seeing them."

"You sat with your back to them. Anyway, I casually mentioned to Dr. Hampton that I'd seen the two of them together. I also cautioned him about Dana."

Ted stifled a snort. "Just how strong was your caution?"

She shrugged. "He took exception to my comments." She continued, "So I guess conflict of interest applies to the situation. But I'm still mad as hell."

"Even the thought of Dana makes you ill, so why would you want to continue with a therapist who's involved with her?"

"Ted, for goodness sakes, I didn't ask for your opinion."

"I'm sick and tired of your carping about Dana and then having an emotional meltdown over the woman."

"Stop this. Now! You're way out of line."

"You're right. I overreacted." He forced a smile. "Let's call it a night."

At three o'clock in the morning, Ted awoke from a restive sleep. The unpleasantness with his wife immediately came to mind. But it was the image of Mark Hampton and Dana sleeping together that made his stomach churn.

Why did their relationship bother him so much? It was really none of his business; he had no claim on Dana. Besides, the woman was out of his league: glamorous, sophisticated, and intrepid.

But the thought of having sex with Dana made his heart race.

Not that he qualified as an expert lover. In all probability, she could teach him a thing or two. He thought about their brief times together. She had a way of brushing her hand against his, of holding his gaze that made everything else stop. He pictured the curve of her cheek in profile… *This has to stop*, he thought, remembering he was in bed with his wife. He turned on his side. How could he even contemplate sex with Dana? Tomorrow they'd have lunch together. That's all. Furthermore, he wasn't the philandering type.

But as Ted began to drift into sleep, he wondered if Susan's description of Mark and Dana together was an exaggeration. Or was Susan just being spiteful? It was entirely possible.

He'd leave it at that.

Chapter Fourteen

At nine in the morning, Susan Connelly strode into the lobby of the Pasadena Republican Patriots Club. Her shoulder bag thumped against her side and she carried a notebook and folders. She congratulated herself on beating out contenders for the back office. Except for special meetings, few members arrived before ten.

From the windows above the doors, rays of light illuminated an area beyond the entrance, brightening the burgundy carpeting and highlighting brocaded cushions on high-backed chairs.

Susan skirted the rarely used chairs, stepping into the shadows in search of a familiar face. She knew it was too early and indeed, the oversized sofa and adjoining upholstered chairs were unoccupied. People also tended to gather before the fireplace where a benevolent Abraham Lincoln, rendered in oils, gazed down from above the mantel. Now, the only presence near the fireplace was Lincoln's.

In the absence of people and conversation, the dark-paneled walls became an intractable presence, closing in on her. As queasiness now took hold, she fought the urge to retreat from this cloistered setting into the sunshine and fresh air.

She chided herself not to give in to the urge and began taking slow, deep breaths. Ah, better. Much better.

Susan set her bag and office materials on the coffee table and then stepped back to admire the line-up of past club presidents displayed on the wall behind the sofa. She knew it was only a matter of time before she joined their ranks. The thought warmed her, fueling pride and patriotism. It also served as a reminder to get to work.

As she moved out of the lobby and into the corridor, she heard her name.

"Susan. Wait up!" Pam Cummings, club secretary and close friend was approaching, breathing heavily, her plump frame aquiver from exertion.

After an exchange of greetings, Susan explained that she planned to spend the morning finalizing the chapter's agenda for the conference in Hawaii.

"Aren't you the dedicated one," Pam said as she followed Susan into the office. "I'm on my way to a budget committee meeting, but I'm glad I ran into you. Are you free for lunch?"

"Gosh, I'm sorry, Pam. I already have luncheon plans. Maybe another time?"

Pam raised her eyebrows and with her cheeks sucked in, gave Susan a devious grin. "If I didn't know better, I'd say you're off to a romantic rendezvous. Like meeting someone on the sly?"

Susan almost snorted and then turned to place her work materials on the desk. It was funny how early on in her therapy sessions, she'd developed a crush on Dr. Hampton. Before, that is, she'd learned of his questionable taste in women. She faced Pam. "Why on earth would you say that?"

Pam laughed. "Why not? Give us a few years and we'll be old and doddering. So now's the time to go for it. But seriously, Susan, you look mighty spiffy in red. I didn't know you could wear that color."

Susan took in Pam's no-nonsense outfit: a tailored navy blouse with gray slacks–a uniform considered suitable attire for the workplace. Today, however, was different.

"I'm taking my husband to lunch. It's as simple as that. Oh, except I'm making it a surprise."

"His birthday? An anniversary?"

"Nope. Ted usually takes Wednesday afternoon off to catch up on paper work. His usual routine is to walk to the corner café for a sandwich."

"Kind of blah, if you ask me."

"Exactly. Gotta infuse a little fun into a CPA's orderly life. And keep the marriage humming along."

A good response, brave words. But when Pam left for her meeting, and Susan settled in at her desk, she reflected on the two weeks that had passed since their spat over Dana.

Spat? What a wimpy word. She'd been deeply hurt, if not outraged over her husband's harsh treatment of her. In addition, she'd been caught off guard by Ted standing up to her.

When Susan had simmered down, she resolved to hold her

tongue if, God forbid, Dana's name came up in a conversation. Also, within this two week time frame, she'd made an effort to be agreeable, resisting the urge to criticize or contradict Ted; moreover, she'd minimized any complaints, however justified.

She questioned this turnabout in her behavior. Hadn't she valued the concept of candor? Hadn't she prided herself on being forthright, leaving it to others to test the gray areas of diplomacy? Instinct over reasoning, she told herself.

Susan studied her reflection in the hand mirror someone had stored in the bottom drawer of the desk. After a quick examination, she put the mirror away, satisfied that through judicious application of blush, her skin glowed, while mascara and eyeliner had opened up her eyes. Best of all, the red V-necked sweater over black suede pants gave her a sassy, flirty look.

With less than two weeks until the conference, Susan had been dieting and today, down seven pounds, she was able to fit into her suede pants. She'd made an appointment for a facial and planned to have her hair styled. After all, if she wanted to rise in the hierarchy of the organization, it behooved her to make a good impression. And God knows, looks counted.

There was another reason for her makeover: Ted. There was something about him lately, something that tugged at her and gave her an uneasy visceral reaction. Lately, he seemed preoccupied, ambling about with a half smile tugging at the corners of his mouth. He was also less solicitous to every day matters that concerned her, including her health. Interesting how the tables had turned, that now it was she who worked to please him, rather than the other way around.

Weeks had gone by since they'd made love. But that would change with Hawaii as an incentive for romance. She pictured the lush grounds of their five-star hotel, the lanai with ocean views, the whisper of the trade winds. Maybe they wouldn't have to wait until Hawaii. *Why not this afternoon?*

Energized over her morning's accomplishments, Susan waltzed into Ted's waiting room, startling Becky and causing her to drop her cell phone.

Ah ha! Caught you playing on the job, Susan thought, as Becky plastered on her great–to–see–you smile. "Gee, Mrs. Connelly, this is a surprise. How can I help you?"

"I'm here to see Mr. Connelly."

"You just missed him."

Out to lunch at 11:15? Or maybe he'd gone for a walk. "Oh, well, I'll wait." In the silence that followed, Susan became aware that Becky was avoiding eye contact.

"Mr. Connelly said he'd be gone for the afternoon," Becky said casually.

Susan knew what this meant: her sailing obsessed husband was checking out yacht sales. In the aftermath of the Dana debacle, Ted had offered to take a more active part in her political activities if she, in turn, would support his interest in sailing.

"He didn't say where he'd be?"

"Mr. Connelly didn't mention where he was off to. Oh." She paused "When I was in his office to pick up some letters to mail, he had a phone call. I was there only for a few seconds, but I heard him say something about the marina. Or maybe it was Marina del Rey."

Susan nodded. Darn and double darn. Just her luck. So much for surprises. Or seduction. "Well, so be it." She gave Becky a hard look, dropped her gaze to Becky's cell phone and then re-established eye contact. "I won't take up any more of your time. I know you have work to do. Hmm?" She turned from the girl and made a speedy exit.

"I know you have work to do." Becky mimicked Mrs. C. when the woman was out of earshot. If there were a contest for the bitchiest woman alive, Mrs. C. would win, hands down.

Becky picked up her cell phone, but then set it back down as she thought about the Connellys. If Mr. C. weren't so old, she would go for him big time. Not only was he hot, he was so darned nice. And, it would seem, someone else shared her opinion of Mr. C. Becky had heard snatches of his phone conversations that led her to believe a woman was on the line. Acting school had taught her about nuances in the voice and how the tone of a person's voice conveys feeling. Especially when it came to romance.

Becky leaned back in her chair and stretched out her arms. Romance was in the air, and Mrs. C. didn't have a clue. Becky sat up straight, smiling. Yet.

Dana had reacted with child–like enthusiasm to Ted's suggestion that they try the aptly named Oceanic Restaurant for lunch.

Located on the Pacific Coast Highway in Malibu, the restaurant boasted picture windows that showcased intrepid surfers as they caught mammoth waves, then rode their boards into shore like marauding horsemen on a do or die mission.

When a warrior crashed, like now, Ted observed Dana react with a mixture of empathy and glee. Throughout lunch she seemed enthralled with the man against nature theme. While he remained enthralled with her.

Ted imagined that next time—if there was a next time—they'd dine in a cozy, dimly lit place that featured fine food, soft music and shuttered windows.

But for now—he lost the thought as Dana turned to him, her expression pensive. "I wonder," she said, "how they feel at the end of the day. Exhilarated? Defeated?"

"The surfers? I don't think they spend much time analyzing their feelings. In the a.m. they're back in the water. It's a way of life."

"Kind of like an addiction, wouldn't you say? Each ride feeds on the next wave and the wave after that, the bigger the better. And each success brings on a euphoric sense of achievement."

Ted wondered at the force behind Dana's words, at the tightening around her mouth, her eyes. Body or board surfing was a sport, like golf, with some participants making this activity an everyday event.

"Clearly, they're motivated," Ted said. "But the more dedicated surfers work on timing, balance, the twists and turns needed to stay erect. It takes skill to master the surf."

"Okay, okay." She laughed. "I guess I got a little carried away. More to the point, lunch was incredible, the best salmon I've had. Not to mention the entertainment."

"Good thing we picked a day when the surf was up." Ted paused to drink the remainder of his wine. "But as the adage goes, all good things—well, you know the rest."

"Don't necessarily have to come to an end."

"Oh?"

Dana smiled. "Don't look so alarmed. I'm not about to suggest we stop at Make–Out Motel, or the like."

"Alarmed? Hardly."

Dana was giving him an appraising look. "But you're not comfortable wining and dining a woman other than your wife. Right?"

"I admit it's out of character for me." He stared out at the ocean for a moment before reaching for Dana's hand. "I'm going to level with you. When I called you two weeks ago and suggested we have lunch after your appointment, the ostensible reason was to review new information I'd received on sail boats." He released her hand. "It was a ploy, an excuse, if you will, to see you."

Dana nodded. "I figured as much. But I went along with the scenario because I thought it a graceful move on your part. I don't like men to come on to me like gang busters."

He chuckled. "Not my M.O."

She gave him a mock serious look. "I don't recall any ruse over our getting together today."

"No. I decided to be straight forward. Take the risk. Besides, I didn't want to bore you with yet another discussion on sail boats." He leaned back against the booth. "We were talking about calling it a day. Or maybe not?"

"Definitely not. Let's stop at my place. We can finish off the afternoon with coffee, or an after–lunch cordial. I want you to see where I live, what I'm fighting Jasper for."

"I'd like that." Ted busied himself by bringing out his wallet as he felt an acceleration in his breathing, a tingling sensation in his extremities. *Watch it, pal,* he told himself. She's offering a drink and a tour of the house, not of her body.

He swallowed hard and signaled for the check.

Dana had led Ted on a tour of her apartment, and now they sat side by side on one of the couches, sipping coffee laced with Irish whiskey.

"I can see why you're reluctant to give up this place," Ted said. "You're made for each other."

"So I've been told." She made a hand gesture. "It's comfy."

"Comfy is not a word I'd use to describe you."

"How would you describe me?" She held his gaze, the green of her eyes more beguiling to Ted than images of seductive women conjured up by poets and artists.

"I'm not clever with words, Dana. You're beautiful, alluring, and vivacious. I'm repeating what you've heard many times. But it's all true."

"I wasn't fishing for compliments." She shrugged. "Or maybe I was. Even beautiful, alluring, vivacious women can feel insecure at times."

He grinned. "Now you're playing with me. But seriously, it must be obvious how attracted I am to you." He paused. "Dare I ask if you feel the same way?"

"Good heavens, Ted, what woman wouldn't be attracted to you? You're handsome, intelligent, and well-bred. I've seen Becky in your office make moon eyes at you. And you can count me in with the rest of the girls."

"Oh, come on." He laughed, then sobered.

She peered at him. "Did I say something wrong?"

"Hardly. What you said makes me feel ten feet tall."

"But?"

He hesitated, and then said, "What about Mark Hampton?"

She started. "Whoa, there. You know Mark? But of course you would know of him. I happened to see Susan going into the office he uses here off our lobby."

"And Susan saw you with Dr. Hampton on an evening when we all were dining at Café-Grimaldi." He shook his head. "Bringing this up, feels awkward as hell. I mean, who you date is none of my business. But I can't help wondering if you and he are in a serious relationship."

"Serious, as in bed partners? We were at one time, and we still go out occasionally, but Mark runs hot and cold, sometimes warm and adoring and at other times distant and cagey. At any rate, I'm tired of all his game playing."

"I never would have mentioned the restaurant episode except that Susan sat facing in your direction. She said you were all over him."

Dana choked on her drink. "Oh. So I'm necking with him? Or better yet, straddling him? Do I strike you as the kind of person who would behave that way in public?"

"Of course not."

"Susan has always denigrated me, and I never found out why." Her voice sounded teary. "Your wife has snubbed me, made me feel inferior and has made it clear I'm not good enough to be introduced to your friends. She's carried this attitude for years." She leaned into him. "It hurts. It's always hurt."

Ted slipped his arm around her shoulders. "Susan looks at you and she's jealous. I'm not excusing her cruelty, but she is insecure." He pulled Dana in closer to him. "Amazing how fragile we all are."

Dana appeared to be caught up in her own thoughts. She said finally, "You're not a playboy. You're a decent person. So I have to assume life with Susan is not heaven on earth. Or you wouldn't be sitting here with me in my apartment."

"Susan and I haven't been close for some time. I've sensed her dissatisfaction with me, that I'm not Mr. Dynamo. Lately, we've been able to compromise on some issues, but I still feel we're moving in different directions. As corny as it sounds, I'm convinced I'm missing a big chunk out of life."

"Do you think you'd be better off going your separate ways?"

"Perhaps." He looked her in the eye. "A lot will depend on you."

"Well, darling, life is complicated–more so for you than for me. You have family responsibilities; I'm a free agent, or will be soon."

"Maybe I'd like to be unattached, too." With his free hand, Ted raised his mug and drank deeply. When he'd set his drink down, he said, "I'd like to see you before Susan and I leave for Hawaii."

"I think that can be arranged." Dana shifted her body so that she was close enough to rest her head on his shoulder.

Ted ran his fingers over her shoulder and up into the nape of her neck, while he grazed her forehead with his lips. Gently, he sought her lips and gathered her into his arms. As their kisses became more intense, their caresses more intimate, Dana murmured, "Oh, how you excite me."

"My darling, my darling." He began to unbutton her blouse–only to feel her hands cover his.

"Stop," she whispered. "We can't do this."

He drew away from her. "My God, Dana, what are you saying?"

"Another minute and I'd be leading you into the bedroom. We can't let this happen. Yet."

He edged away from her. "I don't understand."

"Trust me. Giving in to our impulses would hurt in the long run. I'm talking about passion tempered by guilt, lying, sneaking around, not being able to sleep or concentrate on work."

"Some people thrive on risky behavior."

"Oh, yes, taking risks can be titillating, I suppose. But if we were sleeping together, could you look Susan in the eye?"

"A moment ago I would have said hell, yes. But," he winced, "it's not in my nature to be devious." He took her hand. "I am so taken with you. You're bright, fun to be with, passionate. And, I guess you've noticed I can't take my eyes off you." He held her gaze. "I want so much to make love to you."

"Then it has to be right for both of us. Which means, we can't have Susan as a third presence in the bedroom. She would need to be out of your life."

"I suppose so."

Gently, Dana withdrew her hand from his. "Let's talk practicalities. Sometime next week we'll get together. Then the following week you'll be off to Hawaii. See how it goes between you and Susan at the conference."

"I don't anticipate any breakthroughs. It'll be politics as usual."

"One final suggestion. I own a condo in Kona on the big island. Go there with Susan."

"Why? I'd be thinking only about you."

"Ted, listen to me. It will be just the two of you. You'll be in a private place without the distraction of friends, work, and organizations. There you can focus on the relationship. The end result? You patch up your marriage or you make a clean break."

"I can let you know in a few days about Kona." He nodded. "I like the idea. And another thought. Susan might welcome the idea of a separation or divorce. She seems to have a thing for men who are my opposite."

"It would serve her right if she ended up with a bossy, domineering jerk."

He laughed. "I think we're jumping ahead of ourselves. Let's take it a step at a time." He checked his watch. "I should go."

At the door, Ted placed his hands on her shoulders. "A lot to think about," he said.

"A lot to act upon, my love."

"Maybe some of those steps in time can be pumped up a bit." He gave her a quick kiss and was out the door.

As Ted drove home, he questioned his feelings. How was it possible to be ecstatic, yet saddened at the same time?

Susan was setting the table in the dining room when the phone rang. She'd been debating whether to use the silver candle holders or the textured cut glass from Italy and did not welcome the interruption. She grabbed her cordless phone, while adjusting the centerpiece. "Hello," she snapped.

"Mrs. Connelly?"

"Yes."

"This is Larry from Boat Works in Marina del Rey. May I speak with Mr. Connelly?"

"He's not in."

"Maybe he can give me a call. I've been remiss in getting back to him on some questions he had."

"Oh. He wasn't by your place this afternoon?"

"No, ma'am."

Susan stood perfectly still, digesting that information, but then shrugged. "Okay," she said, "I'll give him your message."

She hung up and finished setting the table, checked the time, and then dashed to their bedroom for a last minute inspection in her dresser mirror. Her clothes were the same as she'd worn this morning, but she'd freshened her make-up. "Looking good," she said to her reflection as she examined her backside.

She was on her way to the kitchen when she heard Ted coming down the corridor that led from the garage and into the house.

"There you are, honey, I didn't hear the garage door opening. I'll take your briefcase and you can sit down in the living room. Your scotch is on the table. I'll join you in a couple of minutes with a gin and tonic."

Ted had stopped in his tracks, a surprised look on his face. She didn't quite catch his muttered response, but he looked pleased.

She smiled. "Off you go," she said, gesturing toward the living room.

Their cocktail hour was going well, Susan thought, with small talk mixed with her recounting of the morning's achievements. Except that Ted had not commented on her appearance. Time to get personal.

"Have you noticed my new outfit?" she asked.

Ted set down his drink. "Yes. I meant to say something. Red is very becoming on you."

"I remembered you'd mentioned one time that you liked me in red. So I wore this outfit to your office today with the intention of taking you out to lunch. As a surprise."

Ted colored. "I'm so sorry. If I'd known—well," he patted her hand, "blame it on the darn sailing thing. I was in Marina del Rey for the afternoon."

"I see. Which reminds me, someone named Larry called from the Boat Works. He wanted to get back to you on some questions you had."

"I was going to stop to see Larry, but I ran out of time. I had to check out another place, and then I met with a sailing instructor."

"Busy, busy, eh?"

"Susan, I'm sorry about today." He looked her up and down. "It's a great outfit. You've lost weight, haven't you?" Again he reddened. "I don't mean to imply you didn't look good before, it's just that I—"

"Ted, it's okay." She laughed, but instinctively felt uneasy.

Something in his manner bothered her, as if he were reading from a script. But now was not the time to focus on her concerns. Besides, they were all so nebulous.

"Well," She started to get up, "dinner is about ready."

"Wait," Ted said. "Speaking of surprises, I have some interesting news. We can extend our Hawaii trip by several days. Would you like to visit Kona? A client has a condo there that we can use free of charge."

"Oh, Ted, I love the idea of going to Kona. What a nice way to end the trip." She gave him a little poke. "In celebration, you're going to be pleased with dinner. I made your favorite chicken dish."

"*Coq au vin*?"

"Yes! And I'm serving a good Riesling wine." She took his hand. "Better yet, we'll dine by candlelight. I like the combination of candlelight and wine. Don't you?"

His answer was a nod and a smile, but she caught a flicker of uncertainty in his eyes.

Later, in bed, Susan contemplated her enthusiastic response to going on to Kona. She recalled telling Mark Hampton that if Ted whisked her off for a romantic weekend in Paris, she would view the experience as more a hassle than as an exciting interlude—a reaction that reflected her ho-hum attitude toward her husband. What had changed?

She turned on her side to draw closer to him. Possibly, in some subtle way, Ted had changed. For whatever reasons, Susan now wanted Ted as a steady, yet romantic presence in her life.

She would be resolute in attaining that objective.

Ted, lying next to his wife, feigned sleep. He sensed how Susan wanted the evening to end. Throughout dinner, she appeared to be wooing him by jumping up to pour his wine, by tending to him like a restaurant server angling for an enormous tip.

He worried what would happen in bed. Could he perform? Surely, it wasn't fair to Susan that Dana occupied his thoughts and dreams, invading the very core of his being.

Then, just before bedtime, a call came through for Susan. The president of the Patriot chapter had declared an emergency. Because of a policy dispute among several members, a special meeting was scheduled for the following evening.

Duty over seduction propelled Susan to man the phone for the next hour. Ted was able to sneak off to bed, and when Susan finally joined him, she did not attempt to initiate sex. The moment had passed.

Now as Ted waited for sleep to come, he thought about Susan's surprise visit to the office. He had diffused some awkward moments over his whereabouts by bringing up Kona. So now he was committed to that course of action.

Dana was right that it wasn't in him to lead a double life. And who knows? Maybe he and Susan could rekindle the joy and passion of their early years together.

He thought it unlikely.

Chapter Fifteen

"Ah!" Elizabeth turned from her computer to favor her mother with a smile. "I think I've found something." Her smile faded. "Mom, are you okay?" Bea had been cheerful during brunch at a nearby restaurant, but now she slumped on Elizabeth's couch, a diminished figure, pale and drawn.

Bea bowed her head. "Without warning, the sadness comes over me." She fell silent, as if to embrace her grief before looking up with a hint of a smile. "But when my spirits sag, I try to focus on Frank's memorial service."

Her mother's eyes shone through her glasses. "I see our precious family, the turnout from Frank's workplace, the gathering of the Elks. I remember how these people uplifted me with their love and support. But now," she looked at Elizabeth with tears in her eyes, "more and more, I just feel down."

Elizabeth left her desk to come to her mother's side. "The service and the speeches were lovely, but that was two weeks ago. And I realize the cards and calls have tapered off. People still care, but everything's already been said, so I suppose we should try to move on."

Bea patted Elizabeth's hand and motioned them toward the computer. "What trick did you pull out of that magical box? You seemed pleased at whatever it was."

"Yes." The creases in her forehead deepened. "But I'm not sure what I discovered would please you."

Bea's expression turned icy. "What-you-discovered. Don't tell me you've found a cancer cure, a miracle doctor. Elizabeth, I've told you and told you I will seek a second opinion regarding my condition, when I'm ready. So back off!"

Elizabeth gasped and clamped her lips shut. She stared at her mother, tears forming.

Bea tilted her head backward, shut her eyes and then opened them wide. "Dear God, listen to me. I've become a cranky old hag, an out–and–out pain in the ass."

"Oh, Mom." Elizabeth pulled her mother to her for a hug and then drew back, smiling. "In my own defense, I was not tracking down cancer specialists. That said, I'm still not sure you'll want to hear what I was up to."

Bea sat straighter, and gave a soft chuckle. "With that tease, who could resist? Let's see. Have you signed up with a dating service?"

"Mom, for goodness sakes." Elizabeth could feel the heat in her cheeks. "I was searching the Internet for information on Dana James–her history, including marriages, and up popped some interesting stuff."

With a wave of her hand, Bea indicated she'd heard enough.

"Okay," Elizabeth said, "I'll shut up about Dana the Demon."

Bea suppressed a smile. "Brunch was great, and," she planted a kiss on Elizabeth's cheek, "I want you to know you're my darling girl." She rose. "Time for me to get on home."

Elizabeth's car was parked out front, and as they walked out of the apartment, Elizabeth noticed how tired her mother looked, how slow her step. But she held her tongue. It was annoying as hell to be told you look tired. Whenever some idiot made that remark about her, she began to feel droopy or beat. Still, she worried about her mother, wondering if her lack of vitality was an ominous sign.

Now as Elizabeth escorted her mother to her door, Bea seemed to perk up. "Are you sure you won't come in for a bit?"

"Another time. Sunday is my catch–up day before it's back to the grind. Also, I have an agenda. Something I need to work on."

Bea sighed. "Your determination is commendable, Elizabeth, but from what little you've told me, I suspect you're delving into something that can only result in trouble."

"If it bites me, so what? Dana James–last name Sterling from her first marriage–is evil incarnate."

"Oh, my dear, surely you're being melodramatic."

"Because of her actions, my father has been taken from us. You have lost the love of your life, and God knows what else she's done to destroy other lives."

"Elizabeth, what are you talking about?"

"All right. I'm only theorizing, thinking out loud. And maybe you're right that I'm overwrought. But some people bring out the worst in me, though I guess that's not so bad if it pushes me to follow a lead."

Bea shook her head. "You've lost me."

"I'm not surprised. Bad habit of mine, thinking out loud. Well. On a happier note, you'll be pleased to learn I'm going out this evening."

"Oh?" A big smile. "Tell me about it."

"Why don't we wait until tomorrow when I call? You need to get some rest, and I should get home."

"To work on your agenda?"

"Don't look so worried. I'm just fooling around and having fun."

"I hope you mean that," Bea said, using her classroom voice.

Bea inserted her key into her lock and then turned to Elizabeth with a smile. "Be sure to call me."

The look on her mother's face–hope, even delight–gave Elizabeth pause as she hunted in her closet for a change of clothes. Her evening out wasn't a date, for heavens sake, but at least her statement had provided a momentary detour from Bea's unending journey down misery lane.

As for her so-called agenda, first on her list was to contact Kyle Sterling, Dana's former husband who'd popped up in her Internet search. Information about their divorce might give credence to what was now merely a hunch. *If* he would agree to talk to her.

Of course, she could drop her investigation, a move that would provide peace of mind for her mother. On the other hand, lingering doubts over her father's death, coupled with the suspicion that Dana was in some way connected made it imperative she address these issues.

Something was fishy, and a Dana barracuda lurked in the dark waters of sinister intent.

Elizabeth slipped into a blue-green top with three quarter sleeves in a gauzy material she thought perfect for a warm summer evening. She liked the effect of a V neckline that minimized the roundness of her face. Ditto for drop earrings in variegated shades of blue. She considered dabbing a small amount of blue eye shadow on her lids but then decided against it. Nothing, short of colored contact lenses would deepen pale blue eyes.

Next, she pulled on light weight black pants–white was a no–no with her generous hips–then decided on flats over heels, the better for walking.

Though a long drive from Tustin, the Art Walk on Melrose Avenue in the Hollywood area promised to be an intriguing diversion. In the lineup were several art galleries displaying paintings by new and seasoned artists, as well as crafts and jewelry exhibits, and even hand painted clothing. Also touted were wine and cheese refreshments.

She'd found the announcement for the Sunday Art Walk in her newspaper, her decision to attend determined by the inclusion of the Melrose Galleria, partnered by Kimberly Williams and Jenna Price.

Elizabeth was not in a buying mood, nor could she afford a costly painting. However, she had every intention of seeking out the woman who was Barry Williams' widow. And Dana James' sister.

Kim came out of her back office to speak to Jenna, only to retreat to her desk at the rear of the gallery as she noted her partner was in the process of completing a sale.

The crowds attending the Art Walk had thinned, and now only a few people walked their aisles, among them a young woman undistinguished except for her vivid blue-green top. Though she studied the displays, she also seemed distracted, glancing around, as if in search of something or someone. She also looked vaguely familiar.

Kim decided to approach what she hoped was a potential buyer. "May I help you? You seem drawn to this portrait of a family dinner scene."

The woman turned her gaze from the painting to Kim. "Isn't it interesting," she said, "how the people at the table, by their facial expressions and body language, even their posture can reveal their innermost thoughts?"

Kim nodded. "Whatever the artist intended, I suppose the stories behind the figures in the painting lie in the eye of the beholder." She paused, unable to second guess this woman's intentions. "Are you considering making a purchase?"

"Perhaps at another time. Actually, I'm here to see you. Do the names Bea and Frank Devlin ring a bell?"

More like a gong, Kim thought, impinging on her delight over the success of the Art Walk, as well as the many sales they'd made this evening. Why bring up the Devlins? What was this woman up to?

"I met them a couple of times," Kim said. "My sister and I were guests in their home when Dana—that's my sister—was enrolled at the community college. Why do you ask?"

"I'm their daughter Elizabeth."

Now Kim could see the physical resemblance to her mother. But she remembered Bea as bland in personality, a contrast to her daughter's more assertive manner. "It's nice to meet you, Elizabeth. What can I do for you?"

"Is there some place we can talk in private? I promise I won't take up much of your time."

Back at her desk, with Elizabeth seated facing her, Kim felt suddenly disheartened, remembering her confrontation with Susan Connelly. Given the circumstances of Dana's falling out with Bea, must she subject herself to a repeat nasty encounter? Or worse, end up defending her sister?

"Ms. Devlin, why are you here?"

"I'm here because we have something in common. You and your husband and my parents stayed in Kona in a condo owned by your sister Dana."

"Yes, I recall your parents were to arrive around July 15 for an anniversary celebration after our stay."

Elizabeth started. "How would you know my parents were to occupy the unit you vacated?"

Oh shoot. Dana hadn't wanted the Devlins to know she'd been behind their winning the silent auction grand prize. "I'm not sure how I knew," Kim said. "From the manager? Though at that time the name Devlin wouldn't have registered with me. Oh, now I remember some chit-chat about all of us being from Southern California."

Kim gritted her teeth, wishing she hadn't been so accommodating in agreeing to talk to the Devlin daughter. But the woman merely looked thoughtful, as if she were digesting that information.

Elizabeth broke the silence, her gaze direct, her tone matter of fact. "I understand your husband died under tragic circumstances, the cause of death—unclear?"

"Heart failure has now been definitely established, though what triggered his death—" she stopped abruptly. "Why on earth are we having this conversation?"

"Mrs. Williams, my father died in your sister's condo of anaphylactic shock." She went on to explain the events leading up to her father's death, including the confusing occurrences that preceded the delivery of the lethal cake.

Kim drew in her breath. Did Dana know what had happened to Frank Devlin? And if so, why would she keep that information from Kim?

Kim shook her head. "This must be a very difficult time for you and your family. I'm so sorry." Condolences rendered, she raised her eyebrows to signal a silent "So?"

Elizabeth got the message. "Your sister was in Kona at the time of my father's death."

"In Kona? You must be confused. Dana was in Honolulu on business during that time frame, but not in Kona. She did come to Kona to be with me when Barry died."

"From Honolulu."

"Yes."

"Mrs. Williams, as you know, bad blood existed between Dana and my mother."

"Unfortunate for all concerned," Kim said. "But you're referring to a situation that occurred long ago."

"Time means nothing to a person who can't let go of resentment, of outrage, who rides these feelings to an imaginary finish line where the only option is retaliation at any cost."

Kim smiled. "A little over the top, wouldn't you say? Look, I'm truly sorry about your father, but I haven't the slightest idea what you're talking about."

"I'm talking in the abstract. Or maybe not," she muttered. "One more question, okay? Then I'll leave. Were Dana and your husband on good terms?"

Kim stood. "I'm still in the dark as to why you're here, but it doesn't matter, Ms. Devlin, because this conversation is over."

Elizabeth nodded and then got to her feet, never once shifting her gaze from Kim. "I apologize for poking my nose into personal matters. Thank you for taking the time to talk with me."

Elizabeth turned to leave but then made an about face. "Oh, you might want to check with Heidi McGowan at Kailua Condos. She told me Dana stopped by her office the day after my father died." This time Elizabeth turned to go and didn't look back.

Kim sank down at her desk, rested her head on the back of her chair and closed her eyes. God, that woman had tested her endurance, leaving her feeling like a soggy piece of bread. Why would she ask about Dana and Barry?

Her musings were cut short by a tap on her arm. Kim opened her eyes and sat up straight, her spirits lifting. Mark Hampton stood over her.

"Just happened to be in the neighborhood," he said with the flick of his hand.

"You're kidding."

"Yeah, well, maybe that's not entirely true. I saw the announcement for the Art Walk in the Calendar section of the *Times*. Since I was at a dinner meeting downtown, I couldn't resist stopping by."

Kim moved quickly to her feet. "I'm so glad to see you, Dr. Hampton. You caught me in recovery mode after a bizarre encounter with a young woman. She–well, I'm just happy she's gone. Why don't I show you around?"

"I'd like that. Maybe I'll find another painting for the office." He smiled. "Or for my home."

Kim took in the warmth in his expression, his genuine smile. On the likeability index, he rated on par with Ted Connelly.

Hmm. So here she was mentally gushing over two men she was seeing professionally, post Barry. Food for thought. But for thought, only. The topic did not lend itself for discussion with her therapist, who was also Dana's lover.

Kim felt energized as the two of them strolled the aisles, commenting on the various displays and sipping wine. But when they came upon the portrait of a family seated at the dinner table, the wine turned sour in Kim's mouth as she remembered Elizabeth's analysis of the painting.

Facial expression, body language, posture. It seemed to her now that Elizabeth, with her steady gaze, had seized upon these facets of

Kim's behavior as she related her father's death and questioned Dana's comings and goings, and her relationship with Barry.

She pictured Elizabeth as she sat across from her, eyes deceptively soft in contrast to a lined forehead, her brown hair chin length, tidy but unstyled. Aside from physical characteristics, Ms. Devlin was articulate and intelligent. But creepy. The woman was creepy and, for God's sake, melodramatic.

Kim told herself to forget about Elizabeth Devlin. She'd focus on the evening's accomplishments. And on the pleasure of Mark Hampton's company.

But at home, when Kim finally settled into bed, her sleep was fitful, her dreams disjointed and on the dark side.

The next morning, Kim thought about her appointment on Wednesday with Dr. Hampton. Dare she spell out her concerns regarding Dana? She dismissed the thought. Elizabeth was a troubled young woman mourning over the loss of her father. And possibly a troublemaker.

Then later that morning, came the phone call that brought about another night of tossing and turning, amid endless speculation.

Mark Hampton had to know.

Chapter Sixteen

Blackout! Followed by applause, curtain down, houselights up.

As people consulted their theater programs or made a dash for the lobby or restrooms, Dana squeezed Mark's hand and gave him an approving smile.

She could see the relief on his face and thought it almost comical.

"I wasn't sure," Mark said, "that even with rave reviews, 'Jupiter Descending' would be all that entertaining. I'm finding the play more depressing than enlightening."

Dana gave a soft giggle. "And confusing? I'm enjoying it for the most part, though the rape scene was hard to take. Still, I suppose that scene served as a metaphor or symbol of repression evolving into savagery."

"Wow." The light in Mark's eyes signaled surprise and respect. "I can hardly wait for a post theater discussion."

"Definitely post," Dana said, getting to her feet. "If I don't leave now, I'll stand at the end of a very long line for the ladies' room. And I don't want to be late and stumbling over people's feet in the dark."

Mark chuckled. "Also, you don't want to miss the start of Act Two. Heaven knows what the characters will be up to."

Mark indicated he would stay put, which pleased Dana; she didn't want him wandering around and seeing what she was up to.

The line for the ladies' lounge moved more quickly than Dana had anticipated and once inside, she turned away from the bathroom stalls and moved into the waiting area. She passed by the counter with lighted mirrors and sat on a couch, then dug into her purse for her cell phone.

"Hang up if a woman answers," Dana sang to herself, as she pressed the numbers for Ted Connelly's home phone. He had explained that Susan would be attending her Tuesday night board meeting, which would allow her to safely call so that they could set a time and place for their Wednesday lunch date.

Ted answered on the first ring.

"Okay to talk?" Dana asked.

After assurances that Susan was out, Ted said, "I tried reaching you at home, with no success."

"Right. I was away most of the day, and now I'm calling during intermission at Westside Playhouse. Are we still on for lunch tomorrow?"

"You bet."

His voice husky, Ted said, "It's all I think about, having you near me, breathing in your scent, looking into your eyes.

He laughed softly. "Highly original, huh?"

"Highly treasured coming from you." Who needed a balcony and adoring fans when you had the adulation of men like Ted and Mark? "Oh. The lights are blinking, Ted. Time for me to get back to my seat."

"Are you enjoying the play?"

"In a word, no."

He chuckled. "Too bad. You can tell me about it tomorrow."

Sure, Dana thought as she ended the call. She would spout gobbledygook about the play, and Ted would listen attentively and nod, while he undressed her with his eyes.

Slowly she moved out of the room and then made her way down the aisle to their orchestra seats. What good were great seats for a show that made no sense and was boring as all get out. And she hadn't come up with all that crap about metaphors and symbols by herself. She'd had help.

Manny Goodman, theater critic for the *Hollywood Review*, was a frequent visitor to her shop. When she learned Mark had to exchange their Sunday tickets for Tuesday, she took advantage of the time lapse to enlist Manny's help. He'd been only too eager to give her a run-down and analysis of "Jupiter Descending," ending his commentary with, "Not your cup of tea, sweetie."

Maybe not, Dana acknowledged, as she joined Mark, but a show of intellect could only further her cause. And oh, baby, did she have a cause, namely, to reel in the biggest catch of her life: Mark Hampton.

Despite the dark thoughts she'd had lying next to him the night her overture toward commitment had been ignored, she'd devised a strategy designed to preclude any need for reprisals.

It was a matter of balance: Be eager to see Mark, but not always available. Show a flair for independence, but melt in his arms. Make him feel ten feet tall, but flirt with men giving her the eye. Always but always, look her best. And oh, try to restrain her bitchy side.

Mark held her hand as the curtain rose on Act Two, the final act of "Jupiter Descending." Though she sat quietly, seemingly absorbed in the play, Dana worked to contain herself, to put the brakes on expressing her jubilation.

If she also felt smug over the success of her game plan, then so be it. Mark was ready to make their relationship permanent. How could she be so certain? Because Mark's attitude toward her had changed. While he'd always displayed a romantic side, gamesmanship or an effort at one-upmanship clouded the genuineness of his affection for her.

Lately, she'd interpreted his behavior as unconditionally loving. And while sexual tension still gave rise to passion, he seemed more at ease with her, as he welcomed her to share in his comforts.

Another advantage to having Mark in her hip pocket: She'd have an excuse to back out of her presumed relationship with Ted Connelly. She'd rehearsed the dialogue in her mind: "You knew Mark and I were having an affair, and that I broke up with him over his lack of sincerity. All that changed—". Well, she hadn't refined the script, but she'd let Ted down gently.

Back to the play, Dana shifted in her seat. Would the damn thing never end?

Forty-five minutes later, Dana joined in the applause as the cast assembled on stage for curtain call.

When the house lights came on, Mark turned to her. His tone soft, his gaze reflecting a lover's intent, he asked, "My place or yours?"

While Mark's place was attractive in its rustic setting, Dana wanted to stage her night of triumph in more opulent surroundings. Her place, it would be.

Dana suggested they settle in the great room, rather than try the terrace. "Even in August, the nights turn chilly after ten o'clock."

That was fine with Mark. "The better to sit closer," he said, the warmth in his gaze indicating he had more than sitting on his mind.

Dana was not about to trot off to bed. Not yet. "So, shall we play the game of who picks which couch?" she asked, giving a flip to the bottom of his tie.

He reached for her, but she eluded his grasp. Kicking off her shoes, Dana swiftly headed for the couch closest to the piano, only to change course and arrive at a setting by the entrance to the terrace. She sat, but then jumped up as Mark caught up with her.

"Oh, no, you don't." This time Mark blocked her escape. He scooped her into his arms and appeared headed for the bedroom.

"No, no, no," she squealed. "First we talk." She broke into laughter. "Put me down, you big lug."

He had backtracked to the couch where they usually sat together, pretended to drop her, but then set her down gently.

Shaping his face into a Groucho Marx leer, Mark took his place next to her. "I like this playful side of you; in fact, I like every side of you. What next? I chase you around the bed?"

She giggled. "You do seem to have bed on your mind. Why don't we have a brandy here first, and then we'll see who chases whom around the bed."

"Deal."

When he returned from the kitchen with their drinks, they toasted themselves and good times ahead. "Seriously," Mark said, "I've never seen this fun side of you."

"You mean silly?"

"Whatever you want to call it, you're a delight. Now. You said you wanted to talk. Is this about the play?"

"I'd rather talk about us."

He nodded. "Okay."

"About our relationship. I'd say we're very compatible. And growing closer."

"I can't deny that."

She waited, feeling a tinge of annoyance while he raised his glass to take a sip, and then set it down. "What if we planned to take a trip together?" She asked.

"Oh. So you're talking travel plans? Great idea. Where did you have in mind?"

"What about a honeymoon trip?"

Mark opened his mouth, and then closed it. A beat later, he said, "I don't understand. You're still married."

"I'm about to be divorced!" She raised her voice, unable to mask her exasperation.

"So you are." He raised his glass, stared at it, and then set it back down.

Dana felt her breathing accelerate. Was the man so obtuse he couldn't see where this discussion was going? Had he never pictured them together on a permanent basis? Heat was everywhere—in her scalp, her face, through her chest—and her breathing was becoming now more fragmented. *The issues, concentrate on the issues*, she told herself.

"Mark, we've invested a lot of time together and lately we've seemed so well suited."

Mark took her hand. "Dana, I'm crazy about you, but I wasn't prepared for this kind of discussion."

She snatched her hand from his. "What are you, a guru standing on a mountain top, dispensing advice to your lowly subjects, but too turned off by their dirty, little secrets to jump into the fray?"

"I think I understand what you're implying—" he shook his head.

"Okay. Let's not mess around. Where do you see us a year from now, five years from now?"

"Dana, I've been so taken with you, and not only because of your beauty. You breathe life into every moment. You're alluring, seductive, at times enigmatic, but never boring. As for a year from now, or five years from now, how do you picture us as a couple?"

Dana could feel the heat drain from her body, supplanted by an iciness that seemed to freeze her vocal cords. She raised her glass, took in a big swig of brandy, set the glass down hard, and then turned to Mark. Her voice a whisper, she said, "I want you to leave."

Mark looked stunned, ashen. "I'm sorry if I've upset you. I was caught off guard by your questions. I promise we'll talk seriously but," he raised his eyebrows, "obviously, this is not a good time." He got to his feet.

Now Dana stood. “Get out,” she said.

At the door, Mark turned back to her. “I’ll call you tomorrow.” He waited, as if hoping for a response, but not getting one, left.

Slowly, Dana sat down. She lifted her drink to finish the brandy. “Bastard,” she said out loud.

Minutes later, she carried the two glasses into the kitchen and took out a bottled Coke from the refrigerator. She drank from the bottle, feeling the cold liquid awaken her senses, buzz her brain into fully alert.

Clearly, she had misjudged Mark’s intentions, despite his change in attitude. On the other hand, he hadn’t come out with some stupid male platitude like, “I’m not the marrying kind.” So maybe she’d shocked him out of his complacency. In fact, she’d bet on that.

As for Ted Connelly, he was her safety net, an adoring innocent so easy to manipulate. True, she had led him on to bring the bitch Susan to her knees. But if Mark fell by the wayside, having Ted around wouldn’t be a bad substitute. Not when she could play queen to his knave.

Failure, she decided as she finished her Coke, wasn’t an option. Though throwing Mark out was an offshoot of her rage, it also served as a brilliant maneuver. She was done with romantic twaddle. If Mark wanted her, and she couldn’t conceive otherwise, it would be on her terms.

Once again, Dana felt jubilant, an almost sexual heightening of intensity. Change was imminent. And she could hardly wait!

True to his word, Mark had cut back on his drinking; sure, he could hold his liquor, but he knew he drank to excess and that eventually health problems would surface. And because he liked to drink, he decided moderation was the key to protecting his health, while enjoying his libations.

Tonight, however, he didn’t hesitate to pour a second brandy. Once again, he sought the comfort of his deck, having changed from coat and tie to a pullover sweater and slacks.

He was the expert, the family therapist who dissected relationships and mental health problems and then put the pieces back together with gratifying results.

So why had he ignored the warning signs? That Dana, the free spirit who relied on no one was, in truth, becoming emotionally dependent on him. That Dana, who bowled men over with the crook of her finger, wanted him–he took a deep breath–in marriage.

He hadn't lied when he told Dana he was caught off guard by her questions; he hadn't lied when he described the qualities that endeared her to him. What she didn't understand was that he had never contemplated marriage. Not a year from now, not five years from now.

Mark sipped his brandy, feeling its warmth course through his body, awakening his sensuous side. Dana was a bright, colorfully plumed songbird, a quixotic creature who, if wronged, might metamorphose into a fierce predator. But whatever her proclivities, at this moment Mark wanted Dana James with every fiber of his mind and body.

He took another sip of brandy as he began preparing in his_mind what he would say he in his call to Dana the following day.

By Wednesday morning, Kim's ambivalence over whether to tell Mark about Monday's phone call was driving her up the wall. She wanted to talk to Dana first and had called her several times but could not reach her. So what to do?

For the umpteenth time, Kim replayed in her mind the conversation that left her shaken and confused.

She'd been rattled when her caller identified himself as Jasper James because, good God, why would he be contacting her?

"Are you here in L.A.?" She asked.

"No. I'm calling from Sydney. However, I expect to arrive in Los Angeles in late August or early September to close out my business. And to see Dana.

"Our legal counsel has been working out the details of the divorce, but I need to reach Dana now." He paused, before continuing, "She won't talk to me, Kim, and I was wondering if you might intercede on my behalf."

Now it was Kim who gathered her thoughts. Finally, she said, "Other than my knowing about the divorce, Dana hasn't confided in me, so I wasn't aware you and she had been out of touch. But I suppose I can understand why that is. At least on my sister's part. Dana did tell me about her call to you from Honolulu."

"When would that be? Oh. At the time you and your husband were in Kona. Kim, I'm so very sorry about your loss."

"Thank you. But no, I'm not talking about when we were in Kona. This was later when Dana was on her way to Australia to see you. She'd stopped over in Honolulu to finalize the sale of property you two owned and when she called you, I understand you were–well, not only drunk, but downright nasty to her."

"What in the hell are you talking about?"

"You don't remember?"

"How can I remember something that didn't happen?"

"All right, I think I've said enough."

"Kim, don't hang up. Hear me out. I've been thinking what an obnoxious jerk I've been, and not because I got drunk or talked nasty to your sister. That never happened. Nor did I know she was on her way to see me.

"What I regret was instigating divorce proceedings by writing Dana a letter. That was callous on my part; I should have confronted her in person. But we'd drifted apart, and I knew living in Australia was not an option for Dana. Not anymore. By writing to her, I thought we'd make a clean break. The sooner the better."

"Your motives or guilty feelings are none of my business. What does throw me is that I know it was Dana who started divorce proceedings against you, Jasper, and not the other way around."

"Is that what she said? My solicitor has a copy of the letter I sent to Dana, dated, of course. Correspondence from her lawyer, responding to my request to end our marriage, postdated my letter to your sister."

"Why would Dana make up such an outlandish story?"

"To save face?"

"The same could be said about you."

"Who started what isn't germane. Kim, I would like to talk to Dana regarding some personal matters." He paused. "Also, I haven't buried reconciliation as a possibility."

"Oh, really?" And how would that fly, she wondered, if Jasper knew about Mark? "All right," she said, "I'll do my best to bring Dana around. Whatever happens, I admire your willingness to be absolutely sure about the steps you're taking."

As she recalled the phone conversation, she remembered the wistfulness in her tone. Barry had denied the possibility of a reconciliation.

Kim was due at Mark Hampton's office in an hour. The question remained as to whether she should confide her concerns about Dana to her therapist. She felt trust and confidence in the man, but how objective could he be, given his relationship with Dana?

Too bad Ms. Smarty Pants Devlin hadn't listened in on her conversation with Jasper. Surely, she could draw a complete character analysis based on inflections and nuances in tone.

Sarcasm aside, the question of what to do grated on her. She would defer her decision until she came face-to-face with Mark, then go with her gut feeling. But first she had to try one more time to reach Dana.

And make one more phone call.

Chapter Seventeen

Elizabeth looked at her watch. Fifteen minutes to go until her appointment with Kyle Sterling, Dana's ex-husband. She sat in her car in a public parking lot, two blocks off Sunset Boulevard.

If she left now and walked fast, she would show up at the appointed time. God forbid she arrive early. In Elizabeth's experience, the majority of office staff who assisted lawyers, doctors, CPA's and the like considered social workers one rung above the people they served. Who cared if she had to cool her heels twenty to forty-five minutes beyond the scheduled time?

Maybe today will be different, Elizabeth thought as she exited her car and headed for Schmidt and Associates Accounting and Tax Services, located in the Sunset Towers.

Elizabeth was not surprised that the woman who sat at the reception window was polite but curt. She certainly wouldn't want to waste energy on a non-client, fitted in at the last minute.

"Please take a seat," she said. "I'll notify Mr. Sterling's office that you're here."

The large waiting room, with its upholstered armchairs and low couches, also boasted watercolor paintings depicting tropical getaways, and a wall aquarium, all designed to sooth the jangled nerves of clients soon to huddle with their accountants.

On this Wednesday afternoon at 4 p.m., the only other person in the waiting room was a man engrossed in business news coming from the flat screen TV.

Elizabeth picked a chair near a stack of magazines where she could observe the receptionist. Thus far, the woman had not picked up her phone or left her place. Oh well, if reading became tiresome, Elizabeth figured she could mentally rehearse the role she would perform before a captive audience of one.

At least getting the appointment had been easy. She'd stated that her purpose for seeing Mr. Sterling was confidential, a matter involving his ex-wife, Dana James. Bingo! She was in.

Five minutes later, Elizabeth was leafing through a *Newsweek* magazine when the receptionist appeared at her side. "Mr. Sterling will see you now," she said, a hint of disbelief in her tone. "Please follow me."

The man who greeted Elizabeth was tall, late forties, she guessed, with an athletic build. He was attractive, but no lady killer, and his coiffed brown hair and manicured nails suggested a standing appointment at the salon. Unsmiling blue-gray eyes, a firm handshake and businesslike demeanor completed the picture.

He had come from behind a clutter-free desk and now indicated she take a seat in one of the three leather armchairs facing his desk.

Back in place behind his desk, Sterling rendered what passed for a smile as he gave her the once over. "You've peaked my curiosity, Miss, uh, Devlin. Do I understand correctly that you're a social worker, and that you're investigating a matter that involves my ex-wife?"

Elizabeth presented her credentials before going into her made up story about moonlighting for an attorney. She named the firm, referenced from the Yellow Pages, then continued by way of explanation, "I enjoy working in the field, gathering information, interviewing prospective witnesses."

He fingered his collar. "I would hope I'm not on your witness list."

"Oh, no. Absolutely not. I'm just gathering background information. Opposing counsel would consider anything you said against your ex-wife as prejudicial."

He appeared to relax. "Okay. What's going on?"

"Allegations have arisen regarding Dana James' treatment of her former housekeeper." Elizabeth consulted her notes. "Elena Delgado maintains Mrs. James bullied her, used profanity, withheld payment because of alleged shoddy service and in one instance, shoved her."

"Really." His mouth curved downward, while his fingers performed a tap dance on his desk. "That doesn't sound like Dana."

"How would you characterize your ex wife?"

"Not as a bully. A cheater? Hell, yes"

"Are you saying she became involved with another man?"

"I divorced her when I learned she was having an affair. And with someone I thought I could trust."

"Was your divorce amicable?"

"Business-like. No fireworks." His smile mimicked a spiteful child. "Once I started divorce proceedings, her lover dumped her." His smile deepened. "Dana's ex-lover then married her sister. Can you beat that?"

"Oh, my." Elizabeth pretended to let that sink in. "Maybe he's the person I should be interviewing."

"Not possible. He died last month. Drowned in a swimming pool at a condo in Hawaii where he and his wife were staying. You might have seen his obituary in 'The Times'. Barry Williams?"

"I must have missed that."

"I suggest you get in touch with his widow, Kim Williams."

She nodded. "I'll take that under consideration. But getting back to the case at hand, you stated Mrs. James was not a bully. Did she have a temper?"

He grew thoughtful. "Not so much a temper, as a penchant for revenge. I remember that when she worked as a buyer at I. Magnin, a manager reprimanded her in front of others for a minor infraction. Dana held her tongue but subsequently spread malicious rumors about the manager that got her fired. The woman also suffered a nervous breakdown and God knows what else."

"I see. Did she act out against you when you divorced her?"

"No. I was merely a comma in a long, dull sentence. Barry was the exclamation mark at the end of a riveting paragraph." He shrugged. "If you get my drift." Again the smile. "I heard Dana was enraged over Barry's rejection of her, but I have no idea if she tried to get back at him."

"So it appears Mrs. James would be capable of mistreating someone for personal reasons."

"If the housekeeper told lies about Dana or talked behind her back, I'd say, 'Look out.' What I can't see is Dana bullying this woman for poor job performance. She'd simply tell her to get the hell out."

Elizabeth stood. "Thank you for seeing me." She smiled. "Though your revelations may have weakened the case against Mrs. James." She thanked him again and started to leave.

"Miss Devlin?" Sterling was on his feet.

Elizabeth turned to face him.

"Do you suppose you could get back to me on how the case is resolved? Dana, bless her little black heart, shouldn't be put to the wheel by some grimy, illegal immigrant out to screw her."

Elizabeth suppressed a shudder as she noted the gleam in Kyle Sterling's eyes. "I'll do my best," she said, and made a hurried exit.

Back in the waiting room, Elizabeth nodded to the receptionist who acknowledged her with a look that was a cross between bemusement and curiosity.

"And wouldn't you like to know what we talked about in his majesty's chambers," she muttered as she left the room. And wouldn't Mr. Jackass Sterling just love to see Dana kicked in the teeth?

Dana's comeuppance would not stem from a court battle between herself and a fictitious housekeeper.

But stay tuned, Mr. Sterling. Stay tuned.

Elizabeth arrived home to discover three telephone messages. The first, from her supervisor, was in reference to Friday's staff meeting. The second message from her mother contained a brief "I need to talk to you." The third, a request to call a San Francisco number that identified the caller, pumped up her heartbeat and brought an infusion of heat to her cheeks.

Something in her mother's tone, perhaps the force behind her words, translated into: This is important. But for once, her mother could wait.

Elizabeth picked up the phone and dialed the San Francisco number.

Robert Chang came on the line.

At his desk earlier that same day, Mark dialed Dana's number, only to hang up as he responded to a discreet knock on his office door. Georgia, his receptionist, opened the door a crack. "Okay to come in?"

"Sure."

She closed the door behind her. "Kim Williams is here. I thought you should know she seems restless, distracted."

"I shouldn't have kept her waiting, but I've been trying to reach a certain party." He raised his hands and shook his head.

"You seem a bit down this morning. Have a bad night?"

Mark chuckled. "Georgia, you're priceless, but I'm going to plead the fifth."

"Well, you know me. I'm just a nosy old woman."

"Uh huh. Who'd be qualified to take over my job."

"Ha! Not for a million dollars. So. Should I tell Mrs. Williams you're ready to see her?"

At his nod, she left the room.

When Kim appeared, Mark was standing. He greeted her with a reassuring smile. Her smile in response was a mere flicker, though the tension in her expression did seem to lessen.

Kim came into the room but then paused. She pointed to the painting over the fireplace. "That's where I'd like to be this very minute, nestled in a café gazing out at that rainy, tranquil street scene."

"Why don't we sit down, and then you can tell me why you'd prefer the Left Bank in Paris over my company?"

His attempt at levity seemed to relax her, as the tautness around her mouth gave way to a genuine smile. "Could we address that issue later?"

"Your call, Kim." He opened his folder and consulted his notes from their last session. "Did you follow through on keeping a daily journal?"

Kim reached into her bag and brought out a medium-sized notebook. "Brilliant suggestion. The journal's kept me focused."

"Good. Later in the hour, if you don't mind, I'd like you to share some entries. But first let's discuss the concerns you brought to my attention last week. What's changed? What hasn't changed?"

As the session continued, Mark gave himself a mental pat on the back for Kim's progress. Now, if she'd only open up to him about what was really troubling her.

Fifteen minutes before the end of the hour, Mark set her folder aside. "All right if we sample a few of your journal entries? The writings don't have to be in order or profound. Just whatever you'd care to share."

Kim opened her notebook and began to read a description of a walk she'd taken over her lunch hour near the Galleria. She'd felt energetic, in tune with her surroundings as she explored the neighborhood, stopping at craft displays, boutiques and art galleries to talk to the proprietors. "I managed to shrug off my self-absorption to focus on others, to get to know people I'd never really talked to. It felt good."

"Out of the cave and into the sunlight? I'd say that's progress."

Kim found another passage to read, then flipped through the pages as if searching for something. She looked up, perplexed. "I can't believe I didn't record this information. What I'm looking at are blank pages."

"What information?"

She looked him directly in the eye. "This isn't about me, you understand. I'm not backsliding. In fact, every day I feel more in control of myself, more alert, more positive in my outlook."

"I'm delighted with your assessment, which I share. But Kim, something's happened to upset you."

"Yes." She looked up at the painting. "And since I can't run off to the Left Bank, I might as well come to terms over some troubling questions. Could we talk? I mean outside of the doctor-patient relationship?"

He smiled. "I've been known to hold a conversation that doesn't involve dissecting one's psyche."

"You did great last Sunday evening at the Art Walk." She'd been smiling, but then sobered. "What I'm about to tell you involves Dana."

Dana. Why did he feel as if he'd been kicked in the gut? He had to catch his breath. The damn room had become stifling. "Tell you what," he said, conscious of speaking in measured tones, "let's sit on my terrace. We can talk there. I can even send out for coffee, if you'd like."

Kim settled for water. She sat stiffly in one of the patio chairs, her expression solemn, while Mark stood at the terrace wall. He took a moment to gaze beyond the terrace, to breathe in the fresh air; then, his composure intact, he turned to face her.

"This is difficult for me," Kim said in a soft voice. "After all, you're my sister's lover." She reddened. "Sorry, that was tactless of me. What I'm trying to say is that it might be hard for you to be objective, given the circumstances."

"Try me."

Kim began with the call she'd received from Jasper James. She explained that in the give and take of their conversation, it came out that it was he who had instigated divorce proceedings. Furthermore, he denied Dana ever placing a call to him in Australia from Honolulu; nor, he insisted, had any incident occurred where he'd been drunk and/or disgusting during a telephone conversation with her.

"So it's 'she said, he said'?" Mark asked.

"Well, he seemed outraged by Dana's accusations. And he says his solicitor has a copy of his dated letter to Dana asking for the divorce and the response from Dana's lawyer, postdating Jasper's letter."

"Okay. Anything else?"

"Remember I mentioned Sunday evening I'd had an unpleasant experience with a young woman? Her name is Elizabeth Devlin." Kim paused to take a drink of water. When she'd set her glass down, she gave him a helpless look. "Where to begin?"

Mark left the ledge to sit beside her. "Why not from the beginning?"

Kim told him about the falling out between Bea Devlin and Dana, describing Dana's anger toward her former teacher. "And yet," she added, "unbeknownst to the Devlins, Dana saw to it they were awarded a stay in her condo in Kona."

"Why would your sister act altruistically toward the Devlins when she harbored so much resentment?"

"On a scale of one to ten, Dana's capacity for forgiveness would rate a minus one. But she's admitted to me her own actions were deplorable and bratty. And you know Dana. She can be impulsive. She can be generous." Kim paused. "Now the story gets a bit murky."

Mark listened intently as Kim outlined what had transpired between herself and Elizabeth Devlin.

When she stopped for more water, Mark said, "I'm curious why Elizabeth would ask if your husband and Dana were on good terms."

"Whatever her reasons, I didn't volunteer that Barry and my sister couldn't stand each other. The animosity was particularly strong on Dana's part. I don't think she ever used Barry's name in a sentence without including the word bastard."

Mark nodded. "Or worse. She told me she had an affair with Barry, and that he'd been heartless in the way he ended their relationship."

Kim sighed. "I can believe that. Barry could be cruel. And then even worse, Dana's husband at the time divorced her over Barry."

Mark hadn't known Dana was married when she was seeing Barry Williams, but he chose not to comment.

"One more tidbit, Mark." Kim gave him an impish grin. "I called you Mark instead of Dr. Hampton. It just came out."

"Is the sky falling?" He smiled. "Not a problem. So what's the tidbit?"

"As I mentioned, I challenged Elizabeth's claim that Dana was in Kona around the time of Frank Devlin's death. But then I decided to call Heidi McGowan, the manager of the units where Dana has her condo. She confirmed that Dana stopped by her office the day after Elizabeth's father died."

"But not on the day of his death?"

"I asked Heidi that same question. She was vague but said she thought Mrs. James had made some reference to driving by Kailua Condos the day before and seeing emergency vehicles."

Mark rubbed his forehead. "Have you talked to your sister about these discrepancies?"

"I've tried and tried to reach her. She's not answering her phone and not responding to my messages. What about you? I'm sure you've talked with her."

"We were together last evening." He hesitated before continuing, "The evening did not go well and no, I've not been able to reach your sister today."

Uh oh, Kim wondered, *what's going on?* Since he offered nothing further, she broke the silence. "Where do we go from here?"

"It's important to hear Dana's side of the story. Be patient. I'm sure she'll surface soon." His tone was confident in spite of the uncertainty he felt. Then the unease he'd experienced earlier was compounded by Kim's revelations about Dana.

"I feel better already" Kim said. "Talking about these concerns and getting your feedback has calmed me a lot. And believe me, I've been anything but calm.

"I could have gotten along just fine without a phone call from that damn Aussie. And Elizabeth! Just who does she think she is, prancing into the Galleria and turning my night of nights into a nightmare?"

She'd been animated as she vented her frustration. Now Kim turned pensive, biting down on her thumbnail. "I'm still not sure I did the right thing."

"By confiding in me?"

"Well," Kim said with a wry smile, "who better qualified than my therapist to hear me out?"

"Right. My suggestion is we keep what was said today strictly between us."

"Amen to that."

"But let's both see what we can find out from Dana."

As if by mutual agreement, they headed back inside.

At the door leading to the waiting room, Kim turned to him. "I can't tell you how glad I am Ted Connelly suggested I contact you."

"Was that the first you'd heard about me?"

"Yes, Ted gave me your card, along with his recommendation."

"So your sister hadn't proposed that you consult me when you were having problems with your husband? She didn't give you my card?"

"No. I suppose she wanted to keep you all to herself." Kim let herself out and, with her back to him, called out over her shoulder, "Good luck with Dana."

Mark stood alone in his office. The talk with Kim on the terrace had taken up most of his lunch hour. He glanced at the wall clock. Fifteen minutes until his next patient.

Back at his desk, Mark reached for his phone.

As Kim walked to her car, she experienced a sudden queasiness and became aware tears were forming in her eyes. It wasn't nice to rat on her sister. And yet, she couldn't bury her head in the sand forever. At least she'd confided in a man whose integrity and trust could not be compromised. Besides, what's done was done.

Now, at her car, Kim looked across the parking lot, zeroing in on the building that housed Mark's office.

Office was such a cold word. She pictured the room with its gentle color tones where she poured out her heart, the now familiar painting that ignited her imagination, the small terrace that nevertheless opened up to the world, blunting despair with brightness. And the strongest image: A man who genuinely cared.

As pleased as she was with her progress, surely she required more counseling.

She smiled. Why rush the process?

Kim had taken the day off from the Galleria, figuring she might be courting an emotional meltdown. Instead, her load had lightened, bringing on an escalation in mood, a quickness in her step.

In no way was she ready to return home. First, a stop for lunch, and then she'd hit the late summer sales—but not in Pasadena. The Wilshire district beckoned, with its upscale department stores where she'd stick to sale items. Or maybe not.

In the parking garage, Kim was storing her purchases in the trunk of her car, when it occurred to her she could leave her car and walk the several blocks to Dana's place. If she were out, so be it. At least she'd made the effort to talk to her sister.

In the lobby of the Wilshire Marquis building, Kim paused to gather her thoughts. Jasper's alleged infamous phone conversation with Dana needed clarification. But she thought she'd skip the controversy over who started the divorce proceedings. If Jasper had been telling the truth, then Dana could have lied to save face.

The Kona issue was more troubling. She hoped her sister might provide a reasonable explanation for her presence at the condos. And if her probing antagonized Dana, too bad. They'd survived past skirmishes.

Enough speculation. Time for action, Kim decided as she moved toward the elevator. The doors had opened, and people spilled out into the lobby, among them was a man who commanded her attention. His movements furtive, he walked swiftly, head lowered, shoulders hunched, as if trying to render himself invisible.

Now several feet away, the man continued on his way, looking neither right nor left. But Kim was able to get a good look at him.

It was Ted Connelly, and he might as well have been wearing the scarlet letter A on the back of his jacket.

Chapter Eighteen

The knock on her door was tentative. Dana drew her robe in more tightly to her body. Ted, returning for one more drawn out goodbye? She waited. Maybe he'd go away. The knock came again, more forceful. *Oh shit, what now?*

She arranged her lips into a half smile, lowered her lids to display her practiced bedroom eyes, and then opened the door halfway.

"Kim! What are you doing here?"

"Surprise! Just happened to be in the neighborhood. Have you checked out the summer sales at Bullocks and I. Magnin?"

Dana brushed a lock of hair back from her forehead. "This is not a good time."

"I don't know why not. Your company has left. And besides, since you're not answering my phone calls, how else can I get to talk to you?"

Dana had to step back as Kim barreled her way inside. Okay, she'd play it cool. Assuming an expression of forbearance, she said, "I guess it would be gauche to call security on my own sister. So. Sit wherever you like, and I'll join you after I grab a Coke. Anything for you? No? Be back in a sec."

When Dana returned from the kitchen, she observed that Kim had chosen the same seat where they'd chatted about Kim's deteriorating relationship with Barry. So much had occurred since. But this was no time to philosophize. She'd set the tone, act conciliatory.

"I'm sorry I haven't returned your calls," Dana said after taking a sip of Coke. "Too much going on with work, with lawyers, and with my social life."

"Especially your social life?"

"Why that smirk?"

"I was in the lobby when Ted Connelly got off the elevator and was making his way out of the building. He looked like a kid who'd been caught stealing change out of a tip jar."

"Ted Connelly, huh? I wonder what he's up to. Do you suppose he's sneaking around behind Susan's back?"

"Why don't you tell me?"

"How would I know?"

"Come off it, Dana."

"If Ted's fooling around, it would serve Susan right. Knock her off her supercilious perch." She raised her glass and drank deeply. "Okay," she said when she'd set down her glass, "stop rolling your eyes and tell me why you're here."

"It appears I'm not the only one having trouble reaching you."

"Oh?" Surely Kim couldn't know she'd ignored Mark's calls as well.

"Jasper called me from Sydney. He says you won't talk to him."

"Why would I have anything to say to that jerk?"

"Apparently, he needs to reach you, regarding some personal issues. Also, he expects to arrive in L.A. in late August or early September to close out his business. He wants to see you."

"Do tell."

"I said it was no surprise to me that you refused to talk to him after what he pulled, getting drunk and spewing out filth over the phone when you called him from Honolulu. But he denies that ever happened. And he was adamant, Dana."

"I'll tell you what happened. He blacked out or passed out and consequently has no memory of my call."

"Really? I can't picture Jasper as a heavy drinker."

"Ooh, yes. He had his moments."

"At any rate, I agreed to talk to you on his behalf."

"All right. You've done your duty. Thank you for stopping by."

"Dana, for heaven's sake."

"Sorry. I know that sounded rude. I just think we could plan a better time for a chat."

"True. But I want to bring up one more thing. Then I'll leave. At the time you planned to go to Australia to confront Jasper, you got only as far as Honolulu. By any chance, did you take a side trip to Kona?"

"No. Why would I?"

"Do you remember Elizabeth Devlin, Bea and Frank's daughter?"

"Vaguely."

"Elizabeth came to see me. She brought up the fact that my husband and I, followed by her parents, stayed in your condo where, in both instances, a death occurred. Did you know her father died of anaphylactic shock?"

"Heidi McGowan informed me of Frank's death."

"According to Elizabeth, Heidi told her that you, the condo owner, had stopped by her office the day after her father's death."

"Who is this Elizabeth? Some kind of oracle? She tells you mice eat pigs, and you believe her?"

"I told myself Elizabeth was a troublemaker–and, in fact, she is a bit odd. Anyway, I called Heidi to back up my trouble maker theory, but she confirmed Elizabeth's version that you did, indeed, stop by her office the day after Frank's death. Furthermore, she thought you might have been in the neighborhood on the day he died."

"My God, you sound like a prosecuting attorney beating the hell out of a witness. All right." She sighed. "I'll come clean. I was in Kona briefly to check on a property I acquired for investment purposes. It's a scenic location not far from the condos at the end of Alii Drive.

"Jasper is not in on this deal, Kim. He doesn't know I have the deed to this property, and I don't want him to know about any of this. Understand?"

Kim's nod, her wide eyed expression conveyed her acceptance of Dana's story. She drew a line across her mouth. "My lips are sealed. I understand now why you didn't admit to being in Kona. And besides, what you're up to is none of my business." She stood. "Sorry if I came across like an interrogator."

"I still don't understand why Elizabeth Devlin would make an issue of my being in Kona."

"She says the events leading up to her father's death are confusing, and that she isn't satisfied with the explanations she's received."

"But why me?"

"Two deaths occurred at the condo you own. Maybe she's toying with some wild theory that you've placed a jinx on that unit."

"Just another nut case, eh?" Dana accompanied her sister to the door. "I promise I'll call soon. We'll set a date to go to lunch."

"I hope you mean that. But I'll leave it to you to name the day and time because you're the one with a busy social life."

A dig? Dana couldn't be sure. Coming from Kim, the remark might be perfectly innocent.

Kim opened the door, only to pause. "How could I have forgotten? This may come as a surprise, but Jasper said he hadn't ruled out the idea of a reconciliation."

Before she could respond, Kim was out the door and out of sight.

Eyes widened, mouth agape, Dana felt paralyzed.

She forced herself to move, but her motions were robotic as she locked her door and then returned to where she'd been sitting with Kim. She stared into her half-finished Coke.

"Cripes," she muttered, "what next?"

Susan had spent a good part of the day charting essentials for their upcoming trip. She'd designated five major categories: 1) wardrobe, which also included make-up, jewelry, shoes and bags; 2) toiletries; 3) conference materials; 4) travel paraphernalia; and 5) must-dos, such as stop mail and newspapers.

As she'd remarked to Ted this evening at dinner, making lists was the way to insure all bases were covered. Wasn't he fortunate to have a wife who was so well organized? She stated this good naturedly, giving him a little poke, but Ted had mumbled something regarding procrastination in response and had not returned her smile.

Now as Susan toiled in her bedroom closet, using a mix and match method to select her wardrobe for Hawaii, it occurred to her that Ted's response to her joshing hadn't made any sense; plus, he'd seemed distracted and fidgety.

It could just be a work-related problem, she decided, her mind already flitting from clothes to accessories.

The ivory jewelry chest with its filigree markings made an elegant centerpiece for her dresser. Double doors with curved gold handles opened to reveal pull-out drawers of earrings, pendants, bracelets and broaches. Not that she wore much jewelry, but good God, look at what she'd accumulated over the years.

The top compartment was reserved for her rings. They nestled side by side, indented in velvet lined rows. Ted, always generous with his gifts for special occasions, favored jewelry. She held up a ring Ted had given her for her last birthday, remembering that Caitlin had oohed and awed over the fiery splendor of opals.

Her own response had not been as enthusiastic. Wasn't it bad luck to wear an opal unless it was your birthstone? Still, she could have been more gracious. The ring was pretty, with double gems that spiraled out of a gold setting. Pretty, but not right for Hawaii.

She wondered what was appropriate but while gazing at her array of rings, her focus suddenly shifted. She shut the lid to the compartment. If she were a dog, she thought wryly, her ears would have perked up and her body would be quivering, on alert. Something had aroused in her a state of wariness: silence, a pervasive silence. No authoritative voice pontificated from the TV; no jazzy or bluesy music throbbed through cracks in the closed door of the den. Nothing ticked, jangled, or clattered; no one coughed, sneezed or even moved.

The house had shut down. Or was it Ted who had shut down? *Dear God*, she worried, *what if he had a heart attack or a stroke?*

She dashed from their bedroom into the hallway. "Ted?" she called out. With no response, she wondered if he might be downstairs, but decided to check out the den at the end of the hall.

The door was open; the room was dark. From the hall light, she could make out her husband, seated at his desk. He wasn't slumped over, *thank God*, but why would he be siting like a statue in the dark?

"Ted? What's going on? Are you all right?"

She heard him breathe in heavily. "I'm—I'm okay. Maybe you could turn on the light?"

"Well, for heaven's sake, you scared me." Under the overhead light his complexion appeared pasty, his eyes watery. "You don't look so good. Do you think you're coming down with something?"

He gestured toward the couch. "Why don't you sit down so we can talk."

As Susan did so, the word "ominous" flashed through her mind.

Wherever this was going, she envisioned a bumpy road ahead.

"I said I was okay because I didn't want to alarm you, but the truth is I'm not feeling one hundred percent, so yes, I may be coming down with something."

"Wouldn't you know it. And here we are just days before the trip."

"I think you should go to Hawaii without me, Susan. The way I feel now, I'd be a drag. I realize we'd be missing Kona, but I promise I'll make it up to you."

"Ted, you don't know you're catching something. You may be having an off day." She tried to tame her frustration, but she could hear the reproach in her tone. And there he sat with this impassive expression. Damn him, anyway.

"Is this your way of trying to get out of attending the conference?" Her breathing was becoming shallow. She had to push herself off the couch to stand. "Because if you're pulling some kind of stunt, Ted, I'll never forgive you."

She carried with her his stricken look as she left the room, conscious now of the wetness on her cheeks, of a mewling sound in the back of her throat that would strengthen into sobs. If only she could catch her breath.

Ted shook off his sluggishness to turn on his desk lamp and douse the overhead light that grayed the room. Maybe Susan was right; maybe he should rid himself of the furniture and carpeting that puddled in drab browns. He could also replace the bland, no color drapes with material that brightened his surroundings.

Susan. The list maker. Well, he could compose a list too–a list that characterized Ted Connelly as: 1) a louse, 2) a cheat, 3) an adulterer and, 4) God help him, a man in love.

God only knew he didn't want to hurt Susan or his daughter, but he was so damned torn between his obligations to his family and his obsession with Dana.

And he was ashamed. Pretending to be ill was a cop out, the coward's way out. This dilemma–no, make that calamity of his own making, screamed for resolution.

Once again, he breathed deeply. Okay. He would go to Hawaii and play out the scenario he and Dana had discussed. He would be supportive of Susan in Honolulu, be a willing participant in conference-related activities, and join in the social scene. He owed Susan that much. And in Kona?

He could only pray he make the right decision.

Mark's evening had turned out to be much better than his day. The poker group he met with once a month had provided distraction from his troubling thoughts about Dana. He even managed to come out a winner at a hundred bucks ahead.

Now at home and settled in his den, Mark picked up the mystery novel he'd started a week ago. The action, suspense and over-the-top characters suited his mood. He'd save soul searching, provocative literary gems for another time.

After ten minutes, he set the book aside. The mystery genre may have suited his mood, but superimposed over characters and dialogue were Dana's face, Dana's voice.

He reached for pen and pad, following the advice he often gave patients about the efficacy of writing down one's concerns.

Now it was his turn. And where would he begin? With Dana, of course.

1) Dana had not returned his calls. Solution? Wait it out, don't call her. As a last resort, see her, insist they talk.

2) What kind of talk? Continue to string her along? Commit to a permanent relationship? With marriage? Without marriage?

3) Dana's lies: Why would she lie about giving her card to Kim? Because she considered her sister a potential romantic threat? No. Because consciously or subconsciously she derived satisfaction over Kim's failing marriage? Maybe.

Why would she lie about who started the divorce proceedings? A self-esteem issue?

Was she or was she not in Kona? A most troubling question.

4) Consider Dana's intense anger over rejection or acts of betrayal:

a. Barry

b. Susan

c. the Devlins

d. Mark?

Mark reviewed what he had written. Unfortunately, he hadn't experienced any flashes of insight. So, he would allow his subconscious to mull over these questions. Maybe in the morning he would awaken to the answers.

In the meantime, it behooved him to check his reference books on deviant behavior. Something grabbed at him, gnawed at him, regarding Dana's behavior.

A part of him wanted to suppress these intuitive signals that set off alarms. But then the clinician in him could not resist a probe into the dark side of Dana James.

Mark fell asleep almost instantly, but then awoke in the wee hours. Time dragged on, but eventually he fell back to sleep, only to dream of Dana.

In his dream he had crossed her threshold into a candle lit labyrinth of pathways and passages that transported him to a grand ballroom. The walls, swathed in creamy silk draperies, took on shimmering rainbow colors, the reflections from a rotating chandelier.

The woman who hailed him from a distance wore a mint green hostess gown, deeply cut in the bodice, with long sheer flowing sleeves.

He'd admired the dress from a time before, but there was something different. This woman was veiled and as she floated toward him, she reached out, her movements seductive, yet playful. She beckoned, and then gestured for him to remove her face and head covering.

Green eyes dazzled him; pink lips that curved into a smile invited passion. But her hair in the pale light could not be mistaken for black.

The woman who smiled up at him was Kim.

Chapter Nineteen

After Elizabeth talked with Robert Chang, she called her mother.

"Thanks for getting back to me," Bea said. "Something has come up that I'd like to discuss with you."

"Sure." Her mother's upbeat tone had tweaked Elizabeth's curiosity. "Better yet, why don't I drop by? I'd like your input on a certain matter."

"Only if you'll stay for dinner. Does artichoke chicken casserole with rice pilaf sound tempting?"

"Who could resist? I'll whip up a salad and bring a bottle of Chardonnay."

"Sounds like a party," Bea said. "But why not? Today I'm in the mood to soak up a bit of sunshine."

And so am I, Elizabeth said to herself. *So am I!*

Elizabeth and Bea sat side by side on the patio, in the glow of the 6 p.m. August sun that hinted at fall's approach.

Elizabeth filled their wine glasses while the casserole warmed in the oven. "Okay," she said, raising her glass, "who goes first?"

"Age before beauty?"

"Yeah, sure," Elizabeth countered, though she couldn't help but smile.

"You remember Dr. Hutchins, the oncologist who diagnosed my condition?"

"Yes. You two had established a rapport." She shrugged. "At least in the beginning."

"I had all but decided to let nature take its course, when Dr. Hutchins called. That was yesterday. I saw him this morning."

"And?" Elizabeth prodded, responding to a gleam in her mother's eyes.

"There's an experimental drug Trycol—something or other. I have it written down. Anyway, I'm told this drug is effective in shrinking breast cancer tumors. And with few side effects. It's still being tested, but the results have been quite promising for patients in advanced stages of the disease.

"Dr. Hutchins wants me to join the clinical trial group; in fact, he sounded," she placed her hand over her heart, "cautiously optimistic."

"Mom, that's wonderful. Go for it!"

After another toast and more questions from Elizabeth, Bea raised her hand. "Enough about me. Age has spoken; now it's time for beauty."

Elizabeth gave her mother a sidelong glance. "If you say so." She paused, uncertain how to begin. Finally, she said, "I'm wondering how you're going to take this."

Bea's smile folded into a grimace. "I promise I won't snap at you. Fire away."

"I'm sure you remember Robert Chang, the detective who interviewed us after Dad's death?"

"Of course."

"Before we left Kona, I made a follow-up visit to his office, and we—well, we seemed to hit it off. When I'd finished my business with him, Detective Chang told me he'd be making a trip to California and kind of indicated we might get together.

"This afternoon he called me from San Francisco. He has relatives there–I think he said an aunt and uncle. But he leaves in two days to come to Los Angeles on business. We plan to have dinner together."

Bea gazed at her wide eyed. "I don't know what to say."

"You don't approve?"

"I certainly don't disapprove. I just never pictured you and Detective Chang as a couple."

"Mom, it's a dinner date. Period."

"Ah, but I can tell how pleased you are. Which makes me pleased, too."

"Good. Now don't get uptight, but in Kona I shared my concerns with him regarding the events that preceded Dad's death. I had to bring Dana into the picture."

She held her breath, expecting an outburst, but Bea merely frowned.

Keeping her tone even, Elizabeth continued, "I'm not going to ruin our evening by bringing up matters that are disturbing to you, but I have my suspicions over you and Dad winning the Grand Prize in the silent auction at the Elks."

Bea's frown deepened. "Whatever can you mean?"

"I don't want to delve into my reasons now, but I sense Dana's hand was in in the pot. Here's how you can help. Do you recall who was in charge of the silent auction at the Elks?"

"Probably Bill Matthews. Stuart Simmons—he's the head honcho—would know for sure."

"I met Mr. Simmons at Dad's service. A very nice man, by the way. I'd like to meet with him or Bill Mathews."

"Elizabeth, I don't like where this is headed, but I will call Stuart and explain you'd like very much to talk to him or Bill."

"As soon as possible? Please? Maybe tomorrow?"

Bea sighed. "I'll try, my dear, I'll certainly try."

Once again Elizabeth gave her mother a hug. "You're the best." Then she stood. "I'm going to pour us a little more wine."

When Elizabeth returned from the kitchen, she said, "I guess you'll be talking to Diane tomorrow?"

"We're having lunch. I thought I'd save my news 'til then."

"Be sure to give her my love." Elizabeth took a sip of wine. "And mom? Don't say anything to Diane about my, uh dinner date?"

Bea raised her glass as to a fellow conspirator. "Our secret. Of course, I expect a full report."

***

Elizabeth saw herself as a mirror image of her mother who, at least by her father's standards, was considered a pretty woman. Stunning or striking were qualities Elizabeth coveted, yet had long since conceded were not in the cards for her. Wishy-washy prettiness had to suffice–with a little outside help.

For her dinner date, a haircut along with highlights, and the application of foundation, blush and subtle eye make-up combined to forge a more sturdy prettiness. She'd decided to wear the blue-green top she'd worn for the Art Walk, one of her more colorful wardrobe pieces.

Elizabeth grabbed her bag and car keys–she and Robert planned to meet at the restaurant–only to return to her mirror for a final critical appraisal, and to spray Summer Dew cologne over her neck and wrists. She rubbed her forehead in a futile attempt to erase frown lines, but then stopped herself.

Damn it, she looked good. Settle down, she told herself. Besides, in no way could she picture Robert Chang primping in front of his mirror.

The thought stayed with her as she left the house, followed by giggles as she drove to the restaurant over the absurdity of the solemn detective trimming his eyebrows or struggling over his hair.

The Flying Tiger, a popular restaurant located in Costa Mesa just outside of Tustin, offered continental cuisine at reasonable prices. At least for Orange County. Along with price, the food and atmosphere rated an A+. Elizabeth had dined there only once, but remembered the hush-hush elegance of cozy lamp-lighted tables, the comforting crackle of a wood burning fireplace, along with Flying Tiger memorabilia that included framed photos of daring pilots from the 30s and 40s.

Opting for self parking over valet service, the walk to the restaurant provided Elizabeth with a time-out to get the circulation going and to establish a mindset: No matter how the date part evolved (terrific, trying, terrible), she would enjoy the posh atmosphere and excellent food.

When Elizabeth entered the restaurant's lobby, she immediately spotted Robert Chang. He stood in profile to her, studying an elaborate sculpture of an aircraft from the early 40s. Tall, slender, and well groomed, his jacket and open-collar shirt exemplified smart casual.

He turned as she approached and she froze. The man who had interviewed her mother and herself, who had invited her into his office, stood before her, his face devoid of expression.

Her smile faded, and she mouthed a "hi."

But then the detective's face lit up in recognition. He came forward, seemingly eager to greet her.

After they were seated and the waiter had taken their drink order, Chang said, "You look very nice."

"Thank you. So do you."

They stared at each other for a moment, and then Elizabeth made a sound halfway between a cough and a chuckle. "Whatever we expected or feared," she said, "I think we've both passed muster."

His broad smile signaled agreement. And when they both started talking at once, their laughter dispelled the awkwardness of the moment.

Though small talk prevailed during cocktails, when dinner was served, Elizabeth brought up the subject of her investigation into what she wryly called Elksgate. "I was able to meet with the grand pooh-bah, who, in turn, put me in touch with Bill Matthews, the man in charge of the silent auction."

"The award that resulted in your parents staying in the Kailua Condo."

"Yes. And Robert, it was all a set up. Bill Matthews at first denied any wrongdoing, but when I described Dana to him, he avoided eye contact, and I swear I detected beads of sweat on his forehead.

"To make a long story short, I stressed the importance of getting at the truth for my father's sake and added that any information he gave me would remain between us."

She paused. "Well, I lied, but at least he fessed up that he made an error in judgment, that yes, he had manipulated the outcome so that the grand prize would be awarded to my parents. In turn, the group had received a sizable donation from the woman I described."

"I take it she neglected to give him her name, and that she paid him cash?"

"Right. Matthews looked so miserable, I underscored that he'd fallen victim to this woman's charms and that I understood he'd accepted the donation for the good of the group.

"I left him with the thought that he might want to discuss the source of the donation with the head guy. Or not."

"Let his conscience dictate the way?"

"Something like that."

Chang's smiling approval—and dare she add admiration?—encouraged her to up the ante.

"Also, I followed through on a hunch and arranged to meet with Dana's, ex-husband, Kyle Sterling."

She explained how she had posed as an investigator for a fictional attorney supposedly involved in a lawsuit against Dana. Her story generated raised eyebrows and a mischievous glint in Chang's eyes that gave way to a more thoughtful expression as she described Dana's affair with Barry Williams, which resulted in her being dumped by her husband and her lover at the same time. She added that Sterling had characterized Dana as a woman with a penchant for revenge.

With dinner now finished, they relaxed over coffee, neither having saved room for dessert.

"What can I say?" Chang asked, "except that you would make an outstanding addition to my staff. You're smart, intuitive and persevering. The offer stands."

Elizabeth felt her cheeks flame. "I think you're serious."

"Damn straight I am."

Elizabeth stared into her coffee. "I wasn't planning on a career change." She looked up. "But never say never. Right?"

He nodded and then broke the silence. "It turns out, I'll be staying here longer than I had anticipated. A couple of cases we're working on in Kona have a Los Angeles connection. At any rate, I wonder if I might see you again."

And again and again, Elizabeth thought. But she responded, "I'd like that very much."

"Good." He placed his hand over hers. "Thank you for taking the time and effort to talk to the person in charge of the silent auction; it saved me some leg work. In addition, your comments regarding Mrs. James, her ex-husband, and her lover were most edifying. Especially since we've decided to exhume Barry Williams' body."

He winked. "Details forthcoming. Say, tomorrow evening at dinner?"

Susan had labored over every detail of the syllabus she'd prepared for her chapter's use in Hawaii. She'd prided herself on being exact, down to the last dotted I and crossed T.

She'd anticipated questions involving policy, budget, protocol, fund-raising, committee needs, etc. Not that dummies existed in their group—well, she could name a few— but spelling everything out precluded endless discussions and tiresome treks into the chapter's bylaws.

And if some idiot strenuously objected to her blueprint to promote Republican values? Let that individual take up the task. For Susan, preparation had paid off; her presentation at the conference was acclaimed by all Patriot Chapters as a towering contribution.

Now in the late afternoon on the last day of meetings, Susan took advantage of her lanai, lounging in this perfumed and sultry setting with an undertone of sex-in-the-afternoon. Too bad her husband wasn't around to take part.

Ted had said he'd be out for an hour or so to explore more of Waikiki before they left for Kona. "Or so" had prevailed—he'd been gone almost two hours.

She sat more erect, determined to inhale the scent of hibiscus and plumeria that trailed from their balcony, determined as well, to allow the sweet ocean breezes to temper her annoyance.

She slumped back in the chair. Dammit, why wasn't he back? Waikiki consisted mainly of shopping centers and resort hotels. What could be so fascinating? Ted had also played hooky from the post-lunch session where nominations for the new board were announced to the membership.

Susan fanned herself. So much for the trade winds and their so-called moderating influence. Humidity might be good for the complexion, but hot and sticky would not cut it for tonight's luau.

Still fanning herself, Susan stepped inside just as Ted walked into the suite. "I'm sorry," he raised both hands, "I'm sorry. Time got away from me."

Forcing a smile, Susan said, "You'll have to share your adventures with me."

"Not a lot to tell, but we'd better wait until later. I need to shower."

She looked at her watch. "Don't forget the luau starts at six. Oh, and Ted, guess what? At the meeting you missed I was nominated, unchallenged, I might add, for president of our chapter."

"Oh? Well, congratulations. You've earned that position."

Could he stretch his mouth into a real smile? Relax his drill inspection posture? "I suppose you think that taking office will impose a hardship on our family life."

"Being president of an organization can turn out to be a full time job." He paused, as if absorbing the import of his comment, then, for whatever reasons, broke into a smile. "Honey, I'm glad for you. You'll make a fabulous president."

His step was jaunty as he reached for her, gave her a hug and a kiss on the cheek before backing away. "Off to the showers," he said, still wearing that goofy smile.

Susan stood in place, transfixed by the hug and kiss. What was with the mood changes? Who was this man she was married to? She thought a moment and then groaned. Midlife crisis was such a cliché anymore.

She shrugged. Maybe it was hormones, high jinks, hot air—whatever. She'd take the good with the bad.

The luau, held on hotel acreage overlooking the ocean, had turned out to be a blast, in Susan's opinion. People relaxed, Mai-Tais flowed, and lines moved quickly through the buffet that featured the highly touted Imu, a pork dish.

Susan wasn't sure she approved of the fiery tomb of red hot rocks for the poor pig. Wrapped in green leaves and covered with dirt, the thing had been roasting for hours. Whatever her misgivings, she was not about to deny herself pieces of pulled pork that melted in her mouth.

Teriyaki steak, chicken, rice, and rainbow colored fruits also highlighted the feast. Both Susan and Ted passed on the poi.

Later when the sun, a blazing red orb, met the ocean, the romance and history of the island came alive through song and dance, a mellow pastiche to distill the excesses of food and drink.

Ted had mellowed, too, shifting from neutral onlooker to becoming fully engaged in all aspects of the luau. Most satisfying for Susan, was that it felt as if they'd stepped back in time and Ted was once again an affectionate, loving husband.

The entertainment began to heat up, moving from graceful, swaying interpretive hand movements accompanied by Hawaiian melodies, to Tahitian style dancing. The dancers hips moved faster and more provocatively as warriors joined the stage, trouncing the enemy to the beat of drums. Sword play and fire-eating were enhanced by drum rolls from the bandstand.

The performance dazzled Susan, but still, her focus was on Ted.

Halfway through the performance, Ted had slipped his arm around her. As she nestled in close to him, it occurred to Susan that they were interacting like a happily married couple. In their case, this was a big deal.

Susan rested her hand on Ted's knee. *Her man. Her love.*

She could hardly wait for Kona.

Chapter Twenty

Susan breathed in the moist sea air and stared at the ocean as waves billowed into grandiose formations, a rampaging force that called for mastery or surrender by intrepid surfers.

At home Susan dismissed surfer mentality as part of California's subculture. But in Kona, she could stretch her perception of the sport to dignify surfing as a noble pursuit.

"Simply gorgeous," she said to Ted. "Not only is the condo lovely, but the location is perfect. I'm so glad we came to Kona."

"I'm glad you're glad."

She stiffened. Lips pressed together, Susan stifled a sarcastic comeback along the lines of thanking him for his insightful response. Oh, well, Ted was not wired to exude enthusiasm.

They sat on their lanai, each with a glass of Merlot. She raised her glass. "A nice way to unwind, wouldn't you say? Before we unpack, that is."

"Absolutely." He gazed down at the surf breaking on the rocks, then leaned back in his chair, face raised to the mid afternoon sun.

"Ted." She tapped his arm. "I want you to know I've done my research."

He raised his eyebrows. "Another list?"

"A fun list for a change. Now listen up. Daytime we'll want to drive out to the volcano. I'd like to see Hilo, as well, or if that's too far, we can explore the northernmost point of the island. Also someone at the conference suggested we sign up for the submarine tour. What have I missed? Oh. Buying you a snazzy Hawaiian shirt at Hilo Hattie's."

"Snazzy as in tacky?"

She frowned as he suppressed a smile.

"And for the evening, of course," she continued, "the sunset cocktail cruise sounds romantic. And where do we even begin with all the waterfront restaurants? Maybe," she gave him a knowing look, "we can find another luau?" She paused. "You don't look happy."

"You've laid out an itinerary we might possibly cover in a week. We're here three nights, Susan. Three nights only."

"Then I suggest we get started." She gulped down the remainder of her wine. "But first I want to get a feel for our unit, maybe check storage space before we unpack. Next I'll make a list of grocery items—mostly breakfast stuff and snacks."

He saluted her with his drink. "It's a good thing one of us is organized. Okay if I join you in a minute or two?"

"Take your time." She blew him a kiss before opening the sliding glass doors to enter the living room.

When they had arrived, she'd made a cursory appraisal of the layout of the unit. The bedroom was a bit small for her taste, but the living room and its furnishings exemplified casual elegance, the side walls of glass providing an openness that she could equate with expansion in her airwaves, allowing her to breathe.

Less impressive, though adequate, was the design of the dining area with its round wood-carved table and matching green-cushioned straight-backed chairs. But the handsome credenza that stretched along most of the wall was quite impressive.

She decided to peek inside and see what the contents might reveal about the condo's owner. She guessed she'd find silver serving pieces, maybe fine china and linens or photograph albums. On the other hand, wouldn't it be a hoot if the owner collected spider specimens or magazines with naughty pictures.

"Only one way to find out," she murmured as she approached for a closer look, only to be distracted by the set piece that filled the space above and on top of the credenza. Her eyes were still adjusting from the outside brightness to the dim interior, but she could see that someone's portrait or photograph provided the centerpiece for a lavish decorative arrangement.

Lavish, as in garish, Susan thought, wrinkling her nose. She stepped in close to view the portrait, gasped, and then backed away as if warding off a blow. *Dana*? Had the wine distorted her vision?

No, her eyes weren't tricking her; the face staring out from the portrait belonged to trash—or by any other name, Dana James. The sour taste of regurgitated wine burned the back of her throat. She swallowed hard, her eyes tearing.

"Well, I'll be damned."

Startled, Susan turned. Her husband stood a few feet away, looking puzzled.

"What in the hell is going on?" She yelled.

"Susan, calm down." Ted held his arms stiffly at his sides, rebuke governing his posture.

"Calm down? How can I calm down when something stinks to high heaven?"

He took her by the arm. "Come on, Susan, let's sit down."

He led her to the sofa where she sat at one end, he at the other.

Susan spoke at the picture that claimed the far wall. "So this is the client who so generously provided you with a Kona get away?"

"It could have been anyone."

"But the owner just happened to be Dana. Why, Ted? Why would she offer her condo?"

"Dana knew we were going to Hawaii. Call it an expansive gesture on her part."

"Because she adores me? Crap. That bitch had an ulterior motive."

"Like what, for God's sake?"

"Well, this place is pretty spiffy. If you ask me, Dana's showing off. 'Wow! See how I've come up in the world.' She's always been jealous of me, of our lifestyle. So now she's strutting her stuff."

"So what?" Ted got up and began to pace. "You like this place, right? And if it weren't for Dana's picture, you'd never be the wiser. I purposely didn't let on who the client was because I knew you'd nix the idea."

"Damn right."

Ted now stood before her, his tall frame hunched, but an imposing presence as he glared down at her. "We don't have to stay. We can change our tickets tomorrow and fly home. It's your call, Susan."

"Why are you so angry? You know I detest that woman."

He raised his arms in a gesture of frustration, turned from her, then walked to the doors leading to the lanai and stared out at the ocean.

Susan wiped away tears. *How can he be so callous? Can't he show some compassion?*

She cupped her chin in the palm of her hand and peered through squinted eyes at her husband's back. Here they were, two hapless beings frozen in an Arctic silence, while that bitch was at home laughing at the way things would play out between them.

Susan crossed her arms over her chest in defiance of her nemesis. She visualized Dana engaged in a forum with herself: *Let's make Susan squirm, push her into a knockdown, drag out with her husband. Ruin every minute of her stay. And how do we accomplish our mission? Easy. By my presence. My portrait will serve as a constant reminder of how we compare as women.*

Susan lowered her arms, hands now balled into fists at her sides. *You want to know how we compare as women?* she asked as if really responding to Dana. *What I might lack in the glamour department, I make up in class, lady.*

She sat straighter. It was just a picture, for heaven's sake. And a picture couldn't wine and dine with Ted or make love to him. Where was it written that Dana held the power to wreck her stay in Kona?

"Ted?" When he turned from the window, Susan assumed her expression conveyed remorse. "Would you come back so we can talk?"

He hesitated a beat, but then consented, "Sure."

As he drew near, she detected a wariness, but not anger.

Susan patted a place near her. When he was seated, she said, "Since you know how Dana and I feel about each other, surely you can understand she's taunting me, making certain her presence," she pointed to the dining room "will make me crazy."

"You don't know that for a fact." He spoke quietly, but reproach was etched in the deepening lines between his eyes, the tightening of his mouth.

"Ted, you're being naïve. That said," she raised her hands, "I admit I overreacted." She took his hand, "Can we pick up from where we left off on the lanai?"

"Let's do that."

Unpacking was the first item on Susan's agenda, so they retreated to the bedroom. As Ted began to unzip one of the suitcases,

Susan placed a hand on his arm. "Isn't it nice," she said, eyebrows arched, "that Dana has provided us this lovely king-sized bed?"

His answering smile was tentative, as if he wasn't sure how to interpret the reference to Dana, but Susan was certain Ted understood her underlying message–that tonight was designated for love.

Love making, as it turned out, was far from Susan's thoughts as she awoke from her dream, disoriented and breathing heavily in tempo with the beating of her heart. Relief came with the realization that she lay safe and warm in a comfortable bed next to her husband—safe and warm, in contrast to the cold and exhaustion she'd suffered in her dream. The images were still vivid as she retraced laboring in the ocean, waiting, watching, positioning her board to catch the next wave, only to be pulled under time and time again.

Generally, Susan enjoyed analyzing her dreams. But the concept of being engulfed by monster waves did not lend itself to cozy contemplation. And if her subconscious was sending her a message, she did not care to be on the receiving end. Not tonight.

Steering her thoughts onto a happier path, Susan reviewed the evening. Cocktails on the lanai had made for an intimate, relaxing interlude, followed by a short walk into town where they'd dined on the deck of a restaurant that jutted over the water.

Their meal, fresh seafood and steamed rice, served with tropical fruits and rum drinks invited lingering. By the time they returned to their unit, though, each felt the effects of the day's journey, the trials of settling in, and the three hour time difference.

If passion wasn't in the cards for tonight, Susan was grateful Ted had warmed up to her. Though she had initiated and guided their topics of conversation, her husband had been an attentive listener and, much to her pleasure, had complimented her on the new silk dress—red, of course—that she'd bought in Honolulu.

At least they could snuggle, she decided, as she turned toward him, only to make contact with bedding.

She figured he was in the bathroom, but when the red numerals of the clock on the end table advanced ten minutes, Susan reached for her robe. God forbid he was sick.

All was quiet and dark throughout the unit. She'd checked the bathroom and kitchen, logical starting places. No Ted. Nor was he in the living room. He had to be on the lanai, but she wondered—or worried—why he'd be out at this hour. And what if he wasn't out there?

Susan drew a shaky breath, not wanting to speculate as she moved to the glass doors. She let her breath out in a whoosh as she spotted Ted seated in the same chair where he'd taken in the sun, and later sipped a cocktail.

Outside, Susan stood back, not wanting to startle him. "Ted?" she called out, then realized he probably couldn't hear her over the sound of the surf.

She stepped away from the doors to view him in profile. She couldn't tell if he was staring at the ocean or into space, but he appeared deep in thought, his hands folded, resting on the table.

Briskly, she moved to stand behind him and placed her hands on his shoulders. He turned slowly and looked up at her as if his being there were nothing out of the ordinary.

She wished she could make out his expression. She wished he would say something. "Ted, are you all right?"

"Yes, of course." He stood. "Let's go inside."

In the living room, Susan turned on a lamp. She saw him more clearly now—he hadn't pulled on a robe or sweater over his pajamas. And in the dim light, his skin looked blotchy, his eyes sunken. "Couldn't sleep?" she asked.

He seemed not to have heard her.

"Ted?"

She peered at him in an attempt to assess his mental state. "Is—is something wrong?" When he failed to answer, her breathing accelerated. "Ted, talk to me. What in God's name is going on?"

"Don't be so dramatic, Susan." He cracked a smile. "I woke up and couldn't get back to sleep. So I decided to sit outside for a few minutes. Simple as that."

It certainly seemed like more than a few minutes to her. "If you're sure—"

"Honey, I'm fine." He took her hand. "Let's go back to bed and rest up for tomorrow. I'm assuming you've planned a full day for us?"

"You bet," she said, giving him a big smile.

Back in bed, Susan turned on her side, away from Ted. What she sought was a dreamless sleep, a sleep that she willed to come quickly to spare her the dreaded 4 a.m. willies.

The concept of warm and safe had weakened, giving way to a nameless foreboding.

Over breakfast on the lanai, they noted the wind had picked up and clouds had formed. "A little change, but nothing ominous," Ted said. "I'm rarin' to go. Wherever, whenever."

Susan offered a silent thank you to a higher power as her world turned suddenly brighter.

So, time to move forward. "Let's explore our own area first, Ted. Then we'll go from there and maybe we'll even drive out to the volcano."

"You're the boss."

He said this with a smile, but Susan wished he hadn't put so much emphasis on *boss*.

By the time they'd covered the village, visiting shops and checking out restaurants, they agreed a trip to the volcano was not an option because of the long drive.

"Maybe tomorrow?" Susan asked.

Ted looked up from his map and shrugged. "Why don't we play it by ear?"

Wondering at his lack of enthusiasm, she said, "We don't have to make that trip."

"What trip?"

"Ted, for heaven's sake."

"Sorry." He chuckled. "It's hard work, trying to fit everything in. But tell you what. Let's drive out to the northern tip of the island."

He looked once more at his map. "On the way, we can turn off to one of the ocean front resorts. Maybe we can have lunch poolside or on a terrace overlooking the ocean."

Susan was tempted to blurt out, "Finally, you're taking charge. And I love you for it." Instead she gave him a wifely smile of approval.

In accordance with their plan, they lunched poolside, ocean view included, against a backdrop of lush hotel landscaping.

Continuing on their way, Susan noted that while the scenery was so-so, the many rock formations, etched with people's names and inscriptions, along with hearts or mysterious engravings, spiked her interest. How would the names Susan and Ted appear? Perhaps not entwined with hearts. Yet.

Now as they headed back, having driven as far north as possible, clumps of gray clouds embroidered with black swatches hovered, darkening the landscape. "Reminds me of that crazy painting in your office," Susan said, immediately wishing she would have bitten her tongue. Ted did not comment. Either he didn't care to respond or hadn't heard her remark.

She hoped for the latter.

A moderate rain accompanied the better part of the trip home but had slacked off by the time they drove into their parking space. The wind, however, had not abated.

Susan shuddered as they entered the elevator. "With this weather, it's a blessing we didn't sign up for the cocktail cruise.

"But we still have tomorrow evening! As for tonight, let's drive south to that terraced restaurant I've been reading about."

When the elevator door opened, Ted made an after-you gesture. "Whatever you say," he said. "You're the boss."

Susan gritted her teeth as she walked ahead of him. What was with this boss business?

"A shame we can't use the lanai," Susan said to Ted as he carried their cocktails from the kitchen into the living room.

He paused a moment to check what was going on outside before joining Susan on the sofa, setting their drinks before them on the coffee table. "I'm surprised the weather hasn't cleared."

Susan eyed the deck. Drizzle, not rain, dampened the flooring and produced tiny drops, lined up in rows over the railings. "Paradise with an edge. Oh, well, cheers anyway." Susan clinked her glass against his, and then sipped her gin and tonic. "At least the day went well."

Silence. Susan observed her husband out of the corner of her eye as he reached for his scotch. How might she describe him? Somber? Detached? "Ted, since we've been back, you've been so quiet."

He set down his drink. "Maybe thoughtful is a better word. Something about the black clouds, the grayness fosters contemplation."

In the fading light, Susan found the outside ambiance dreary and depressing. "Kind of a downer, in my opinion." She thought for a moment. "On the other hand, the gloom does bring on reflection."

He turned to her. "How so?"

She'd captured his interest. She patted his hand. "I want you to know I've given a lot of thought about us, about our marriage. Somewhere along the line we began to drift apart. Wouldn't you agree?"

"I suppose so."

"I fault myself. I've taken you for granted in failing to appreciate how hard you've worked for Caitlin and me. I've put my own interests ahead of yours, and I know I can be impatient and demanding."

"And I've failed you!"

His vehemence took her aback. "What on earth do you mean?"

"I can't match your energy and dedication to a cause. More and more I see myself lacking in so many ways when it comes to making you happy."

"That's just not so. Besides, we've been doing so much better since we agreed to support each other's interests."

Ted stared down into the glass in his hand. "Did I ever tell you I'd like to learn to play the clarinet or saxophone?"

"No, but this doesn't come as a surprise. I know jazz is a big deal with you."

"Could you tolerate my learning to play a musical instrument?"

She shrugged. "I think sailing would take enough time away from your career and home life, without adding another hobby."

"How do you really feel about me taking up sailing?"

She sipped her drink. "Isn't this conversation becoming a little heavy?"

"Please answer my question."

"What's to discuss?" Susan's glass made a loud clunk on the

table. "You're going to buy a sailboat; you're going to learn how to sail. And I will support you. Now let's change the subject."

He hesitated, pinching his lips together. "I'm glad the conference went so well for you."

"For us, Ted. You're no mere footnote in the grand scheme of things."

"I wish with all my heart I could stand beside you and share your drive and passion for politics. I've tried; I can't do it."

"Because you've reserved your passion for that slut, Dana?"

"Why would you say that?"

"I don't know. But I'm not a stick of wood, Ted. I have feelings, and in my gut I know something isn't right.

"Also, I'm confused. One minute you're affectionate toward me, and the next minute you're distant or preoccupied. You're blowing hot and cold, which makes me wonder if you're harboring a crush on Dana."

She expected him to dismiss the idea, even express annoyance over her assertion, but Ted's skin had taken on a mottled look, akin to his early morning appearance. And now as he turned to her, his eyes mirrored the soulful gaze of their former pet dog when he'd misbehaved. "Some men can have it both ways. I can't."

"What are you talking about?"

"I love you, and I love our daughter. But I'm torn."

Susan felt heat spread from her neck upwards to her face as the room began to close in on her. Breathe, breathe, stay focused, she told herself. "Whatever is on your mind, Ted, you'd better spell it out."

"Oh, God, I hate this." Eyes closed, he pressed his fingers against his forehead, and once again turned to her. "I don't want to hurt you, but what I'm about to say involves Dana."

"I said, spell… it…out."

"All right. All right. Dana's office visits developed into more personal get-togethers. We—we developed a fondness for one another."

"And what did this fondness lead to?"

"We explored the possibility of a more permanent relationship. It occurred to me you might welcome the idea of gaining your freedom. Chances are you'd meet your soul mate, someone dynamic and charismatic whom you could relate to."

The closeness in the room was almost suffocating, but she wanted details. "Why did you bring me here?"

"Dana knew I was conflicted, and in all fairness to her, she thought our being here by ourselves would bring matters to a head. One way or another."

"Crap. That bitch knew her picture would set me off, that a daily reminder of her would tilt the board in her favor."

He bowed his head. "I confess I'm still torn."

"Oh, poor baby. How you must be suffering."

"This is not the time for sarcasm. Do you think we could talk this out in a civil manner?"

"Shut up. I'm asking the questions. While on your jaunts about Waikiki, did you call Dana?"

"Yes."

"One last question. Have you slept with Dana?"

His voice took on a hoarse edge. "We slept together once. One time only."

The room dimmed around Susan, but not because of the storm. She wanted Ted to disappear, for the words he had said to vanish. She could still make him out, his worried expression, a widening of his mouth, but she could only hear a buzzing in her head. She stood, Ted stood, his mouth continuing to open, close, change shape.

In a flash it came to her that she had to get to the kitchen. She moved swiftly, at a half run. The movement got her blood flowing again, restored her hearing and as she entered the kitchen, the noise of opening and slamming of drawers awakened her from her stupor.

She hadn't memorized the contents of the drawers, but knives were plentiful and looked sharp. She grabbed one with a black handle, larger than a steak knife but smaller than a butcher knife. In another drawer she found a mallet.

Carrying both knife and mallet, Susan shoved past Ted in the doorway and let out a high pitched giggle at his look of consternation.

At the credenza, she flailed at leaves and flowers, knocking them out of their vases which, with a swing of the mallet, plummeted to the floor, porcelain pieces now askew in a jagged maze of fake gold leaves and orchid flowers.

She heard her name, with God's word invoked, the voice harsh and dissonant. She felt hands grasping firmly at her shoulders. She turned, brandishing her knife and when her husband retreated in terror, she turned to the task at hand, using her knife and the mallet.

Shards of glass glistened on the floor like frozen rain desecrating spring florals. Dana's face, a mass of slashes, now ceased to exist, ripped of eyes, ears and mouth. Portrait backing, loosened but not cut away, hung like butchered skin.

This exertion had cost her. Breathing hard, clutching her tools of destruction, Susan stepped away from her handiwork to find Ted frozen in place, horror distorting his features.

He raised a hand. "Susan, please. Don't do something stupid. One of us has to be around for Caitlin."

Astounded by his inference, she started to laugh, but then had to stop as laughter broke into coughing, escalating into a choking fit.

When she was able to contain herself, she said, "I'm not a murderer, Ted. See?" The knife and mallet made a clatter on an uncarpeted portion of the floor. "Besides, life in prison would deprive me of finding my soul mate."

Her breathing was shallow, and she was sweating, but she had to continue. "Bastard that you are, I almost feel sorry for you. Because you've made a rotten choice, Ted. Dana will dump you, and when that happens—" She was wheezing, the tightness in her chest accompanied by a growing numbness in her legs. "When that happens don't think you can come back—come back to me," she said, her voice a mere whisper. "Bronchodilator," she gasped.

She could no longer stand nor could she coordinate her movements to use the inhaler. Ted kneeled at her side as she lay on the floor.

Ted was shouting at her. "Try, Susan, try. You know what to do. I've called 911, but you have to hang on." He held the inhaler to her nostrils. "Damn it, breathe in." He continued to carry on, but she couldn't help him or herself.

Wisps of light engaged in a battle with darkness and in that darkness she revisited her dream. Once again, seaborne, she grazed the crest of the wave, only to crash, sucked under into a suffocating pool of blackness.

Would she resurface? Probably not. Nor did she care, one way or the other.

Chapter Twenty-One

Heidi McGowan sat hunched in her chair, talking on the phone at her desk. Reaching down to her right foot, she massaged the little toe that she'd stubbed against the chair leg. The toe hurt like hell, and it was a struggle to maintain her composure.

"I know," she said into the phone, "you're only trying to get the facts. Believe me, I have the utmost respect for newspaper reporters. But all I can say is that a ruckus occurred in one of our units. Possibly a domestic dispute. The woman was alive when the ambulance arrived, but barely. I don't know if she survived or not. Call the hospital, for God's sake."

"Jesus," she muttered as she slammed down the phone. Then sensing a presence, she looked up. A woman stood back from Heidi's desk, her expression a mixture of interest and amusement. "Sorry for sounding off," Heidi said, "but calls have been coming in all morning over an—uh—incident that occurred last evening."

Heidi remembered to smile as she reached for the reservations book. Then she took another look at the woman. Amazingly, she resembled Beatrice Devlin, minus the glasses, with the same plump frame, round face and short gray hair. She was dressed in a tailored white blouse, tucked into charcoal gray pants. She wore no jewelry or accessories and carried a simple satchel.

"I take it you had some excitement last night," the woman said as she approached.

Heidi nodded, and then opened the reservations book. "How can I help you?"

"By allowing me to help you."

Eyes narrowed, Heidi leaned back in her chair and tilted her head to one side. "Go on."

The woman set down her satchel. "I have a business proposition for you. Could we talk over there?" She pointed to the sitting area with its love seat and chairs. "Or I could bring a chair to your desk."

Heidi stood. "I'd like you to state your name and your business."

"I work for the *Honolulu Tattler*."

"The tabloid?"

"Perhaps you recognize the name Charley Maddex?"

"I've read—" Heidi cleared her throat. "I mean, the name rings a bell."

"Only a bell? Sounds a bit vague. But we'll fix that. You see, I'm Charley Maddex; that is, I write under that byline."

Heidi sank into her chair, her jaw heading south. "You've got to be kidding. You? You're the one who dishes out the dirt?"

"None other." She smiled sweetly. "You can call me by my real name, Charlene."

Because of her tortured toe, Heidi decided sitting was preferable to standing. She thrust the upper part of her body forward, hoping to wilt the woman by the intensity of her gaze. "Well, Charlene, you can just toodle out of here. I want nothing to do with that rag you call a newspaper."

"You recall I used the words business proposition? That means we're talking money, honey. Excuse me while I fetch a chair."

Before Heidi could protest, Charlene was settled in at the side of the desk, close enough that Heidi could smell cigarette smoke from the woman's clothes and read determination in her steely blue eyes.

"We pay good money for a big story," Charlene said as she brought out a notebook from her satchel. "I'll tell you what I know. Three different parties occupied the same unit, one right after the other, and a death occurred among each party. Though from what you said on the phone, the latest victim may or may not be dead. At any rate, we've established a pattern."

"Since you have all the facts, what could you want from me?"

Charlene raised a finger. "In a minute." She opened her notebook. "Death number one took place in the swimming pool here under mysterious circumstances. The newspapers covered that incident. In death number two, the man croaked—sorry, sometimes Charley Maddex takes over—as a result of an allergic reaction to peanuts. Not much newspaper coverage on this one, but according to our research department, the death happened under questionable circumstances."

Charlene's smile was bright. "And now with last night's

incident, here we go again. Is that unit jinxed or what? Oh, and I understand the furniture got busted up."

"Not the furniture, for heaven's sake, just the owner's portrait." Heidi slipped her foot out of her sandal, wondering if she should see a doctor. "How could you know about what happened last night?"

"We employ stringers—part-time correspondents. These people have contacts. They keep us informed."

"Ah," Heidi said. "But you want to know more, the inside scoop. And that's where I come in."

"Beautiful." Charlene's expression softened. "You're the kind of person I like to work with."

"Did I say I would work with you?"

Charlene reached into her satchel and drew out some papers. She slid one sheet onto the desk in front of Heidi. "Like I said, we pay generously. In turn, I would want background information on the people involved in these, uh, tragic events. And anything pertinent leading up to the incidents. In some cases, you'd confirm information we have.

"Most importantly, I'd like to know who owns that unit and what his or her reaction has been to these happenings.

"If you decide to work with us," she flipped another sheet of paper onto the desk, "we have certain stipulations. Take a look."

Heidi studied the contract. Most of the conditions set forth pertained to the *Tattler* having exclusive rights to the information she might provide. In all, she couldn't believe her luck. $1500 for an hour or so of chit chat?

"Well?" Charlene tapped her pen against her notebook. "Do we have a deal? If so, we'll both sign copies of the agreement and I will write a check for half the amount today. The rest you'll get when we publish, which should be soon."

"Hmm. I'm almost convinced to go along with this, though I could risk losing my job. Let me think." After a pause, Heidi said, "Another $500 would seal the deal."

Heidi held her breath, wondering if she'd overshot the limits, but Charlene merely shrugged. "All right. We'll up it $500."

When they'd signed the papers, Charlene produced a tape recorder from her satchel, found an outlet and plugged it in.

"Let's get started," she said. "You mentioned the owner's portrait was destroyed. I would guess the owner is a woman?"

At Heidi's nod, she continued, "We'll begin with a description of her. Better yet, I want a picture of the owner. Any photo will do."

"I don't have anything on file."

"Then we'll just have to find a snapshot, or maybe something more elaborate?"

"Where? How?"

"Ms. McGowan, where do you think? You have the key to the unit. Surely you can find a photo album or family portrait?"

Heidi looked down at her foot. "Before you arrived, I think I broke my toe. I'm not sure I can walk very far."

"Oh, too bad." She brightened. "No problem. You can give me the key and point the way."

Heidi felt her stomach tighten. "If that came out, if you were seen, I'd be fired."

"Then you'll have to make your way slowly. And if by chance the victim's husband walked in on you, you'd tell him you were inspecting the unit for damage. Simple. Now, I want the name of the owner and anything you can tell me about her."

The knot in Heidi's stomach tightened. She could quit now, tear up the contract. On the other hand, she didn't owe that arrogant Dana James a thing. Nada, baby, nada.

"Okay," she said to Charlene. "Dana James, the owner of the condo, gifted us by her presence at the time deaths number one and two occurred. When I commented that her unit was the site for two deaths she said—as if it didn't matter—that death did seem to hover over these premises. Then she added, 'I wonder who will be next?'"

Heidi raised her hand to her mouth. "You're going to quote me?"

"Ah." Charlene was beaming. "I wonder who will be next? I love it. Perfect caption for my article. Care to comment, Ms. McGowan? No?

"Honey, you don't look so good. Is it the toe? Never mind, dear. The pain will pass. In time.

"Shall we continue?"

"Mr. Connolly?"

Ted raised himself from the couch where he'd been dozing in the waiting room outside ICU. He placed his hand on the arm of the couch to steady himself, unable to discern from the doctor's expression whether the news was good or bad.

"Your wife," the doctor said, referring to a chart, "is not quite out of the woods, but she has vastly improved from when she was brought into emergency last night."

"Oh, thank God. So you're saying she is out of danger?"

The doctor smiled. "Yes. Rest and follow-up evaluations are indicated when you return home. We'll know in the next couple of days when she's ready to make that transition.

"You can see her now. She's been awake off and on throughout the morning, and the last time I checked, she was stable and alert."

The doctor opened the door for Ted to enter ICU. As he turned to leave he said, "Better make that a short visit."

Ted blanched at the sight of tubes and monitors in place to facilitate Susan's survival and recovery.

He stood beside her bed, heart pounding as he waited for her to open her eyes. His relief that she had come through with a good prognosis was tempered by concerns of what lay ahead for him and Susan in view of last night's debacle.

He sat down in the one chair provided, fighting exhaustion. He'd been at the hospital all night.

"Ted?"

Had he nodded off? Ted sat up straight and blinked several times to clear his vision.

Susan's eyes were open, but she looked at him blankly, as if he were a stranger. Maybe he dreamed she'd called his name?

He brought his chair in as close as possible to the bed and took her hand. "It's okay sweetheart. I've talked to the doctor, and he says you're going to be fine."

Matter of factly, Susan said, "I almost died."

He had to lean forward to grasp what she said. "I'll make sure that what you went through never, ever happens again."

She withdrew her hand. "Why?" Her voice had gained strength. "Don't tell me you're no longer torn?"

"Oh, Susan. I'm so ashamed." He bowed his head. "What you must think of me."

"Because you had an affair with a woman I despise? Because you chose that piece of trash over me? I'm too weak to tell you what I think of you, Ted. Now, anyway. So I'll keep it short and simple. I don't want you in my life anymore. I'm not a person who can forgive or forget. So don't even try to convince me we should stay married."

"You don't mean that. Listen to me. Susan, don't turn away. Look at me. I promise, I swear, I'll make this up to you."

"Too late."

"I know you're deeply hurt, but you can't end our marriage," he snapped his fingers "like that."

"Watch me."

Ted, hands clenched, got up, but then sat back down. "You're in intensive care, you're on heavy medication and probably still emotional. How can you make a life altering decision under these circumstances?"

"You made a life altering decision. Now it's my turn."

The spitefulness in her tone was like a fist to his gut.

He pushed back his chair and stood. "You have every right to punish me. But we need to talk this out when you're stronger and I've had some sleep. I'm going to crash at the condo for a while, but I'll be back later."

At the door, when Ted turned to look back at her, Susan's eyes were closed, but he sensed she was awake.

"Susan, I love you, and I don't want to lose you. Our marriage is not over."

The sound of his voice, strong and confident echoed in his ears. But after he'd shut the door behind him, a weakness in his legs brought him to a standstill. In fact, a wobbliness had invaded his body.

The corridor ahead that led to the elevators stretched endlessly, the overhead lighting creating a glistening effect, as if reflecting water.

Ted's journey from hospital to car, from car to condo could be characterized, he later thought, as the long wade home. It seemed to take forever.

The bedside clock read twelve noon when Ted lay down to rest. When he awoke, it was seven in the evening. A call to the hospital confirmed what he'd surmised, that after tests and consultations throughout the afternoon, Susan wanted to rest and had, in fact, turned in for the night.

The next morning when Ted arrived at the hospital and was told his wife had moved from ICU into a private room, his spirits rose a notch.

The door to her room was open, and Ted was surprised to see a man holding a briefcase standing by her bed.

Susan had spotted him. "Ted," she called out, "come in, please."

The man turned as Ted entered. Where had he seen this person? Then it came to him. At the conference.

"You look puzzled, Ted." Susan sat up in bed, wearing a smile, her hair neatly combed, the ends tucked behind her ears. "I'm sure you've met Dick Hastings? Though, for these purposes, Richard will do."

Ted nodded. "I think we sat at the same table at the luau?"

"Right," he said. No smile.

Ted looked at Susan. "So?"

"Richard and his wife are staying in Honolulu for a week, but Richard was kind enough to fly over for the day." She paused. "He's a divorce attorney."

Ted was suddenly lightheaded. He grabbed for the back of a chair until his adrenaline had surged and he could steady himself. "What is your hurry, Susan? We've barely talked; we have a hell of a lot to sort out."

"What's to discuss? Adultery is adultery is adultery."

Ted turned to the attorney. "Dick, Richard, or should I call you Mr. Hastings? You need to convince your client that a cooling-off period is mandatory."

Ted towered over the attorney, whose rotund build and bland features invited raised eyebrows when weighed against an operatic base baritone delivery. "Mr. Connelly," he said, "let's step out of the room for a minute."

The voice brought back memories of Ted's 11th grade basketball coach whose barked commands generated immediate compliance.

In the hallway Hastings said, "I tried suggesting a time-out and the possibility of reconciliation. At this point your wife is adamant that we start divorce proceedings immediately." He shrugged. "All that could change, but I wouldn't count on it."

He rubbed his eyes and then gave Ted a tired smile. "A lot to work out once you've consulted with your attorney. Of course, Susan will seek custody of your daughter, but she says you're a good father and that she'll be generous when it comes to visitation rights."

The thought of Caitlin brought tears to Ted's eyes, but then he hardened. "You'll find it easy to work with Susan, Mr. Hastings. She's very efficient, a great organizer and list maker. She'll lead; you'll follow."

Ted looked at his watch. "I have my own arrangements and calls to make, so I'll be on my way. Tell Susan I'll see her either this afternoon or tomorrow. We have decisions to make that can't be put off."

He nodded to Hastings, before briskly leaving the hospital.

Ted had been pumped up, riding on waves of anger and indignation over Susan's shutting him out, over her obvious enjoyment of whacking him in the balls with Richard Hastings.

Now back at the condo, his determination to initiate action on his own flagged. Where to begin? He started for the phone, but then slowly made his way out onto the lanai. He couldn't think.

Ted stood at the railing and rotated his shoulders, the sun's warmth an anodyne to the tightness in his neck and shoulders. Idly he viewed the surfers at play, the symmetry in motion of oarsmen guiding canoes, and doll-like figures navigating the skies, hanging from parasails.

Beyond the breaking waves, three sailboats glided languorously, their white sails an adornment to an azure sea. He watched intently as the boats proceeded on their course, the undulation of the vessels governed by gentle swells.

For the first time in hours a sense of purpose quickened his pulse. He wanted to be at sea, piloting the craft, engaging in camaraderie with fellow sailors. And now, why shouldn't he pursue that dream as he started a new chapter of his life?

Ted dashed into the condo and made a beeline for the bedroom, where in a dresser drawer he found the address book that listed his lawyer's cell phone number.

But first he would call Dana.

Kim stood at Dana's door, about to press the doorbell, but then drew back as she heard her sister's raised voice. "What? She did what?"

Good heavens, Kim thought. She hesitated, but went ahead and rang the bell. After all, Dana was expecting her.

When her sister opened the door, Kim was relieved to see Dana pressing a phone to her ear and not in a confrontation with man, woman or beast.

Dana waved Kim inside, continuing her conversation. "Kim's just arrived. She said it was urgent she see me so I'll have to call you back later." She nodded in response to something the caller said. "Hang in there, Ducks. Everything works out for the best.

"Gawd!" Dana flung her cordless phone onto the nearest sofa, and then turned to Kim. "That woman!"

"Who?"

"Susan! She and Ted stay in my condo at my invitation, and that fiend ends up destroying my portrait by ripping it to shreds."

Kim took in Dana's disheveled appearance: her hair looking as if it had been torn at, her complexion pasty, chest heaving. Kim spoke in measured tones. "Why in the world would you invite Susan and Ted Connolly to stay in your condo?"

Dana raised both hands to smooth her hair. "Give me a minute." She took a deep breath, then another. "Let's go to the kitchen," she said. "I was working at the counter, checking inventory for the shop. We can talk in there."

Kim sat across from Dana, noting her sister's color was better, her breathing regular. A glass that contained Coke was about half full. Dana raised the glass to her lips, drank, and set it back down. "You sounded upset on the phone. Why the urgency?"

"I'll get there," Kim said, "but not until you tell me why the Connollys were staying in your condo."

Dana checked off an item on an inventory sheet. "As a favor to

Ted. He's been very helpful in advising me on financial matters."

Yeah, right, Kim thought. *And next you're going to tell me the moon is made of cheese?* "Next question. Why, in light of your generosity, would Susan destroy your portrait?"

"Because she's demented."

"Dana—"

Her sigh was deep and drawn out. "When you arrived, I was on the phone with Ted. He was calling me from Hawaii. I'll cut through the histrionics and make this brief. Susan and Ted fought after Ted admitted he was attracted to me. A huge row ensued, and Susan, in a rage, wrecked my portrait. Then she collapsed and had a near death experience."

Kim gawked at Dana, at a loss for words. Finally she asked, "How is Susan?"

Dana shrugged. "People like her always survive. As for my portrait, I never really liked that pose. My new one will be spectacular." She paused. "Oh. And Susan has started divorce proceedings."

"Wait a minute. Susan is breaking up her marriage because Ted is attracted to you? I think you're leaving something out."

Dana took a sip of Coke, and then produced her cat-like smile. "I'll leave it to you to fill in the blanks."

As usual, Dana's intrigues provided a distraction from Kim's concerns. Now her sister was looking at her questioningly. "I delivered on my part," she said. "Now it's your turn."

Kim swallowed hard. "I got a call from Detective Chang. An order was issued to exhume Barry's body. They've removed tissue samples to examine under a microscope."

Dana's eyes took on a deeper green. "Why?"

Kim shook her head. "It's all a bit nebulous, but the detective mentioned too many loose ends. Something about Barry's death being untimely, given his age, and the difference in yours and my assessment of Barry's state of health. He referred to the glass at the pool, that the contents could have been contaminated; though that doesn't make any sense to me."

Kim bowed her head for a moment, and then looked Dana in the eye. "He didn't bring up my emotional state, but he did allude to 'other factors'. Do you think they suspect foul play? That I'm—what do they call it?—a person of interest?"

Dana rolled her eyes. "There you go, invading my territory. If anyone gets to play Drama Queen, it's me. As for Chang, he delights in throwing out meaningless expressions just to stir things up."

Dana fell silent and patted Kim's hand. "Sweetie, let's not borrow trouble. Remember, the police looked over the unit and nothing was found to indicate foul play. Let's leave it at that."

Kim nodded. Dana, as always, was the voice of reason. So why didn't Kim feel any better? The authorities having second thoughts as to the cause of Barry's death certainly didn't help.

Dana looked up from making a notation. "I wish I hadn't mentioned Barry's cocaine use. But maybe the police have questioned a drug distributor who's brought Barry into the picture."

Kim shook her head. "I still can't accept that Barry was into drugs. But who knows? We'll know the answers in time.

"Meanwhile, my dear, I don't know if you're still involved with Mark—you haven't mentioned him in a while—but you've got Ted at your beck and call, not to mention Jasper waiting in the wings."

Dana cracked a smile. "Complications with a capital C."

"I only wish I had such complications."

"Maybe you should grab onto Ted. If a certain situation works out for me, and I expect it will, Ted will not be a part of my life."

"Thanks. I've always hankered for castoffs."

"In any event, I'm seeing Mark tomorrow evening. You're right that it's been a while. We were merely at an impasse, so to speak."

Kim forced a smile. "And now?"

"I think, little sister, the best is yet to come."

The smugness in Dana's tone and expression irritated Kim, who was growing restless as she waited for her sister to elaborate.

Instead, it appeared Dana had experienced a shift in mood. "By the way," she said, "give me a call when you hear from Chang."

Her request, delivered in a casual manner, ran counter to a sudden rigidity in posture, a soberness in expression.

Kim had come to her sister for comfort. Now she wished she had stayed home.

Chapter Twenty-Two

Mark studied his dining-room table with a critical eye. Sturdy beige placemats were set off by Kelly green cloth napkins. It wasn't nearly as elegant as the settings at Dana's, and he noticed the cloth napkins clashed with the turquoise vase housing his floral centerpiece. Fortunately, crystal water and wine glasses, along with his mother's good silver added some class to the setting.

He knew something was still missing… candles. He'd forgotten the damn candles. No time to look for them now, he decided as he hastened into the kitchen.

While Mark was tearing up lettuce into a salad bowl, he wondered if he should have held off on making it until Dana had arrived. Two people putting together a salad, or one watching while the other worked, suggested comfort and compatibility. He wasn't sure if he and Dana met that criterion. Mark would worry later; now he needed to finish the salad, adding dried cranberries, cucumber slices, and crumbled blue cheese to the greens.

Dana's phone call had caught him off guard. She'd sounded upbeat, a flirtatious lilt to her voice, as if the hiatus in their relationship had not existed. She told him she missed him and wondered if they might get together.

"I'll treat you to dinner at my house," he'd said.

Upon reflection, dinner in a restaurant would have been more appropriate. A home setting invited intimacy, and he could only ponder what might surface, given their fractious parting. He reached for a knife to slice a green apple, only to have the knife fly out of his hands to the floor.

Klutzy. That described his actions for most of the day. Good thing Dana had rejected his offer to pick her up. He could only imagine the consequences of having to get behind the wheel to take her home—especially if the evening did not go well.

He still wasn't sure whether or not Dana would be staying over.

With the salad completed and stored in the refrigerator, Mark traipsed into the living room where they'd be seated for cocktails. Hors d'oeuvres were in place on the coffee table. He'd picked up newspapers that had been strewn about, emptied his waste basket and straightened pictures. No dirty socks peeked out from under the sofa. Still, he couldn't he relax.

Mark rubbed his forehead. His problem was that after writing down his concerns over Dana's behavior and the state of their relationship, he had placed this masterpiece of introspection into some soggy compartment of his brain where it had languished until Dana's call.

He glanced at his watch. Whether for good or bad, Dana should arrive any minute. But something nagged at him and he wondered if he had neglected to do something…

Back to the dining room, Mark switched on the light that illuminated his deck. Maybe, they'd elect to sit outside at some point in the evening. About to exit the room, he stopped himself—the candles!

It was too late now. At the sound of the doorbell, he hurried to the front door, figuring fate had intervened. In all likelihood, and going by the sort of day he was having, his use of candlelight would result in the drapes catching fire. Or worse.

When Mark opened the door, his heart raced at the sight of Dana decked out in white. She wore a sleeveless top with a plunging neckline over a flared, pleated skirt, her jewelry a combination of silver and turquoise. She held out a multicolored gift bag that he presumed contained a bottle of wine. They hugged as he ushered her inside, Mark commenting on how lovely she looked.

When they reached the living room, Dana surveyed their appetizers. "Liver pâté." She breathed the words as if exclaiming over an exquisite gem. "That's a winner in my book, Mark. I could eat a pound of the stuff. And heaven help me if I get started on the brie. You've set out my favorite cheese." She blew him a kiss as she slid into place on the sofa.

"Oh. About the wine I brought? It's a Riesling." She paused, eyebrows raised in a question. "Aha. You're smiling."

He saluted her. "My favorite white wine and perfect to go with Cornish game hens. Let me chill the wine, and then I'll bring in our martinis."

When he returned with their drinks, Mark raised his glass. "To good times."

"And to us," Dana added.

"And to us," Mark repeated, with more conviction than he felt.

"Do you marinate the hens?" Dana asked. Responding to his nod, she said, "I'm amazed you'd find time for so much preparation."

"I wanted our dinner to be special."

"That's so sweet, Mark." She took a sip of her drink, and then set down her glass. "Tell me what's going on with you."

Mark drew in his breath. The situation was becoming surreal. The woman had kicked him out of her home and had refused to return his phone calls. Now she wanted to engage in small talk?

"Dana, honey, first let me say how pleased I was to hear from you."

"I know. I could tell from the sound of your voice."

Once again he rubbed his forehead. "But the way we parted was disagreeable, to say the least. We can't simply ignore what happened."

Her mouth a pout, Dana said, "I cut you short, I overreacted. Obviously, we weren't in sync regarding the issues I brought up." She shrugged. "Well, darling what can I say? Are you serving humble pie for dessert? If so, be sure to cut me a thick slice."

Mark chuckled, and then patted her hand. Damn, she could get to him. He forced himself to stay focused, to start a meaningful dialogue. "If we're casting blame," he said, "my grade for sensitivity that evening would rate a big, fat F."

Dana spread pâté on a cracker. "I'm not a dummy, Mark. I realize we need to come to terms on a variety of things." She bit into the cracker. "But isn't cocktail hour a time for relaxation and pleasant conversation? For now, can't we just enjoy each other?"

"Yes, of course." He decided to back off. Actually, Mark found it a relief to continue their conversation in a lighter vein. At times though, he half listened, or commented laconically, his mind rehearsing the steps for their dinner. Until Dana brought up Kim.

"She came to see me yesterday." Dana gave him a little poke. "Come to think about it, Kim didn't seem exactly thrilled when I mentioned you and I would be getting together this evening."

"Can't imagine why." Mark made a mental note to call Kim to see if she'd extracted any relevant information regarding Dana's discrepancies in her statements regarding when she was in Kona.

"Here's the kicker: Kim told me an order was issued to exhume Barry's body. Don't ask me why. But Kim was quite upset over this latest turn of events."

Mark shook his head. "What's going on?"

"I asked the same thing. I made light of the situation; that is, I tried to reassure her it was no big deal. But seriously? I'm very, very worried for Kim. Food for thought, eh?"

Dana raised her glass and smiled sweetly. "A refill please. I'll bet you're ready, too. And while you're mixing I'll keep you company and help with dinner."

He answered her smile with his, but could not match her cheeriness.

Rather, his steps were heavy as they headed for the kitchen.

Dinner, Mark had to admit, was excellent, with Dana expressing delight over every dish. In fact, he was able to put aside his concerns for the time being.

When Dana left the table to freshen up, Mark put away the leftovers and prepared their after-dinner drinks: Cointreau for her, brandy for him.

They agreed the deck was worth a try, with Dana bringing out a light wrap from the oversized bag she'd brought. He wondered if she'd packed her overnight items as well.

"This is so lovely, Mark." She gestured about her. "My terrace has a certain panache, but here the tranquility, the sights and sounds of nature are balm for the soul."

Mark held back a snicker. Where was this coming from? Not from the Dana he knew. "I'm glad you're comfortable in this environment," he said.

"Comfortable? Yes. But I'm not just talking about this evening. I feel—I know this is where I belong. With you."

She was seated with her back to the light, so he couldn't read her expression. He groaned inwardly. This beautiful but troubled woman was pushing him into a corner. Again.

"Dana, sweetheart. You know how much I care for you. More than I've cared for any woman. But before we consider the idea of a permanent relationship, I think we need to address problem areas in our personal lives that need to be resolved."

"For God's sake, Mark, you're the problem. Clearly, you harbor a fear of commitment. By all means let's keep the comfy status quo. All fun and gratification without the responsibility. Am I reciting the Mark Hampton credo?"

"I wouldn't put it that way."

She cocked her head. "What are you afraid of? Life? I could give you one hell of a ride." She'd been rushing her words, as if racing against a timer, her tone brittle. "But wait. You mentioned problems in our personal lives. What on earth are you referring to?"

"Dana, you're charming, alluring, witty, an absolutely delicious woman. But what concerns me are the resentments you cling to, your excessive anger."

"Well, gee whiz, yes. I have expressed negative feelings toward people who've betrayed me or treated me cruelly. But the fault lies with them. Not me."

"Maybe you need to examine some gray areas in your relationships. Not everything can be measured in terms of black and white."

"Crap. You won't find me shilly-shallying around. I pride myself on being decisive, of having the backbone to act on my beliefs."

"Admirable traits."

"So where does this leave us?"

His irony had been lost on her. "I'd like for us to view ourselves in a more objective light, remove our masks, so to speak. Be open and honest so that we can grow closer." He couldn't very well bring up her inconsistencies, her possible lies.

In the silence that followed, Mark supposed Dana was struggling to frame a response. Unexpectedly she leaned over to kiss him lightly on the lips.

"I didn't want to bring this up earlier," she said, "but I'm scheduled to meet with my soon-to-be-ex tomorrow morning. Earlyish. So I'd better get on home."

"I wasn't sure if you'd be staying over—"

"Not this time, love. I want to be sharp for tomorrow morning, and I need a change of wardrobe."

At the door, Dana gazed into his eyes. "Your dinner really was special. Thank you for an incredible evening, Mark. A hug, please?"

He held her in a close embrace and then sought her lips. She responded with a passionate kiss. When she broke away, she said, her voice soft and silky, "Next time, dinner at my place?"

"I'd like that."

"Promise me? We have a date?"

"I promise."

He held the door open for her and then started to follow.

"No need to walk me out. You've got a kitchen full of dirty dishes." She darted ahead, turned once to wave, and then quickly got into her car.

He waited until she'd sped off to go back inside.

The dishes could wait, Mark decided, going instead to his desk in the den. His book on deviant behavior lay open before him. He'd read the chapter titled "Narcissism" several times.

The characteristics of a narcissistic personality disorder popped out at him: *exaggerated sense of self importance, inability to take blame, easily offended, can't take criticism or rejection, defiant or enraged reaction to real or imagined slights. Can be vengeful.*

On the plus side: *can be charming, creative, highly productive, confident, excel in CEO positions or high profile jobs.*

He reviewed what he knew about Dana, and then thought about her uneven behavior this evening, particularly her lack of response to his suggestions. A number of these traits fit her. On the other hand, he was not convinced Dana suffered from a severe clinical disorder—though mild might qualify.

He closed the book. He'd had enough for now, and the chores that awaited him in the kitchen would be a welcome diversion.

Mark stood, but then sat back down at the ringing of his phone. To his surprise, his caller was Susan Connelly. She explained she was in Hawaii, hospitalized after a life-threatening asthma attack.

"I'm so sorry," Mark said. "Are you all right?"

"I'm practically recovered, but I didn't call to discuss my condition." She paused. "A significant change has occurred in my life, Mark, and what I am about to say could possibly affect you. So please hear me out."

Though he detected a smugness in her tone, Mark, always a good listener, gave her his full attention.

When they'd terminated the call, Mark drew a shaky breath, gained his strength to stand up without wobbling, and walked into the kitchen.

He would take extra care to see that his china remained intact.

But he intended to beat the hell out of the pots and pans.

Elizabeth stood before her mirror, assessing her appearance. Her frown lines were less evident, which gave her a sense of elation. She could credit the dim bedroom lighting, but preferred to attribute her skin's glow to an inner sense of joy.

As for her new outfit, the blue cotton off-the-shoulder top was appropriately casual for dining in, as well as smart looking. However, the matching pants were snug around her middle and created a puckered effect.

Better fitting black pants would do just as well. She started for her closet, only to make an about face to answer the ringing phone.

"I'm probably calling at a bad time," Bea said. "I just hope all went well in the cooking department."

"I would have been lost without your instructions, Mom. I tasted the beef stroganoff, and it melts in your mouth. I'm sure Robert will be impressed."

"How many dates have you two had?"

Elizabeth felt her cheeks grow warm as her mind provided an instant replay of their good night kisses. "We've been together every evening since he arrived here. Which reminds me, when we have brunch on Sunday, could we include Robert?"

"I'd like that very much."

"Uh, Mom. Outside of work, Robert can be shy, and sometimes

he comes across as a bit formal. But he's great to be with, and I am so attracted to him."

"I like that happy sound in your voice."

"Me, too. It's probably too soon to say where we're headed, but I have a good feeling about us."

"So do I." Bea sounded wistful. "Since I helped with your dinner, I'll want to hear how everything turned out. If you can get back to me before ten this evening, fine. If I don't hear from you, I'll assume your detective didn't run off in a huff."

She laughed, "Mom, Robert is not like that—whoops. I hear the doorbell. Gotta go. Talk to you later."

There was no time for changing now; she'd just have to suck in her stomach.

Elizabeth opened the door to a smiling Robert Chang. In one hand he held a bouquet of flowers, resplendent in fall colors of gold and russet shades, while in the other hand he clutched a bottle of red wine, adorned with a burgundy and white striped bow taped to its neck.

Elizabeth pressed her hand to her heart. "Oh, my goodness, look at all of this. Come in, come in." She started to lead them to the sofa, but then spun around. "I think the kitchen should be our first stop. I want to find a vase for these beautiful flowers."

Robert followed her into the kitchen and set the bottle on the counter. "You may already have selected a wine for this evening."

"I did, but we can serve yours."

"It's up to you." He said this softly, gazing into her eyes. "You look lovely this evening. Blue becomes you."

"Thank you." Suddenly she was breathless. She stared back at him, struggling against an overpowering urge to kiss him. She broke the spell by turning to reach into the cupboard for a vase.

The flowers, which Elizabeth and Robert could view from where they sat on the sofa, graced a small table positioned next to the fireplace. "I'll have to keep in mind how a touch of color spruces up the place." She made a wide gesture. "Austere comes to mind."

Robert gave her a sidelong look. "You've seen my office. My apartment isn't much of a step up."

Elizabeth swallowed her laugh. "I guess utilitarian would be an apt description?"

"You're too kind." He took a sip of his vodka and tonic, his drink of choice, Elizabeth had learned, and then patted her hand. "A woman's touch would greatly enhance my work and living environment."

"You talk about wanting me to join your staff, but you failed to mention interior decorating as part of the job description."

"Again, that would be up to you."

"I see," she said. It wasn't what he said but the nuances in his tone that induced a shiver of delight. She reached for her drink. Time out, she told herself. "Anything new or exciting on the detective front?"

Robert nodded. "Yes, indeed."

"Let me guess. You have the results of the tissue samples taken from Barry Williams' body. Right? I'm dying to hear what they found. Oops." She put her hand to her mouth. "A bad choice of words."

He grinned, then sobered. "Mr. Williams did not die from natural causes, Elizabeth. Apparently, someone spiked the drink he took out to the pool with antifreeze. Or it's possible this element was added to the bottle of Drambuie in his kitchen."

"Antifreeze?"

"It's an automotive additive used to lower the freezing point in a car engine."

"Good heavens." Elizabeth made a face. "Wouldn't the man have caught on right away that his drink had a weird flavor?"

"Actually, ethylene glycol–that's the technical name–tastes okay. It's sweet, it's colorless, odorless and can blend well into a variety of drinks. Even if Williams recognized a sweetness to his Drambuie, he might have credited that to the brandy he'd been drinking before he went to the pool."

"A carry over from the brandy? That makes sense. Obviously antifreeze is lethal?"

"Oh, yes. It can cause heart failure, brain damage, stroke, and even death if the victim is not treated immediately."

Elizabeth stared into her drink, processing what Robert had related. "So Barry Williams was murdered. What next? I suppose Kim Williams is a suspect?"

"She certainly had motive and opportunity, but at this point we lack hard evidence. That said, we're just getting started on what is now a homicide investigation, so it's a whole new ball game.

"Change in subject." He smiled broadly. "Do you enjoy weddings?"

Elizabeth giggled. "It beats going to a funeral."

"I may have mentioned the aunt and uncle who live in San Francisco? Well, their daughter–my cousin Lee Ann–is to be married in three weeks." He looked at her expectantly.

"Oh? Uh, that's nice."

"It would be even nicer yet if you'd come to the wedding with me as my guest."

"To San Francisco?"

"Yes. I would pay for all your expenses."

A wedding in San Francisco. With Robert. "I'd love to accompany you to your cousin's wedding."

"Wonderful. These people do it up big, so I expect a round of parties. Sound like fun?"

She gave a short laugh. "I'm not much of a party girl, but I'm a fast learner."

"Do I strike you as a party boy?"

"Can I plead the fifth?"

He laughed, and they continued bantering until Elizabeth brought up the subject of paying her own way.

Robert shook his head. "I'm paying." He raised his glass. "Another, please?"

"We'll see. About paying, I mean, not the drink." She took his glass and then grabbed her own. "Instead of gin, I'm switching to vodka. I want to try your drink."

"Then I'd better go with you to supervise," he said, with a twinkle in his eye.

As Elizabeth preceded him into the kitchen, she was glad Robert couldn't see the tremor in her hands or detect her uneven breathing. She hadn't felt this giddy–maybe ever.

Later, giddiness took a back seat to concentration as she applied herself to the task of putting dinner together. She was rewarded for her efforts when Robert likened the meal to gourmet fare.

Now as they sat side by side on the sofa after coffee and dessert, Robert, at her request, provided details about his family in Hawaii and San Francisco. His father had died when Robert was a teenager, and he'd grown up in Honolulu where his mother currently lived with his married sister.

When she asked if they would attend the wedding, he implied that it was more than likely. He then put his arm around Elizabeth and drew her close. "I have a busy day tomorrow, but I'd like for us to get together in the evening. That is, if you're not growing tired of me?"

"Are you kidding? Robert, I love being with you."

His kiss left her breathless and yearning for more.

Once again he sought her lips, only to draw back. "I should be going." He rose and Elizabeth followed.

At the door, he placed his hands on her shoulders. "You are a remarkable woman, Elizabeth. Your dinner was better than any restaurant offering. You are bright, beautiful, caring. What more can I say? Except that I, too, love being with you."

Before she could respond, he brought her to him, his lips finding hers. When they drew apart, he seemed flustered. "I'll say goodnight now."

"Robert."

"Yes?"

"Do you really want to leave?"

"No. No, I don't."

"Then stay with me."

"Maybe forever," he whispered as she led him to the bedroom.

In the morning after Robert had left, Elizabeth remembered to call her mother.

"A late night?" Bea asked.

An incredible night, she wanted to sing out, filled with loving beyond anything she'd experienced in her admittedly limited sexual encounters.

But instead she simply responded, "It was a great evening," and then gave her mother a detailed account of her success with dinner.

"What about brunch?" Bea asked.

She'd forgotten to ask Robert to join them. "However, I expect a call from him sometime today, and we'll be getting together this evening."

Bea chuckled. "Should I start shopping for a mother-of-the-bride dress?"

Elizabeth laughed. "By all means. And take Diane with you so you can help her select her matron-of-honor outfit." They were just joshing, but…well, what if?

Robert did reach her at work in the early afternoon, "Just to check in, to hear your voice," he said.

Elizabeth responded in kind before extending the brunch invitation.

"I'd be delighted. As for this evening, just to add a little spice, I'm going to bring along some pages that were faxed to me out of the *Honolulu Tattler*."

"Would the words spice and *Tattler* suggest something racy?"

"Yes, as in tabloid."

"I'm waiting for the punch line."

"A feature story appears that—well, you'll have to steel yourself as to the subject matter. But Dana James figures prominently in the article. That, in turn, has produced some interesting ramifications."

"Robert, I can't wait. What does it say about Dana James?"

"Uh-oh. My cell phone is ringing. I think it's a call I've been waiting for. Sorry, sweetheart. I'll fill you in when I see you this evening."

Elizabeth stared at the silent phone. How was she supposed to concentrate on work? She sighed and then smiled, thinking that Robert was a bit of a tease. In fact, the staid detective harbored a playful streak she found endearing.

Elizabeth pushed aside the report she was supposed to sign. Face it, she found everything about Robert endearing.

Settling back in her chair, she closed her eyes and granted herself permission to feast at the banquet of love, savoring the sweetness of her fantasy, of emotional and physical fulfillment.

And then she sat upright, rattled by the force of a question that until now had lurked only in a shadowy corner of her mind.

What would it be like to call Hawaii her permanent home?

Chapter Twenty-Three

Kim paced her living room and listened for the slam of a car door as she waited for Dana to arrive. The tightness in her neck and across her shoulders had persisted throughout the morning. Now she hugged herself and shivered as a sudden chill pervaded her body. The familiar sound of the kitchen wall clock chiming the hour bolstered her comfort, but then she lost track of the count. A glance at her wrist revealed she'd neglected to put on her watch.

As Kim entered her bedroom, she noted the clock on the end table by the bed showed 10 a.m. But where in the heck was her watch? Maybe it was buried under the towels, pillow cases, and other items on her bed she'd meant to take to the laundry room.

She jumped at the sound of the doorbell. Forget lost watches and dirty laundry, she told herself as she hastened to the door.

"Well, look at you," Dana said, strolling past Kim into the living room. "No smile? No sisterly hug?"

"Not much to smile or hug about. But thanks for making a house call. And because you've put yourself out, lunch is on me." Kim pointed to the sofa. "Can we sit?" She waited until they were settled. "I have news. Oh. Can I get you something to drink? A Coke?"

Dana shook her head, her expression veiled. "You said you didn't want to talk on the phone. What's up? Something heavy?"

"Brace yourself. Detective Chang called with the results from Barry's tissue samples. Apparently, it was the drink he took to the pool that killed him. Can you believe this? His Drambuie was spiked with anti-freeze."

Dana didn't move, didn't blink, her expression impassive.

Kim broke the silence. "I have the technical name written down. It's described as an automotive additive."

"I know what it is. I read in the paper about a woman who added anti-freeze to her husband's drink. The dumb fool didn't know what was happening to him because anti-freeze is supposed to have a pleasant taste, plus there's no odor, no color, and so on."

"Dana, for heaven's sake, focus on the implications from the report. Where does this leave me?"

"In a case like this I suppose the spouse is a person of interest, so the detective in charge might want to question you. But it would appear no one saw who concocted the lethal cocktail, so without a witness, they don't have a case." She studied her nails.

"Don't forget motive and opportunity." Kim pointed to herself.

Dana made a dismissive gesture. "I still think Barry's death was drug related. Someone, maybe a supplier, was out to get him. In any case, the person who knocked him off did you a favor."

"Why do you persist with that theory? Barry was not on drugs." Kim glared at Dana, but her sister wore, once more, the mask of indifference. "Dana? *Dana*."

"What?"

"You seem so out of it."

Still no response.

"Ah. I just remembered. You met with Jasper yesterday morning. Did he give you a hard time?"

"Not at all." Dana perked up. "Mainly, we discussed property matters. He also brought up the idea of a reconciliation. I told him I'd think about it."

"Really?"

"Don't sound so spooked. I don't know that I'd seriously consider such a move, but—" she shrugged and looked away.

"I may be treading on delicate ground, but the last time we talked, Mark was very much in the picture."

Dana sniffed. "Commitment is a dirty word in Dr. Mark Hampton's vocabulary."

"I'm sorry to hear that," Kim said, unsure if she really was sorry.

"I'm beginning to realize that Mark is a very troubled man."

"He doesn't give that impression."

Dana's expression hardened, her lips stretched into a thin line. Kim readied herself for an outburst, but all Dana said was, "You don't know him like I do."

"True."

Silence. Kim rubbed her shoulder, wishing she had never bothered to enlist her sister's help. Dana had her own problems, so to hell with Kim's looming induction into the criminal justice system.

Both women started at the sound of Dana's cell phone. She pulled the phone from her bag and moved from the sofa to stand by the front window, her profile to Kim. Kim gazed in fascination, her resentment ebbing, as sunlight streaming through the window framed a dazzling portrait of a women in white, the flokatis at her feet extending this pristine image.

With the call completed, Dana moved out of the spotlight to pick up her car keys from the coffee table. "Sorry I can't stay longer. I'm off to another meeting. We'll do lunch another time."

"Another meeting with Jasper?"

She hesitated, and then said, "I'm going to see Ted at his office."

"Oh, my. The plot thickens."

Dana gave her a wry smile. "Should be interesting."

Kim followed Dana to the door. She reached for her sister's hand. "I'm sorry your evening with Mark was a disappointment."

Dana snatched her hand from Kim and gave her a dark look. "You know the saying, what goes around comes around? Well, he'll get his." She nodded, her gaze fixed and intense.

"Is Mark that important to you? You have other men in your life. You'll always have admirers."

Dana's expression softened. "That's true," she said. "Sorry if I got carried away."

She started out the door, but turned back to Kim, giving her a quizzical look. "If Barry's death was not the result of a drug hookup, then what? That bastard would not have taken his own life."

Kim clenched her hands as a sudden queasiness took hold. "Surely, you don't think *I* poisoned Barry's drink."

Dana gave her an appraising look. "You wouldn't have had the guts. Well, I'm on my way. Hang in there and be sure to keep me posted on whatever comes up."

"I'll walk out with you," Kim said. "I want to check the

mailbox."

Kim waited until Dana had driven off to walk down to the curb. Mostly, junk mail filled the box, with the exception of an 8x11 sized manila envelope.

A few steps from her front door, Kim heard her phone ringing. She had to scramble to make it in time, but she answered before the caller had hung up.

"Kim, it's Mark. I know you're scheduled to come in next week for our regular session, but I'd like to follow up on our conversation regarding Dana. Would you be free to stop by the office around three tomorrow afternoon?"

Kim didn't bother to check her schedule. She'd be there.

Kim found her watch and tended to the laundry, but she was hardly distracted from her troubling thoughts. Again and again she replayed the conversation with her sister. *Was Dana's lack of focus due to her bitterness over Mark's behavior? And just how deep was the rift in their relationship?*

She wished everything wasn't so complicated.

Moments later, after opening the mail, Kim again wished things were simpler.

The manila envelope contained a copy of a weekly newspaper called the *Honolulu Tattler*. Prominently displayed on the front page was Dana's picture. And the accompanying article suggested that Kim's sister had been less than truthful when questioned about her presence in Kona.

No signature or cover letter. No return address.

Once again, Kim hugged herself against an indefinable cold.

What in the hell is going on?

Dana sniffed the stale air as she entered Ted Connelly's waiting room. The emptiness and the dim lighting brought forth an image of a Greyhound bus station at 4 a.m.—or maybe a place of mourning.

Missing at the receptionist desk was Beth or Becky— whatever her name was—which Dana considered a plus. The girl's fake show of respect and "gotcha" smirk did not sit well with Dana.

The door to Ted's office was open and seconds into her arrival, he popped into the waiting room.

His face lighted up as he held out his hands to greet her. "Dana, how good to see you. You look beautiful, as always."

Dana responded with words of greeting as Ted led her into his office and then shut the door. "No clients are scheduled for today, so I thought it would be a good time for us to get together." The lines at the corners of his eyes had deepened, and his frame appeared leaner than she'd remembered. Not that he'd become frail, but neither was he robust. She pictured Mark. Still, Ted was an attractive man.

As they sat down at their usual places, Dana fought a sudden urge to bolt. Not one to hide his emotions, Ted might dissolve into tears, or launch into a fervid account of his feelings for her.

He did neither. Instead, his tone soft, he said, "What a mess."

"I'm sorry, Ted. But knowing Susan, I'm not surprised she put you through hell."

"Had she been the one who cheated, I'm not sure how strongly I would have reacted."

"Naturally, you'd be hurt, disappointed, maybe even enraged. But vindictive? I don't think so."

"Try unforgiving. She didn't have to think twice about ending the marriage."

"Well, Ted, we did discuss the fact that it might be you, walking out of the marriage."

His smile was sheepish. "I recall words to that effect. As a matter-of-fact, I am contemplating a fulfilling new life." His smile faded.

"But?"

"No buts. It's just that I'll be forever haunted by Susan's near death experience–the fact that I brought it on."

"Break-ups can be nasty."

"Including the aftermath."

She gave him a teasing smile. "It seems you're cursed by being a warm and sensitive person. Some men would run, not walk, to the nearest exit and be done with it."

He sighed and then held her gaze. "What about us?"

Oh, God, Dana thought. What about us? "Because of what you've been through and are going through, I have no idea how to answer that question."

"I hold myself solely accountable for the breakup of my marriage." He reached across the table to take her hand. "Despite all that's gone on, you've been constantly in my thoughts. Nothing's changed. Dana, I adore you; I would love to spend the rest of my life with you."

"You must know I have strong feelings for you, and that I've loved every minute of our time together." Dana gently released her hand. "But I think we need to keep our distance for a while. At least until the dust has settled. In other words, until you're a free man, I don't think it's wise for us to be seen together."

Ted bowed his head, pursed his lips, and pushed back his chair. "You're right." He stood, as did Dana, and then came around to her and gathered her into his arms.

He held her close for a long moment, and then slowly backed away, his gaze lingering on her eyes, her lips. "I'm going to miss you like hell."

"Likewise." Dana held his gaze, then reached for her purse and turned from him.

She stepped into the waiting room and paused to look back. Ted had not moved from where they'd embraced. He raised his fingers to his lips and then slowly extended his hand.

Dana thought his gesture both sexy and endearing. "Call me," she said, "when everything's settled? We'll take it from there."

His smile was loving. And trusting.

Outside the building, Dana inhaled the sunshine, the beauty of the day.

Ted, unlike some of the bastards in her life, would never lead her on, only to show her his back. Nor would he make snide, hurtful remarks about her behavior or throw her away like a worn rag. He was a good, sweet man, and she had performed a service in ridding him of Susan. She doubted, however, that he would become a permanent fixture in her life.

Dana jaunted out to her car, picturing Ted's lovelorn expression as she had left the office. Two men, Ted and Jasper, found her irresistible. Well, Jasper might have cause to conclude otherwise, but she could fix that.

And Mark, well, he still presented a challenge, though that whole concept had worn thin. At any rate, he'd accepted her invitation to dinner. She thought about their dinner and humored herself calling it His Last Supper. Well… she'd have to give that some thought.

Dana checked her appearance in the car mirror, smiled, and then adjusted her sunglasses. Top of her form, she thought, comparing herself to her younger sister whose deepening lines around her eyes and pasty complexion reflected her fragile emotional state.

Poor, poor Kim, Dana thought. *Always dependant on big sister to come to the rescue. Maybe it's time for tough love; let Kim fight her own battles.*

She didn't really think Kim would be held responsible for Barry's death. But should the unthinkable happen, Dana would see to it that Kim be represented by the best criminal defense attorney in Los Angeles County.

Mark wished he'd better prepared himself for his meeting with Kim. Each held back, it seemed, unwilling to cast her sister, his lover in a vertiginous maelstrom of doubt and deception. The time had come to dig in.

"You questioned Dana," Mark asked, "regarding her presence in Kona?"

"I did. Dana denied, and then admitted she was in Kona during the time frame we discussed. She said she was looking at a property she'd invested in, that her being there couldn't be exposed because Jasper was not aware of this acquisition."

"A bit thin?" Mark asked.

"A part of me thought so at the time, but I wanted to believe her, and that outweighed any doubts."

Mark looked once again at the article from the *Honolulu Tattler*, then back at Kim. "I don't know about you, but I sure as hell won't be getting a good night's sleep."

"Make that two of us." She sighed. "Where do we go from here?"

"That'll take some thought." He grew pensive, and then said,

"Dana was at my place for dinner the other evening."

Kim nodded. "She indicated, without going into detail, that she was disappointed with the outcome of the evening."

Mark rubbed his forehead. "I'm not surprised and yet, your sister insisted that for our next get together, I come to dinner at her place." He chose not to bring up the phone call from Susan Connelly and her gut wrenching message.

"I'll take Dana up on her dinner invitation. Maybe I can use the tools of my trade to get to the bottom of her erratic behavior. Meanwhile, I suggest you confront her with the *Tattler* article. She'll have plenty to say on that score. But what she says may not be as important as the way she acts. Listen to voice inflection; study her body language."

"I'll do my best."

Back at me, Mark thought, hearing the tightness in Kim's voice, observing the slump in her posture. In all, a reluctant conspirator.

Kim sat straighter, her smile sardonic. "Okay, Dr. Hampton. I can interpret from your facial and body expressions, compassion and concern. Thank you for caring. As for our 'mission', she made quote marks with her fingers, "I hate the prospect of confronting Dana, but I'm up for the job."

"Sounds like we're a team."

"I hope so because I'm about to toss another complication your way. It's a shocker. Barry's body was recently exhumed."

"Dana told me you had come to her with that bit of news. What's going on?"

Kim recounted the findings from the testing of tissue samples, adding, "It's Dana's belief that Barry's death was the result of a drug deal gone wrong."

"You knew he was on drugs?"

"Mark, he was not a drug user. Dana insisted he used cocaine during the time they had their fling. But I would swear he was clean, at least during our marriage."

"I see." He didn't buy the drug use scenario either, but something else had come to mind.

"Kim." He reached for her hand, but drew back. "If Detective Chang wants to meet with you–and I think you'll hear from him–would you ask him if I, as your therapist, could be present? I might present a broader perspective concerning people and events."

"Like what?"

"I know I sound vague, but I'd rather keep it that way for now. On the other hand, I could go to Chang on my own."

"No." She grabbed his hand, "I'd much prefer to have you by my side."

"Then if Chang doesn't object, we'll do it that way."

Kim released his hand; she appeared slightly out of breath. "I'd better be on my way."

"There's no need to rush off. I'm free for the rest of the afternoon. Or do you think we've covered everything for now?"

"For now, yes." Her eyes, their coloring softer and more milky than the intense green of Dana's, held his gaze. He remembered his dream and fought an impulse to reach out to her.

Instead he said, "Could you hang on for a minute? You've probably heard the Connellys are divorcing?"

Kim nodded.

"According to Susan, the breakup was the result of Ted's infatuation with Dana and their subsequent affair." He paused.

"If Dana has spoken to you about Ted, I'm sure she'd want to keep what passed between you confidential. However, if Dana has not confided in you, and if you're willing, I'd like your take on did they or didn't they–to put it bluntly."

Kim thought for a moment. "The animosity between Dana and Susan could poison a river, so I suppose it's possible Susan is lying. But to what purpose? As an excuse to get rid of her husband? That said, Dana has not admitted to, nor has she denied having an affair with Ted. She appears, however, to enjoy the game of wouldn't-you-like-to-know? by way of a cryptic remark underscored by a saucy look or an enigmatic smile."

"Pure Dana."

"Yes. And add to that, I saw Ted exiting the lobby of the Wilshire Marquis, looking as if he were catching the next bus to purgatory. Oh." Kim clamped a hand over her mouth. "Oh, God, this can't be easy for you."

"Kim, it's okay." He smiled. "Trust me."

The weight of uncertainty lifted, smoothing Kim's brow, and in the next instant, her demeanor changed. The lift of her chin, head cocked slightly to the side, an unwavering gaze into Mark's eyes signaled, he thought, an openness (or something more?) he found intriguing.

"I forgot to mention," she said, "that when Dana was at my house yesterday, she broke off our visit when she received a call on her cell phone. It was Ted, asking her to meet him at his office." She looked away. "There. I've made your day."

"Kim. Please don't fret over what you perceive is making me feel bad. The atmosphere enveloping Dana and myself, if not stormy, is unsettled."

She gave him a direct look. "I see. Or maybe I don't. Anyway, I really need to get going."

At the door to the outer office, Mark at Kim's side, said, "Call me if and when you hear from Chang?"

"Count on it. And I'll make a mental movie of my confrontation with Dana."

He touched her arm. "You'll do just fine.

"Oh", he said, stepping back, "be sure to tell Chang about the *Tattler* article, sent to you anonymously. He'll want to have a look–if he hasn't seen the piece already." The information, he presumed, would take some of the heat off of Kim.

"Okay." She laughed. "And now I'm outta here before you dream up any more assignments." Her step was assured as she left the office.

Back at his desk, Mark toyed with the idea of asking to meet with Ted. He wanted confirmation of a Dana-Ted liaison before he confronted Dana. On the other hand, actually meeting with Ted suggested a heavy handedness he wanted to avoid.

Mark looked at his watch, and then picked up the phone. Ted might still be at his office.

Ted answered his phone, his tone reflecting surprise, yet warmth.

After a modicum of small talk, Mark said, "My purpose in calling, Ted, is to clarify a matter of interest to me." He described Susan's call, addressing his concern over Susan's emotional health—a white lie, at best.

"Susan went through a horrifying experience," Ted said. "But she's a strong woman; thanks to you for getting her back on track." He paused. "I'm sure I've come across as a callous S.O.B. In my own defense, I tried to make things right between us; I told her I wanted to salvage our marriage, and for the most part, I meant it. But because of what happened between Dana and me, staying together was anathema to Susan. She wanted me out of her life. Period. End of marriage."

"So where does this leave you and Dana?"

"Until things settle down, we've agreed not to see each other."

"But you do contemplate a future with Dana?"

"I can only hope so." He laughed softly. "I feel awkward talking about Dana to you. On the other hand, she made it clear you're no longer together."

"Really?"

"She did mention you get together for dinner occasionally."

Mark laughed. "You might say that." On that note, Mark ended the conversation. Ted may have found their exchange odd, but that was the last thing Mark was worried about at this point.

Mark leaned back in his chair and stared at the misty Parisian scene depicted in his painting. Like others, he wished he, too, could be transported to that boulevard café, a cozy sanctuary from contradictions, betrayals, and whatever else the fates had in store.

"God help us all," he muttered.

Chapter Twenty-Four

Elizabeth wagged her index finger at Bea. "What are you doing in the kitchen, Mom? Robert and I are in charge of clean-up."

Bea stepped back from the sink to face her daughter whose bearing communicated she would brook no dissent.

Robert tore his gaze from Elizabeth to speak softly to Bea. "Mrs. Devlin, your shrimp-artichoke casserole was so good, perhaps you noticed I had not only seconds but thirds?"

"I wasn't counting, Robert, but good for you. This casserole is one of our favorite brunch dishes."

Elizabeth's furrowed brow suggested they get moving. "Tell you what," Bea said. "I'll let you two clean up in here–you'll want to refrigerate the leftovers–but save the dishes for later. Come join me on the patio. We can finish off the peach cobbler."

The response of headshakes and groans conjured up a laugh from Bea. "All right," she said, "but I want to talk to Robert about his investigation."

Elizabeth relaxed her stance. "Which reminds me, Mom. I have something to bring up too. We'll join you shortly."

As Bea approached the patio doors, she could hear Elizabeth, her tone low but still audible. "Mom looks tired. We probably should have gone out for brunch."

Bea sighed as she entered the patio. Elizabeth continued to hover over her mother, though lately, with not as much intensity. Bea took a moment to check on her small garden before lowering herself into a chair.

On the plus side, the pronoun "we" had woven its way into much of the conversation throughout brunch. Her daughter and Robert were a pair, all right. Maybe even lovers. Whatever their relationship, Bea liked Robert and looked forward to getting to know him. Both appeared excited over their pending trip to San Francisco to attend Robert's cousin's wedding.

Robert's inviting Elizabeth to a family wedding seemed like a good sign. Again she sighed. If only Frank were here to share in his daughter's happiness. And be here for her as well. She missed that dear man with every fiber of her body and soul.

The sound of the patio doors opening brought Bea out of her reverie. "My goodness, what have we here? More champagne?"

When they were settled, Bea raised her glass to Chang. "A very nice selection, Robert."

His smile lit up his face. "The least I could do, Mrs. Devlin."

"Bea. My name is Bea, Detective Chang."

He reddened, and then chuckled. "Bea it is. And mine is Robert."

Elizabeth had followed their exchange with a glimmer of amusement. Now she sobered. "Mom, I told Robert about the program you're enrolled in for testing an experimental drug. If you don't object, can we speak freely?"

"Of course."

"I'm wondering, if you've experienced any changes, like in appetite or energy level?"

"No, but I haven't been in the program long enough to notice any subtle or dramatic differences. Also, I may not be taking the drug. It's possible I've been assigned to the group that's on the placebo."

"Oh, no." Elizabeth looked heartsick.

"Honey, you know how these testing programs work."

"Yes, but when the outcome involves my own mother—" She bowed her head.

Robert placed his hand over Elizabeth's. "Sweetie, if your mom is on the placebo and the drug turns out to be as promising as the research has shown, she'll start taking this new drug."

Bea noted the affectionate "Sweetie." "Elizabeth, I'm seeing the doctor tomorrow. I had blood work done last week, and I'm being well taken care of. Now let's change the subject. Robert, Elizabeth told me you mailed Kim a copy of that tabloid article that spotlights Dana. Negatively, I assume."

He cocked his head, eyebrows raised, a twinkle in his eye.

"Let's just say we wanted to stir things up a bit. We thought it likely that Mrs. Williams would show the article to others, including her sister."

"Which in turn," Elizabeth said, "might incite action on someone's part, or maybe even a showdown between sisters."

"Well," Bea said, "Dana has been a busy little bee. Imagine manipulating the Elks Lodge's silent auction for Frank and me to win the grand prize. She wanted us to stay in her condo. But why? To make up for past sins or for more sinister purposes?"

Robert shrugged. "I've asked myself that same question. Dana pops up here, there, everywhere, but so far we lack hard evidence to bring charges against her."

"Oh!" Elizabeth set down her drink. "Tell my mother how Dana's picture in the *Tattler* brought about some interesting developments."

Robert nodded. "Supposedly, Mrs. James flew from Honolulu to Kona to be with her sister the day after she was informed of Mr. Williams' death. But the manager of the hotel down the street from Kailua Condos reported Mrs. James was registered at their hotel for several days, starting on the day before the drowning death.

"Also, Tony, the handyman at the condos, apparently reads the *Tattler*. He says a woman who could have stepped out of the photograph on the front page of the tabloid got on the elevator at the condos around 11:30 a.m. on the day Williams died. She carried a large bag and appeared watchful, looking to her sides and behind her."

Bea drew in her breath. "I assume if this woman was Dana, she did not make her presence known to Kim and Barry Williams."

"Who," Robert added, "spent the morning and early afternoon at the beach."

Elizabeth broke the silence. "Mom, what are you thinking?"

"I was thinking back to when that lethal cake was delivered to Frank. So much confusion surfaced over who ordered it, and why it was delivered to our unit. But now maybe someone who recognized Dana from her picture will come forward with answers. If Dana was involved."

"Good thinking, Mom. We probably can thank Heidi for producing the picture since she had access to the unit. I can picture her nosing through drawers and closets for a photograph album."

"Sounds sneaky or even illegal," Bea said. "Speaking of Heidi, is she still employed at the Kailua Condos?"

"As far as we know," Robert said.

Elizabeth snickered. "I'd throw the woman out on her ass. But who's to say if her notoriety constitutes a draw or a liability for the condos? Well." Elizabeth raised her arms in a leisurely stretch. "Time to get busy, Robert."

Bea noted the softness in Elizabeth's tone, the looks exchanged between her and Robert, and suppressed a shiver of delight. Now if only the person or persons responsible for Frank's death could be brought to justice, Bea's world would be an almost happy place.

Robert started to follow Elizabeth as she left the patio, but then held back. "Mrs. Devlin–I mean, Bea, we haven't forgotten about your husband or the circumstances leading to his death. The investigation continues."

"Thank you, Robert. I know you're doing your best." She hesitated, and then said, "Everything I've learned points to Dana as the culprit in bringing such tragedy into our lives. But I guess the evidence is what you call circumstantial?"

"So far, yes. But a strong case can be built on circumstantial evidence. We're getting there, Bea." He smiled, then made a hurried exit. Bea had to admire Robert's positive attitude.

She only wished she felt the same.

On Monday morning, Kim left Jenna in charge at the gallery so that she could meet with Detective Chang at the Los Angeles Police Department's Wilshire Division.

Fortunately, Mark had been able to reschedule his morning appointments so he could join them. His presence and reassuring smile helped Kim to maintain her composure.

They were seated at a long table in a windowless, narrow room. Detective Chang sat at the head of the table, with Kim on his right and Mark on his left. Chang had been cordial when he greeted them, but now as he looked up from his notes, his manner turned cool and professional as he told them the test results had determined that Barry Williams had been murdered.

"Moving on," Chang said to Kim, "we have on record the time line as to how you spent that last day and evening with your husband. I'd like you to go over it again, starting with when you and Mr. Williams arrived at the beach."

Chang listened intently, and when she was finished, Kim held her breath, expecting to be informed she was a prime suspect in Barry's murder. But Chang responded, "We can't discount that you were emotionally distraught over events that evening, perhaps–and I emphasize perhaps–to the extent of wanting your husband dead. But only *after* he asked you for a divorce. Which leaves little time or opportunity to commit a murder.

"The old cliché of where there's a will there's a way could apply here, but you were impaired from your fall in the parking garage and ethylene glycol would have been difficult to obtain on such short notice. These considerations weigh in your favor. Unless, of course, you had a partner in crime."

Kim looked at Mark whose nod and half smile signaled encouragement. "Detective Chang, I swear to you. I am not a murderer. I did not kill my husband."

"Sir." Mark turned to Chang. "As Mrs. Williams' therapist, I can attest to her character and emotional health. This woman could not have killed her husband."

"Duly noted, Dr. Hampton." Chang shut his notebook. "Mrs. Williams, I see you brought along Honolulu's intellectual gem, the *Tattler*."

Kim smiled. "I have no idea who sent this or why it was sent to me and not Dana. And I know if my sister had been sent a copy of this–this rag, I'd have heard about it in spades." She scratched her head. "You'd think there'd been a cover letter or at least a return address. Have you seen this issue?"

"Yes. It must be disturbing to have your sister cast in such an unflattering light."

"Tell me about it. The article portrays Dana as a heartless, insensitive clod who couldn't care less if someone drops dead. As for her 'I wonder who will be next?' remark, she was obviously mouthing off to Heidi McGowan."

Chang turned to Mark. "I assume you've read the article. Care to comment?"

"I agree with Kim that the write-up was biased to put a negative light on Dana James. She's also characterized as a glamorous woman of mystery whose presence invites disaster." He raised both hands. "This is a writer who knows how to cater to the readership.

"One last comment. The destruction of the condo owner's portrait was played up in the article, allowing the readers to form their own opinion regarding Dana James' relationship with the Connellys. None of it positive, I might add."

"Whoever wrote the article is a whack job," Kim said. "I guess Dana could sue for defamation of character, though why acknowledge that kind of garbage?"

"Ah, Mrs. Williams, if only it were that simple."

Chang's stiffening in posture, his deliberate tone brought on a surge in Kim's heart rate. Mark, too, appeared on alert. The detective had their attention.

They sat in silence as Chang explained that Mrs. James' picture in the *Tattler* had led to information that 1) She had registered at the hotel located near Kailua Condos on the day preceding Barry Williams' death; and 2) That the handyman at the condos had identified Mrs. James as being on the property the day of Williams' death. "At the time you and your husband were at the beach, Mrs. Williams."

Kim placed a hand over her heart to still the thumping in her chest. "Wait a minute. You're taking the word of a handyman? And as for the staff at that hotel, they're either lying or cashing in on the publicity. I know Dana was in Honolulu the night of Barry's death. I called her there, and she promised to fly to Kona the next morning to be with me."

"You called her hotel in Honolulu?" Chang asked.

"No. I had her cell phone number." Kim tipped her head back. "Oh, shit. Could she have faked being in Honolulu?" She addressed the question more to herself than to Chang.

Mark cast a worried look in her direction, and then turned to Chang. "Just how reliable is this handyman?"

"He seems to be a dependable witness, based on his report of the altercation between the Williams in the parking garage when they returned from dinner."

Kim gnawed on her thumb nail, clasped her hands. She wished

they'd shut up. Their words stung and felt like pin pricks to the back of her head. And now it felt like someone had turned down the thermostat. "It's cold in here," she said. The room was tilting and she grabbed at the edge of the table with a shaking hand.

Both men stared at her, and Mark hurried to her side. "Kim, are you all right? You seem disoriented."

"I'm feeling light headed." She closed her eyes, took a deep breath, and then opened wide. "Better. I'm steady. I think."

Chang pushed back his chair and stood. "Can I get you something, Mrs. Williams? A glass of water? Or do you think you need to lie down?"

"No. I'm all right." She touched her forehead, feeling the dampness below her hairline. "If we're finished here, I need to get some fresh air."

"You're free to go." He gave Mark a questioning look.

"I'll stay with Kim until I'm sure she can navigate on her own."

As Chang ushered them out, he said to Kim, "I'll be in touch. You're in good hands with Dr. Hampton. Both of you take care."

Kim was grateful for Mark's supporting arm and his silence as they left the building. Outside, she looked up at him, and then away as tears began to form. Mark turned to face her, taking hold of her hands. "I think it would be helpful if we talked. The Comstock Hotel is just around the corner. Their Gold Room is highly rated for lunch and doesn't attract a rowdy crowd."

"Sounds nice but I couldn't eat a thing."

"Did you have breakfast?"

"Coffee and a bagel."

"Not very substantial. Come on, we're going to put some color in those pale cheeks."

Kim didn't argue and as Mark shepherded her down the street, his arm placed lightly over her shoulder, Kim began to relax for the first time in days.

After they'd rounded the corner, Mark stopped and looked back. "It was just a glimpse," he said, "but I thought I saw a woman dressed in white who looked a lot like Dana."

"Probably a look-alike," Kim said as they continued on. "Dana is in downtown L.A. this morning conferring with her attorney."

The walls of the Gold Room depicted scenes from the California Gold Rush, with paintings and photographs of forty-niners staking their claims or panning for gold. Saloon-like structures with bawdy cut-outs of ladies peering from upstairs windows added spice to the setting, providing a distraction from Kim's woes.

They had settled into a spacious cream colored booth and Kim exhaled, "A perfect choice. Some hotels feature sports bars or tea rooms. This is much better."

"Can you picture me in a tea room?" Mark asked.

Kim laughed. "I can't even picture myself in a tea room." She pantomimed holding a cup, little finger extended.

"Your color's better already," Mark said. "Think you're up to unwinding with a glass of wine?"

"Absolutely."

When the wine had been poured, Mark started to look at his menu, but then closed it. "When do you see Dana?"

"Tomorrow. At her shop when she closes at four."

"I'd advise you to stick with our original plan. Let Chang confront Dana as to her whereabouts before and on the day Barry died."

"Okay." She made a face. "I didn't mean to belittle Tony, the handyman. He seemed like a decent person. But he could have been mistaken when he identified Dana as the woman on the property. As for the hotel" Kim put her hand up to her mouth. "Oh, God, Mark. Where is this going?"

"It doesn't look good for Dana."

"Or for me. I can see the headlines on the front page of the *Tattler*: 'Sisters: Partners in Crime. A Charley Maddex Exclusive'."

"Charley Maddex sounds like she'd qualify for a case study in one of my text books."

"Not a nice woman. So. What's going on with you and Dana?"

"She called to thank me for my dinner and to remind me we'd be getting together at her place." He gave her a twisted smile. "I may have screwed up, but I decided to tell her about Susan's call."

"I can imagine her reaction."

"Lots of denials. Susan, ever vindictive, lied to cause trouble between Dana and me. As for Ted, she spoke disparagingly of him as a love-sick puppy whose advances she'd spurned. I told her I'd spoken with Ted, and that he'd confirmed the two of them had been in a relationship."

"Enough said, right?"

"Wrong. He'd lied too, to break us up. If he couldn't have her, no one could, etc., etc."

"Gosh, everybody's a liar." Kim shook her head. As she sipped her wine, her thoughts strayed to this morning's meeting. Slowly she set down her glass. "I thought Detective Chang was receptive when I defended myself."

"He seems decent."

"When he interviewed me after Barry's death, he came across as efficient but stiff, like his face would crack if he moved a muscle. My point is, today he seemed less reserved and much warmer."

Mark smiled. "Maybe the guy's in love."

"I can't picture him with a girlfriend, but you never know. So. When do you see your girlfriend?"

"I'm not sure the term girlfriend applies, but I'll see Dana later in the week."

"I'll let you know how tomorrow's visit goes."

"Please do." He patted her hand, and then reached for his menu, only to push it aside once again. "What if Chang's telling us about Dana's presence at the hotel and on the condo property was a deliberate move to prod one of us to spill the beans to Dana?"

"Because?"

"She might be spurred to take action. For example, seek out a criminal attorney, try to flee the country, or even attempt to buy her way out of her dilemma."

"And then Chang pounces? My God, like a game. Her move, his move. I hate this cat and mouse stuff."

"But I'd say he's on the right track. *If* I've made the right judgment call. At any rate, I'll try to get Dana to invite me over as soon as possible. Then I'll take it from there."

"You mean tell her about our meeting with Chang?" At his nod, she toyed with the edges of her cocktail napkin, and then looked up. "Dana's my sister, and I should be the one to carry out Chang's plan. If that's what he's up to. Besides, I'm seeing her tomorrow."

Mark's response was a grimace. After a long pause, he said, "I suppose you're right. And I know you'll carry a load of trepidation and guilt feelings, but don't beat yourself up, Kim. Dana won't blow away; she's made of steel. In addition, she's quick witted and undoubtedly will come up with a clever explanation. Just don't argue with her."

"I'll stick to listening to nuances in tone and observing body language," she smirked.

Mark chuckled. "Good girl. And now I decree that to preserve our sanity and safeguard our digestive systems, all Dana talk be suspended for the duration of lunch."

That was fine with Kim. Since their meeting with the detective, a question she felt compelled to ask Mark had embedded itself in her mind, like a musical refrain, repeating itself over and over. Now she had gained a reprieve.

Lunch had restored balance and normality–at least temporarily. When their server dropped off the check, Kim said to Mark, "Thanks for babysitting. Lunch is my treat."

"Nonsense. It's been my pleasure."

"You're too kind." Kim planted a kiss that was almost full on his lips, and then sprang back. "Wow. I haven't even finished my second glass of wine, and I'm tipsy. Sorry."

"I'm not sorry."

Nor was she. She was sorry that playtime was over, that she had to come to terms with the unthinkable. The question that weighed on her mind had graduated from a repetitive refrain to a dark and foreboding counterpoint.

"I need to ask you something," she said. Her tone must have signaled her seriousness. The mischievous gleam in Mark's eyes gave way to fixed attentiveness: the clinician attending to his patient.

Kim met his gaze. "Based on everything you know about Dana, do you think she'd be capable of committing a violent act?"

"By violent act, do you mean murder?"

Kim nodded.

"I think—" Mark stared into space for a long moment, then turned to her, his eyes moist. "The answer, sadly, is yes."

On that somber note they prepared to leave.

On a scale of one to ten, Dana's day had registered at a minus one.

But in the gathering twilight, nursing a Coke on her terrace, her edginess began to recede as she watched hop-scotching city lights phase in against a blue gray backdrop. In minutes full darkness would bring a nip to the air, a prelude to autumn.

Fall's bite suited her. Besides, the terrace was her domain–Planet Dana—from which she could view a fully illuminated world at her fingertips.

Empowered by her own majesty, Dana dismissed the burden of hurt and anger that had weighed on her throughout the day.

Instead, she turned her thoughts to Ted, knave to her queen. The wimp had left messages on her house and cell phones. Had he overruled her edict that they avoid contact? Naughty boy had given his phone number where he could be reached at his new "digs". She'd chortled over his use of that term which was passé, at best.

Ted was the least of her concerns. Kim had called with a reminder she'd be seeing Dana at the shop tomorrow afternoon. A day ago Dana had thought to cancel their meeting. Kim's constant whining, fearing she'd be accused of Barry's murder, was becoming tiresome. Today, however, she detected an urgency in Kim's tone that whetted her curiosity. Dana now welcomed a face-to-face encounter with her sister.

Dana moved to the edge of the terrace, relishing her commanding position. In the old days, disloyalty was punished by banishment to the tower or dungeon. In today's world retribution came about by more creative methods.

Reluctantly, Dana turned from the sights and sounds of her city. She needed her rest to prepare for tomorrow. But first she would finish her Coke while she reflected on all the tomorrows to come.

Her first order of business: Tie up loose ends.

Chapter Twenty-Five

Kim was not encouraged by Dana's perfunctory greeting or cool stare. Kim had arrived at her sister's shop a few minutes before closing time. She waited now in the back while Dana locked doors and display cases.

It had been a while since Kim had visited Dana at her workplace and now as she scanned the room, something struck her as odd or off kilter.

She made a mental inventory of the sofa, armchair, desk and small refrigerator. But Kim remembered a Tiffany lamp that had graced a corner of the desk; now, it was nowhere to be seen. Also missing, an Oriental throw rug, a Degas reproduction of dancers at the bar, a corner stand that showcased merchandise from the shop, collectibles from Dana's travels and, on a separate shelf, a replica of the portrait Susan had destroyed.

Maybe Dana was embarking on a redecorating project. Clutching a copy of the *Tattler*, Kim slumped onto the sofa, wishing with all her heart that questions pertaining to decor were the only hot topics for discussion. Kim hadn't heard Dana approach, thanks to thick azure blue carpeting that served as a soothing counterpoint to displays of glittering rings and other high fashion jewelry.

In contrast, Dana's entrance was fast paced and emphatic, her heels performing a staccato passage over hardwood floors as she swirled past Kim to sit at her desk. "What's so urgent?" she asked.

"Dana, for heaven's sake, what is the matter with you? Why are you in such a foul mood?"

"Why do you think?"

Kim threw up her hands. "I didn't come here to play games. I want to show you something I received in the mail." She held up the tabloid for Dana to see.

"That's my picture."

"Yes, look at it. Better yet, read the article."

"Toss it my way."

Jesus. "No. You come to me."

Kim assessed her sister's grandiosity and movements like a queen in her court. With her head held high, Dana joined Kim on the sofa.

"I guess the story was too dramatic to resist," Kim said, explaining how the feature writer from the *Tattler* had sought out Heidi McGowan for information regarding two deaths and one near death in the unit owned by Dana James. The piece posed the question of whether all the tragedies were a coincidence or not.

Dana skimmed the article and just as quickly thrust the paper aside. "I had no idea Heidi McGowan housed an imagination in her teenie-weenie brain. What a crock. Can't you just picture that chunky frump in her garish muumuus, her smirky expression, her crow's feet jumping off her face?"

Whew, was Kim's silent rejoinder, relieved that Dana was only focused on Heidi. "I have to say I was appalled at the tone of the article."

"And so you express your indignation by waving this trash in my face?"

"Unfortunately, the article raises questions regarding your behavior. Also, it highlights inconsistencies in your explanations to me."

"Oh, for God's sake. Cut the gobbledygook."

"Dana, the manager of the hotel where you stayed in Kona told Detective Chang he recognized you from your picture in the *Tattler*, and that you checked in the day before Barry was murdered. Also, the handyman at Kailua Condos saw you on the property at the time Barry and I were at the beach."

"And I saw you making lovey-dovey with Mark Hampton."

"What are you talking about?"

"Yesterday's appointment with my attorney was canceled. So I was out and about running errands on Wilshire Boulevard. I saw you and Mark clinging together with his arm around your shoulders. I couldn't believe my eyes. How could you betray me, you little sneak?

"As for Mark Hampton, he's just another listing under B for bastard."

"Dana, listen to me. No one is betraying you, because nothing is going on between Mark and myself. Please. Let me explain.

"You remember we both figured Detective Chang would want to interview me over the circumstances of Barry's death? Well, the meeting took place yesterday at the L.A.P.D., Wilshire Division. Mark, as my therapist, was allowed to be present."

Kim noted Dana's lack of eye contact, her regal posture and stony expression. But she had to press on.

"When Detective Chang gave me this new information about the timing of your whereabouts in Kona, I became upset, both physically and emotionally. What you saw on the street was Mark being protective because I was still shaky. In no way was his arm around me a romantic gesture."

"I know what I saw, and I don't believe you."

"Fine. We went straight to a hotel and spent the afternoon having sex."

Dana guffawed. "In your dreams."

"Okay. Forget that. What matters is that you haven't explained those reported sightings when you were supposed to be in Honolulu."

"Oh, all the roaches coming out of the woodwork, just for a little attention. That handyman saw my picture and Bingo! Dana James slithers onto the property, complete with furtive glances and a mysterious bag.

"As for the hotel register, someone obviously faked my signature, signing me in a day early.

"For what purpose?"

"Why don't you ask the publisher of that filthy tabloid? They'll exploit anyone for a story. And the scum who perpetuate these myths walk away with a bundle."

Body language: jerky, restive, lack of eye contact. Tone: defensive, sharp, fast paced. Kim had her report for Mark.

"Dana, I'm not the enemy, and the way you're acting concerns me. You make accusations that Mark and I have something going on, and that people are out to exploit you. I'm not sure where I go from here."

"Why not go home?"

"Okay. But answer me this. Can you prove you were in Honolulu the day before and the day of Barry's death?"

"I don't have to prove a God damned thing."

"Give me a name. Where did you stay in Honolulu? I'm serious. Detective Chang may come calling, and it's your word against these witnesses who've come forward."

"All right. If you must know, I checked into Aloha Towers; then I heard from a client of Jasper's who lives in Honolulu. The guy was going out of town, his ocean front condo became available, and so I moved in for a few days."

"No witnesses?"

"How would I know? I wasn't counting on being interrogated by my sister."

"It's not me you have to worry about; it's Detective Chang."

"Like I said, no one witnessed Barry's death. Of course, as I've reminded you, the spouse is always the most logical suspect." Dana gave her a self-satisfied smirk before leaving the sofa to return to her desk.

Kim watched as Dana opened a leather bound book, and then reached for a pen to make an entry. *What is she doing?* Kim wondered. *Was the book for making appointments or an inventory? Was it a diary?* The whole thing seemed as out of sync as the starkness of the room.

Dana now switched her focus from her book to Kim, giving her a probing look. "After seeing you with Mark, I thought why not let Kim take the rap for Barry's death?"

"Dana, good lord, what are you telling me?"

"You figure it out. But like you always say, it's big sister to the rescue. So why not assume I did you one gigantic favor?"

Kim stood. "You're talking in circles. What do you mean you'd let me take the rap for Barry's death? Did you kill him?"

Dana gasped, placing a hand over her heart. "Mercy, how could you say such a thing?"

"Look, Dana, I didn't come here to play games, so stop toying with me."

Dana leaned back in her chair, eyelids at half-mast. "I've always said you have no sense of humor, Kim."

"I fail to see anything amusing about this conversation."

"Listen up." Dana leaned forward, elbows on desk, gripping the sides of the opened book. "I don't take rejection lightly, and Mark will pay for his cavalier treatment of me. As for you and Mark, if I couldn't corral him, you don't stand a chance in hell, baby."

Kim started to reply, but clamped her lips shut instead. She was no match for Dana's thrusts and parries. She turned to leave.

At the door, Kim couldn't resist a backward look. Dana sat upright, hands flat on the desk, her gaze devoid of expression.

Words that had no connection to their previous conversation came tumbling out of Kim, "I couldn't help but notice how empty this room looks. Are you planning to redecorate?"

Dana's eyes flickered with amusement as her lips curved into a smile. "Wouldn't you like to know?"

"Not particularly." Glad to have the last word, Kim made a hasty exit.

At home, Kim was on the phone to Mark. "The woman is infuriating. Talking to Dana was like one of us speaking English while the other answered in Swahili."

"How was her mood?"

"Dreadful." Kim continued with a description of Dana's body language, her reaction to the *Tattler* article, her castigation of people who placed her at the hotel or on the condo property, contrary to Dana's version of her whereabouts.

"Dana implied she was involved in Barry's death–thereby doing me a favor–then acted shocked when I asked her outright if she'd killed him."

"Dana can be melodramatic. Maybe she implicated herself to get a rise out of you."

"Whatever her mind games, she wasn't happy with either of us, Mark. You were right when you thought you spotted her. She saw us walking down the street with your arm around my shoulders. Ergo, I betrayed her and you're a bastard."

Mark sighed, "Well, she hasn't canceled our dinner tomorrow evening."

"Dana's beginning to frighten me. I almost feel I need to change the locks on my doors. Maybe you should too."

"She must really have been on the warpath."

"I wouldn't take her behavior lightly, Mark. Lately, Dana's been saying 'you'll get yours' or words to that effect. I have a really bad feeling about you and Dana getting together."

"I appreciate your warning, Kim. I'll watch my back."

"Call me?"

"I promise I'll report back."

That was fine with Kim. The not so fine part would be the waiting to hear from Mark. Dana's dark side had manifested today in ways Kim had never experienced.

And it scared the bejesus out of her.

By the time Dana entered her penthouse, she had downgraded her encounter with Kim from nasty to unpleasant. Besides, sparring with her sister was a hoot. Lord knows, Kim didn't stand a chance against Dana's circuitous twists and turns.

Maybe Kim had been sincere in her protestations regarding her designs on Mark. And maybe not.

How interesting that Kim had noticed the missing pieces in the back office. The explanation for their removal would soon become evident. As for the tabloid fodder, nothing existed to connect her with Barry's death or Frank's unfortunate demise. Still, she wasn't thrilled over her characterization in the press or the possibility of being questioned by Chang regarding discrepancies over her whereabouts within the time frame of Barry's death. In fact, Chang was becoming a damn nuisance.

And though it shouldn't matter, it rankled her that Mark was now privy to questions regarding her truthfulness.

Suddenly, she felt exhausted, as if she'd climbed twenty floors to arrive at her front door. A Coke would serve as a pick-me-up.

As Dana neared her desk on the way to the kitchen, the blinking of her phone's message light proved a distraction. Jasper? Mark? Ted?

She guessed correctly that the caller was Ted. This time she made a note of his new phone number.

Ted was in his kitchen surveying his selection of frozen dinners when the phone rang. His heart skipped a beat. *Let it be Dana.*

At the sound of her voice, he heard himself blubber like a besotted school boy.

"Dana, darling, you got my message. I can't tell you how happy I am to hear from you."

There was silence from the other end before her voice came on, soft and beguiling. "Why Ted, I thought it was settled we stay out of contact for a while."

"It seemed logical at the time, but I find it impossible to stay away from you. And I would hope you feel the same. Surely, we can meet now and then. We could keep a low profile. I have my place, you have your place, so why deny ourselves the pleasure of being together?"

"I'm a free agent, but in your case, it's not that simple, Ted. If we were seen together in a compromising situation, Susan might retaliate by upping her financial demands or argue that my influence over you makes you an unfit father."

"If we were living in a small town in Bible Belt Middle America, I'd agree with you, but in a cosmopolitan city—"

"Ted! Stop, stop, stop. I can't let this go on."

The sharpness in her tone caught him off guard. Something was off. Way off. "What are you trying to tell me?"

"Ted. You are one of the nicest men I've ever known, and I don't like hurting you. But you have to know, I'm going back to Jasper."

"You can't be serious. What about us?"

"Did either of us make a firm commitment regarding a future together?"

"We were sure as hell headed in that direction."

"Well, darling, things have a way of working out as they should. Now you can pursue your passions unhampered by Susan. You can look for a woman to love and cherish who shares your interests." She paused. "It just won't be me."

"Dana, I—" he was breathing heavily, "I can't accept what you're telling me. Something isn't right here."

"Ted." Her voice was once again soft and silky. "Like the song goes, 'It was just one of those things.'"

The line went dead.

Chapter Twenty-Six

Dana surveyed her bedroom. Open drawers yawned at her, their contents piled willy-nilly on the bed, while clothes sprawled over chairs or were still closet bound, clustered in smug groups of seasonal wear.

Her groan was audible as she rotated her shoulders and then massaged the base of her neck. *Break time*, Dana decided as she headed for the terrace.

But once outside, she realized she hadn't been keeping track of the time. The sun's rays had retreated in deference to the city's emerging sound and light show. Mark was due to arrive in less than an hour.

Back inside, Dana got into the shower and reviewed her recent accomplishments. Decorative furnishings from her office had been crated several days ago. But getting household goods ready for shipment to Australia proved tiresome.

Still, she was motivated to prepare for the packers and movers. With luck, she'd be long gone when Chang came calling. Not that she doubted her prowess in outwitting the detective. But she certainly didn't want to waste her time—or his.

In concluding that the benefits outweighed the risks, Dana had decided to reconcile with Jasper. Furthermore, her insistence they speed up the move had brought a gleam to Jasper's eyes, a bounce to his step. But what sealed the deal was her willingness to call Australia home. *The irony of it all*, she thought, as she dried off and then turned her attention to hair and make-up. What had spurred their break-up was Jasper's indifference to her feelings. What did he care that she'd be deprived of country and home, of her shop and yes, even Kim? Now she welcomed the chance to escape the consequences of her deeds, as justified as they might be.

But first things first. As Dana preened in front of her mirror, she pictured Mark fawning over the white silk, close-fitting dress that she'd paired with a short, sheer white jacket.

She stared at herself in the mirror and declared her reflection "Beauty in White"–a perfect title for a portrait worthy of joining the ranks of masterpieces in a museum like the Norton Simon in Pasadena.

Too bad she had to settle for one pair of adoring eyes over crowds of admirers. But truth be told, she'd dressed for Mark alone. She had decided that he should take with him a bittersweet remembrance of love lost.

As if on cue, her doorbell chimes signaled show time. "Poor little lamb," she murmured, enjoying a measure of sardonic glee.

Their greetings were cordial, though perhaps reflexive, as in a throwback to happier times. Whatever the warmth of the moment, she steeled herself for what was about to unfold.

Dana led Mark to the terrace, indicated he should take his usual seat, and then excused herself.

Moments later when Dana brought out their martinis, she noted Mark's sober expression. Kim had undoubtedly filled him in on the sisters' quirky meeting. Dana wondered how her sister would have described her—wily? willful? wicked? "I know my invitation was for dinner," Dana said as she took the chair next to the small table that separated them, "but I have something different in mind for us this evening–a farewell drink."

Mark did not return her smile, his eyes reflecting puzzlement as he sat up straighter.

Dana suppressed a smile, enjoying his uneasiness. "You think I'm guilty of destroying lives." She raised her glass. "Shall we drink to that?"

"Dana, as always, you look like you've stepped from the pages of a fashion magazine, but this posturing on your part is not at all attractive."

"Oh hush." She took a sip of her drink, then another sip. "You're not joining me? Here, we'll trade." She switched their drinks.

His smile was uncertain. "What kind of games are you playing?"

"I'm just having a little fun with you. But mainly, I wanted to say goodbye in person."

"What is that supposed to mean?"

"It means goodbye to all of this." She gestured widely. "And hello to Australia."

Mark still hadn't touched his drink. He stared at her in disbelief, as if she'd confessed to being an alien from a distant solar system.

"So you're back with Jasper."

"Yep."

"Aren't you being a little ho-hum about relocating halfway around the world? Have you thought this move through?"

Before she could respond, he softened his tone. "I remember the day we met, the way we instantly connected. I also remember how unhappy you were over the idea of giving up your home. He stared down at his drink and then raised his eyes to meet her gaze, his expression reflective. "I didn't even know you, but the thought of your leaving brought on a feeling of loss."

"That was a magical moment." She sipped her martini and then set down her glass. "Oh, well. Times change. People change. But I loved that when we were together, you found me, shall we say, irresistible?" She directed her gaze at him in a challenge to refute her statement.

"Dana, I still have feelings for you."

"But?"

"Part of what I feel for you now is concern." He reached across the table to place his hand over hers. "I can compare you to an exotic flower that's beginning to darken at the edges, that will collapse upon itself and break apart if not tended to."

Her laugh sounded brittle to her ears. "Never mind explaining what you mean by 'tended to'." She wrenched her hand from under his. "What nonsense."

"Okay. Let's get back to your move to Australia. Why the sudden turnaround?"

"My priorities have changed."

"In what way?"

She shrugged. "I don't have to explain myself."

"What about Kim?"

"Kim will have to learn to survive without her big sister. It's time she grew up and stopped being a cry baby."

Mark bowed his head, looking pained as he clenched his lips. Finally he looked up. "Dana, I'm going to speak frankly. I won't bore you with medical jargon, but you're exhibiting signs of a serious personality disorder. Particularly, your game playing and devious behavior have me concerned."

"Oh, come on, Mark, we all play games. As for devious behavior, I have no idea what you're talking about."

"I think you know exactly what I'm talking about."

Smug, stupid man. Her hand shook as she tasted her martini.

His lips formed an "oh" as he let out his breath. "How can I put this? You bring so many endearing qualities to a relationship. You're dynamic, alluring, creative, to name but a few traits. On the dark side, you nurture your resentments and act on perceived betrayals with a vengeance that's all consuming. In short, you're getting away with murder, and I don't mean that metaphorically."

She gasped and brought her glass down hard on the table, spilling some of her drink. "Where is this coming from? Evil voices in your head? Geez. I'll take this tirade as a one time–what do you call it? Aberration?"

She could hear near hysteria in her voice. And that would not do. She modulated her tone.

"Now let me be frank, Dr. Hampton. You feign concern while you make these wild assertions about me. But I know what you're up to. You use these tactics as a ploy to make me seem unfit to become a permanent part of your life."

"Why would I do that?'

"Because assholes like you can't commit to a relationship. I believe the term is commitment phobic?"

Her words didn't seem to affect him. He sat like a lump with a discerning expression. *What am I, case #125?*

"Well," she said, "this conversation sucks. Since you've decided not to join me in a farewell drink, I think you should get the hell out."

He pushed back his chair but stayed put at the sign of her raised hand.

"I feel sorry for you, Mark. I could have given you the world. Now someone else will benefit from your loss."

She held his gaze, but he didn't flinch. His eyes conveyed something she couldn't be sure of—could it be regret?

Dana gripped the stem of her glass. "I see you years from now, an old man hunched over your brandy and cigar, alone on your deck, reliving what might have been."

Mark stood and maintained an even tone as he spoke. "I'll overlook your less than flattering portrait of me. Although if your prediction turns out to be correct, I'll still hold close my memories of the wonderful times we shared."

"If you recall, I was willing to make it a lifetime of beautifully shared memories."

Mark eased back into his chair. "It was not my intention to cut us off, Dana. But I recognized that if we were to make a lifetime commitment, a number of personal issues needed to be resolved."

His tone was gentle, his expression mirroring compassion.

Cripes, is he trying to kill me with kindness? "Personal issues?" She spit out the words. "Here you go again. My God, Mark, you're turning into a Johnny one-note bore. Just go. Get out."

Mark rose. His tone deliberate, he stated flatly, "Running off to Australia is what sucks, Dana. You can't run away from yourself. You're in trouble and you need help."

Dana had raised her drink to her lips. Now she stared at him over her glass. "Screw you," she muttered.

Quickly, she averted her gaze, cleared Mark from her thoughts, and allowed only sounds to enter her mind: the scrape of a chair, footsteps, a pause, then more footsteps.

She sat very still until she heard the front door close. She exhaled then unaware she'd been holding her breath.

The sounds from the street below, now augmented by an emergency vehicle wailing down the boulevard, partnered by the squeals of braking cars were an affront to her sensibilities. The terrace had lost its charm.

Back inside, Dana placed the drinks she'd carried from the terrace on the table that fronted the same sofa where she and Mark had engaged in cozy conversation as a prelude to love.

She knew it behooved her to get back to work, but she might as well finish her drink. And while she was at it, she'd finish Mark's untouched martini as well. Anything to soften the edge of his hurtful insinuations.

Vengeance. The word sounded irksome to her ears. Ditto, for those other swell "V" words: vindictive, vitriolic, and vicious.

What about victim? she thought. Reaching for her martini, she knew that she, Dana, was the victim of cruel, perverted acts of betrayal and injustice, thanks to the evil trio: Barry, Bea and Susan.

She drank deeply and then giggled. "Do unto others as they do to you," she said to herself. She liked the way that came out.

"Oops-a-daisy," she said, noticing that she hadn't shut the terrace doors. She went to pull the doors closed, and then on her return, had to grab the arm of the sofa to steady herself. She blamed the three inch heels.

Leaning on the sofa, she kicked off her shoes and then reached for the lamp on the end table to switch on the light. In so doing, she discovered her brown leather book hidden behind the lamp. *Sun of a gun.* She'd been looking for that little rascal.

With book in hand, Dana returned to her place on the sofa and opened to the page where she'd cited under the heading, "Loose Ends", the countless wrap-up chores involved in a move. Also on the to-do list: breaking ties with Ted and Mark. Ted had been a cinch. Mark, on the other hand…

From Mark's uneasy demeanor, it appeared he suspected the evil queen had poisoned his drink or intended to clobber him by other means.

With all the fuss over her comings and goings, she wasn't about to up the ante by sharing her penthouse with a corpse.

Not that he deserved to get off so easy. Still, for a romantic like Mark, sweet revenge could come in the form of his being incapable of settling for less of a woman than herself. She'd drink to that!

Then there was another loose end: her dear sister. Kim would make a scene and babble on about Dana's impulsiveness, her abandonment of Kim, how the move to Australia would ruin Dana's life. Just thinking about Kim made her tired.

She tossed the book aside. All this aggravation was a drag, depleting her energy. Or maybe it was the martini. She'd made them extra strong to jolt Mark. Too bad he'd wimped out.

Dana rested her head on the back of the sofa and closed her eyes.

Ah, this felt good. Five, ten minutes of shuteye, and then she'd resume packing.

Dana had barely shut her eyes when rapping or tapping sounds intruded. She fought arousal but to no avail. She could still taste the gin and wondered if the knocking was at her door or in her head.

The rapping started up again, now more distinctly. Dana peered with one eye at the door. Jasper was tied up with a business associate. Besides, he had a key. She couldn't imagine Mark returning, and Kim would have called first.

Maybe they'd go away. She relaxed as the rapping ceased, only to jump at the sound of the doorbell chimes. She'd better investigate. Stumbling a little, Dana crossed to the door in her stocking feet.

She opened the door a mere inch or two to peek out. A woman in a blue jacket dress, clutching a medium-sized matching bag stood beyond the door as if hesitant to approach. Dana didn't recognize the woman.

Dana opened the door wider in an attempt to place the person, and then froze. *Oh, no.* She squinted in an attempt to test her vision. "Bea?" she managed to gasp.

"Mind if I come in?"

While Dana stood like a dummy, mouth agape, Bea slipped past her into the penthouse and stood with her back to Dana as she scanned the room, gazing to the left, upwards and to the right. "What a remarkable place," Bea said, turning to Dana. Behind her glasses, Bea's eyes shone with what Dana interpreted as admiration mixed with awe.

Dana strode forward." What are you doing here?"

"You and I have a little unfinished business."

"You're not welcome here, Bea. If you don't leave, I'll call security."

"Dana." Bea's slump in posture, the quaver in her voice, made her look and sound weaker and older than she was. "Please hear me out. I don't have much time left on this planet. I've been diagnosed with terminal breast cancer."

Dana flinched. "That's terrible. But why come to me?"

"Because my time is limited, I need to put my affairs in order.

You are one of my loose ends."

Dana relaxed her stance. "I can relate to that. So?"

"Do you mind if we sit down?" Bea pointed to the sofa.

"This is not a good time, Bea. I'm in the process of packing my household goods for a move out of the country." She eyed her empty glass. "I guess I won't be getting much more done tonight. So, okay. But let's make it short."

Dana shut the front door and led the way to the sofa. When they were seated, Bea stared curiously at the two cocktail glasses.

Dana gave a little snort. "I'm not in the habit of fixing myself two martinis. I had a guest, but he, uh, declined his drink. His loss, my gain." She drank from the full glass and then set it down. "Where are my manners? You want a martini, Bea?"

Bea's smile was demure. "If I drank a martini, you'd have to carry me out of here. However, I'd welcome a soft drink, if you have one. My mouth gets so dry because of the medications I'm taking."

"Sure. I'll bring you a Coke."

In the kitchen, Dana took out two Cokes, thinking she'd better switch to something non-alcoholic, but then reconsidered and put one can back in the fridge. Gin would ease the way through what she hoped would be a brief encounter with the woman who had almost ruined her life.

Now seated next to Bea, Dana reached for her martini, while Bea raised her drink in a salute. After taking several sips of Coke, Bea set down her glass. "Can you guess why I'm here?"

"To make amends for robbing me of my scholarship?"

"You robbed yourself, Dana. Have you no conception of wrongdoing? Do you think you were entitled to the scholarship even though you cheated?"

Dana rolled her eyes. "You came here to lecture me?"

Bea made a dismissive motion with her hand. "I didn't mean to get off on that. I'm here because we need to sort out a few things."

Dana sighed and raised her glass. At the rate this was going, she'd soon be opening another bottle of gin. "Please do make your point."

"My point is that I know it was you who killed Frank."

"What?" She drew out the word. Carefully, Dana placed her glass on the table. Now Bea was rambling on about the silent auction at the Elks Lodge and how Dana had seen to it that the Devlins won a free stay at Dana's condo in Kona.

"That cake you had delivered to Frank was the murder weapon."

Dana blinked to clear her vision. "Jesus, lady, your medications are making you delusional."

"Why would you want to take the life of a loving, decent man? To punish me? Was that it?"

"He wasn't supposed to die. It was—" Dana clamped a hand over her mouth. My God, what did she just say? Bea stared at her with an intensity that was almost blinding.

"Detective Chang knows it was you, Dana, who sent the cake."

Bluffing, Dana told herself, *the woman is bluffing*. "I don't know what you're talking about."

"You're one tough customer, aren't you? But I would guess you're not feeling so great right now."

Dana raised a hand to her throat. She did feel slightly nauseous. "I'm fine. You think I can't hold my liquor?"

"Your drinking habits don't concern me. However, when you were in the kitchen, I took it upon myself to enhance your drink."

Dana shook her head to clear out the cobwebs, unsure if she'd heard Bea correctly.

"Of course, you wouldn't notice any change immediately. Ethylene glycol is odorless and colorless, but perhaps just a trifle sweet?"

"You put anti-freeze in my drink?" Dana thought she'd screamed the words, but the sound coming from her mouth was fragmented and weak.

"I've got to get help." Dana tried to stand but couldn't raise herself. She pushed hard to get up, but her legs wouldn't hold, and she fell back onto the sofa.

Bea, her tone conversational, said, "So you were packing to leave the country?" She looked Dana in the eye. "I guess there'll be a change in plans."

"Bea. Please. Please. You've got to help me. Call 911."

Bea had removed her glasses. Her eyes, rheumy and sad, she said, "I hear the panic in your voice and see the look of horror in your eyes. Now you can relate to your victims."

"Bea, for God's sake. Do something." Everything in the room seemed disconnected, rubbery. The room was melting and so was she. "Help me," she begged.

Glasses back on, her tone firm, Bea loomed over her.

"Call it an obsession, but before I go to my grave, I need the truth. Barry Williams had no one to save him when he ingested the liquor you poisoned. You'll die like he did. Or I can call for help. You tell me what you did, and then we'll see about calling 911."

There is no evidence. Chang knows he hasn't got a case. Dana was lucid enough to cling to those thoughts. She caught Bea looking at her watch. The woman was insane. She'd confess, but later it would be Bea's word against hers. If there was a later.

"I got rid of Barry because he deserved to die."

"How did you kill him?"

"Switched Drambuie bottles. Traded his for my poisoned one. Then switched them back again."

"And Frank?"

It was getting harder now for Dana to think, to talk. "Ordered cakes. One with peanut base."

"You had them delivered to Frank?"

"Yes."

"When you knew I'd be out?"

"Yes. Yes. Yes." Four glasses wobbled on the table. Two Beas hovered over her. Neither woman moved. "Go. Go. 911," Dana croaked.

After what seemed an eternity, the two Beas left the sofa.

Dana's last conscious thought was two-fold: Bea, whose demise was imminent, would not risk departing from this world with Dana's death on her conscience. Or she would let Dana die. And then the two of them would meet in hell.

Bea had moved out of Dana's range of vision and now stood

behind the sofa to assess Dana's condition. Her feet touched the floor, but from the waist up, she lay crumpled to the side, eyes shut, lips slightly open, with drool at the corners of her mouth. Her skin had taken on a waxy sheen.

Coming around to the front of the sofa, Bea thought to straighten Dana's dress that had inched up to reveal her thighs, then shuddered and moved to where she'd been sitting to retrieve her bag. She glanced again at Dana. She didn't want to admit it to herself, at war with her conscience, but Bea decided that yes, she was savoring this moment.

Her motions business-like, Bea reached inside her bag for her cell phone, and then placed her call.

"Mission accomplished," she said.

Chapter Twenty-Seven

The street outside the Wilshire Marquis was set ablaze with a pulsating aurora of flashing blues and reds. To Bea, it was sheer madness.

She stood stoically next to Chang as police and medical personnel filled the lobby.

"Elizabeth should be here any minute," Chang said. "I told her that as part of my investigation I needed to drop by here in the early evening. We agreed she'd join me around sevenish so we could spend the rest of the evening together."

He smiled. "I explained I couldn't elaborate on my presence here because I was pressed for time."

"And of course," Bea said, "your vague wording would compel Elizabeth to come running." She paused. "You didn't tell her about my part in all this?"

"I thought it best to wait until we were all together." He'd been eyeing the entrance. "I would say that moment is upon us."

Elizabeth had spotted the two of them and came running toward them. "Mom! What are you doing here? What is going on? I'd swear we're smack in the middle of a crime scene. Robert?"

"Sweetie, it's okay. We'll explain."

At that moment the elevator doors opened. Bea stretched her neck to peer over onlookers and was able to identify Dana being transported on a stretcher.

Elizabeth stood on tiptoe. "They're carrying out a woman." She moved to the side for a better view, then grabbed Chang's arm. "Robert, is that Dana?"

He nodded.

"Is she dead?"

Chang inclined his head toward Bea.

"Let's talk at dinner," Bea said.

Robert hadn't been able to get away immediately, which left Bea to fend off Elizabeth's queries.

She'd held her position but was relieved now that the three of them were seated in the Italian restaurant across the street from the Wilshire Marquis.

Elizabeth's attempt at a smile failed as she shifted her gaze from her mother to Robert. "Okay, you two. Time to come clean." She paused as the waiter served their drinks, and then continued, "It's obvious you both were involved in whatever led to Dana's demise."

Bea sipped her wine before addressing her daughter. "Wrong on both counts. I acted without Robert's blessing, and Dana is not dead."

Elizabeth looked dumbfounded. "Would you care to fill in a very large gap?"

"Exactly what I had in mind." Bea raised her hand. "Let's take it from the beginning, okay? As I looked back, I'd concluded more and more that Dana was responsible for Frank's death. And more and more I'd come to believe it unlikely she'd be held accountable.

"Convinced I had no other choice, I formulated a plan to bring Dana to justice. I brought this plan to Robert."

The detective squeezed Elizabeth's hand. "I was intrigued with your mother's proposal, but in good conscience refused to put her in harm's way."

Elizabeth gave him a tremulous smile. "Thank you, Robert." She turned to Bea. "I can't believe you'd put your life on the line."

"Honey, you're being too dramatic. Now hear me out. I was able to arrange a meeting with Robert's superior. It took a while to persuade him I was on the right track, but thankfully I was able to convince him the end justified the means.

"To make it short, this evening I paid Dana a surprise visit." At Elizabeth's look of consternation, she added, "With Robert close by to spring to my rescue if I so much as raised my voice. He insisted on taking that precaution."

Bea described her encounter with Dana, the drinks episode, Dana's confession and eventual loss of consciousness.

Elizabeth looked wide eyed at her mother. "Let me get this

straight. You told Dana you'd spiked her drink with anti-freeze, but you didn't. What, then, caused her to act dopey and pass out?"

"I have in my medicine chest a number of prescription drugs, including codeine and medications for insomnia called alkaloids. These drugs, which I ground into a fine powder, can induce intoxication and even bring on hallucinations.

"The combination of drugs I provided her, plus her belief that I'd poisoned her drink, led to her collapse. She will recover, but slowly, and it won't be pleasant."

"What follows will be more unpleasant," Robert added.

Bea nodded. "With this in mind, Robert, I'd better give you my watch. After I show it to Elizabeth. Take a gander at this, my dear daughter. Have you ever seen a voice recorder watch? It's ingenious." She pointed. "To turn it on, I pressed this button to start recording my conversation with Dana. With this model, the blinking light that indicates it's recording can be switched off, so no one's the wiser."

"How sweet that is." Elizabeth took a long look, and then handed the watch to Robert. "I can't see any difference from the watch I'm wearing." She turned to Bea. "Robert is always proclaiming what a great addition I'd be to his staff." She pressed his hand. "What about my mom, Robert? Wouldn't she make a great consultant?"

"Absolutely." He raised his glass. "A toast to your lovely mother for her inventiveness, pluck and perseverance."

Elizabeth followed suit. "I'll second Robert's toast, though I'm tempted to add foolhardiness to the list." She brushed away a tear. "What I mean to say is that I'm so proud of you, Mom."

Bea's lips quivered, but she managed a soft "Thank you."

Being with the daughter she loved and the man she was sure she'd grow to love, Bea could only bask in the warmth of their smiles and kind words. Whatever her destiny, peace and hope now transcended fear and despair.

It was as if an angel had whispered in her ear, "Stay strong, Bea. Live each day with courage and with the expectancy that anything is possible."

"So." Bea said to Elizabeth and Robert. "What's next on the agenda? San Francisco? Let me tell you it's a city of many delights. Did you know, Robert, that Elizabeth's dad and I honeymooned there?"

And as Bea recounted their adventures, she felt Frank's presence beside her, blue-eyed and blond, his laughter drawing her laughter, his warmth, his ardor bringing a new and joyous dimension to her life.

She would hold on to that image.

Epilogue

Wedding album in hand, Elizabeth plops onto the sofa in the living room of the one bedroom apartment she and Robert are renting in Kona. The place is still a bit stark, even with the addition of house plants and decorative shells, but Robert claims his wife could qualify for Decorator of the Year. She smiles, thinking to herself that his newlywed status was surely coloring his judgment.

Actually, newlywed may no longer be appropriate. It's been a year since they married.

She thinks back to that beautiful January day here in Hawaii and feels a rush of joy as she contemplates their upcoming anniversary; more so, for the baby that's due in late summer.

But now as she views their wedding pictures, lingering over the photos that include Bea, pleasure retreats in the face of bereavement.

Elizabeth misses her mother and though she doesn't nurse her grief, at times an overwhelming sadness takes hold. If only the experimental drug had lived up to its promise. But reports of toxic side effects shut down the trial.

Her distress is short lived. Robert is back from a meeting and brings in Saturday's mail that he places in front of her on the coffee table.

He also notices the wedding album and leans down to give her a kiss on the cheek. "Everything okay?"

"I'm fine," she says. "Come join me. I want to hear about your meeting." He slides in next to her but before he can report, Elizabeth, her curiosity getting the better of her, reaches for a large square envelope that perches on top of the pile of mail, teasing to be opened.

"I'll bet this is a wedding invitation," Elizabeth says, as she fingers, then opens the envelope. "Aha! I was right." She pulls out the card and takes a moment to absorb its content.

"Well, what do you know?" She passes the card to Robert. "Shall we go?"

He slips his arm around her and murmurs into her ear. "Who

doesn't love a wedding? And besides, isn't it time to visit Diane and family?"

Kim reflects on accepting into the present what has been missing in the past: fulfillment, stability, contentment.

As she dares to be happy, she thinks back to a year and a half of emotional upheaval, of the drudgery of working with Jasper on the disposition of Dana's possessions and properties, now that she is incarcerated. She shudders as she recalls the complexities of the task, the mountain of details.

In the same time frame, she sees Mark occasionally. No longer his patient, their relationship is clouded. In a dance of uncertainty, they achieve a measure of closeness, only to back off and go their separate ways.

Then by chance they meet in the mail room at the Wilshire Marquis. "You won't believe this," Mark says, "but we're standing in the same spot where Dana and I first met."

Kim nods. "I know the story. You meet, then waltz off to La Casita for lunch and," she gestures, "so it begins."

His expression turns meditative. "That's how it all started." He pauses a beat, and then regards her warmly, holding her gaze. "Credit time to promote healing and restore sanity. I find that once we're released from the constraints of the past, we gain back our perspective, and most of us can then move on."

He gives her a sheepish smile. "Excuse the pontificating. What I'm really trying to say, Kim, is that I'd like to take you to lunch."

"I'd like that very much–with one proviso. We bypass La Casita?"

"I think we can manage that. In fact, I know the perfect place. Do you like Greek food?"

It wouldn't matter if he suggested fish head stew at a beach shack. Instinctively, she knows the time is right.

And so it begins for them.

Mark and Kim plan a small chapel wedding, to be followed by a far grander Country Club reception. They are pleasantly surprised that

Elizabeth and Robert Chang will be in attendance. Ted Connelly is bringing a date, a pretty redhead, Ted confides to Mark, who is a member of his sailing group. Susan is not on the guest list.

All well and good. But something nags at Mark, lurking on the fringes of his consciousness. For whatever reasons, just days before his wedding, he decides to visit Dana in prison.

Dana is not surprised to see Mark Hampton. In fact, she's been expecting him.

In the visiting room, he peers at her through the screen that separates them. "You look well; in fact," a kind of wonder creeps into his tone, "you're as lovely as ever."

"Why thank you, Mark. You wouldn't have formed that opinion during my first god-awful months in here. But I was able to surmount certain obstacles. Now I have a number of loyal followers. Not only do they cater to me, they value my guidance and clever solutions to their problems. Of course, others aren't as charitable, but that's because they're jealous of my power and envious of my looks." Her gaze sweeps the room, her hands in constant motion.

"Dana—"

"Did you know your wife-to-be furnishes me with toiletries and cosmetics? They have to pass scrutiny, but Kim sees to it that—"

"Dana," he raises his hand, "slow down, please. Listen to me." He waits until he has her full attention. "I need to say this. Kim and I are marrying for all the right reasons. But that doesn't erase what you and I had together."

"I know." She holds his gaze.

He takes in his breath as her eyes encapsulate him in a sea of emeralds.

"Kim doesn't have you for life, Mark. I do. You still desire me. Maybe more now that I'm unavailable. I can hear the longing in your voice, see in your expression how you hunger for me. You see, Mark, I've ruined you for any other woman.

"And that's what keeps me going."

Winter sunlight bathes the wedding chapel in a gentle luminance, granting the pews and altar a flower laden pastel elegance.

Mark is at the altar as Kim, resplendent in a gown of deep rose chiffon, approaches. He can only marvel that he has reached this milestone in his life.

Like in his dream, it is Kim, not Dana who reveals herself in all her goodness and radiance to bring love and meaning into their lives.

And yet—

About Jackie Ullerich

A native Californian, Jackie Ullerich was born in Los Angeles, grew up in San Diego and attended UCLA, where she graduated with honors, earning a secondary teaching credential in theater arts and English. She also attained Master Teacher status, which qualified her to train and supervise student teachers at the high school level.

In a major change of venue, Jackie left the classroom for the world stage to travel and live in a variety of places, both in the U.S. and overseas, with her Air Force husband.

Her years of living in Turkey and Greece coincided with changes in government, including tanks in the streets. But hostile environments were offset by exploration of ancient cultures and the colorful tapestries of contemporary life.

Of her many experiences, teaching English as a foreign language at the Turkish War College in Ankara, was an adventure in itself. While her novels reflect first-hand knowledge of exotic and historic locales, California provides a backdrop for most of her writing.

Presently, Jackie and her retired Air Force JAG husband reside in Palm Desert, California where her husband golfs while Jackie writes.

Jackie has a strong readership following based upon her previously published works "The Bride Stands Alone" and "At Risk," which are currently available in e-Book and print from leading book retailers.

CPSIA information can be obtained at www.ICGtesting.com
Printed in the USA
LVOW13s1027271013

358778LV00001B/129/P

9 781621 830245